The LOVER

The LOVER

ROBIN SCHONE

KENSINGTON PUBLISHING CORP.
http://www.kensingtonbooks.com

BRAVA BOOKS are published by

Kensington Publishing Corp.
850 Third Avenue
New York, NY 10022

All Kensington titles, imprints and distributed lines are available at special quantity discounts for bulk purchases for sales promotion, premiums, fund raising, educational or institutional use.

Special book excerpts or customized printings can also be created to fit specific needs. For details, write or phone the office of the Kensington Special Sales Manager: Kensington Publishing Corp., 850 Third Avenue, New York, NY, 10022. Attn. Special Sales Department. Phone: 1-800-221-2647.

ISBN 0-7582-0427-2

First Printing: April 2000
10 9 8 7 6 5

Printed in the United States of America

I dedicate this book to:

RBL ROMANTICA—a web board with Bodacious Bods aplenty and a clan of women extraordinaire—thanks for your support, rebel ladies!

Nora Coffey, founder of HERS, Hysterectomy Educational Resources & Services, an international women's health organization whose mandate is: "To provide information about the alternatives to, and consequences of, hysterectomy;"

Mimi (Meserak) Ramsey, founder of FORWARD USA, a "(non-profit) organization with a two-fold mission: Eliminating Female Genital Mutilation (FGM) wherever it exists on the planet; and providing support services to those young girls and women who are victims of FGM;"

Linda Hyatt, wonder girl agent, and Kate Duffy, wonder girl editor, whose generous praise and support were unflagging—thought for sure I'd gone too far this time;

Mom, here's the virgin you requested! She's sort of clueless. . . .
And, of course, to Roselle Library! who valiantly struggled to find me books covering the history of heterosexual male prostitution (a very well-kept secret, believe me).

As to my worst critic and best fan—sorry you missed this one, Don!

Author's Notes

We ain't come that far, baby!

You don't want to know how many books I pored over, trying to trace the history of heterosexual male prostitution—well, actually I just wanted to find out about its existence in the nineteenth-century—only to discover that gigolo is a term coined circa 1920, and that historians prefer to believe that the practice did not occur prior to the twentieth-century because traditionally women did not have control over their own wealth until recently, so therefore they could not possibly afford to buy a man's favors other than through a wedding dowry.

Yeah, sure. . . .

Not surprising, there are historical words for such men. They are listed in *A Dictionary of the Vulgar Tongue*, by Francis Grose, first compiled in the 1790s. One word in particular caught my attention: it's a term that still exists today—stallion.

So maybe our great-great-great-great-grandmothers weren't supposed to have the wherewithal to purchase sexual favors—or the desire—but guess what? They did.

I am continuously amazed at how little technology and morality has changed since late Victorian times. Modern bathrooms—complete with hot and cold running water and toilets that efficiently flushed—existed for those who could afford them, as did electricity and the telephone.

Department stores made their grand entrance. Horse-driven buses—called omnibuses—cheaply taxied people who could not afford either their own stables or the price of cabs. An underground train was built in the 1860s to carry workers to and from London proper and surrounding boroughs.

In essence, there are very few conveniences we have now that a century earlier our British Victorian ancestors did not have on one level or another.

Gynecologists examined women via a speculum, just as they do now. The diaphragm, a feminine contraceptive, was developed in the 1870s by a German doctor and soon became very popular among our "staid" Victorian ancestresses. (Unfortunately, the use of diaphragms did not become common in the United States until the 1920s—at about the same time that the term gigolo was coined. A coincidence, do you think?)

Toilet paper existed. Sanitary napkins existed.

In other words, life was not as primitive in Queen Victoria's era as we necessarily believe. Nor were women as sexually ignorant or passive as myth would claim.

One thing, however, our two eras still share—repression.

Please join me in my celebration of women's sexuality. It is a gift, and as such is to be treasured. Because like every other human right, it can so easily be taken away.

Chapter 1

Death.

Desire.

Michael did not know which of the two had brought him back to London.

He sat and waited for both.

Voices rose and fell around him. The tips of burning cigars shone red like the eyes of hungry rats. Candle flames flickered, crystal glinted, jewels sparkled.

Women draped in gaudy silk gowns and gentlemen attired in black dress coats and white waistcoats steadily streamed up and down a curved oak staircase, footsteps muffled by plush red carpeting.

There was no question of what had brought them to the exclusive tavern. In the House of Gabriel drinks were charged by the dram and rooms were rented for sex.

A feminine titter drifted out of a dark, velvet-draped corner.

Michael was acutely aware of what the men whispered over surrounding candlelit tables as they waited either to gain release or to recover from it. Of what the whores laughed at, sipping vintage champagne.

Michel des Anges.

Michael of the Angels.

A man whom women once paid to pleasure them, he was now a man who must pay women to give him pleasure.

"Mon frère." Gabriel appeared without warning at his right shoulder. He did not touch Michael—he had not touched anyone in a long time. "She is here."

Deliberately Michael turned his head to confront Gabriel.

His violet eyes clashed with silver ones.

Gabriel did not flinch at the sight of Michael's face. Any more than Michael flinched at Gabriel's blond, ethereal beauty.

My two angels, the madame of the *maison de rendezvous* had claimed twenty-seven years ago when she saved them from starvation on the streets of Paris. *A dark one, for the women. A fair one, for the men.*

They had been thirteen-year-old runaway boys then. Now they were forty-year-old men.

And they still ran from the past.

"Is she alone?" Michael asked.

"She is alone."

Michael's testicles tightened.

In anticipation.

In frustrated anger.

She did not deserve this, this woman who came to him seeking sexual satisfaction.

"It's not too late," Gabriel murmured. "I can send her away and she will come to no harm."

Five years ago Michael would have agreed.

Five years ago he had thought his secret safe.

Too late.

They were both trapped: the woman by her need for pleasure and he by his need for vengeance.

Michael smiled.

He knew the effect of that smile, of the crinkling of dark skin that repelled rather than attracted.

It was a smile devoid of humor.

"You are precipitate, *mon vieux*. After one look at my face she may decide that she is being shortchanged."

"She does not come here blind." Whiplash sharpness edged Gabriel's voice. "Her solicitor would have told her what to expect."

How could anyone prepare a woman for what he now was?

How could any woman want him, *knowing* what he was?

"Is that why you did not cringe, Gabriel?" Acid threaded Michael's response. "Because you knew what to expect?"

"Let it be." Light and darkness danced across Gabriel's flawless features. It was impossible to read his expression. "Together we will find another way."

But there was no other way. Any more than there had been twenty-seven years earlier.

Michael dispassionately considered the consequences of his plan. And he knew that nothing would halt the outcome of this rendezvous.

One woman's life in the name of revenge.

It had already killed six. What was one more?

"Show her to my table."

A stillness settled over Gabriel. "Are you so desperate for a woman, Michael?"

Michael bit back a snarl of pain.

Yes, he was desperate for a woman.

The madame of the *maison de rendezvous* had given him the gift of redemption. He had learned to bury the horror of his childhood in the scent and the taste of a woman. Through their pleasure he had found, if not peace, solace.

Now whores cringed at his touch.

He could no longer endure the life he had been forced to live these past five years, trapped in a body which kept him from the one act that made his existence bearable.

He would rather die—and take with him the man who was responsible for it all: the life that had made him a stud to be sold to any woman who could afford his price, and the night that had taken it away.

Face impassive, Michael returned Gabriel's unblinking gaze. "Aren't you, Gabriel?"

It could have been a hiss that sent the candle flame dancing. Or it could have been a draft created by a man and a whore rising from a nearby table.

Their time had come.

Now it was Michael's.

Gabriel silently melted into the shadows that he presently lived in. Minutes later, he reappeared in the arched doorway, blond hair shining like a silver halo. The woman at his side wore a gray velvet opera cloak, hood discreetly draped over her head.

It was elegant. Expensive. Designed to conceal rather than reveal.

Clearly it was not the cloak of a prostitute.

She hovered in the doorway, as if hesitant to enter this tavern where every desire could be fulfilled.

Pleasure. Pain.

Nothing was forbidden in the House of Gabriel.

Rage flared up inside Michael, burning hotter and brighter than any flame.

Fire did not always kill. He would not make the same mistake.

Unbidden, his manhood hardened in preparation for the night to come.

He remembered how it used to be, lying with a woman who wanted him.

He imagined how it could be tonight, lying with this woman.

There was nothing he would not do to ensure her pleasure. No part of his body he would not use to bring her to orgasm.

His lips. His tongue. His teeth. His hands. His sex.

He would use all of them and give her more.

Kisses that burned. Licks that tormented. Nibbles that tried the boundaries of pleasure-pain. Caresses as soft as a sigh. Deep, compelling finger probes followed by the even deeper thrusts of his cock.

He wanted revenge, but God help him, he wanted a woman's passion more.

Michael did not flinch when the woman stopped at his table. Her features were a pale blur in the shadow of her hood, whereas his face was fully visible.

He could feel her stare, as he had felt every woman's stare for the last five years.

Michael did not doubt for one moment what she looked at.

Flame had licked his right cheek like the tongue of a lover.

He tensed, prepared for he knew not what, a gasp of horror, angry denial: This is not Michel des Anges.

This is not a man whom a woman pays to have sex with.

Fighting the compulsion to turn his head away from her perusal, he allowed her to see what she would get for ten thousand pounds, the amount of money her solicitor had offered him for one month of service.

A hum of energy swelled across the busy drone of feminine titters and masculine speculations. Bets were made, odds placed.

Michael's left temple pounded in time to the mesmerizing flicker of light and darkness. Images clicked through his mind like painted frames inside a magic lantern: a young girl, laughing; a middle-aged madame, gasping. Worms wriggling. Breasts jiggling.

Death.

Desire.

Both beckoning. Both waiting.

"Monsieur des Anges."

The waiting was abruptly over.

As if unaware of the attention the trio was receiving—an obviously well-to-do female in the company of Gabriel, the untouchable angel, and Michael, the scarred one—the woman sat down on the chair that Gabriel held out for her, velvet rustling, wood squeaking.

"Monsieur des Anges," she repeated, voice low, cultured, surprisingly seductive. "How do you do."

The fluttering candlelight revealed a firm chin and rounded cheeks. Her nervousness, underneath her outward genteel repose, was palpable.

Forcefully Michael tamped down the intense sexuality that had made him a fortune in two countries.

Her solicitor had said the contract was not binding until he satisfactorily passed the test of this first meeting.

She might yet bolt. If she did, he would pursue her.

He did not want to take her by force.

He wanted her to want him.

He needed her to want him so badly that he shook with it.

Michael spoke calmly, lightly, as if it had not been five years since he had last sat across a table from a woman. *As if it had not been five years since a woman unflinchingly met his gaze.* "Would you like champagne . . . madame?"

"I am not married, monsieur, if that is your question."

He was fully aware of her marital status.

Her name was Anne Aimes. Her age was thirty-six.

She was a plain spinster with pale blue eyes and silver-kissed hair that was neither blond nor brown.

There was nobody who would question her whereabouts. Nobody who would miss her.

Nobody wanted her, save for himself.

"It would not matter if you were," he said truthfully.

"I think . . . yes. Thank you." Awareness shimmered in the air—a woman's realization of how soft her own femininity was in comparison to a man's hard masculinity. "I would like champagne, please."

Behind her, Gabriel raised his hand for a waiter before once again disappearing into the shadows of his life. Immediately a liveried man wearing a tailored black dress coat and a crimson waistcoat appeared. He held aloft a tray bearing two glasses and a bottle of champagne in a silver ice bucket.

"The service here is very good," she commented stiffly, politely.

Michael wondered if she realized that the waiter was available for sex as well as table service.

He wondered if she would be that stiff and polite between silk sheets.

He wondered how far she would continue this charade before revulsion sent her screaming into the night.

Brief, bitter amusement lit up his eyes. "The House of Gabriel is known for the service it provides."

Michael waved the waiter away when he would have poured the champagne. Grasping the slender neck of the bottle in his right hand, he cupped a crystal glass in his left, purposely holding both hands in full view, knowing what she would see: what he saw every day of his life.

If she could not bear the sight of his marked hands—of the puckered masses of red and white welts that ran from his fingertips to just above his wrists—she would not be able to accept their touch.

Her gaze followed his movements, flowing back and forth between his fingertips to the glimpse of white cuffs underneath the sleeves of his black dress coat.

Now she would turn away, as every woman turned away—in pity. Disgust. Scorn.

"You were burned."

His fingers tightened around the bottle, the glass, absorbing the cold, drawing upon the strength of sand that had been transformed by fire. The memories of his defeated cries of agony blended with those of the woman he had brought to ecstasy.

"I was burned," he agreed tonelessly. He was vaguely surprised at the steadiness of his hands as he poured the champagne.

Chest tight, he offered her the glass of bubbling wine, waiting, waiting. . . .

For a miracle to obliterate the never-ending terror.

For this woman to take him, as he would take her, endlessly, tirelessly.

Sensation bolted down his spine. He almost dropped the glass at the silky contact of her gloved fingers.

It had been five years since a woman had touched his hand. Whores stuffed his manhood inside them rather than risk his scarred flesh touching theirs.

She seemed impervious to the phenomenon that had just occurred. Tilting her head, she sipped champagne—the golden liquid sparkled underneath the shadow of her hood—before firmly setting the glass down on the white silk tablecloth. "Why do you call yourself Michel . . . des Anges?"

The question momentarily caught him off guard.

It had been so long since he had been Michel.

Why didn't she repudiate him?

Thick black lashes shielded his eyes, a Michel trick, studied and perfected underneath the madam's tutelage. " '*Voir les Anges*,' " he murmured cryptically, wondering how far he dared go, how risqué to be.

Some women liked blunt, sexual talk. Others preferred sensual euphemisms.

He did not understand this spinster woman.

She carefully translated his words, as if she had not spoken French outside of finishing school. " 'To see the angels.' "

" 'To see angels,' " he silkily corrected her, monitoring her reaction. "It is a French expression for having an orgasm."

It was not the answer she expected.

"You named yourself because of your ability to have an orgasm?"

Slowly he poured champagne into his own glass, making her wait for his response. Thrusting the bottle deep into the ice—as if it were his phallus and the bucket her sheath—he snared her gaze. "I am named, *chérie,* for my ability to bring women to orgasm."

Shock gave way to blazing cognizance.

Of her sensual needs.

Of his ability to satisfy them.

Sex was an exciting game. A dangerous game.

One that even an unfashionable spinster could engage in. *If she could afford it.*

She played with the stem of her glass. "You have been with many women."

It was not a question.

"Yes."

First in France, then in England.

"Have you brought each one of them to orgasm?"

Echoes of passion long gone but never forgotten reverberated inside his head. Each woman made a particular sound when she reached her peak.

"Every woman." Michael curved his fingers around his glass, shaping it as he would a feminine breast. "Every time."

Sparkling liquid sloshed onto her hand. A dark stain spread over the back of her pale gray silk glove.

"I am a virgin."

Jesu. Jesus. He had not expected *that.*

She was a plain spinster, but surely there had been someone

in her life—a childhood friend to experiment with, a boy who was more interested in exploring the mysteries of femininity than in courting the local beauty. A footman, a stable boy, *someone*.

He had never had a virgin.

"Why?" he barked, Michael now, not Michel who had never slept alone.

Why would any woman give her virginity to a man who looked like him?

Her head snapped back, the chimera of sexual tension broken. "I beg your pardon?"

He leaned toward her, eyes narrowed, face only inches away from the candle flame that could so easily burn out of control. "For ten thousand pounds, any bachelor in this tavern will marry you. The Speaker of the Commons sits three tables away. Baron Stinesburg sits directly behind you. Why are you doing this? With me, of all men?"

Candlelight flared. It reflected off of a slender nose, revealed the tightening of pale lips that were neither full nor thin. "Perhaps, Monsieur des Anges, I have seen too much death to be cheated by a few scars. Perhaps I wish to see angels."

Michael's breath caught in his chest.

Death.

Desire.

It had come full circle.

She did not deserve this.

But neither had the ones before her.

Purposefully he set down the champagne glass and spread his hands onto the white silk tablecloth. "I will caress you with these hands. I will penetrate your body with these fingers. Can you honestly say you will not flinch at my touch?"

The candle flame lurched and hissed.

She tilted her chin. "I cannot say, sir, never having had anyone's fingers inside my body. I daresay it will depend upon how many you use to penetrate me with."

Michael did not want a woman's innocence.

"Do you know what will happen when I take you to bed?"

"If I did not, I would not be here."

Grudging admiration filled him.

There was strength in Anne Aimes; a strength born of ignorance.

She could not possibly know the pleasure that he would demand of her or the climaxes he would rend from her.

"It's not too late." He did not know where the words came from. Perhaps there still existed inside him a shred of the man he should have become. "You may still change your mind."

But even that unexpected bit of gallantry was a lie.

He would not allow her to walk away from this night. She had sealed her fate when she sent her solicitor to rouse him from his five-year-long sentence of solitude.

Her shoulders straightened beneath the concealing folds of the gray velvet cloak. "I have no desire to change my mind."

Michael imagined her naked, with no cloak of genteel refinement to hide behind. Breasts bared, thighs open, release just a scream away.

The sexual energy that he had so carefully leashed washed over him.

She felt it. Responded to it.

She was not beautiful, this woman who had come to him for her pleasure. But he did not require physical beauty.

Anne Aimes wanted him.

Despite his scars.

That was more than enough.

He would not disappoint her. For the allotted time they had together he would be Michel, the man who made women see angels, not Michael, the man who brought them death.

"One month. Of pleasure." Michael pushed his glass across the table. It connected with the base of the heavy silver candle holder with a crystal ring of finality. "I will do anything you wish. However many times you wish it."

She wet her lips, a quick flick of a pink tongue. "That is what I am paying you for, Monsieur des Anges."

A smile twisted his lips.

Anne Aimes had newly come to her wealth. She had yet to realize that money did not control men.

Sex controlled them.

Vengeance controlled them.

Money merely made it possible to act upon the two disparate needs.

"I assure you, *chérie,* I will not forget what it is you are paying for."

Sliding back his chair, he stood up and held out his hand.

She hesitated only a brief second before taking it.

Exultation surged through him. It was followed by a rush of lust so strong it nearly brought him to his knees.

Michael steered her through the candlelit rows of tables, careful to keep her face in shadow while he deliberately flaunted his own to the men whose sweethearts, wives, and daughters he had once fucked.

By the morrow word would have spread throughout the farthest reaches of England: Michel des Anges was back. And, disfigured though he was, a woman had purchased his services.

Anne Aimes balked when she realized their destination. "I was led to understand that there were rooms upstairs where we could . . . be together."

Yes, there were rooms upstairs. Opulent chambers lined with beveled mirrors and equipped with every device to bring men and women sexual gratification.

Michael did not want her first time to take place in a night house. He could give her that much.

Deftly turning, he backed her into the alcove outside the arched doorway and caught her face between his hands.

She did not flinch from the touch of his burn-roughened skin.

Coldly, calculatingly, he anchored her against the wall with the press of his groin.

Her body, underneath the cloak, was shielded in feminine armor. The whaleboned corset did not hide the thrust of her nipples. The layered petticoats did not mask the yielding welcome of her gently rounded stomach.

Her cheeks were soft and smooth, like velvet—softer even than her cloak. Blood thrummed beneath his fingers.

Fear.

Arousal.

A prostitute knew the dangers of giving in to unbridled passion. Outside a brothel or a night house, a woman was defenseless. She could be bound. She could be raped. She could be killed.

But Anne was not a seasoned whore; she was a virgin spinster who had yet to taste the pleasure—or the pain—that a man could give her.

She did not know that trusting a stranger could bring death.

He leaned his head forward, inhaled the commingled scents of soap and innocence. And beneath those, the tantalizing perfume of her desire.

Anne Aimes's hunger was not as great as his. *Yet.*

"You must trust me," he whispered. "By the time the night is over I will know every inch of your skin. I will explore every crevice, every orifice in your body. If you cannot trust me outside this house, then you will not trust me to bring you to pleasure. If you cannot bring yourself to trust me—completely, unconditionally—then the terms of our contract cannot be met. And I will bid you *au revoir,* here, now."

More lies.

He would not leave her.

Not tonight. Not tomorrow.

Lightly he kissed her, his lips, at least, untouched by the fire that had taken everything away from him.

It was a tease of a kiss, a whisper of breath, a flick of his tongue. A prelude and a promise.

Electricity arced between them.

Her need.

His need.

She wanted to lie with a man.

He wanted to lose himself inside a woman.

His body swelled to the point of pain, knowing that at least this night both of their needs would be fulfilled.

She gasped, her breath sweet with champagne, and underneath that, the caustic tang of tooth powder.

A curious pang shot through his chest.

She had brushed her teeth before their meeting. For fear that *she* might repel *him*.

Sidling away from the hard threat of his masculinity, she squared her shoulders underneath the velvet cloak. "I assure you, the terms of the contract will be met, Monsieur des Anges. Shall we go?"

Michael let her go ahead of him, outside the smoke-filled safety of the night house into cool spring air.

He wondered if she would still want him in a month's time.

He wondered if she would still be alive in a month's time.

Chapter 2

Michel des Anges filled the grinding, jarring hack, stealing oxygen, usurping space. His body burned Anne through her cloak, hip to shoulder; the memory of his kiss burned her lips, inside and out. Orgasm was a living, palpitating promise.

Every woman, every time, the carriage wheels grated.

Eighteen years ago she had thought he was the most beautiful man she had ever seen. Now he was hers, paid for with the money that would have been her dowry had she married.

Anne wanted to scream for the cabby to stop. Or perhaps she wanted to scream for him to hurry, so that she could get the night over with.

The man beside her spoke precise English, as cold and clipped as if he were an Englishman born.

He was not the man she remembered.

Save for those incredible violet eyes of his.

They blazed with raw sexuality.

"You said you will do anything I wish." Anne stared at the door of the hansom cab. Light briefly shone inside the grimy window beside her; the passing lamppost turned ominous darkness into worn brown upholstery. "As many times as I wish it."

The cracked leather underneath her shifted, creaked. She could feel his eyes upon her.

"That is what you are paying me for."

But she didn't know what to ask for.

She only knew that she wanted.

A man's touch.

A man's body.

Her own satisfaction.

"What if . . . what if a woman did not know what to ask for?" Anne's voice was unnaturally loud over the monotonous clip-clop of the horse's hooves and the singsong grind of the carriage wheels. Her shoulder throbbed where his rhythmically rubbed against it. "What if . . . she did not know how many fingers she wanted inside her?"

"Then I would introduce one finger at a time"—his voice was a dark rasp—"until she could not comfortably take any more."

Anne clenched her thighs together at the sharp stab of desire his explicit words evoked. She remembered his hands spread out on the white tablecloth, and saw not the scars—trivial flaws that did not cripple with arthritis or weep with cancer—but the length and the breadth of him.

"How many fingers does a woman normally require?"

"Three. Sometimes four."

His fingers had been long. Far thicker than her own.

"Surely that many would not be comfortable."

"Sexual pleasure is not always a matter of comfort. I assure you, when you are properly prepared, your body will accommodate that many fingers. And yearn for more."

Anne struggled to control her breathing. "How will you know when I am properly prepared?"

"When your body is hot and wet," he said bluntly.

Her body was already hot and wet.

"How many times can you . . . bring a woman to orgasm?"

A sigh of breath was followed by the slipping of her hood. She fought to keep her hands in her lap and not shove the hood back over her head.

He was no longer beautiful, this man who was named for his ability to bring women to orgasm, but he was darkly, dangerously attractive.

Her only attraction was her money. But even that, surely, could not blind a man to the threads of silver hair that marked her spinsterhood.

"However many orgasms she wants. However many *you* want, *mon amour.*"

It was only when he uttered the odd French word that he gave away his heritage. His voice deepened, became melodic, seductive. It promised a woman everything she had ever wanted, sexual acts a virgin spinster could not even begin to imagine.

"Please do not call me that. I am not your love; I am your patroness."

And she was frightened.

By the strength of her desire.

By the man sitting beside her.

Of all the things he might do to her; of all the things he might not do to her.

Dear God. What was she doing?

Her elderly, sickly parents had been dead for less than a year. Yet instead of mourning them she catered to her own selfish needs.

Needs that a spinster should not possess, let alone confess.

Hot breath tickled her ear. "You said you know what will happen when I take you to bed."

Anne sat perfectly still, perfectly straight, as she had learned during her one brief, disastrous season, a rich heiress in a sea of barnacles. Men and women had courted her to her face and laughed behind her back.

She did not want this man to laugh at her.

"I am not ignorant about the mechanical aspects of mating, monsieur."

"Really." Something hot and slick flicked her ear. "Describe to me what will happen when I bed you, mademoiselle."

Anne licked lips that were dry as coal dust—her ear burned and tingled. What had he done to it? "You will join your body to mine."

Like the animals.

But animals did not worry about failure or inadequacy.

Darkness enveloped Anne. It had nothing to do with the diminishing gas lamps lining the narrow London street.

Moist heat feathered her hair, fanned her cheek—his breath. He forced her to look at him by the simple act of blocking her view of the hansom door while his body curved around hers. "Have you ever seen a naked man, *chérie?*"

Anne should reprimand him for the familiarity. She was paying him to pleasure her body, not to ply her with French endearments.

She found that she could not.

No one had ever called her *dear,* or *darling,* or *sweetheart,* not in English, certainly not in French.

Her parents had called her Anne. The servants called her Miss Anne. Everyone else called her Miss Aimes.

As they would continue to address her for the rest of her life.

She inhaled the acrid aroma of tobacco smoke, and underneath that, the suffocating scent of clean, healthy masculinity—expensive soap and a hint of musk. "No, I have never seen a naked man."

It was only a partial lie. What she had seen was not a man.

"Do you know how deeply I will possess you, when I am buried inside your body?"

Anne did not look away from the black hollows that were his eyes. "If you mean do I know how deeply you will penetrate me, then the answer is no."

She did not lie this time.

"But I want to know, Monsieur des Anges. I want to know how deeply both your fingers and your body will penetrate me. Else I would not be here with you in this carriage."

It could have been her breath that caught in the darkness. Or it could have been his.

"Penetration is not possession, mademoiselle."

Fleeting light lit up the right side of his face—it starkly delineated the ridge of scars edging his cheek—and then once again he was swallowed in obscurity.

"Then I am afraid I do not understand your question."

"Physical penetration will vary—five to ten inches, depending upon the size of a man's erect penis. A woman can take a man into her body and still remain in control of her emotions. But when she lies underneath him gasping for air with only his breath to sustain her—with only his body to give her the orgasm that her very life depends on—at that moment, *chérie,* that man possesses that woman."

Anne gulped air—his breath.

She imagined his body filling her—*five to ten inches*—as his breath filled her lungs.

Completely.

Unconditionally.

A frisson of fear raced down her spine.

"That is only if a woman is not in control of her emotions. This is a business arrangement, monsieur, not an *affaire de coeur.*"

"You hired me to overcome your control, mademoiselle."

Her heart skipped a beat, raced to catch up. "You make it sound . . ." *Dangerous.* Not at all like the business arrangement that they had. "I hired you to give me pleasure. As a man hires a woman to give him pleasure. No more. No less."

"There is a difference between a man's pleasure and a woman's pleasure."

Yes, men were freely allowed to pursue theirs, while women were not.

"And what is that, pray tell?"

"A man needs only a woman's body; he does not need her to bring him to orgasm. His own motions will do that."

Anger flicked along her nerves. "Do you think that a woman needs a man only because of his male appendage, monsieur?"

"If that were so, mademoiselle, then you would not be here with me in this carriage."

His silky response was a parody of her own.

Anne gripped her reticule. "I do not understand the purpose of this conversation."

"I am trying to prepare you for the coming night."

"By telling me that a woman needs a man and not vice versa?" Sharpness spiked her voice.

"I never said that a man did not need a woman; I said that a man does not need a woman's motions to bring him to release. But you will need me in the coming hours, mademoiselle. Your needs will render you far more vulnerable than my body will. No matter how deeply I penetrate you. And I assure you, *chérie,* I will penetrate you very deeply."

Desire. Fear. Anger. Pain overlapped the myriad emotions his words provoked. And the realization that he did not speak to hurt her; he spoke the truth.

She would not be here if she thought any man could satisfy her.

Her needs did make her vulnerable—especially when she revealed them to a man who did not share them.

That was why she had chosen Michel des Anges, so that there would be no pretense.

"How deeply will you penetrate me, monsieur?"

"Nine and a half inches, mademoiselle."

Nine and a half inches reverberated inside the cramped cab.

A thrill of alarm rushed through her body. "This is a business arrangement, monsieur," she repeated, more for herself than for him.

"This is a sexual liaison, mademoiselle. It is neither a romantic interlude nor a business venture. I will not present you with a bouquet of flowers and beg for the honor of a kiss. Nor will I shake hands with you come the morning and leave my card on your pillow. What I will do is give you pleasure beyond your wildest fantasies. Do not confuse carnal relations with love or business."

His words were harsh. Erotic.

Heat welled up inside her—and the hope that he would indeed give her pleasure beyond her wildest fantasies.

Her parents had been married for fifty-nine years, betrothed to align wealth instead of bodies. They had shared riches and sickness but no love or pleasure.

And then they had died. As lonely and miserably as they had lived.

Anne did not want to die, always wondering what she had missed.

She squared her shoulders. "I am fully aware of the nature of this liaison, monsieur. And I assure you it fulfills my every expectation. I want you to take my maidenhead, not give me flowers. Hopefully you will kiss me rather than shake my hand, but I do not expect you to beg me for anything, certainly not liberties that I am paying you to take. As for your claim of being able to please me beyond my wildest fantasies, that remains to be seen, does it not?"

The hack abruptly jerked to a halt.

For one heart-thudding second Anne thought she had shocked the very horses into stillness.

Without comment, Michel des Anges swung open the door and stood up, shoulders bent. Stepping out onto the small stoop behind the bobbed horse, he held out his hand for her to take.

The white and red welts were raw in the light of the carriage lamp.

What would they feel like inside her, those long, scarred fingers?

Would he give her three . . . or four?

How could they possibly prepare her to take an erect penis . . . *that was nine and one half inches long?*

She placed her hand in his—as she had done at the tavern.

Blistering heat penetrated her thin silk glove.

Would his fingers be that hot, penetrating her? *Would his erect male flesh?*

Suddenly Anne was free and she could breathe again. She dug into her reticule for coins to pay the cabby, only to find that the hack was already pulling away from the curb.

Heat blanketed her back—a man's arm. It was whipcord strong.

Her heart tattooed a painful warning against the confines of her corset.

Michel des Anges was seven inches taller than she.

He could hurt her in ways she had no knowledge of, as she had had no prior knowledge that a man used his fingers to penetrate a woman's body.

He could kill her.

And there would be nothing she could do.

For one heart-stopping second she thought about running after the cab.

Truth held her immobile.

Anne could indeed marry any bachelor inside the House of Gabriel—a surprising number of whom she had recognized, as this man knew. They would claim her inheritance by day, and by night they would go there, to pay for their pleasure with her money.

She would be a wife—perhaps even a mother—and still know nothing about the satisfaction that a man could give a woman.

And she would yearn for more.

As she had yearned for so very many years.

This man was renowned for his ability to please women. A stallion, he was called. The most expensive stud in England.

Ten thousand pounds would be his at the end of a month.

He would not hurt a woman who laid the proverbial golden egg. Especially when the liaison had been set up by a solicitor.

Spine rigidly straight, she allowed him to guide her up the concrete stoop of a tall, narrow town house. He did not fumble with the key, easily fitting it into the lock as if he had as much experience opening a door as he did a woman's body.

Dimly she surveyed a small foyer lined in rich oak paneling. A large hyacinth plant occupied a side table, variegated blue petals in full bloom. Silver glinted in their shadow—a tray waiting for the morning post. Beyond the foyer, marble steps flanked by intricately worked iron balustrades marched up into darkness.

It did not look like an abode of ill repute, this house where she would lose her maidenhead. It looked like a home.

Beeswax polish and flowers scented the air.

Her house in Dover smelled of illness and carbolic disinfectant; her town house in London of age, dust, and mildew.

Silently he turned off the gaslight. His hand pulsated with heat at the base of her spine; it urged her up the dark abyss that was the stairway.

An elusive luminescence cast the top landing in dull shadow.

She gripped the wrought-iron handrail that could not be seen, only felt. Legs trembling, skirts swishing, she ascended the stairs toward the waiting light.

A corridor hung with pale silk cloth ran the length of the first story. Their heels clicked a hollow litany on the mirror-smooth oak floor: *Penetration, possession.* A fan-shaped wall sconce at the end of the long, narrow hallway battled encroaching darkness.

A cream-painted cornice and closed doors measured their steps: the stilted gait of a woman determinedly taking control of her sexuality and the confident pad of a man who brought every woman to orgasm, *every time.*

He pushed open the solid oak door that the lamp guarded; a massive four-poster brass bed gleamed in the crack of light.

Shutting off the gas to the wall sconce, he gently, implacably, nudged her inside the bedchamber. The pitch-black darkness was heavy, sweet, stifling. For one panic-stricken moment she thought she had stepped inside a greenhouse.

Or a wake.

Soundlessly he maneuvered ahead of her. The sharp strike of a safety match splintered the silence.

Warm light spilled from a stained glass globe, starkly delineating an oak nightstand and a crystal vase filled with bloodred roses. Immediately to the left of the hurricane lamp stood the brass bed; white silk sheets and a leaf green velvet quilt were turned down in readiness.

Dropping the flaming matchstick into a small, green bowl, Michel des Anges turned, face dark, black hair haloed by golden light. He noiselessly, purposefully closed the distance separating them. "Let me take your cloak."

Anne stared at the jagged shadows digging into his cheeks. She steeled herself against the image of him exploring her every crevice and orifice. "Thank you."

Scarred hands reached for her, a jarring reminder that he was not the man whom matrons and debutantes alike swooned over eighteen years earlier. One by one he released the buttons on her cloak, there at her neck . . . lower, between her breasts. . . .

Heat spiraled through her nipples.

Things were progressing too quickly.

"I didn't bring a nightgown," she blurted out.

His black eyelashes slowly lifted. Anne was trapped by startlingly violet eyes.

"You won't need one," he murmured. He tugged her reticule from between her clenched fingers and tossed it behind her. A small plop sounded in the flickering light. Her cloak followed the reticule, a heavy *whoosh* of velvet.

Anne felt naked and immeasurably plain in her modest gray silk gown, a peahen to his peacock.

She closed her eyes. The look in his left no doubt whatsoever as to what he would next remove.

She did not want him to see her breasts that were too small and her hips that were too large.

But she wanted to see him.

She was paying a considerable fortune for the privilege of doing so.

No matter what he said, this was business: the business of pleasure.

Her pleasure.

Anne opened her eyes and stepped back on trembling legs. "Please undress for me."

Violet fire flared in his eyes. "You want to see me . . . naked?"

She drew herself up to her full height of five feet, five inches. "I am a spinster, monsieur, but I am also a woman, with the same desires as any other woman. Of course I wish to see you undressed."

The lamp blazed; light and shadow wildly leaped around him. "Do you know how a man is fashioned, *chérie?*"

She defiantly tilted her chin. "I will not faint at the sight of your male appendage, monsieur, if that is what troubles you."

"But will the sight give you pleasure?"

"Does it not please other women?"

"You are a virgin, mademoiselle. If you have never before seen a naked man, you might be . . . alarmed."

She firmed her lips. "I will not know, will I, until I see you?"

Cold calculation glittered in his eyes; it was followed by hot deliberation. "And if you are alarmed?"

"I will not frighten other inhabitants of this house by running screaming into the street."

The brightness of the lamp dimmed as abruptly as it had flared. "No, mademoiselle, I do not believe you will."

Skillfully, deliberately, he shrugged out of his black dress coat, let it slither to the floor in a seductive whisper of silk on silk. Without taking his gaze away from hers, he unfastened the top button on his white waistcoat.

No doubt many women had requested that he disrobe for them.

Beautiful women, experienced women.

Anne focused on his hands instead of his painfully intense gaze.

"Does it hurt?" she abruptly asked. "Your hands, I mean. Would you like assistance?"

His scarred fingers stilled.

Resolve replaced Anne's nervousness. This was familiar, something she knew how to do. All her life she had assisted her parents. In the drawing room, at the dinner table, and, ultimately, on their deathbeds.

Stepping forward, she brushed aside his fingers.

The small, pearl buttons refused to come undone.

She had never been this inept in the sickroom.

Frowning, she pulled her gloves off.

Iron-hard fingers cuffed her wrists; the gray silk gloves fluttered free of her suddenly nerveless hands.

Alarmed, she jerked her head back.

His face was only inches away from hers. The scars that rode his high cheekbone were livid.

"I have no need of a nurse, mademoiselle."

Paralyzing awareness swelled over her.

He *could* hurt her. *And no one would know until it was too late.*

She licked her lips, tasted his breath, hot and moist. "I have no desire to be your nurse, monsieur."

"In the cab you said you did not know what you want."

She would not look away. Nor would she pretend to misunderstand him.

"No, I asked you what would happen if a woman did not know what to ask for. I never said that I did not know what I want."

He lowered his head, lips just a kiss away. "What do you want, mademoiselle?"

It was a challenge.

How far will you go, spinster woman? was what he really asked.

How prepared are you for the attentions of a man who is named for his ability to bring women to climax?

Anne took a deep breath.

This was all she would ever have, this one month of pleasure.

She would not back away, not from him, not from her silly virgin fears.

"I want you to bring me to orgasm."

"How many times?"

"As many times as my body will allow."

"How many fingers do you want?"

"As many as my body will accept."

"How deeply will you take me?"

"However deeply you can penetrate me."

His violet eyes burned. "Has a man ever touched your breasts?"

How difficult it was to admit the truth. "No."

Men had wanted her parents' fortune, but no man had ever wanted the woman she yearned to be.

"Has a man ever kissed you with his tongue?"

Anne swallowed remembered revulsion. "Once."

"You did not enjoy it."

No, she had not enjoyed it. The young gentleman who had stolen the kiss had bragged to his friends that Anne was desperate for a beau, claiming that only a man desperate to wed an heiress would kiss such a homely cow.

She stared at the thick fringe of his lashes. They were black as soot, and so long that the ends clustered together. "He gagged me," she said stiffly. "And he . . . drooled on me."

"I will not gag you, *chérie*. Nor will I drool on you."

The heat blistering her face and banding her wrists abruptly disappeared.

He stepped back and shrugged out of his waistcoat.

The withdrawal was so abrupt that Anne could only stand and stare.

Black lashes veiling his eyes, he reached behind his neck to unhook the band of his white dress tie.

Her lips and tongue throbbed.

She had wanted him to kiss her, as he must know she had.

A brazen, reckless energy overcame her. "What *will* you do, monsieur?"

"When I kiss you, I will suckle your tongue." Arms lowering, he dropped the banded tie to the floor. His thick black lashes swept open. "When I remove your dress, I will suckle your breasts. And when you are naked"—he deftly plucked free the first of the three gold studs securing his white silk shirt—"I will suckle your clitoris."

Anne's breath caught in her throat.

Suckle your breasts reverberated in the chill night air. Immediately it was followed by *Suckle your clitoris.*

He removed the second gold stud. "Do you know where your clitoris is, mademoiselle?"

She struggled to keep her gaze trained on his face and not on the black hair peeping through the ever-widening vee at the neck of his dress shirt. "I am not ignorant, monsieur."

Shortly after returning from London eighteen years earlier, she had stolen a conspectus of the medical sciences from her parents' physician in Dover. It had named the parts of her body that desired attention, but it had not told her what to expect from a man.

It had not told her what a man expected from a woman.

He freed the last gold stud and thrust the three into his pocket, purposely drawing her gaze to the front of his trousers. "Do you know what will happen when I lick and suckle you?"

Her nipples and clitoris throbbed at the image his words conjured. She jerked her gaze away from the large bulge in his black trousers.

She would not be embarrassed by her needs.

Anne squared her shoulders. "No doubt I will experience an orgasm. The first, I hope, of many. Is that how you gained your name, monsieur? Because of your expertise at licking and suckling a woman?"

"Among other things," he returned enigmatically.

Crossing his arms, he grasped the sides of his shirt and jerked it over his head.

Anne's heart slammed against her ribs.

His cheek and hands were scarred, but his body was perfect: all dark skin, curly black hair, and sculpted muscles.

Without warning, his dark head reappeared and the silk shirt joined the rest of the clothing scattered across the oak floor.

He knew the effect he was having on her, the effect he must have on all the women who purchased his services.

She didn't want to be the only one shocked and titillated this night.

"Are you fully erect, monsieur?"

"Yes," he returned, seemingly undaunted by her daring. "I am fully erect."

Hot moisture pooled between her thighs.

"Do you always . . . get erect when you are with a woman?"

"Yes," he said flatly.

"I would like to see you."

"Then take off my trousers, mademoiselle."

His violet eyes dared her to touch him—and see exactly what she was paying for.

All nine and one half inches.

"Very well, monsieur," she retorted evenly. She stepped forward.

Heat radiated from his body. Anne fought the memories of a diseased, dying man, and then she fought silk-covered buttons. Her fingers fumbled, as they had when she had tried to remove his waistcoat. But now she could not blame her clumsiness on gloves.

Anticipation coiled in her breasts and lower abdomen.

Each released button revealed more and more of the thick, dark hair that matted his chest and arrowed down his stomach. She could feel him underneath the lined silk of his trousers. He was long and thick and hard. His penis pulsed with a life of its own.

Breath bated, she peeled his trousers down over his hips . . . his thighs. . . .

And sucked in blistering heat, the faint scent of soap, and the musky scent of a man's sex.

The muscles inside her vagina clenched.

In desire.

In fear.

He had been right. She was not prepared for the reality of such a vital man.

Her gaze leaped up to his.

His violet eyes were waiting for hers.

"You said that you brought every woman to orgasm."

"Every time," he agreed silkily.

"Even when the woman was a virgin?"

"I have never had a virgin."

He had never had a virgin.

She had never had a man.

If she took him inside her, she would not be the same woman that she now was.

Anne fought to keep the rising panic out of her voice. "If you have never had a virgin, how do you know you will be able to give me pleasure?"

Calmly, methodically, he pulled his trousers back up, walked over to the bed, sat down, and proceeded to remove his shoes. One soft thump followed another. The socks made no sound at all.

His bare feet were long, large as his hands were large, the same dark, dusky brown color as was the rest of his body.

Except for his manhood.

Jutting out of the opened vent in his trousers, the thick, fleshy stalk bulged with blue veins, the tip a purplish red hue, like a garden-ripe plum: hearty and heavy. Black hair peppered his testicles. They, too, were striated with blue veins.

"How do you know?" she repeated shakily.

Standing up, he shucked his pants off and walked toward

her, six feet of dark, hair-studded skin and sinewy muscle. His engorged manhood swayed with his approach.

He stepped so close that the bulbous crown of his erection prodded her silk gown, and underneath that, her lower stomach.

It throbbed.

She throbbed.

The very air throbbed.

"I will please you, *chérie.*" Scorching breath feathered her upturned face. "You must trust me."

How did men do this, take their pleasure with women who were strangers to them?

"If I may borrow a robe, I will undress in your dressing room," she offered stiltedly. "You may extinguish the light and wait for me in bed."

A dark, scarred hand lifted, sifted through the tight bun that she wore her hair in, found a pin. "I think not, *chérie,*" he murmured, hot breath abrading her cheek.

The pin slid free and dropped to the oak floor, a tinny *plink* that was inordinately loud over the thrumming of her heartbeat.

She did not know what she was supposed to do . . . or how she was supposed to act.

Anne stood still, as she had learned to do when surrounded by the ton who deliberately mistook her ignorance for clumsiness.

Anger came to her rescue. "It is my money, monsieur. You will do as I please."

Another pin fell to the floor. "You are paying me to ensure your pleasure."

"Yes. And disobeying my wishes does not bring me pleasure."

Yet another pin slid free; her bun sagged. "It will, *chérie.*"

She grabbed his hands, her fingers impeded by her hair. "Please do not do that."

He did not stop, using both hands to free her bun. "There is no pleasure in being a pincushion."

The hard thrust of his penis rubbed against her stomach, a tantalizing tease, frightening in its proportions—in its base masculinity.

Her hair slithered down her back.

No man had ever seen her hair loose.

Desperately striving to retain a semblance of control—*she was not the gauche eighteen-year-old girl who had inspired ridicule among the ton*—Anne awkwardly rested her hands on his lean waist. His muscled flesh was as hard as it looked, the corded skin blistering hot. "I have never been naked in front of a man."

She had never been naked in front of anyone save her old nursemaid.

He thrust his fingers into her hair, working out the tangles. His scar-roughened flesh grated against her scalp. "I assure you, you have nothing that I have not seen before."

But he had not seen a woman like her before.

He had never seen a thirty-six-year-old virgin spinster . . . *not like this.*

"I'm not young."

He forced her head up. Darkness shadowed his face. Only his eyes were alive. "Neither am I."

Tears pricked her lids. "I'm not beautiful."

His fingers tightened in her hair. "Neither am I."

"Your eyes are. They burn. With need."

Something like pain flashed across his dark, tense face. "So do yours, *chérie.*"

He lowered his head and would not let her turn aside as he lightly licked her lips, tongue a silky tease of liquid fire.

Her fingers dug into his waist. His muscles were hard, unyielding. "I do not know how . . . to take a man's body inside my own."

"It is like a kiss," he whispered, breath searing her saliva-coated lips. "I will taste you. Lick you. Tongue you. And then I will penetrate you."

Her control was slipping, *slipping*. "With your tongue?"

He released her head. Grasping her right hand, he dragged it between them and closed her fingers around throbbing flesh that was both hard and soft, pliable yet rigid. "With this."

Chapter 3

Uncontrollable lust sparked through Anne's body. She couldn't move; she could only feel.

And marvel at the miracle that was a man's arousal.

Nothing in her life had ever compared to Michel des Anges—not her erotic dreams, not her sexual fantasies, certainly not the long, endless hours she had nursed her father.

He was softer than satin, harder than steel. Far longer than the width of her palm. Thicker than the circle of her fingers. He pulsed in time to her heartbeat.

Anne gulped air. "Please turn out the light."

"I can't do that."

She opened her mouth to protest—it was her money that paid for their union—only to be silenced by scalding heat.

He licked her. He tongued her. And then he pierced her.

Lightning bolted through Anne.

He caressed her tongue, the roof of her mouth. . . .

Too much. Knife-sharp sensation stabbed through her breasts.

And still the flesh inside her fist pulsed and throbbed.

Her lungs ached with the need for oxygen.

He gave it to her, only to suck it inside his mouth—along with her tongue.

Michel des Anges suckled her.

As he had promised he would.

First her tongue, her breasts, and then her clitoris.

Her clitoris, breasts, and tongue pulsed and throbbed in time with the satiny-smooth flesh in her hand.

The tight constriction around her chest eased; the waist of her dress drooped.

Sound vibrated inside her mouth. "Raise your arms."

Squeezing her eyelids shut, Anne turned loose the thick male appendage that mirrored her heartbeat and raised her arms.

Her silk dress snaked up her torso, over her head. She could feel his stare all the way down to her slippered toes.

"Tell me your name, mademoiselle."

Her eyelids snapped open.

"Anne. Anne Aimes."

She immediately remembered that her solicitor had warned her to remain anonymous in this venture, a silly warning. What was more dangerous than this ache that stripped a woman of everything but raw, animal need?

Deft fingers untied the tapes of her bustle.

"You may call me Anne," Anne blurted out, cringing as the words left her mouth but unable to stop them. "May I call you . . . Michel?"

The bustle fell with an audible plunk onto the wooden floor.

"We are going to be close, Anne Aimes." Deft fingers untied the tapes of her top petticoat. "As close as two people can get. You may call me whatever you wish."

The petticoat fell about her feet, a soft swish of sound and motion.

Anne clenched her hands at her sides lest she struggle to retain the remainder of her clothing. Desperately she concentrated on his voice. *We are going to be close . . . as close as two people can get.* "You said this was not a romantic interlude."

"Nor is it." The second petticoat joined the first, creating a mound of wool. "There is nothing romantic about lust."

He cupped her derriere, his fingers perilously close to the seamless vent in her wool drawers. "Lust is earthy."

Suddenly his hands were inside her drawers, a rasp of scars and calluses. "Lust is primal."

A rough finger mapped out the valley between her cheeks. "We will sweat. We will groan."

Hands sliding down, he tested the plumpness of her soft buttocks, simultaneously pressing her against his groin so that she tested the hardness of his manhood. "We will fight each other for your pleasure. And when we climax, we will be one body, joined by our sex."

His violet eyes trapped hers. "*That* is what will happen when I take you to bed, mademoiselle."

Anne's spine was so brittle it felt as if it would snap. Desperately she tried to marshal her thoughts. "Do you always join a woman in climax?"

The harsh drag of his fingers inched up and out of her drawers, grasped the ends of the tape to her corset, proceeded to unlace it. "When the time is right."

The whalebones collapsed, like a deflated accordion. The corset fell to the oak floor. Its loss restricted rather than aided her breathing.

"How do you know when the time is right?"

"When a woman's screams echo in my head." His breath serrated her cheek. Holding her gaze, he lightly ran his hands over her breasts, lingered infinitesimally over her painfully engorged nipples. "And she is so swollen and exhausted that she cannot reach another climax.

"Lift your arms," he abruptly ordered.

Anne had no choice but to comply. The linen shift was jerked up and over her head.

Cold air. Hot skin.

His fingers weighed her naked breasts, kneaded them.

The sensation was too intense. Too painfully personal. The look in his eyes was too discerning.

She had not known it was possible to want a man this badly.

Even as she thought it, she knew it for the lie that it was.

She had wanted him this badly eighteen years ago when she saw him dancing with Countess Raleigh, a beautiful, rich woman fifteen years her senior. And she had known, for all that Anne was one of the richest heiresses in England, that he would not so much as glance at her.

And he had not.

She squeezed her eyelids together to buffer the truth.

He would not be here with her now if she could not afford him.

"Open your eyes, Anne."

She reluctantly did as he bade.

"Don't close them again. There's nothing to hide from, *chérie.* I know what you feel. I know what you need."

How could this man—this perfect man who did not drool when he kissed or tremble with passion when he stood naked before her—how could he know about a spinster woman's needs?

Anne fought to speak, to rationalize instead of palpitate like the bundle of raw, exposed nerves that he had reduced her to.

She did not want to be this vulnerable.

"How do you know what I feel?" The words were torn from her throat. "How could you, of all people, possibly know what it feels like to want someone to touch you so badly that you pay for it?"

Emotions that she could not even begin to fathom darkened his eyes. "We all have needs, Anne."

"Do you?" she harshly demanded.

He did not look away. "Yes."

"Have you ever needed to be touched so badly that you paid for it?"

The scars ridging his right cheekbone tightened. "Yes."

"Why?" Her hoarse cry echoed in her ears.

The darkness in his eyes deepened; at the same time the fire intensified. "For this, *chérie.*" He brushed the rock-hard tip of her breast.

Air caught in Anne's chest. It escaped in a gasp when he lowered his head and sucked her nipple into his mouth.

Molten fire coursed through her breast and down her spine.

Her hands—*what did she do with her hands?*

Did she leave them at her sides?

Did she thread her fingers through his hair, as he had earlier done to hers?

Did she pull his head against her breast to make him take it more deeply inside his mouth, as she wanted to?

Her chaotic thoughts were interrupted at the invasion of

scarred, callused skin. It breached the vent in her drawers, and then it breached the nether lips that only she had ever touched.

Her heart pounded so hard that her entire body shook from the force of it.

Would he penetrate her? Or would he touch her where she desperately ached to be touched?

Her legs instinctively widened, giving him the freedom to choose.

For long seconds he simply rested there, finger nestled between her swollen nether lips while he suckled and suckled her nipple.

A direct line of electricity arced through her body, breast to labia, labia to breast.

She tensed, waiting for something . . . *something*. . . .

And then it came, the touch that she needed: the slippery glide of a hard, wet, scar-roughened finger.

Anne convulsively grabbed his head while her neck arched back in a silent scream of release.

A popping sound broke the single-minded enjoyment of her orgasm. Dimly she associated the sound with the release of her nipple. The chill spring air was almost painfully cold after the furnace of his mouth.

A harsh rasp of air drowned out the sound of her own ragged breathing. Anne opened her eyes . . . and stared straight up into Michel's.

"You didn't scream."

"No." Anne struggled to regain her breath. "That is not . . . dignified."

Especially in a spinster woman.

"I told you, *chérie*. This is lust, not romance. There is no room in my bed for dignity. And even if there were, I wouldn't allow it. You came to me for sex. Hot sex. Wet sex. The kind you won't find in the marriage bed, where a man's sole concern is producing an heir or satisfying his own needs."

His finger moved, a slippery descent to her vagina. He pressed inward so that both she and he could feel the membrane that was her maidenhead. "When I take this, I want you to cry out. I want to know when I hurt you. And then I want you to cry out again. To let me know that I please you."

His words were alarming, yet unbelievably arousing.

Her mother had been forty when she conceived Anne, her first and only child. Always a sickly woman, what little health she possessed had dwindled with the pregnancy and subsequent birth.

Her father had been ten years older than her mother.

They had not needed a child; they had needed a nurse. And they had gotten one in Anne.

She had never screamed. Never laughed out loud for fear that she would disturb their rest.

Every childish joy, every adolescent heartbreak, every adult need had been borne in silence.

"I don't know if I can," she whispered.

"I will make you scream, *chérie.*" The words were gravelly, a promise of unimaginable pleasure. *Or pain.* "Before the night is over I will make you scream again and again."

Anne tensed; he throbbed against the unbreached portal of her femininity. "Are you going to penetrate me with your finger now?"

"Do you want me to?"

She firmed her chin. "Yes."

She wanted it all: his tongue, his fingers, his manhood. Everything he had ever given a woman.

Everything she was paying him to give her.

Suddenly the tantalizing threat of his hand was gone. Anne stood alone in her drawers and the aftermath of an orgasm that had not come from her own fingers.

And like all the ones that had come before, *it was not enough.*

"I brought a tin of French letters." She fought her body to keep her hands at her sides instead of covering her swollen breasts. "They're in my reticule."

Practiced fingers found the four buttons on the band of her wool drawers. Thick black lashes veiled his eyes. "I have my own."

He did not fumble with her buttons as she had fumbled with his.

She would not be dependent on this man. Nor would she be possessed by him.

She would prove that she was a woman in control of her emotions.

"I prefer we use the ones I purchased."

"But I do not, *chérie*."

She stiffened her spine; her hardened nipples stabbed the wiry hair covering his chest. Prickly heat rocketed through her womb. "Why not?"

Anne watched him as he watched the cream-colored wool glide down her body, knowing what he saw—hips that were too generous . . . a pale stomach that was rounded . . . a patch of brown pubic hair. . . .

A dark flush outlined his high cheekbones. The white scars on his right cheek and temple stood out in stark relief.

The heels on her shoes all at once felt as if they had grown by several inches. Her pelvis jutted forward in a most unseemly manner, flaunting . . . *everything*.

Her naked body.

Her naked needs.

His thick, dark lashes lifted. She was pinned by his violet gaze. "It is a matter of size, *chérie*. My condoms are specially tailored."

Her fingers clenched into fists. "I wish to put it on you."

Michel held out his hand, palm upward; it was scarred both front and back. "*Tout ce que tu veux*. Whatever you wish. However many times you wish it."

Grasping the fingers that would soon penetrate her, she awkwardly stepped out of the hobble of her drawers and over the mound of her clothing.

Her hair tickled her buttocks. The garters holding up her cotton stockings bit into the tops of her legs. With her pelvis tilted forward by the heels of her shoes, her thighs rubbed together, creating slick friction. Never had she been more aware of her femininity or the potential consequences of her actions.

The brass bed with the turned down covers loomed impossibly large before her, beside her. The heavy, sweet scent of roses was overpowering.

Releasing her hand, he opened the top drawer in the oak nightstand and took out a tin stamped with a portrait of Prime Minister Gladstone. Taking off the lid, he held the austere box out to her.

Incongruously, she remembered that her tin was stamped with a portrait of Queen Victoria. The monarch's expression was no less stern than Gladstone's. Anne tentatively chose a tightly rolled-up piece of rubber.

Replacing the lid—as if it were perfectly commonplace to offer a woman a condom—Michel set the tin on top of the table by the vase of roses.

Anne lowered her head; her hair slithered over her shoulders, framed her face.

Carnal need warred with maidenly modesty.

Overriding both was the need to impress this man with her expertise, to prove that she was as worthy as the women who had come before her.

Sublimely unself-conscious, Michel positioned his manhood for her.

The flesh deep inside her vagina pulsed in time to the tiny heartbeat that throbbed in the engorged, purple-hued crown he offered her. A single drop of clear moisture glistened in the glare of the lamplight.

The conspectus had not mentioned that a man secreted moisture when aroused.

She touched him lightly, hesitantly. "You are wet."

"So are you, mademoiselle."

Ignoring the flash of embarrassment his observation provoked—*it was too late to be embarrassed*—Anne awkwardly attempted to roll the thin rubber sheath onto him.

The head of his penis was too large.

No matter how forcefully she tried, Michel's French flesh would not fit inside the French letter.

Anne stilled. Stinging tears blurred the erect penis that pulsed against her fingers.

Utterly humiliated, she still wanted him.

Hot, labored breath gusted her hair. Motion caught her eyes—

his right hand reached between her legs. A long, scar-roughened finger delved between her nether lips.

Hard flesh pressed down on her bowed head—his forehead. He gently swirled his finger, making her feel the wetness of her arousal. Then she saw it, when he brought his hand back up. His middle finger was coated with her feminine essence.

"It wants lubrication, *chérie.*" Michel took his already slick finger and smoothed the clear drop of his own essence around the crown of his penis. "Pinch the end of the condom," he instructed her raggedly, "to leave room for the sperm. Now roll it up."

Slowly, carefully, hardly daring to breathe, Anne rolled the thin sheath of rubber up over the plum-shaped head.

The French letter did not mask the pulse underneath his skin, or the smell of masculine arousal: musk mingled with the sweet pungency of roses.

The backs of her fingers brushed his. Instantly he withdrew—first the hand holding his erect flesh, then the hard pressure of his forehead. Feeling strangely bereft, Anne sheathed the remaining two inches of his manhood, up to the thick bush of wiry black hair that matched in color and texture the hair that covered his chest and arrowed down his stomach.

"I am finished," she announced unnecessarily, afraid to meet his gaze, afraid she would see the laughter that must surely be lurking in his eyes.

Warm, rough fingers gathered the twin ropes of her loosened hair and pulled it away from her face so that she had no choice but to lift her head.

Violet fire glittered in his eyes. Sexual need—not laughter at a plain spinster woman's ineptness. "No, *chérie,* you have just begun. You will not be finished until you are too swollen and exhausted to orgasm. But I will make you come again. Even when you beg me to stop."

She did not glance away from the hard intent in his gaze. "I will not beg you to stop, monsieur. No matter how many orgasms you give me."

When she returned to Dover, she would do so knowing that she had experienced the full extent of her womanhood.

A smile twisted his lips. He had such beautiful lips, the top one bluntly edged, the bottom one soft yet hard. "You are so certain, *chérie.*"

Slowly, gently, he tugged on her hair until she turned in synchronization with his body. Light shone in Anne's face; it sharply delineated the scars on Michel's right cheek.

Her heart skipped a beat. "I am prepared for a degree of pain, monsieur."

Smoothing back her hair, he rested his hands on her bare shoulders, heat weighting her down. "But are you prepared for the pleasure?"

She locked her legs to keep them from buckling underneath her. "Yes."

Oh, yes.

He lowered his head; his breath teased her lips. "How can you possibly be prepared for the pleasure I will give you, mademoiselle, when you do not know what to ask for?"

"But I do know what to ask for," she whispered.

She wanted him to perform all the sexual acts she had always yearned for but had not known existed until this night.

Suddenly her knees gave way and she was falling, grabbing for an anchor, finding it but still falling. . . .

The bed rose up and caught her buttocks.

Michel kneeled in front of her on the wooden floor. His forearms were corded underneath her fingers. The black hair sprinkling his dark skin was prickly soft. Heated rubber nudged her knees.

"Tell me," he rasped. "Give me the words, *chérie*. Be a woman for me. Tell me what you want . . . and then take your pleasure."

Her heart hammered in her chest, her breasts, between her thighs. "I want you to taste me."

"Open your legs."

She released the coiled muscles that were his arms and clutched silk in one hand and velvet in the other. "Should we not get between the covers?"

"No." He gripped her thighs up high, just above her white lace garters. "You saw me. Now I want to see you."

"Surely you have seen other women."

"I have seen many women. But I have never seen the woman that you are, Anne Aimes."

This was as close as any man would ever get to seeing the woman that she was.

Anne opened her legs.

Sitting back on his haunches, he grasped her knees and spread them more widely apart—wider, wider yet, until her muscles screamed in silent protest and icy air invaded her most private regions.

Her heart kicked wildly at her ribs.

There was nothing he could not see in this position.

She was open, vulnerable.

Completely.

Unconditionally.

"Scoot forward. . . . Keep your legs open."

Black, silky hair brushed the tops of her thighs, there where her skin was not protected by the cotton stockings. Petal soft lips met petal soft lips, a whisper of a touch.

Anne gasped. Agonizing sensation ripped through her stomach and shot to her breasts.

"I tasted you." Hot breath laved the gaping folds of her labia. "What else do you want, mademoiselle?"

Her entire focus centered on the dark head between her thighs and Michel's mouth that was only an inch away from oblivion. "I want you to lick me."

Scalding heat leisurely lapped at the arousal that leaked from her, as if it were rich cream and he was a cat daintily dining. He licked the wet, slick valley between her swollen lips, stopping just short of her clitoral hood, licking and licking.

She closed her eyes, straining downward, downward. . . .

"What else, *chérie?* Tell me what else you want."

Anne barely recognized her voice. The woman who shamelessly strained to gain her orgasm she did not recognize at all. "I want you to tongue me."

Galvanizing heat. Unbearable pressure.

He thrust at the opening of her vagina, a burning prelude, as if he would take her virginity with his tongue.

Her muscles clenched.

He tongued and probed, tongued and probed the small, taut membrane that protected her, until she did not know if it was pain or pleasure that she felt.

She had never imagined a man doing this, tasting her, licking her, testing her maidenhead with his tongue—

Piercing pain replaced the burning pressure. *He had bitten her!*

Eyes flying open in shocked awareness, Anne grabbed Michel's head. For one heart-stopping second his lips closed around her clitoris; his teeth sank into the stem while he suckled her. Sharp pain turned to equally sharp pleasure as his tongue swirled round and round, *there,* where she was most sensitive.

She had never imagined a man suckling a woman's clitoris as if he were a baby—a hungry baby with sharp teeth—who suckled and suckled for nourishment. . . .

Michel abruptly kneeled upright, his lips shiny wet . . . *from her.* His hips held her legs splayed, so closely wedged between her thighs that his wiry pubic hair mingled with hers and the hard, rubber-sheathed flesh that was his penis jutted against the nether lips he had licked and tongued and nibbled.

Cupping her right cheek with his left hand, he leaned into her. His mouth was hot, slippery; it tasted . . . of her.

Of hot, wet sex.

"It's all right to cry, Anne."

Anne swallowed her breath. Something large and round and blisteringly hot separated the lips of her femininity, prodded the portal of her vagina.

She remembered Mrs. Kildairn's prized plums. The largest in Dover, the widow boasted. They were four inches in diameter.

The same size that the plum-shaped head of his penis felt like.

Anne clutched his shoulders. She had thought he would take her virginity while she lay on her back—the way she had always imagined it while safely tucked inside her empty, lonely bed. The way he had described it in the cab. "Can it be done . . . like this?"

"Yes." Michel's lips moved against hers, slippery soft, beguiling as the serpent that had enticed Eve. "If that is what you want. Do you?"

She wanted whatever he did to her.

"Yes," she said, panting.

His left hand slid down her cheek, a slow caress, down over her chest—her nipple stabbed his palm; desire stabbed through her breast—smoothed over her waist, spread over the small of her back and the swell of her buttocks. He pressed her closer while the pressure against her maidenhead pushed inward.

"Relax, *chérie*. It is like a kiss. First I tasted you." His mouth opened over hers, hot and wet. The blunt pressure between her thighs throbbed. "Licked you." Slick heat glided over her lips. The bulbous head of his manhood swirled against her tautly stretched portal. "Tongued you." He prodded her mouth, her teeth, almost entering her but not quite. "And now I will penetrate you."

His tongue pierced her; at the same time the pressure between her legs knifed forward.

Anne forgot dignity. She forgot control.

She cried out—she who had never cried out.

The sound was muffled by Michel's mouth. He took the breath he had forced from her lungs and gave her his breath in return.

Anne involuntarily tried to push him away, to escape the pain, to regain a sense of self-control.

He grabbed her hip with his right hand while his left hand burrowed underneath her buttocks. "Hold still."

She felt spitted, unbearably stretched and vulnerable—as if her body were no longer hers alone.

This was not what she was paying for, this invasion that rendered her helpless.

Babies were helpless.

Invalids were helpless.

She did not want to be helpless.

Anne gritted her teeth. Tears stung her eyes. "It hurts."

"Look at me. Tilt your hips down. Feel what I'm doing." He captured her hand, guided it between their bodies. "I'm not all the way in. The pain will pass, *chérie.* Feel me sandwiched between your lips. . . . There."

Dear Lord, he *was* sandwiched between her lips. Hot, wet, and slick, they furled around the solid thickness of him in a sexual embrace.

"Don't close your eyes, Anne. I want you to look at me. I want to see your passion." The scars edging Michel's cheek were livid. "You had the courage to tell me what you wanted. Now let me see how much you want it."

Anne took a deep breath. She blurted out the only coherent thought she could form. "The French letter. It feels . . . like rubber."

"It is rubber."

"I didn't . . ." *Know.* "I feel . . ." *Like a stranger inside my own body.* "I'm sorry. I'm sorry I cried out."

Shadow engulfed his face. "Don't say you're sorry . . . not to me. Not ever. I want you to scream. And moan. And groan. I want you to lose yourself in what I do to you. I want you to want me."

For a blinding second she was hurtled outside her body. "You don't think that a spinster woman wants to be wanted? Perhaps I want you to moan and groan for me. Perhaps I want to hear you cry out, too!"

He pressed his forehead against hers. His skin stuck to her, hot and gluey with sweat. Or perhaps it was her skin that was hot and gluey with sweat.

"Then make me cry out," he whispered hoarsely. "Tilt your hips. Ride the shaft of my penis with your clitoris. Let me give you pleasure, *chérie.* Let me make you come. And when you come, grip my cock so tightly that I cry out with you."

She bit her lip, flesh throbbing. Inside. Outside. Mouth. Vagina. *Forehead.* "Your cock—you are referring to your penis?"

"My penis, my cock, *ma bitte.*" His fingers dug into her buttocks. "Tilt your hips. . . . More."

Searing pleasure jolted upward from her clitoris, sizzled along the lips of her femininity that curled around him, bolted through her painfully stretched vagina.

She had never imagined such intimacy. Man and woman, two bodies made one by their sex.

But he had known, this man who was named for his ability to please women.

"What do I do now?"

His expression hardened, skin tightening, lips flattening. "You take your pleasure."

The muscles inside her vagina rippled around him.

Michel forced himself another inch inside her, then pulled it out. In again. Another inch—*how deeply could she take him?* Out again. He was creating a burning, stinging rhythm that she instinctively responded to—riding, sliding, gliding along his shaft while she stared into his eyes that were impossibly violet.

"There is so much passion inside you, *chérie.*" His lashes lowered, banking the friction inside his gaze while his body continued pushing and pulling, pushing and pulling. . . . "I know you want to come." Leaning forward, he grazed her mouth, pulling her closer, closer. . . . "You gave me your cry of pain." *He gave her three more inches.* "Now give me your cry of pleasure."

Without warning, Anne exploded . . . and cried out at the harsh pleasure that tunneled inside her body.

The bed exploded with her.

With a grunt, Michel came to his feet, her buttocks secured with his left hand so that she remained firmly impaled. One shoe fell off of her flailing feet; it was immediately followed by its mate. He dropped down hard on the edge of the bed so that Anne sat straddling his waist.

Her head snapped back; she gasped in agonized pleasure.

He was all the way inside her.

All nine and one half inches.

Scalding heat scaled her throat, her breast . . . he latched onto her nipple and suckled while he ground his pelvis up into her, grinding side to side so that her labia and clitoris were smashed flat. She arched her back, no longer certain if it was pleasure or pain she felt; immediately his hand was there, hard and rough, supporting the small of her spine while he continued to suckle and suckle her as he ground himself up higher and higher inside her. He could not possibly go any deeper, *but he did,* and she cried out again in uncontrollable release.

Only to cry out yet again when the room turned upside down and a band of cold silk dug into her head and shoulders; equally cold velvet imprinted her backside. Her hair held her immobile—it was trapped between her and the bedcovers.

She stared up from where he had deposited her onto the bed. The muscles in her vagina fluttered in the aftermath of one climax, preparing for another.

Michel leaned over her, hips firmly implanted between her thighs, manhood deeply lodged inside her vagina. He was a blanket of wiry, prickly heat, chest pinning her breasts, stomach molding her womb.

Sizzling perception jolted through her.

Anne desperately gulped air.

There was only his breath to sustain her. Only his body to give her the orgasm that was again building up inside her.

"Now, *chérie.*" His violet eyes glittered. "Now I will show you angels."

Chapter 4

A gasp woke Michael just as pink dawn stretched across the ceiling.

It came from a woman.

Even as the woman's presence registered in his consciousness, she jerked out of his arms and sat up in bed. Long, silky hair concealed her back, a pale brown shield that glinted with gold and silver in the dull glow of an oil lamp.

Michael was abruptly aware of the sting of dried sweat and the scent of sex and roses. A deafening pounding commenced inside his ears—the sound of his own heart.

"What is it?" he murmured, body tensed, knowing the answer. Anne Aimes had had her night of pleasure and now she wanted to go home.

But she couldn't go home.

He had brought her to orgasm eight times, deliberately drugging her body and her mind with carnal excess. She should not be awake.

Turning, Anne's eyes swept over him. They were pale, unfocused, rimmed by lavender shadows. "I overslept. I have to get up. They need me. I need to get their medicine. . . ."

Her parents had been dead for ten months. The mother had followed the father, two days apart.

Helen and Henry Aimes had been old when they died, outliving every other relative. They had been old when they bore Anne, their only child.

And now she was alone, this spinster woman who was no longer a virgin.

As he was alone.

A sharp pain twisted inside Michael's chest.

"You haven't overslept, *chérie.*" Gently, carefully, he pulled her back down into the curve of his body, cocooning her with his arms and the silky web of her hair. "Shhh. It's all right."

She remained stiff in his arms, determined to cater to a family who no longer existed. "But their medicine . . ."

Michael smoothed a baby-fine strand of hair off her forehead; it clung to his scar-roughened fingers. He nuzzled her temple, savoring the smell of their commingled sweat and sexual satiation, and underneath that, the fragrance of soap, shampoo and her own unique scent, a sweetness that varied from woman to woman. "It's all right, *chérie.* You don't have to get up. It's all right. . . . No one needs you tonight. Go back to sleep."

Anne's resistance evaporated in a sigh.

"They died," she mumbled, eyes closing, breathing slowing. "I was so tired. . . ."

For a moment Michael thought about shaking her awake and bundling her out of his home and his life. He simultaneously realized what had disturbed her sleep.

The latch on the French doors rattled.

Someone was trying to break into his bedroom.

It was too soon, he thought on a surge of raw energy. The woman nestled against him was too inviting.

He needed more time.

The grate of metal grinding against metal sounded again.

How many men were waiting to take him? One? Two? Three?

The energy pumping through his body peaked. For one heart-stopping moment, he didn't know if he was prepared to fight or to flee.

Scalding shame was replaced with scorching anger.

He would not run, ever again.

Gently he disentangled himself from Anne's hair and lifted her head off of his shoulder. Sliding out of bed, he dimmed the lamp until the comforting yellow glow was a red tongue of fire.

A dark shadow shone through the curtains.

Only one had come for him. *This time.*

The oiled glide of hinged wood stirred the cool air—the drawer in the nightstand.

He had been prepared for Anne with a tin of condoms. He was equally prepared for the intruder.

The ivory hilt of the knife balanced in the palm of his hand, custom-fitted, as had been the French letters. One for fucking; the other for killing.

It did not matter.

He would not go until he was ready to be taken.

Crouching down on the cold wooden floor, he eased up the latch, knife poised, ready to strike.

"Either use it or put it away, Michael." The whisper was only a breath of air.

Gabriel.

He instinctively glanced toward the bed to make sure that Anne had not wakened. She lay as he had left her, on her back. He had forgotten to flip the covers up. Her breast gleamed in the dim light, as if carved out of alabaster; her right arm lay curled on top of the white silk sheet, palm turned upward.

Michael was not prepared for the rush of emotion that surged through him.

He had serviced women since he was thirteen years old—he had no right to feel pride at being Anne Aimes's first man.

He had belonged to any woman who could afford his price—he had no right to feel possessive of this one spinster.

But he did.

He did not want Gabriel to see her naked as he had seen her.

"Stay." Michael's command was a sigh of sound.

Rising, he grabbed Anne's velvet cloak off of the chaise lounge where he had earlier thrown it and wrapped it about his naked body. It reached midcalf. He stepped out onto the balcony, toes curling on the damp, icy wood, and softly closed the French doors behind him.

Pink pearled the sky. It was edged by fresh black smoke, London stoves stoked to cook breakfast for five million residents. A bird shrilly sang in the garden below.

Michael and Gabriel stood eye-to-eye, one head dark, the other fair. "I could have killed you, Gabriel."

Gabriel's breath mingled with Michael's, a plume of gray vapor. "Perhaps I wouldn't mind."

The anger simmering inside Michael eased. "I would."

"And you do not think that I will mourn you, Michael? You saved my life. Perhaps I would like to return the favor."

Gabriel had not considered it a favor when Michael had found him chained in the attic of a rich client's house. He had fought to die even as Michael had fought to save him.

"Why not enter by the front door?" Michael asked mildly. He stepped back, out of the moist cloud that was their combined breath. "You have a key."

"Perhaps because I wanted to see how prepared you are to deal with the men who will come for you. These French doors offer no protection. Why haven't you put grids over your windows?"

"Because if I do that, they cannot take me, can they?" Michael softly reasoned.

"What if it isn't you they take, but the woman?"

Michael remembered the feel of Anne's maidenhead stretching to allow him entrance.

She had screamed: first with pain, then with pleasure. Just as he had promised her she would.

He ruthlessly buried the memory. "Then she will gain me entrance. Perhaps she will die, perhaps not. I will still kill him. Or die myself, trying."

"You smell of her."

"I'm wearing her cloak."

"You smell of her sex, Michael. Of her pleasure. And yours. She did not come to you as a decoy. Will you let him do to her what he did to Diane?"

Michael closed his eyes, trying to shut out Gabriel's words.

For one infinitesimal moment he relived the experience of Diane, a woman who had walked away from her titled husband to be with him, a man whom she believed was nothing more than a French male whore. He remembered her uninhibited laughter and her unrestrained passion; her unadulterated lust for life.

When the man had taken her, she had broken in two months. Only in death had she regained peace.

Damn Gabriel.

Michael had loved Diane.

And her killer was free.

He opened his eyes. "Yes. Yes, I will let him take Anne Aimes."

They stared at each other, two fallen angels who wanted too much, dared too much, and had paid the price.

Gabriel stepped back, sudden comprehension flowing across his fair, flawless face. "He already knows."

Michael did not lie. "Yes."

He had known for the past five years that a spy had been planted in his household. He had also known that as long as he remained submersed in his own private hell he would be safe.

But then the solicitor had appeared on his doorstep.

Michael had followed the spy, who in turn had followed the solicitor.

The solicitor had led them both to Anne Aimes.

There was no doubt that the man knew who had procured Michael's services. Just as he knew that she was a lonely spinster who would not be missed until it was too late.

"And when you kill him, Michael? How will you live with yourself, knowing the price another woman will pay?"

Michael's lips quirked in a brief, ironic smile. "Perhaps I will not kill him. Perhaps he will kill me."

"Let me take her away. He knows that you are no longer content to play farmer. You lie to yourself if you think that women do not want you. There will be others, now that you're back. You do not need Anne Aimes. It is your sexuality that is the bait, not this woman."

Anger threatened to destroy Michael's sangfroid. He lashed out, wanting to hurt, knowing the tool to use. "Do not judge a woman's tastes by yours, *mon frère.*"

The hurtful words hovered between them.

Both knew them for the lie that they were. Neither had chosen the life that they led.

Gabriel's eyes narrowed; they gleamed silver in the new dawn.

He did not bother denying what was so patently false. "You're a fool, Michael. Buy a mirror. Look into it. *He* didn't condemn you to hell; you did."

Michael's lips tightened. "Stay away, Gabriel. I will not lose this time."

"You're afraid I will warn her?" he mocked.

There was no trace of the thirteen-year-old boy Gabriel had once been. No vestiges of laughter or tears.

Michael did not have to buy a mirror; he was looking into one.

The coldness numbing his feet settled in the pit of his stomach. "Yes, Gabriel, I am afraid."

"And if I do warn her?"

Michael turned without comment and eased inside the French doors.

Darkness closed around him.

There was too much death.

He had almost threatened to kill his only friend. *He* was *going to kill the only woman who took pleasure in his touch.*

Movements jerky, he turned up the lamp, needing the light to hold the past at bay.

Anne had asked him to extinguish the light when he undressed her.

If he had been another man, he would have respected her modesty that one time, her first time.

But he was not another man.

There was only one thing he feared more than fire. And that was darkness.

Michael silently appraised the woman in his bed.

She lay peacefully asleep, impervious to the man who watched her. Impervious to the fate that awaited her. Impervious to the cold that would blanket her.

A curly black hair rested on the plump white flesh of her breast—a hair from his chest. Below it, her nipple was dark and swollen, like a bruised strawberry.

She was very sensitive—she had almost orgasmed when he had suckled her.

Her slender fingers were devoid of jewelry, her short, buffed nails a healthy pink. Carved half-moons throbbed in his back and shoulders.

She did not look like the passionless, anemic woman who had entered the House of Gabriel, any more than she looked like a woman marked for death.

He remembered her choked gasp when he had initially brought her to orgasm.

In the cab she claimed she had never before seen a naked man. Yet not once had she displayed the modesty or timidity society expected a well-bred virgin to exhibit.

Married women had come to him, ignorant of the names for their sex organs. How had this spinster gleaned her knowledge?

What kind of life had she lived, that she did not think she could cry out with pleasure . . . or pain?

Michael inhaled heavy, sweet air. The scent of roses failed to mask the pending stench of decay.

Anger fisted inside his stomach.

His muscles ached from the labor of satisfying a woman instead of the labor of working his farm in Yorkshire. The latter had exhausted his body while his mind ran rampant. Anne had occupied both his mind and his body.

Damn the man for using the one means guaranteed to destroy him.

For one rage-filled moment he wondered if Anne Aimes had been hired to bring him back to London.

The man was capable of such a scheme. He knew Michael's weakness.

Immediately the anger dissipated, leaving behind only the need.

No amount of money could buy the passion he had seen in Anne's eyes.

The trembling started deep inside him, familiar but never welcome. There was only one way to stop it.

Tossing the velvet cloak aside, he snatched a condom from the tin and skillfully rolled it over his erect manhood. Unbidden, he remembered Anne's clumsy attempt to sheathe him with rubber.

She had been so afraid of losing control, standing before him naked and trembling with her hunger. So very determined to exert power that she did not possess.

Michael slid underneath the covers. The sheets were warm, inviting, the scent of sex alluring.

It had been five years since a woman had warmed his bed. Five intolerable years since a woman had gifted him with her ecstasy.

Michael rolled over onto his side and reached out—

His heart skipped a beat before accelerating to a loud roar.

Anne's pale blue eyes were open. They regarded him alertly, undimmed by sleep or dreams of the past.

Had she been awake when he stood over her?

Had she heard him step out onto the balcony?

Had she overheard his conversation with Gabriel?

"The birds are awake."

He did not move for fear of alarming her. "Yes."

"It's late." Her voice was distant, composed, not at all like the voice that had cried out with passion. "I have to leave."

Michael was suddenly tired of pretense.

He wanted.

She wanted.

Why couldn't it be enough?

He wasn't Michel, no matter how hard he pretended or how much he wished otherwise. The man he had been five years ago was dead. Everyone he had ever loved was dead.

Michael cupped Anne's face in his hands—*Michael's* hands, not Michel's. Hands that repelled rather than attracted.

But she *had not been repelled.*

Even now she unflinchingly bore his touch, her expression cool, guarded.

Gabriel was wrong. There was no other woman who would take him as Anne Aimes had taken him.

She had been bluntly honest about her desires. She deserved honesty in return.

"In the cab, I didn't tell you something—something that I should have told you," he whispered.

Uncertainty flared in her eyes.

She had such clear, pale eyes. So achingly expressive. They spoke of loneliness and pain and the gut-wrenching need to be touched, held, accepted.

Michael's language, not Michel's.

"What?" she whispered back, her breath hot and sweet with the remnants of champagne, tooth powder, and a woman's satisfaction.

"I didn't tell you that when a man is inside a woman"—he slowly stroked her velvety soft cheeks with his thumbs while cradling her shell-shaped ears in his palms—"it is her breath that sustains him . . . just as his does her. I didn't tell you that I need you, Anne Aimes. I need you to touch me. And I *will* pay for it."

She stiffened, unprepared for Michael the Englishman. Unaware that it was he who had taken her maidenhead, not Michel, the French *courailleur*. "There is no need to patronize me, monsieur. I am well aware that a man like you does not need a woman like me."

Michael spread his fingers, trapping her baby-fine hair and eggshell-fragile skull in his hands. "You think that a man who is scarred does not need the touch of a woman?"

She held perfectly still, as she had in the night house, surrounded by philanderers and whores. As she had in the hansom cab, pressed against a man hired to take her virginity. As she had in his arms when he had undressed her, immobilized by fear and desire. "I did not say that."

He tilted her face so that it was aligned with his, lips to lips, nose to nose. "Then you think that because I'm a whore, I don't need to be touched."

She rolled slightly toward him to relieve the pressure on her neck and grasped his forearms. "I did not say that, either!"

Panic and embarrassment were rampant in the spinster's eyes.

She was right to fear him—Michael, unlike Michel, would take and take until she had nothing more to offer. He would not seductively cajole her from maidenly shame or modesty as Michel would do. Time was too short.

His fingers held her head immobile, his gaze locked to hers. "Then what did you say, Anne Aimes?"

Her breath fanned his lips in short, hot spurts. "I merely imported . . . You have many women who come to you—beautiful women. Younger women."

How could she be so naive?

Did she need spectacles? Couldn't she see what he was?

"I have not had a patroness in five years," he said bluntly, acutely aware of his throbbing, engorged penis and the confession that would change everything.

Her eyes widened in disbelief; the frantic tug of her fingers slackened. "Why?"

"There was a fire," he returned roughly, dreading pity even more than repulsion.

"You did not wish to . . . be with women, because you were burned?"

How could Michel's pain—a man who had been dead for five years—hurt so much?

"Women did not wish to be with *me* . . . because I was burned."

"I find that difficult to believe, monsieur."

"Why?" He dug his fingers into her scalp, not exactly rough, but not exactly gentle either. "Why do you find it difficult to believe that a woman would not pay to lie with a scarred whore?"

"Because you are still the most handsome man I have ever seen."

Michael froze; the bird warbling outside the balcony was suddenly, piercingly loud. Nine miles away in London proper, Big Ben announced the time—one distant bong, two, three, four, five. "You have seen me before?"

"Once. Eighteen years ago. At a ball."

"I do not remember you."

"No. Of course not. Why should you?"

It should not matter that she had seen him before the fire.

But it did.

"I am not the same man."

"I have no complaints."

Lightninglike sensation rammed through Michael.

Why did this spinster accept him when every other woman spurned him?

He eased the pressure of his hands and threaded his fingers through her hair; it was warm and alive as he was not. "I asked you what you wanted. Before I took your virginity."

"I told you what I wanted."

"No." Michael gently massaged her scalp, easing away their pain, hers . . . and his. "You repeated the words that I gave you. The things I said I would do to you."

Her affirmation was swift and firm. Heartbreakingly predictable. "But I did want those things."

"But you didn't know that a man kissed a woman's clitoris," he ruthlessly insisted. "That a man tasted her, licked her, tongued her. Until tonight. Did you?"

A pale spark of desire flamed in her eyes.

She liked the words. Explicit words. Sexy words. The carnal phrases that between a man and a woman created an intimate dialogue.

Finally, reluctantly, she admitted, "No."

Michael breathed in the scent of her, of her sex, the sweetness of her unperfumed skin and feminine lust.

"If I had not told you about these acts, what would you have asked for?"

How she hated confessing her ignorance. Yet her inherent honesty would not let her lie.

"I don't know. I didn't think you would ask me. . . ." She closed her eyes, hiding her vulnerability. "I didn't know what to ask for."

And she still didn't.

"But you knew that men touched women. That men lay with women. Tell me what you thought I would do," he said softly.

"I thought . . . that you would kiss me . . . on the mouth."

"Did you know that a man suckled a woman's breasts?"

"No."

"Had you ever imagined a man suckling your breasts?"

Distress pulled at her lips. "Yes."

He gently feathered her eyelashes—they were short, spiked, tipped in gold—with his thumbnails. Her eyes sprang open at his touch.

"Tell me," he whispered, wanting to share her simple desire. To forget, however briefly, the evil that men did to men. Women. Children.

"I've seen mothers nursing their babies, and I thought . . . I thought how nice it would feel . . . to have a man suckle at my breasts. What a special closeness it must create."

Michael's breath quickened, his own need fanned by her innocent sensuality. "Did you ever touch your breasts when you had these thoughts?"

The mattress shifted underneath him.

"No." Michael held on to her, forcing her to turn on to her side and fully confront her passion. "Don't pull away from me."

They were all each other had—possibly they would be the last person either would ever touch. Hold. Love.

She rolled against him—her nipples bore into his chest; his manhood prodded the vee of her thighs.

"Your feet are cold," she murmured breathlessly.

And she still did not flinch from him.

He could feel the pounding of her heart as if it beat inside his own body; the pulse of his desire throbbed in his temples. "You didn't answer my question."

"I don't understand what it is that you expect of me."

"The truth, Anne Aimes. You may ask me anything you wish and I will not lie to you." *Not in bed, not about sex.* "You asked me if I had ever wanted to be touched so badly that I paid for it. *Yes.* The last five years I've paid for my pleasure. Knowing that whores found my touch repulsive, I still went to them. Wanting to touch. And be touched.

"Sometimes, when the sex was over and I lay awake in my own bed, I touched myself and wondered why it wasn't enough, taking a woman who didn't want me. I closed my eyes and imagined that there existed a woman who did want me . . . a woman who wasn't repulsed by my scars . . . and I would come again in my own hand."

Conflicting emotions raced through her eyes, like clouds tearing across a clear blue sky. Shock, that a man would openly speak about his need for a woman; understanding, that he would touch himself and yearn for more.

As this spinster had no doubt yearned.

"I want you, Anne. I want to be more than your whore. I want to be your lover." He rubbed his lips against hers until they parted and his breath invaded her mouth. "Stay with me. Now. Tomorrow. Stay with me for the month. I'll tell you what to ask for. What every woman has a right to demand. And then I'll give it to you. Every touch. Every kiss. Every lick. Things you've never imagined. Sexual acts I haven't performed in five years."

Pain glistened in Anne's eyes. "You didn't cry out . . . when you reached your orgasm."

At his moment of climax he had not been able to cry out.

Michel cried out, not Michael.

"Is that what you want? As my procuress, you are entitled to whatever you wish. A whore will cry out, if that is what pleases," he murmured relentlessly. "Whether orgasm is achieved or not."

"You're not a whore," she protested tightly.

Michael smiled humorlessly, knowing the lie for what it was. "But I was."

A whore. *Courailleur.* Stallion. *Macqueral.* Pettycoat pensioner.

The names for men like him were endless, in both English and French.

"What are you now?"

What was he now?

What was a man who preyed upon a woman's need for sexual pleasure, and who then used her need to be wanted?

There was no excuse for what he was about to do.

If he didn't keep her she would die.

If he did keep her she would be taken.

Only fools believed there was nothing worse than death.

Michel had not been a fool—only foolish. Michael was neither.

He felt the coffin lid slam down on them both as he uttered the words that would bind this spinster woman to him.

"I am a man"—Michael harshly expelled—"who wants to turn back time for one month. A man who wants to hear a woman cry out with passion and know that it is not feigned. I want to feel like the man I was five years ago. Whole. Desirable. Like I did tonight, when you climaxed for me. And later, when you slept in my arms. I want to share my body with you, Anne, but I can't do that if I'm your whore. And I won't be your lover if all the time you'll give me is a few hours here and there."

His needs were echoed in Anne Aimes's eyes. The longing to be attractive. To be wanted. To experience the special closeness of sex.

"I can't stay," she murmured. "I have to go. . . ."

But he couldn't let her go.

"You woke up . . . earlier . . . and said that you were late." He lightly licked her lips, absorbing her taste and smell, deliberately imprinting her with the flavor and scent of his own body. "That you had forgotten 'their medicine.' Do you take care of someone . . . nurse someone?"

Guilt spread over her pale features; immediately it was gone as she retreated into her spinster shell. "No. Not anymore."

He didn't want to hurt her.

"Then you have no one who needs you," he whispered. "No one to go home to."

Michael braced himself against the flatness in her gaze. "No. I have no one."

"My family died when I was eleven."

He was surprised at his admission.

She did not seem astounded that a man hired to pleasure her would discuss his family. "How did they die?"

"Cholera," he lied.

"Does it bother you, being alone?"

"Yes." There were so many things he would not have to lie to her about.

"What would you do . . . if I stayed now?"

The ache in his groin crawled up through his body, lodged inside his chest.

Pillowing her head with his left hand, he ran his right hand over the line of her shoulder—memorizing the delicate protrusion of bones, the indentation of her waist, the soft, luscious curve of her hip. "Do you want to stay with me . . . *now?*"

A delicate pink flush suffused her face. "Yes."

Michael grasped her knee, pulled it up and over his hip until her thigh notched his waist. "For sex."

"Yes."

The moist heat of her vulva seared his manhood. She was open. Unprotected.

An unwitting victim.

Forcefully he blocked the memories of what the man had done to him. To Diane.

Of what he would do to Anne.

"And will you lie to me?" he asked, needing her willingness, her openness, her naked passion.

Anne tentatively grasped his shoulders, leery of touching him, still afraid that *he* would reject *her*. "Why would I lie to you?"

Firmly securing her thigh, he grazed her swollen mouth with his, and eased his left hand out from underneath her head.

"Sometimes a lie is all that protects us." Michael tunneled his left hand underneath the pulsating warmth of her and clasped her buttocks—the velvety skin there was softer even than her face and breasts. "But there's no need to lie. Not to me." He feathered the crevice between her buttocks before slipping lower to seek out the core of her. "We both want . . . we both need . . . this."

Her vagina was burning hot. And wet.

Anne flinched at the insertion of his finger. "I don't know if I can take you right now. I'm . . . tender."

Michael could not promise that he wouldn't hurt her. In the end they would both be hurt. Or dead.

Shielding the truth with his lashes, he caressed her lips with his. "Do you trust me?"

"If I did not, I would not be here in your bed."

An invisible fist slammed into his gut.

He should give her to Gabriel.

Michael moved his finger back, circled tightly puckered flesh.

Anne tensed, frantically wriggled, was held firm by his arms and by her hair. "What are you doing?"

"I told you at the tavern that by the end of the night I would know your every crevice . . . your every orifice."

Jesus.

His finger was enveloped in blistering heat—hotter even than the fire that had burned him a lifetime earlier. He swallowed her gasp.

She tore her mouth away from his, hands lodging between their chests, pushing to escape the unexpected invasion.

But there was no escape.

"Put me inside you, Anne."

"But you have—"

"It is the French way. Relax. Take me. Many things will seem strange to you at first. I haven't touched a woman like this in five years. There's a special place inside you I want to caress. Let me give you pleasure, Anne."

"I don't want—"

But she did.

"What?" he mercilessly interrupted. "You don't want to explore the boundaries of passion? Wouldn't you like, just this once, to experience everything . . . every touch . . . every pleasure . . . that a man and a woman can experience together?"

Anne bit her lip, caught between propriety and a woman's curiosity. "Yes. That is why I came to you."

Even in this she would not lie.

"Then take me. Put me inside you."

Michael helped her, using his right hand to guide her trembling fingers until his manhood was gripped in a different kind of heat than that which bathed the middle finger on his left hand.

She convulsively gripped his waist with her strong thigh, inadvertently pulling him deeper. "Oh, my God!"

Michael kissed Anne's eyelids closed, unable to bear the stark emotion in her gaze.

He hurt her and she still trusted him to please her.

"Move with me." Her eyelashes tickled his lips. He carefully commenced the rocking motion that would ultimately bring them to completion. "Take your pleasure."

Make me forget. . . .

Her body unwittingly responded to his, as it had in the night house. As it had when he had taken her maidenhead.

Michael watched her face—and did not think of the man who waited for him. He thought only of Anne Aimes.

A slight frown gathered between her eyebrows—they were a darker brown than her lashes, the same color as her pubic hair—as she concentrated on obtaining her release. He could feel her orgasm gathering inside her, could feel the pulse of his own need through the thin membrane that separated his finger and his manhood.

Her expression told him everything: where to touch. When to slow down. When to speed up. How deep to plunge. At what angle to penetrate. When to be gentle. *When to be rough . . .*

Anne's eyelids snapped open.

Her pale blue eyes burned with passion.

For him. With him.

"I want—" Anne gasped, instinctively arching her back when he flexed inside her.

He wanted, too. So many things.

Her muscles tightened around him; Michael had to work to maintain the rhythm. He gritted his teeth; stinging sweat trickled down his temple.

"When you orgasm . . ." She matched him breath for breath. "I want you . . . to cry out . . . like you made me . . . cry out!"

He had not cried out when the man had taken him.

Would it have helped?

Had it helped Diane?

Would it help Anne?

A face was reflected in her dilated pupils—it was naked with need, curiously vulnerable in its single-minded intent, open mouth gasping for air, nostrils flared in undisguised want.

With a start of shock Michael recognized himself.

He didn't want her to see him like this.

The madam's tutelage came to his rescue.

"Come with me!" he harshly urged her. Expertly he twisted his wrist at the same time that he flexed his pelvis. "Now!"

Surprise etched Anne's flushed face. She threw her head back and cried out her release.

Michael buried his face in the hot, moist crook of her neck. Her muscles clamped his manhood and his finger in a fist-tight vise, fusing their flesh into one. For a brief second *he* was Anne Aimes, lost in innocent pleasure. An agonized groan vibrated in his chest, his lips, the tendons cording his throat. Then his seed burst from him and pooled inside the rubber condom, a hot bath of sperm.

Reason returned with release.

Stealing a woman's innocence would not bring back his own.

He inhaled the scent of roses, sex, and sweat, trapped in the spinster woman's hair and the ripples of her orgasm. He wondered how many more little deaths they would have before the final one.

Chapter 5

Anne awoke with a start to palpitating, rose-scented sunshine. A white-enameled ceiling bordered by a cornice of gilded leaves stared down at her. Pale green silk climbed the walls. Brass gleamed—the footposts of a bed.

She shifted her hand across a cool, slippery-soft sheet and touched a hip.

A naked hip.

Her hip.

"Good morning."

Throbbing recognition pulsed through her body. It settled in the raw, swollen flesh between her thighs.

The pungency of sex and sweat abruptly overwhelmed the sweetness of roses.

Anne swiveled her head on the silk-encased pillow.

White-enameled wood and sparkling panes of glass materialized out of blinding sunshine—French doors. A man's dark head solidified out of shimmering dust motes—Michel des Anges.

Scalding embarrassment flooded her face.

He had told her he would make her cry out.

And he had.

Again and again.

Anne gripped slick handfuls of silk to prevent herself from flinging back the covers and running away as fast as her legs would carry her.

The medical conspectus had not cited the repercussions of coition. There had been no reference to the emotional cleaving that occurred with shared orgasm. No mention of the whispered exchange of confidences that exposed loneliness and incited lust.

She was not prepared for this.

Penetration, yes. *Possession,* perhaps. But not this—awakening in the bed of a man who had stripped away her every inhibition to reveal her for the love-starved woman that she was.

"Good morning," she offered stiltedly, acutely aware of her unwashed face, uncombed hair, and unbrushed teeth.

Michel set aside a neatly quartered newspaper and rose from a yellow silk-upholstered chaise lounge.

His black hair was damp. It curled over the edge of his white linen shirt collar.

It had been damp last night, too. With sweat.

Hers and *his.*

Memories flooded her consciousness—of him striding toward her, naked, with the full, heavy thrust of his penis swaying side to side.

How deeply will you penetrate me, monsieur?

Nine and a half inches, mademoiselle.

She instinctively glanced at the vee of his thighs as he strode toward her now.

The gray wool trousers were tented.

Do you always . . . get erect when you are with a woman?

Yes.

Immediately her glance darted upward.

He loomed over the bed, taller than she remembered, larger than she remembered.

Save for his penis.

She remembered that as being very large.

The scars ridging his right cheek sharpened. "A hot bath will ease your soreness."

Anne forced herself not to look away from his violet eyes—eyes that had seen both her nakedness and her need. "Thank you. I will take one when I get home."

A muscle jumped at the corner of his mouth. "I did not please you?"

She took a deep, fortifying breath—*if she could solicit a sexual liaison in the dark of night, she could face the consequences of her actions in the light of day.* "You must know that you did."

"But not enough for you to take me as your lover."

Her heart tripped inside her chest.

She was not the same woman who had demanded that he taste her, lick her, and who had then taken her pleasure.

Any more than he was the same man who had confessed his need to be touched, and who had then pierced her where surely no woman should be pierced.

With the sunlight clearly delineating the fine wrinkles around her eyes and the silver threading her hair, she was once again a spinster who must pay for her pleasure. Whereas he looked like a beautiful, scarred statue, remote and removed from the pleasures of the flesh.

Lucifer after the fall from grace.

He could not possibly want to be her lover.

"Is it . . ." *No, he had said a woman had not solicited his services in five years.* "Was it customary for a . . . patroness . . . to stay with you?" she asked coolly, carefully masking her discomfiture.

"If I invited her, yes."

A flush of pleasure warmed her cheeks.

It was quickly followed by the cold slap of reality.

Any woman who paid ten thousand pounds would be welcomed by him.

"I do not wish to inconvenience you," she said stiffly.

"You do not inconvenience me. My home and my servants are at your disposal."

A chill premonition pricked the hairs at the nape of her neck. "You own . . . this house?"

The hand-carved cornice with its individually molded leaves that bridged the pale green silk-covered walls and white-enameled ceiling were unique works of art. As had been the marble staircase with the intricately fashioned wrought-iron balustrades they had traversed the night before.

"I also own an estate in Yorkshire county," he said, as if aware of the direction of her thoughts.

But that would mean . . . "If you own this house . . . and an estate . . ."

Her mouth snapped shut.

How stupid of her to presume anything about this man.

Michel des Anges had no doubt made several fortunes. His expertise was a testament to the number of women he must have serviced throughout the years.

Gambling had stripped more than one man of his wealth.

"I see," she said.

His long, black lashes shielded his eyes. "What do you see, Anne Aimes?"

"Obviously you have fallen on hard times."

"Is that why you think I took you last night?" he asked silkily.

There was nothing soft or silky about his face. It was filled with stark challenge.

And the compelling knowledge of her most secret desires.

She had cried out, his violet, black fringed eyes said. With the need for satisfaction. The need to be young. Beautiful. Touched. Wanted by a man.

By him.

A man who could overcome a woman's control and fulfill her wildest fantasies.

And he had.

For a price.

Anne retreated behind a wall of curtness. "Please leave me. I must get dressed."

Michel sat on the bed beside her, mattress sinking, silk and velvet covers bunching. She clutched the top sheet to her breasts and inched her buttocks across the mattress to stay the slide of her body.

Pain shot through her. It took a second to separate the stabbing ache between her thighs from the sharp hurt that yanked at her scalp. She stilled, held captive by her hair.

Why had he released it from the bun? She would never be able to get the tangles out.

How ridiculous she must look, with her hair loose as if she were a young woman.

A strong, scarred hand reached out, smoothed fine strands of hair off of her left cheek. "Don't run away from me now, Anne."

Blood thrummed underneath his hot, rough fingertips; his hip throbbed against hers, striking a rhythm deep inside her where he had ripped and torn and thrust and teased until pain had become pleasure so intense it had seared her soul.

Her throat tightened, there where he had muffled his agonized groan of release. "I don't know what you mean."

He continued smoothing her cheek, forging a raspy link of shared recollections: *his breath filling her lungs; her breath filling his lungs; their bodies merged into one, joined by sex.* "You're frightened."

Anne tensed, fighting his touch; fighting inexplicable tears. "Yes."

"Of me?"

Yes.

"I'm not . . ." She focused on the thick, black hair that curled at the base of his throat. Remembering its texture, crinkly and wiry. Remembering it abrading her breasts, an undulating blanket of prickly heat. "I'm not like that."

"But you are."

His fingers burned; his hip burned; the flesh between her thighs burned. It did not alter the truth. "No."

A thirty-six-year-old spinster whose only accomplishment was being a nursemaid did not scream and cry.

"Shall I tell you what I found most attractive about you at the House of Gabriel?"

Anne's gaze flew up and locked with violet eyes.

He would not lie to her, he had said.

But she didn't want to hear the truth.

"It is not necessary."

Sunshine brightly illuminated the left side of his face; light filtered through the tips of his lashes. Faint lines radiated out from the corner of his eye. "But it is necessary."

"I don't want—"

"We both want," he interrupted harshly. "That is why you

made the assignation. And that is why I was there, waiting for you."

It was not *she* he had waited for.

He did not know her.

He had not even remembered her.

Anne stiffened, both angered and hurt at his deception. "You said you would not lie to me, Monsieur des Anges. It is a simple matter of business that brought us together. You waited because of the promise of ten thousand pounds. It is my money that you found attractive. Nothing more. Nothing less."

His fingers stilled.

Shadow darkened the bedchamber, an ominous cloud on the horizon.

And still his skin throbbed and pulsed.

Against her cheek. Inside her breasts. *Her womb.*

Every inch of her body remembered his touch, responded to it.

"Nothing is ever simple," Michel exhorted on a sharp inhalation of air. "Not lust. Not life. You've lost to death. You should know better."

Anne's heart kicked against her ribs, galloped to outrun her fear.

How could he possibly know? . . .

The moisture in her mouth evaporated. "How do you know I've lost to death?"

"You told me."

Frantically she cast about in her thoughts. Remembering, remembering—

The wet lick of his tongue. Embracing heat; her breast boring into his chest; his masculinity nudging her femininity.

You woke up . . . earlier . . . and said that you were late. That you had forgotten "their medicine." Do you take care of someone . . . nurse someone?

No. Not anymore.

"I told you I would not lie to you, Anne Aimes." The raised ridges edging Michel's cheek whitened. "And I will not. Last night

I waited for you in the hope that the woman who solicited my services would see my scars—and still want me."

And she had.

A shimmering burst of sunshine underlined her unspoken affirmation.

"You would not have been there, waiting, if not for the money," she insisted, forcefully concentrating on the nature of their relationship instead of that enervating, throbbing pulse that promised more.

More passion.

More pleasure.

The black of his pupils swallowed the violet band of his eyes. "If not for your offer," he agreed, "I would not have been there. Waiting."

The truth should not hurt.

"A man is more attracted to a woman's beauty than he is by her passion," she said defiantly.

Now where had that come from?

"No," Michel said, fingers and voice equally grating. "Only a fool values beauty over passion."

"Yet you did not notice me eighteen years ago."

She bit her lip to stop the words—*too late,* her pain echoed among the gilded leaves.

A rough, scarred thumb traced the heat racing across her cheek, gently brushed her compressed mouth. "Yet here you are."

Anne's lips quivered. "I remember . . ." *The woman he had danced with. Laughed with.* "Are your duties not more easily performed when a woman is . . . beautiful?"

"Every woman has her own unique beauty. Do you know how velvet is made?"

It was becoming increasingly difficult to tell whose pulse palpitated and pounded.

"It is . . . woven from different fabrics."

"There is a velvet woven from silk. Silk velvet."

"Yes."

It was very expensive.

"In the night house I looked at you while you sat across from me, and I wanted you because *you* wanted *me*. But in the vestibule I touched your cheek." His fingers rasped the length of her jaw. "And I thought . . ."

Anne stiffened, waiting, breath suspended.

"I thought I had never felt anything that soft . . . like velvet . . . until I touched your buttocks. Your skin there is like silk velvet."

She would not be disappointed.

"A man does not judge a woman's beauty by the softness of her . . . *bottom*."

Violet fire bled into the black of his pupils. "I assure you, a woman's bottom holds great appeal to a man."

Anne's muscles clenched.

In memory.

In desire.

She moistened her lips; her tongue briefly scaled the coarse, salty texture of his thumb. "What can you give me as a lover that you have not already given me?"

Darkness engulfed her. Michel leaned down, blocking the sunlight. "Intimacy," he murmured, a whisper of breath that smelled of coffee.

He licked her lightly.

When she closed her eyes and opened her mouth, he licked her deeply, touching places inside her that had nothing whatsoever to do with her lips or her tongue. Scorching breath inflated her lungs. "Friendship."

Anne had never had a friend.

A governess had schooled her, and shielded her from the village children lest they steal her away for her parents' money.

She squeezed her eyelids tightly shut; the taste of coffee lingered in her mouth. It was mellowed with passion.

Hers . . . or his?

"Friendship can't be bought," she protested.

"Anything on this earth can be bought. . . ."

Michel nipped her bottom lip, sucked it between his teeth to lave away the tiny pain before hungrily suckling it. *As he had suckled her tongue. Her nipples. Her clitoris. . . .*

Her tongue, nipples, and clitoris throbbed in time to the pulsating veins inside her bottom lip

She had no one waiting for her at her town house, only servants the solicitor had rented for her amorous adventure in London.

What would it be like, she wondered, to live with a man, *this man,* if only for a month?

What would it be like to leisurely explore the boundaries of passion and experience *everything* . . . every touch . . . *every pleasure* . . . that a man and a woman could know together?

Things she'd never imagined. *Sexual acts he hadn't performed in five years.*

Breaking free of his mouth which was draining her very will, she desperately repeated the words he had claimed in the cab: "This is a sexual liaison."

Michel grasped her chin, preventing her from turning away to seek air that he did not give her. "I offer you more."

Intimacy. Sex. Friendship. Lust.

Anne swallowed. "You don't know what you're asking of me."

A nightly rendezvous could be kept secret. But if she openly lived with him, servants would talk. Gossip would spread throughout London, and from there to Dover.

She would lose all vestiges of respectability. As she had lost all vestiges of her virginity.

"I do know what I'm asking of you." Scorching words bathed her slippery wet lips. "I'm asking you to give me what I'm willing to give in return. Complete access to my body . . . in exchange for complete access to yours."

Complete access reverberated inside her mouth, against her tongue.

"The women whom you invited to stay with you . . . did they accept this offer?"

He rubbed his lips back and forth, moistening his mouth with the saliva he had imparted to hers. "I have never offered a patroness what I offer you now."

Anne felt as if she were drowning. In his heat. His scent. His breath. His taste.

Day melted into night, morning into day, past and present pleasures merging.

She clung to the reality of dialogue. "You have never experienced intimate sex . . . or friendship . . . with another woman?"

Cold air replaced Michel's lips and body.

Anne stared up at him, chilled by his abrupt withdrawal. "I beg your pardon. I had no right to ask that."

"I told you. You may ask me whatever you wish." The right corner of his mouth twisted, relaxed. "I have known such a relationship. Once. A long, long time ago."

A small barb of jealousy stung her. "What happened?"

His voice was flat. Emotionless. "She died."

And he had loved her.

"I'm sorry."

Curiosity flared in his eyes, as if he were not used to a woman expressing her condolences. "Are you?"

"Yes."

She must have been an incredible woman to gain the love of a man like him.

"It does not upset you, knowing that I have cared for another woman?"

"No. Of course not. Why should it?"

"Have you ever cared for another man?"

Anne steadily met his gaze, heart pounding in her breast, her vagina, her eyes. She echoed his earlier words. "Once. A long, long time ago."

Fleeting regret darkened his face. "What happened to him?"

"I do not know."

She had no idea whatsoever of what had happened to Michel des Anges these past eighteen years.

Her solicitor had not told her that he was scarred. Nor had he told her that Michel owned property in both London and Yorkshire.

He had not told her that the man who was once renowned for his ability to pleasure women had not had a procuress in five years.

Before she could fathom Michel's intentions, he tugged the covers down.

Pure instinct took over. Anne lunged for the velvet quilt, the silk sheet—and lost both.

She held rigidly still, refusing to give in to her embarrassment . . . or the indignity of trying to hide with her hands what was physically impossible to conceal.

Her fingernails dug into her palms.

He had no right to look at her in the unforgiving rays of sunlight.

Thick black lashes shielding his eyes, Michel perused her nakedness.

Unbidden, her gaze followed his.

Her nipples were dark and swollen, her breasts startlingly white in comparison.

They did not look like they belonged to an aging spinster. They looked like they belonged to a woman who had known a man's passion.

"A man takes pleasure in a woman's breasts." Reaching out, he plumped her soft flesh, his touch achingly gentle. As if she were fragile. Precious.

A woman to be treasured rather than a client to be serviced.

Her heart thumped against the heavy weight of his hand. She could see his scars—a mass of hard, puckered ridges—as well as feel them. The individual ridges were hard and hot. The nipple protruding from the cup of his fingers was equally hard and hot. Both his hand and her nipple rapidly rose and fell in cadence with her breathing—one flesh, a part of a whole.

"He loves the softness." Lightly he touched the pad of his thumb to her engorged nipple, pressed it into the mound of her breast. "The hardness."

Painful pleasure forked through Anne's chest.

Michel abruptly removed his thumb so that her nipple sprang up harder than before, longer, swollen to the point of bursting.

Anne's gaze shot up, away from the blatant sign of her arousal.

His face was dark, intent, lashes long and thick against the smooth, unmarred skin underneath his eyes. Inky dark hair blocked the scars on his temple, caressed the ones on his cheek; blue highlights danced across the black hair framing the left side of his face.

"You've watched mothers suckle their babies. And imagined a man suckling your breasts." His voice was curiously remote. "The closeness it must create."

An invisible band squeezed her chest.

He looked so utterly alone.

A man who bore the grief of an eleven-year-old boy.

A man who wanted to be whole. Desirable.

"Men want that closeness, too. That's why they suckle a woman."

Slowly Michel's eyelashes rose, revealing a baffled hunger, as if he, too, were overwhelmed by emotions outside his control.

"You've felt my heartbeat. Against your breast. Inside the palm of your hand."

Heat pulsated inside her palm where the night before his manhood had palpitated against her skin with a life of its own.

"I feel your heartbeat now." His gaze did not waver from hers. "This morning I felt it against my chest. My lips. My tongue. My finger, buried inside you."

Remembered sensation tore through her. Of shallow, penetrating probes. Of deeper, alternating thrusts.

"I told you thoughts I've never told another woman." Sunlight flickered in his left eye; his right one remained in shadow, dark and flat. "I confessed my need to touch. To be touched."

He lightly rotated his thumb round and round the tip of her nipple. "I admitted my desire to be wanted. Despite my scars. Needs and desires I will never share with another woman."

His words reverberated inside her body, primal and poignant, plucking and strumming an invisible wire that stretched tighter and tighter with each circle of his thumb.

"I *am* a whore. By trade. You are a spinster. By marital status. If we were not what we are, we would not be here. But I want more. I want, for the time that we have left together, for us to simply be a man and a woman. Lovers. Living together. Sharing sex. Sleep. Laughter."

Anne could not breathe, either to expel the air that was locked inside her lungs, or to draw in needed oxygen.

"I will not ask you again, Anne Aimes. Stay with me. Or we will both regret it for as long as we live."

Regret.

Such an ugly word. An emotion she had vowed never again to experience.

"I do not laugh . . . very often," she managed.

"Neither do I."

"I never wanted to be a spinster."

His relentless, circling thumb stopped. Violet pain flickered in his eyes. "I don't want to be your whore."

"Have you really wanted a woman so badly that you touched yourself?" she asked unsteadily.

"Oh, yes." He gently flicked her nipple until it felt ready to burst—once, twice. . . . "Many times."

Erotic sensation that was neither pleasure nor pain arced back and forth between her womb and her nipple.

Promising more . . . *if she dared.*

"Have you ever touched . . . your breasts?"

His violet irises ate up the bleakness of his pupils. "A man has the same needs that a woman does."

To touch. To be touched.

To be wanted.

Despite the past. Despite physical imperfections.

Anne fixedly stared at his scarred thumb, strumming her breast; at her turgid brown nipple, flicked back and forth.

She imagined touching him as he was touching her.

Tasting him.

Kissing him.

Suckling him.

Feeling the pulse of his heartbeat against her lips. Her tongue.

"As lovers . . . may I do anything to you . . . that I wish?"

"Anything. Everything."

She labored for breath; the insistent thrumming inside her breast and womb was building to a crescendo. "Do the French really do . . . what you did this morning?"

Suddenly his hand and his thumb were replaced by cold air. Heat brushed her pubic mound—his gaze. It was followed by the solid heat of his fingers.

Anne instinctively gave him access. She opened up her legs to a rush of cooling air.

His wrist curved, stiff linen cuff a shock of white against the pale brown vee of her pubic hair.

A pulse leaped to life deep inside Anne where he had previously penetrated her. She flinched. *Where he now penetrated her.*

Gently, insistently, he eased all the way in before slowly easing all the way out.

His middle finger was slippery wet; a thread of crimson striated the creamy moisture of her essence.

Suddenly she felt his gaze on her face, watching her study the evidence of the pain he had wrought the night before, and the desire he created anew.

"The French are very practical when it comes to their pleasures." His voice was low. Husky. "They are not as fastidious as the English."

Without warning the bed shifted underneath her. Between one heartbeat and the next Michel grasped her right leg; at the same time he twisted his torso so that he lay between her thighs, his face only inches away from her splayed femininity.

Mortification vied with excitement.

Anne involuntarily tried to close her legs.

His fingers dug into the softness of her thighs. "Don't."

"You can see me."

"I saw you last night."

"But this is not . . . night."

And sunlight was not kind to a thirty-six-year-old spinster.

Michel pushed her thighs more widely apart. "There is no need for modesty between lovers."

No need for modesty. *No room for dignity.*

She ached.

With renewed passion.

With lingering pain.

"I need to . . . bathe."

"Having sex with me did not dirty you."

He nuzzled the inside of her thigh, close, *so close*. Hot moisture trickled out of her pulsing, throbbing vagina.

Excitement was rapidly overcoming mortification.

"I—" *Bled*. "You surely do not intend to—"

"I surely do not intend to—what?" His breath fanned her raw, aching nether lips. "Taste you? Lick you? Tongue you?"

Surely he would not—*not in the light of day*.

Surely he would not—not before she washed.

But she wanted him to.

She wanted him to kiss her in the exact same manner he had the night before.

And he knew it.

"But I do intend to taste you. Lick you. Tongue you." Michel's violet eyes were bottomless pools of unplumbed carnality. "A Frenchman, unlike an Englishman, does not hesitate to lave away a woman's pain. He knows that it is because of him that she bleeds."

Lowering his head, he delicately lapped at her exposed, vulnerable flesh. Her labia first, a quick lick, parting the lips. Slowly, thoroughly, his tongue swirled at the portal of her vagina, plunged inside it, impaling her very heart. He lapped and lapped until the raw tenderness was gone and pleasure, just as sharply invasive, ripped through her and she was straining for more, *more*—

Anne frantically reached out—

Only to grab fistfuls of hair.

It was silky soft and warm with the scorching heat that belonged solely to Michel des Anges.

Michel raised his head, lips shiny with her arousal.

Emotion swelled inside her, a sharp bite of wonder, apprehension, and sexual excitement. "Is there nothing that you will not do?"

"Nothing," he said hoarsely. "Providing that it brings pleasure."

Hands shaking—or perhaps it was the bed that shook—she cupped his head; the imprint of his ears branded the palms of her hands. She did not want him to be her whore, crying out, kissing her, pleasuring her because it was what *she* wanted. "But do you enjoy doing these things?"

"Yes."

The truth, he had said.

"I enjoy them, too."

Michel pressed a kiss into the springy tuft of her pale brown pubic hair. "I know you do," he murmured softly, hot breath sifting, teasing her swollen flesh, which pulsed and throbbed for attention. "You are a passionate woman. And that is a man's true measure for beauty."

Anne almost believed him.

Staring at the long, lean fingers that curved around her thighs—at the masculine nails that were short and manicured, at the thumb nails that were noticeably longer—it was possible to believe anything.

As no doubt countless others had believed.

"I cannot imagine any woman not wanting you," she whispered.

His dark, ridged skin sank into her soft flesh.

Daring his rejection—damning society's—she braved his gaze. "I want you to be my lover. I want to experience the intimacy you speak of. Living together. Just a man and a woman. For one month. If that is what you wish."

A blast of energy rode the wave of her sexual excitement—it came from Michel.

From his eyes, which blazed with heart-stopping intensity.

From his shoulders, which tensed rock-hard between her thighs.

Lowering his head, he grazed her clitoris in a silky-soft kiss. *"Plus que la mort elle-même,"* he murmured.

Before she could translate his words—she was not even certain she had heard them correctly over the hammering of her heartbeat—he sucked her up into a vortex of pleasure where the past that had held only sickness and death and damning decisions ceased to exist and the future was his mouth. His tongue. And the orgasm that glimmered just over the horizon.

Chapter 6

Each bump of the carriage wheels jogged another memory.

Michel's cry, hoarse and strained.

Michel's penis, hard and erect.

Michel's long, scarred finger, stained with her virgin blood.

Over and over Anne heard the words he had murmured before taking her into his mouth.

Plus que la mort elle-même.

She could not have interpreted his French correctly. Or else she had not heard him clearly.

A man did not want anything *more than death itself.*

The cab pulled up to the curb.

Anne stared through the small, square window; it was smeared with tiny fingerprints—the hands of a child.

The brick town house looked different.

Older. More conservative.

Anne felt different.

Younger. Less confident.

Last night she had thought to buy the pleasure Michel des Anges could give a woman. She had never, ever thought he would give her access to his body.

To his life.

Anne tripped as she stepped out of the cab.

Clumsy, clumsy old maid.

Her hands inside her gloves were clammy.

With fear.

With anticipation.

Last night had changed her body.

Living with Michel would change her life.

She could never again take her place among those of the respectable ton who were her parents' contemporaries.

Anne gave the grim-faced cabby a sixpence.

How much had Michel paid the cabby last night? she wondered inanely. More than what she now paid?

The door to the town house opened just as Anne reached for it.

"Miss Aimes." The butler, an attractive man in his fifties with receding sandy hair, stepped aside for her to enter. His spine was ramrod straight.

Anne tried to envision him doing to a woman what Michel had done to her.

She could not.

In his stiff black coat and tie, the butler was a picture of English moral rectitude.

He revealed neither surprise nor disapproval that Anne returned home after a twelve-hour-long rendezvous, his features set in the expression that all servants wore to mask their emotions lest they displease their employers. "Shall I take your cloak, Miss Aimes?"

Her Dover servants, many of whom had been in her parents' service before her birth, addressed her as "Miss Anne," not the impersonal "Miss Aimes."

Their faces were equally impassive.

A wave of loneliness broke over her. It was followed by a rush of shame.

Never before had she wondered about a servant's sexual practices.

"No, thank you." Anne stiffened her spine. "Please have my abigail come to my bedchamber."

The butler bowed again. "Very well, Miss Aimes."

The smell of age and mildew followed Anne up the worn, wooden stairs.

They were familiar scents, safe scents.

Doubt creaked—a loose board. It sliced through the lethargic glow of sexual satiation.

What if Michel had said all those things—that he needed a woman to want him—because that was what *she* wanted to hear?

What if he wanted her to stay with him merely as a ploy to leach more money from her?

The hallway was paneled in mahogany; Michel's hallway was hung with pale blue silk.

Her doors were dark wood; Michel's doors were painted white.

The life she had chosen was exemplary; the life he had lived was shamelessly immoral.

Yet here they were. . . .

Anne threw her cloak and reticule onto the wooden four-poster bed, then crossed the maroon carpet to stand in front of an old-fashioned cheval mirror.

Her corset pinched her swollen breasts; her wool drawers abraded her tender nether regions—proof that she was not the same woman who had dressed in front of this mirror some twelve hours earlier.

The internal changes did not show in the looking glass.

She had left an aging spinster; she returned an aging spinster.

Why would any man want a woman like her to be his lover? To sleep with her? Wake with her? Breakfast with her?

A soft knock interrupted her reflections.

"Come in."

Anne continued looking in the mirror, searching, *searching*. . . .

Only to find her bedroom door pushing open. A dark, wiry woman in her early fifties stepped into the dank bedchamber.

It dawned on Anne that Michel did not have a mirror in his bedchamber. Or bathroom.

"How may I help you, Miss Aimes?"

Anne peered into the shadows inside the mirror. The maid's black dress blended into the dark mahogany of the closing door.

"I would like a bath, please."

The cavernous holes that were the abigail's eyes bore into her back. "Will that be all, ma'am?"

The woman in the mirror who outwardly resembled Anne was pale and composed; the woman inside her quaked and trembled with the momentousness of her decision. "No. Please pack my trunk. I am going away for a month."

So that a man to whom she paid ten thousand pounds could be her lover instead of her whore.

No, not her whore. She had *never* considered Michel a whore.

The abigail curtsied. "Very well," she said, and turned toward the bathroom.

Anne pivoted in a swirl of wrinkled gray silk. "Jane—"

The rental abigail paused. "Ma'am?"

"Do I look different?"

"No, ma'am," the maid responded blandly, incuriously. "Is there anything else, ma'am?"

"No." Anne suddenly felt ridiculous. The maid had known her less than a week. Even if there were a difference, the abigail would not notice. "Thank you."

She resisted the temptation to turn back around and search anew for the changes that Michel had wrought inside her body.

Because she *was* changed.

She had paid a man to take her virginity.

She had garnered the courage to tell him what she wanted.

She had confronted her desires in the blaring light of day.

The muted creak of rusty pipes eerily interspersed the rheumatic ticking of the French clock on the mahogany mantel of the empty fireplace.

It did not matter why Michel wanted to be her lover, Anne determined mutinously.

She wanted this month with him—a sharing of sleep. Of waking. Of breakfasting.

Intimacy. Friendship.

Pleasures she would never experience with a husband.

A rustle of cloth alerted Anne that she was no longer alone.

Jane stood in the doorway adjoining the bedchamber and bathroom. When Anne caught her gaze, the abigail's dark eyes shifted.

"Shall you undress now, ma'am?"

"Yes. Please."

The abigail deftly unfastened the tiny buttons lining the back of Anne's silk dress.

Michel, she remembered with a flush of heat, was equally adept—at both dressing and undressing a woman.

Slowly, methodically, Anne was relieved of her dress, bustle, corset, and petticoats. The French marble clock chimed the time.

A quarter of an hour had lapsed. The exact same time that the antiquated geyser required to heat up the bathwater.

An answering clock ticked away inside Anne's body, marking the minutes, counting the dangers.

Jane turned in a swish of black wool and disappeared into the bathroom. The splash of cascading water filled the yawning void.

The bath would be filled in five minutes.

Jane returned on cue. "I will have a footman bring down your trunk, Miss Aimes."

The overwhelming finality of Anne's decision swelled over her. "Very well," she said—and fought to keep from running after the departing maid to rescind her decision.

Muggy moisture filled the cubbyhole-sized bathroom. It stank of gas. The geyser, a water-tube boiler painted to resemble green marble and outfitted with shining brass and royal arms, continued to emanate heat.

Quickly she brushed her teeth, rinsed her mouth with water, and spit it out in the yellowed porcelain sink. The Bramah toilet—outdated as was everything else in the town house—belched and gurgled when she pulled the copper chain hanging from the reservoir box on the ceiling. She kicked aside the wool drawers bunched at her feet—and stared at the fingerprint on her thigh.

It was red.

The muscles in her vagina clenched.

She lightly touched the fingerprint.

Her fingertip was far smaller than Michel's. The aching throb inside her pelvis was testament to just how much larger he was than she—everywhere.

The narrow, wooden seat biting into the backs of her thighs, she leaned over, removed her garters, and unrolled her stockings.

Michel had both rolled them down . . . and up. The first after he had shown her angels; the second a scant hour and a half earlier.

Standing up, she grabbed the chemise and jerked it over her head.

The bathwater stung—Anne forced herself to sit all the way down into the narrow copper tub until tepid water lapped at her hips.

As Michel had lapped at her nether lips.

But there was nothing tepid about his tongue. It was scalding hot.

She dipped the washcloth into the water, then rubbed a bar of soap onto the wet cotton until lather frothed and foamed.

Creamy. Cleansing.

Like the combined essence of a man and a woman.

No geyser monopolized Michel's bathroom. No gas fixtures lighted his bedchamber.

Had he been burned in one of the many gas explosions that killed and maimed English citizens throughout cities both large and small?

The washcloth abraded her tender nipples. It was slippery rough, smooth yet scratchy. Like his fingers when they had been inundated with her pleasure.

What would it be like to bathe with a man? she wondered.

Michel's bathroom was large, the porcelain tub proportionally sized. It would easily fit two.

She dropped the soapy washcloth and cupped her breasts, imagining that her hands were Michel's; that her nipples prodded his palms instead of her own. Imagining . . . *him inside her* . . . larger than his finger . . . plunging more deeply than his tongue . . . while water churned around them.

"Ma'am?"

Anne snatched her hands away from her breasts and slapped her arms over her chest; the liquid heat that suffused her body owed nothing to the bath. "Yes?"

Jane stepped toward the copper tub, eyes staring everywhere but at Anne's nakedness. She held out a tin. "I thought you might like to add Epsom salts to the water. It is quite soothing when one is tired. Or sore."

Anne froze.

How did the maid know? . . .

She forced herself to relax.

How could the maid not know?

Anne had been gone for an entire night and half the morning. The abigail had removed her outer garments. Anne's skin smelled of sweat, both hers and Michel's muskier odor.

She would not be embarrassed because of one servant.

Soon all of London would know.

"Thank you, Jane. But I am almost finished here. Are you through packing?"

"Very nearly, ma'am. What shall you be wearing on your journey?"

What did a woman wear to meet her lover?

"My gray wool walking dress with the black velvet collar. And my black grenadine morning cloak."

"Very well, ma'am." The maid hurriedly scooped up Anne's discarded undergarments and withdrew.

For one crazy second Anne thought about calling the abigail back and asking her if it was "very well" for a spinster to cohabitate with a man whom she was not married to.

The response such a question must surely evoke brought a bubble of laughter to her throat.

The realization that the maid would no doubt curtsy and indifferently reply, "Very well, ma'am," brought tears to her eyes.

Anne vigorously scrubbed herself clean.

What was wrong with her?

She had lost her maidenhead, an event that she had diligently plotted and planned. Nothing more, nothing less.

She would not regret her decision.

There were far too many other circumstances to repent. Choices she had not made. Responsibilities she had not fulfilled.

Misery fed regret. Not pleasure.

Rising in a splash of water, she briskly dried off before swathing her body in the damp towel. In the bedroom she silently donned her stockings, drawers, and chemise behind the obscurity of a wooden screen. Jane greeted her with corset outstretched; Anne winced—her breasts were still swollen and tender. She stepped into the circle of petticoats held down for her. Quickly, impersonally, the maid tied on the horsehair-stuffed bustle and pulled the gray wool dress over Anne's head.

Michel was an excellent lady's maid, Anne thought giddily. Far, far better than either Jane or her abigail in Dover.

Perhaps men should fulfill the position instead of women.

She gingerly sat down on the horsehair-covered bench in front of the dressing table. Michel had laved away the pain but not the tenderness.

"Shall you be back . . . at the end of the month, Miss Aimes?"

The pale blue eyes staring at Anne in the mirror widened, reflecting her surprise. This was the first time any of the rental servants had expressed curiosity about her comings and goings. "Yes. Of course I will be back."

The abigail unpinned Anne's hair—electricity trickled down her spine. She remembered Michel's hands, equally expert at unpinning a woman's hair. "And will you be leaving an address, ma'am?"

She frowned. Last night she would have welcomed the maid's interest; now she found it irksome.

Contrition was instantaneous. It was not the abigail's fault that her mistress was involved in a clandestine *affaire.*

"I will leave my address with my solicitor."

Hard bristles bit into Anne's scalp, stroked the length of her back. "But what if your solicitor is unavailable?"

Anne averted her gaze from the glint of silver that streaked her pale brown hair. How long before pale brown hair streaked the silver? *How long before she did not recognize herself at all in the mirror?* "That is highly unlikely. In any event, the solicitor's housekeeper has access to his files. She will be able to locate me, should an emergency arise."

The abigail quickly pinned up Anne's hair, dark, thin fingers darting here and there in the mirror. "I will have the butler summon your coach."

Heat mushroomed in Anne's cheeks; a blush spread over the pale flesh of the woman in the mirror.

The coachman was the only Dover servant who had accompanied her to London.

She did not want the old to intrude on the new.

Not yet.

"My journey is not far. A cab will suffice."

A last pin slid into the tight bun Anne's hair had been secured in, lightly grazing her scalp. The abigail stepped back; dark eyes met pale blue ones in the mirror. "Will you take lunch before you leave, Miss Aimes?"

She had not dined last night, sick with nervousness. Nor had she accepted Michel's offer of refreshment, her appetite overcome by sexual satiation and belated shyness. "Yes. Thank you."

"Very well, ma'am."

Anne gritted her teeth. "You may leave black silk gloves, my black beaded reticule, and my black bonnet with the butler. I do not require your assistance again."

In the dining room Anne picked at scalloped potatoes, Yorkshire pudding, and rare roast beef steak. Blood leaked onto her plate.

Would she bleed again when Michel penetrated her?

How would she be able to take him come the night, sore and swollen as she was?

Perhaps she should wait.

Another night.

Another time.

She pushed her plate aside.

A footman liveried in a black coat silently scooped it up. When she abruptly rose, another liveried footman pulled the chair back for her.

Everyone wore black, she realized. A respectable color for respectable people. It forcibly reminded her that instead of mourning her deceased parents she cavorted with a man who had made a fortune off of wealthy women.

A man who claimed he had had no procuress in five years.

But she wanted him. She did not find his scars repugnant.

Were there not other women such as herself?

In the foyer, a dark-haired, liveried footman conversed with the butler over her trunk. They jerked to attention at the sight of her.

"The cab is waiting, ma'am. James, take the trunk out."

James hoisted the trunk onto his shoulder.

He was amazingly strong. Ruggedly handsome in spite of the nose that had obviously been broken at one time.

Further proof of her descent into decadence.

She had never before appraised a footman's physique, let alone wondered about a servant's sexual habits.

The butler opened the door, admitting the only ray of sunshine into an otherwise dismal house.

"Do you have any instructions, ma'am? I understand you will be gone a month. Shall you leave a forwarding address?"

His cold courtesy grated on her nerves. He made her feel like a stranger in her own home.

When Michel touched her, she felt like a stranger inside her own body.

"My solicitor, Mr. Little, will have my address," she answered shortly. "He will stop by periodically. If you require anything, he will take care of it."

The butler impersonally held out her black grenadine cloak. Anne slipped first one arm through a sleeve, then the other. Silently he offered her gloves, a round black felt hat with a white aigrette curled around the crown rather than the black bonnet she had ordered, and her black beaded reticule.

Had Jane misunderstood her instructions?

Grimly positioning the hat on top of her head, she looped the handle of her reticule over her wrist and pulled on her gloves.

The butler did not step out of her way.

"The address, ma'am. If you would be so good."

Anne's heart did a somersault inside her chest. "I beg your pardon?"

A sunbeam bounced off of a glazed marble eye, adding macabre life to the stuffed owl perched on a side table.

"The address, if you please, Miss Aimes." The butler produced a lethally sharp, five-inch-long hat pin. "So that I may give it to the cabby."

Anne stared at the hat pin.

For the first time in her life she realized how fragile human skin was, stretched over muscle and bone. How easily it could be pierced.

By flesh.

By steel.

Icy fingers stroked her vertebrae.

It was ridiculous, of course. But Anne was suddenly afraid of this blond-haired English servant who looked as if he had never touched a woman's naked body.

She mentally shook herself.

Her solicitor had hired him. He would not have done so unless the servant had excellent references.

Anne tore her gaze away from the needle sharp hat pin. "I am going to see my solicitor," she said, and reluctantly relayed his address.

The butler bowed. "Your hat pin, Miss Aimes."

"Thank you." Fingers not quite steady, Anne accepted the pin. She gingerly stuck it through the crown of her hat before stepping out into the sunlight.

The butler trailed behind her and opened the door to the cab. Just as would any other butler.

So why couldn't she calm her thumping heart?

The hack smelled of damp hay and worn leather. Innocuous odors. When it pulled out into the stream of traffic, she did not know if it was relief or trepidation that balled inside her stomach.

Each bump and grind of the carriage wheels drove home the lingering ache inside her pelvic region. Pressing her face against the window, she concentrated on the passing streets and carriages.

Anne had never visited her solicitor's office.

The two-story brick building was old and unassuming, rather like the solicitor himself. It was surrounded on either side by less carefully preserved brick buildings.

A sparkling glass front window advertised MR. LITTLE, SOLICITOR, in bold black letters. White venetian blinds blocked the interior view from inquisitive eyes.

Taking a deep breath, Anne stepped out of the cab.

"Please wait," she instructed the cabby. "This is not my destination. I have a moment of business to take care of."

The cabby, face grooved with perpetual boredom and overwork, silently tipped a worn bowler hat.

A little bell announced the opening of the solicitor's sturdy wooden door. The smell of freshly baked bread and lilac scent struck her in the face.

"May I help you?"

It took a second for Anne's eyes to adjust to the dim interior light. Polished wood raced up a stark white wall—a banister. Near the foot of the stairs sat a small desk weighted down by a massive metal typewriter. A woman wearing a white lace cap sat behind it. Anne estimated her age to be in the late fifties.

"Mrs. Huttchinson?" she asked, surprised.

The solicitor had always referred to a housekeeper, not that most ambitious breed, a woman clerk.

"Mr. Little no doubt told you that I am his housekeeper." The woman smiled; the lines creasing her cheeks and eyes added character to a face that was still quite attractive. "And so I am. I am afraid he is not in at the moment. May I help you?"

Anne gripped her reticule. "I am Miss Anne Aimes. When do you expect Mr. Little?"

Mrs. Huttchinson's brown eyes softened. "How do you do, Miss Aimes. Mr. Little left early this morning. He caught the train to Lincolnshire. To visit with a client there."

"I see."

Anne did not see at all.

Mr. Little had been most insistent that she contact him after her liaison with Michel des Anges—to assure him that the arrangements had proved satisfactory, he claimed.

She suspected the reason he wanted her to contact him was to verify that she had safely returned from the liaison.

"Did he say when he will be back?" Anne asked.

"Indeed not. I am afraid he departed before I awoke. He left a note saying that he had gone, is all."

The solicitor had visited Anne in Dover when her parents died; it had taken several days to go through all the necessary papers.

Then he had visited her again when she summoned him two months past. He had stayed overnight, and returned for another overnight visit after gaining Michel's signature on the contract.

Anne was not his only client.

He would be back soon.

"May I leave a note for Mr. Little, please?"

Mrs. Huttchinson graciously rose to her feet in a waft of lilac perfume. "Certainly, Miss Aimes. If you will follow me, please."

Her figure was neat and trim underneath a starched white apron. She was the same height Anne was.

Anne incongruously remembered that she and Mr. Little were the same height. Client, solicitor, and housekeeper were all five feet, five inches tall.

Mrs. Huttchinson's heels were muffled by a thick green wool runner. Walnut paneling swallowed the light in the narrow hallway.

Mr. Little's office—indeed, the entire lower floor of the building—was surprisingly large and comfortable. Surrounding bookshelves were crammed with ancient leather tomes; the green carpeting was thick and luxurious. Two brown leather wing-back chairs waited in front of a long, glass-topped desk.

A curious smell of scorched meat permeated the room. White ashes were thick in the iron fireplace; a shiny brass tong protruded from the grate.

"Please be seated, Miss Aimes." Mrs. Huttchinson gestured toward the desk and the writing materials neatly arranged there.

Sitting on the edge of the first of the two leather chairs, Anne briskly drew off her right glove and reached for the necessary writing tools. She paused, brass pen poised between her fingers. A large, black leather trunk crowded the wall behind the desk.

The solicitor had traveled with just such a trunk when he had visited her in Dover.

"Mr. Little—he does not plan on being gone long, I take it?"

Mrs. Huttchinson followed Anne's gaze. "Oh—Mr. Little would have taken another trunk, a smaller one, so possibly not. He wrote in his note that I should have this one sent to a fellow solicitor in London."

Anne dipped the pen into the inkwell—and stared at the blank vellum paper.

How could she reassure the solicitor that she was well when even she did not know what or how she felt?

A single drop of ink teared on the sharp steel nib. It splattered onto the stark white, bled into the paper. *Black instead of red.* A reminder of the pain Michel had brought, as well as the unimaginable pleasure.

Quickly scribbling a short note, she lightly sanded the paper before folding and sealing it in an envelope.

"Just leave it there on the desk, Miss Aimes. No one will disturb it. Mr. Little will see it first thing when he returns. He is very conscientious in these matters."

"Thank you." Anne wondered if the older woman was indeed married—or if she had adopted the title of Mrs. purely to gain respectable employment, as so many women did. She offered a smile. "Mr. Little speaks very highly of you."

Wicked humor gleamed in Mrs. Huttchinson's warm brown eyes. "Mr. Little speaks very highly of you also, Miss Aimes. He says you are a most courageous young woman."

Anne blinked.

Surely the solicitor had not told Mrs. Huttchinson about Michel des Anges.

She immediately dismissed the thought.

Mrs. Huttchinson, obviously a respectable woman, would not be so cordial if she knew about the illicit contract. No one knew save for Michel, Anne, and the solicitor.

Anne thrust her hand inside her glove and followed Mrs. Huttchinson to the front of the building. The older woman courteously opened the door for her, admitting a draft of cool air and dazzling sunshine.

She paused on the threshold, suddenly needing approval, knowing she would not receive it. How could she ask another woman to condone her actions? "Please give my regards to Mr. Little."

Mrs. Huttchinson smiled kindly. "I will most certainly do that, Miss Aimes."

Anne reluctantly stepped forward. Behind her the closing door clicked with finality.

The cabby—face as blank and uncaring as those of the rental servants—stared down at her. His hat was pulled low over his eyes. "Where to, ma'am?"

Suddenly it was not a black bowler hat that Anne gazed up at. She saw instead the black bodice of her abigail reflected in the mirror of her dressing table. *But what if your solicitor is unavailable?*

Across the street, a horse, startled by a boardman passing out bills, reared up and kicked the air.

A man stood nearby, leaning against a lamppost. Metal glinted—the head of his cane. His hair was so black it gleamed with blue highlights.

Anne's mouth went dry.

Michel had hair that color.

As if aware of her regard, the black-haired man abruptly turned away.

A shoeblack blocked his escape. Between one blink of the eyes and another the man became not Michel, but just another Londoner hitching his foot up on a shoeblack's box and hunching over the kneeling boy to watch him clean the filth and manure that mucked the cobbled streets off of his boot.

It dawned on Anne that Michel, a Frenchman, had only once spoken French after he had taken her virginity.

Rose Huttchinson stared through the slits of the venetian blind. Anne Aimes hesitated by the cab, as if unsure of her destination.

Her heart ached for the spinster and the choice she had made.

John Little had frequently talked about Anne Aimes. First of her dedication. Then of her solitude. And finally of her incredible decision.

Rose wondered what Miss Aimes would have said if she had told her that she, too, had once faced a similar choice.

When her husband, a barrister's clerk, had died, she had been childless and destitute. John had offered her a job in his home, and then he had offered her a place in his bed.

They had been two middle-aged people bound by loneliness, young enough to want but too old to trust in new beginnings. He had been committed to his work; she had been afraid of losing another man to death.

That had been ten years ago. Now John Little was sixty-five, and she was fifty-nine.

As if coming to a decision, Anne Aimes stepped into the cab and pulled the door shut.

Rose did not for one minute regret taking comfort in her solicitor's bed. She hoped that Miss Aimes did not regret taking comfort in Michel des Anges.

Sometimes a woman had to grab happiness and let the future take care of itself.

An omnibus waddled down the street, blocking Rose's view of the departing cab.

She frowned.

John had complained of chest pains lately.

It was not like him to go off without telling her, she thought fretfully. He worked too hard. He should not have stayed up all night, working on that will, and then traipsing off without a by-your-leave.

A sixty-five-year-old man was too old to travel at every client's whim. Who would warm his feet while he was away?

Who would warm *her* feet?

A reminiscent smile curved Rose's mouth.

John had discussed the legal merits of marriage on several occasions these last few months. Perhaps, if he worked up the courage to propose, she would reconsider her decision to remain an independent woman.

Perhaps *she* would make *him* an honest man.

That would certainly teach him to go off and leave her alone.

Chuckling, she turned back to her desk and the typewriter that was John Little's pride and joy.

There were so many things to do. A will had to be typed. The ashes in John's office needed to be cleaned and the room aired.

What had he burned? she wondered irritably. It positively reeked.

She checked the paper in the typewriter, then squinted down at the neatly stacked papers and the scrawled script that was John's handwriting.

In the note, he had instructed her to arrange for his trunk to be delivered to a solicitor.

Strange, that. She had never heard the man's name before.

John always kept her informed about his legal associates.

A shadow darkened the scrawled handwriting.

Rose started.

The bell over the door had not rung. There was only one other entrance into the solicitor's home and office, and that was through the back door. But John and Rose were the only two who possessed a key.

The shadow was broad—much broader than that which belonged to the frail man she had come to know and love.

Clutching her chest to still the thumping of her heart, she looked up, up, up . . . and stared, mesmerized. "May I help you?"

The man smiled disarmingly.

Rose's heart fluttered.

He really was quite handsome.

She remembered the first time she had seen her husband, a blindingly clear spring day—much like this day. Gay young women had strolled in the park, flirtatiously pretending to ignore the studious young men who took their lunch there.

It was the last thought Rose had.

Chapter 7

Michael watched, body motionless, from the upstairs sitting room window. The thin, powder blue silk drape clung to his fingertips.

Anne Aimes's hair had also clung to his skin.

It was far, far more fine than the silk curtain.

The spinster stepped out of the cab. She wore a plain black cloak and a round black hat with a white egret feather that danced in the sunlight. Raoul, his dark, wiry butler, gesticulated wildly, directing two footmen to unload her trunk.

Michael's heart hammered against his ribs: from delayed reaction. From the rush to reach his town house before her cab.

He had been careless. Anne had seen him outside her solicitor's office.

What would she have done if she had recognized him? Would she have come to him, knowing he followed her?

He remembered the morning sunlight—and Anne lying in his bed, sleeping.

She slept quietly, unobtrusively, as she lived.

Except when approaching orgasm.

There was nothing quiet or unobtrusive about her uninhibited pleasure.

Anne and Raoul disappeared underneath the arch of the doorway.

Last night he had tasted her innocence. This day he had tasted the woman he had made of her: the saltiness of sweat; the sweetness of passion; the coppery tang of her virgin blood.

Michael had never before made a woman bleed.

He should feel remorse.

He did not.

For the time they had left she was his.

A whore's woman.

A killer's woman.

The two footmen clumsily lowered the brown leather trunk off the cab.

It was no doubt filled with drab, colorless clothes that befitted a drab, colorless spinster.

Each grasping an end of the trunk, the footmen walked underneath the arch where Anne and his butler had disappeared.

Michael glanced at the silk drape in his hand, at the pale, transparent blue that was reminiscent of Anne's eyes.

He imagined her dressed in beautiful clothes. Revealing clothes. Clothes that defined her innate sensuality instead of her marital status.

A hand fisted inside his chest.

The identity of the man she had cared for *a long, long time ago* had been so painfully obvious.

Beautiful, cocksure Michel des Anges. A French *courailleur* who had seemingly escaped the threat of the Franco-Prussian War merely to take English ladies for the ride of their lives.

He had been so confident he would not be identified. So very sure he could finish what the boy he had once been could not.

Michael bitterly begrudged the man Anne Aimes had cared for—the man who had died in a blazing inferno—whereas she did not in the least begrudge the woman who haunted his past.

He was not used to generosity. Or kindness.

Anne had unstintingly given him both.

Distant steps traversed the marble stairs; not-so-distant steps echoed down the hallway toward the sitting room where Michael awaited Anne.

His spinster was a fighter.

Diane had been a beautiful woman whose reckless passion had matched his. They had shared laughter. Champagne. And sex.

Everything else had been superfluous.

When the man destroyed Diane's passion, she had possessed nothing more enduring to sustain her.

Anne was strong as well as passionate. Intelligent. Familiar with death and suffering.

She might survive.

If she did, she would need more confidence to see her through the aftermath.

He could give her that.

The air behind Michael stirred. He could sense his butler, Raoul. But he could feel Anne in the very blood that pulsed through his veins.

His erection was instantaneous.

"Mademoiselle Aimes, monsieur."

Michael dropped the curtain and turned toward the only female alive who couldn't imagine another woman not wanting him.

Her pale blue eyes were guarded, her shoulders squared. She had not allowed Raoul to take her cloak.

Only sheer strength of will kept her from turning and running from the force of her desires.

Anne's passion tonight was his enemy, as in the end it had been Diane's enemy. It would make her nervous and restless.

He had to circumvent her thoughts before they led them both down a road that neither would enjoy traversing.

Michael smiled; behind his practiced charisma, he plotted. "You came."

"As you see."

But he did not see . . . how far he would go in order to restrain her.

He did not see how far she would venture on this sexual odyssey that both their needs had catapulted them into.

He did not see how long it would be before she pieced together the pattern of deception and seduction, and her passion turned to hatred.

Deliberately he played on her kindness—as he had earlier played on her sensuality. "Will you be seen with me outside these walls, Anne Aimes?"

His question took her by surprise. As it was supposed to.

Her expression took Michael by surprise. As well as the pain it engendered.

Even she hesitated to be openly seen with a man who bore the scars of his past.

Anne tilted her chin, denying the horror that had flitted across her face. As she denied her feminine attractions. But they existed—both the physical appeal she held for him and the repugnance he incited in her. "Yes. Of course I will be seen with you."

Michael shrugged off the hurt. What he did to Anne would cause far more pain than any she could inflict upon him.

"Then I want to show you something. Something that is quite extraordinary. If you dare," he challenged.

Anne rubbed the peacock blue velvet between her gloved fingers and silently damned both herself and Michel.

If she had known that he would take her to a dressmaker she would not have accompanied him.

She felt hurt. And used.

He had tricked her. Worse, he was obviously ashamed of her.

She pushed away the bolt of cloth. "I would prefer something more subdued, please. Perhaps a navy blue."

Michel and Madame René, a petite, autocratic old woman with shocking red hair who wore a collar of pearls worthy of a queen, exchanged looks.

Anne correctly interpreted their silent communication.

She was an unsophisticated, gauche woman, their glances said, who did not know the slightest thing about what was fashionable.

And she did not.

But she knew how harshly the world judged an unmarried woman.

She knew that wearing peacock blue velvet would not make her less of a spinster.

It would not make her younger.

It would not make her more attractive.

What a fool she had been, to agree to stay with a man she knew nothing about other than that he had a perfect body and knew exactly how to make a woman forget she was not similarly blessed.

"Mademoiselle, we will take your measurements and then we

will decide, *oui?"* The modiste held up a small, slim hand. A large diamond glittered on her right forefinger. "Claudette, take mademoiselle's reticule—Angelique, her gloves—Babette, her cloak—ah, there is no need to worry, mademoiselle; Monsieur Michel will watch over your things."

Short of creating a public row, there was little Anne could do to restrain madame's feminine army. In due order her reticule was pried out of her clenched fingers; her gloves tugged off of her hands, and her cloak whisked away.

"*Voilà,*" Madame René said briskly. "If you will step this way, *s'il vous plaît.*"

Anne found herself ushered behind a maroon velvet curtain into a plain, claustrophobically small dressing room. A crystal gas chandelier hissed and popped overhead. "There is no need to take my measurements, Madame René. I can tell you what they are."

The modiste, shorter than Anne by several inches, reached up and pinched her left nipple.

The air froze in Anne's lungs. It escaped in a blast of outrage. "How dare you—"

"*Non, non,* mademoiselle, this gown, it is not made to fit you *ici*—here—see? The wool—it balloons over your breast. Claudette! Ah, there you are, *ma chère.* Bring the new corset—the French one—that arrived yesterday. Now, mademoiselle, we will take off our dress."

Anne stepped back from the modiste's small, busy hands before they took even more shocking liberties. The hard press of a wall stopped her short. "I will send you my measurements, madame. Monsieur and I have a previous engagement that we will be late for. Pardon me. . . ."

Madame René did not step aside.

The modiste cocked her head, a conspiratorial gleam in her bright, tawny eyes. "It is Monsieur Michel, *oui?"* she whispered. "He is a much changed man. You dress the drab ensemble when you are with him, *non?* To attract less attention. No woman wants to draw the eye when she is with such a man, *oui?"*

Anne's head jerked back. "You are mistaken, madame."

"Non, I do not think so, mademoiselle. If I were, then you would want to please him, to be *la belle* for him. You would want every man to look at you when he is at your side, to say, *quelle une femme incroyable*—what an incredible woman! What a man he must be to possess a woman like her!"

"Monsieur des Anges is a remarkably handsome man," Anne said icily. *Despite his scars.* "He is quite capable of holding his own in any company."

"If you say so, mademoiselle. He is rumored to be built like *un étalon*—a stallion." Madame's mouth wrinkled in a moue of distaste. "But those scars. . . ."

The ice in Anne's blood thawed; molten heat infused her.

Michel *was* built like a stallion.

"I am not ashamed of Monsieur des Anges," she insisted, masking mortification with haughtiness.

Madame shrugged. The Gaelic gesture was more telling than words.

Clearly the modiste did not believe her.

"Madame René, I am not . . ." Anne forced the words out—painful words, hurtful words, *truthful* words. "I am not an attractive woman."

A satisfied smile broke across the woman's wizened face. "That is before you come to me, the so talented Madame René. After I finish with you, mademoiselle, you will be *très magnifique!"*

Anne raised an eyebrow ironically. "And how much will you charge for this miraculous transformation?"

"A fortune, mademoiselle. But if you did not possess it, you would not be with Monsieur Michel, *non?"*

Anne breathed slowly, deeply.

She would not be hurt.

The modiste said to her face what others would soon be saying behind her back.

She did possess a fortune. If not for her money, she would not be with the man who was named for his ability to bring women to orgasm.

Everything could be bought, Michel had said. Sexual satisfaction. Intimacy. Friendship.

Why not the illusion of beauty?

"Very well, Madame René."

The modiste was not content merely to strip Anne of her dress. "*Tout,* mademoiselle. *Tout.*"

Everything went—bustle, petticoats, corset, chemise, *drawers.*

The dressmaker did not understand English modesty—very practical for a woman in her business, Anne thought bitingly.

As convenient as it was for a man in Michel's business.

Goose bumps marched over her body.

She shivered, clothed only in a hat, drooping stockings, and garters that squeezed the very air from her lungs. The feminine articles did nothing to hide her swollen, tender breasts. The heels on her half boots forced her pelvis forward—as had the heels on the slippers she had worn when Michel undressed her.

But there was a world of difference between being stripped naked by a woman as opposed to a man. With Michel it had been exciting, titillating. Madame René inspected her as if she were a horse, first from the front, then from behind.

She felt like a great, clumsy horse, with the feather sticking out of her hat.

A measuring tape snaked around her neck, choked her, slithered away. It was summarily stretched across her shoulders. "Lift your arms, mademoiselle." The tape was pressed into Anne's armpit—a warm shock of fingers and cold metal tab—and extended to her wrist.

She had not undergone the humiliation of being measured for many, many years. Ridiculously, she found herself hoping—as she had hoped when being measured for her London wardrobe eighteen years past—that the modiste would find perfections her own mirror did not.

Anne stoically stared over Madame René's head as the elderly woman leaned into her naked bosom. Above her the popping hiss of the gas chandelier was discordantly loud.

She did not have to glance down to see what the modiste saw. There was no mistaking the physical evidence of her night of passion—her breasts had been hungrily suckled by the man who waited on the other side of the drawn curtain.

The measuring tape circled her torso, pulled tight to nip her bruised, distended nipples.

"Small in the breast." The modiste quickly scribbled a measurement onto a little ledger before dropping it into her apron pocket. Sinking to her knees, she drew the tape around Anne's waist. "We are thickening here, mademoiselle. Perhaps we should forgo our desserts."

Anne gritted her teeth. *So much for hidden perfections.*

The tape circled her hips; Madame René's head dipped perilously close to parts that surely no woman should be near. Especially when those parts—tender and swollen from a man's attentions—lasciviously jutted forward. "Hips a trifle broad."

The tightness banding her left foot eased—Madame René expertly unlaced her half boot.

"Lift your foot, mademoiselle." Anne awkwardly complied, grabbed madame's perfectly coiffed, impossibly red hair to keep from toppling on top of the dressmaker when she jerked the shoe off of her foot. "*Maintenant. Le droit.*" The modiste tapped her right foot. "Up."

Anne curled her stockinged toes into the wool carpet and concentrated on the maroon curtain instead of the small hand that pressed into her inseam in the exact same spot that Michel had nuzzled her. The intimate touch spiraled through her groin, rendering her breathlessly, painfully aware of the pulsating throb between her thighs and the man who waited behind the velvet curtain.

The modiste jotted down more measurements before springing up as sprightly as a child. "Claudette!"

Anne with a start became aware of a small, nervous woman who appraised her much in the same manner as Madame René did. She clutched a black satin garment to her thin chest.

"Claudette, lace mademoiselle into the corset—ah, we shall sew padding into it, *ici*—" Anne stiffened as the modiste thrust her hand inside the corset, sharp knuckles digging into her right breast— "and reinforce it with whalebone, so that it pushes her up and out, *oui?*"

"*Oui,* madame."

"*Vite,* we must have a bolt of fabric—Angelique, bring the peacock *velours!*"

The curtain was thrust aside, affording Anne a fleeting glimpse of Michel—and he of her.

Un étalon, Madame René had said. A stallion.

Is there nothing that you will not do?

Nothing. Providing that it brings pleasure.

The violet in his eyes flared; then he was obliterated by a tall, bony woman who strode through the doorway with the bolt of peacock blue velvet as if on a mission of mercy. The maroon curtain flapped closed behind her.

The heat of Michel's gaze remained.

Madame took the material and draped it about Anne's hips and legs. "We must showcase her legs—they are passably fair, *non?* The panel must be tight—tighter, with an overdress caught up to the side, so. For *une robe de jour,* a day dress, we will sew little kick pleats so that she may stride unhindered. *Oui?*"

A resounding chorus of "*ouis*" followed.

The dressing room was too crowded; the attention Anne received was too overwhelming. French perfume and gas from the overhead chandelier swirled inside her head.

What more could Michel possibly do to her that he had not already done? she wondered dizzily.

What would she talk about, these coming hours, days, weeks?

He was an anomaly: a sophisticated man who possessed both the uninhibited manners of his French forebears and the cool civility of the English.

What if her wealth could not hold his attention?

Suddenly the bolt of material was gone, as was the corset.

"Never fear; we will do well by you, mademoiselle. You may join Monsieur Michel and I when you are dressed."

Madame René regally exited through the curtain while the two contrasting assistants, one short and wiry, the other tall and gangly, dressed Anne.

Coldly. Methodically. As if she were a mannequin instead of a woman who for the first time in her life flouted society and all it represented.

Anne dimly realized that her hands were icy cold.

She was afraid.

And she did not like being afraid.

It made her feel as if she were eighteen instead of thirty-six.

Anne joined Madame René and Michel only to find that they sat side by side. They were surrounded by bolts and bolts of fabrics. Bright, vivid colors spilled over the gold brocade couch and the Aubusson-covered floor. Some hues she had never before seen; others she had admired but never dared wear.

Their heads were pressed together. Afternoon sunlight glinted on their hair. Michel's was untainted by gray; madame's was brazenly dyed red. They conferred over a cluster of sketches.

As if she did not exist.

The client, having provided the necessary monies, was no longer of any import.

The fear and excitement that had dogged her decision to stay with Michel found a focus.

He was not the one who would be wearing these exotic colors that represented every hue of the rainbow. And he certainly was not paying for them.

"I believe it is I you should be consulting, madame," Anne said frigidly.

Madame René regarded her as if she were a child who had rudely spoken out of turn.

Anne's anger grew disproportionately. "I will take a gown in navy blue serge, but I would like to see fashion plates, please."

Madame René stiffened, rather like a small bantam hen. The collar of pearls circling her throat glowed. "I am a *couturière*, mademoiselle. An *artiste*. Do you question my talent?"

Michel smoothly intervened. "Mademoiselle merely wondered when you could deliver your masterpieces, madame. She would like a day dress for tomorrow."

"Impossible." The couturier's French accent was strangely lacking.

"Nothing is impossible, madame," Michel said softly.

Greed replaced the stubborn implacability in her bright, golden brown eyes. "Are you willing to pay the price, Monsieur Michel?"

Michel's violet gaze rested on Anne.

Every word they had exchanged—every touch, every intimate act—was reflected in his eyes.

The shocking insinuation of his finger.

His uninhibited tongue-bath.

Complete access . . .

Suddenly the busy city of London invaded the small, elegant shop. Muffin boys rang their bells. Vendors shouted their wares. Carriage wheels sang. A whistle sliced through the noise—a street sweeper hailing a cab in the hopes of earning an extra halfpence.

"Yes, madame." Michel's voice was hard, implacable. "I am willing to pay the price."

"Then it is done." Madame René rose from the couch, back straight, head regally held high. "It has been a pleasure, mademoiselle. Do not stay away so long next time, monsieur. Claudette! Angelique! Babette! Bring the bolts of material—we have other customers who await our services."

Customers who were not as ungracious as the spinster Mademoiselle Aimes.

Madame's feminine French army hurriedly gathered together the bolts of beautiful fabrics and trailed after their mistress.

Anne's beaded reticule glittered on a Louis XVI side table; the fingers of her black silk gloves dangled limply over the glazed, gilded wood. Her black grenadine cloak hung on a brass hook nearby. Michel's cane was propped beside it, gold head gleaming.

The private sitting room shrank until there was no place for self-deception.

A peahen did not belong in the French provincial setting.

It was all too obvious Michel did.

He had sat there, in this shop, perhaps on that very same divan . . . many times.

Assessing many different women.

Anne squared her shoulders. "Why did you bring me here?"

Michel's violet eyes were impenetrable. "Madame René is in reality *la Comtesse de l'Aguille.* Her grandparents escaped to London during the revolution. They lost everything—their estates, their wealth, their jewels. Foolishly they reared their sole surviving daughter to believe that she would marry an English aristocrat worthy of her position. The daughter succumbed to a rake who had no intention of marrying her; then she succumbed to death after delivering his child. The grandparents turned their ambition onto the grandchild—a beautiful, titian-haired girl who would obviously attract wealthy, titled men.

"But the girl was practical. She was determined to become a courtesan and have not one, but many English aristocrats. When her attractions matured, she opened this establishment. First she ruled the men, now she rules their women. A woman who does not have a gown designed by Madame René is not thought to be fashionable."

Anne continued to stare at him mutinously.

She did not want to feel sorry for Madame René.

All these years she had been reconciled to being a plain spinster. Or so she had thought. With a single fitting the modiste had shown her how little she differed from the eighteen-year-old girl she had once been who had failed to take her place among London's beautiful, fashionable elite.

"She does not dress just any woman, Anne," Michel elaborated gently. "Not even for the exorbitant prices society belles are willing to pay."

"Did you take just any woman who could pay you?" she asked coldly, knowing she was behaving badly but unable to stop the question.

"At first, yes," he said bluntly.

"And later?"

"I took only those who met my criteria. As does Madame René."

"What is her criteria, pray tell, if not wealth?"

"The same as mine."

"And that is?"

"We both require passion in a woman."

For one heart-stopping moment Anne believed that he found her attractive.

She wanted to believe him.

But Michel would not have taken her without her money any more than Madame René would have.

The throb between her legs intensified. "You said you would not lie to me."

"I have not."

"If I wanted you to . . . would you?"

A faraway door slammed shut on the noisy London life that had invaded the shop.

Something like pain crossed Michel's dark features. Or perhaps it was regret. Or merely boredom at her lack of sophistication. "No, I will not lie to you."

Anne blinked back tears. "Why not?" she asked tightly.

"Because I like you, Anne Aimes."

No one had ever said they liked her. Wanted her. *Needed her*.

She quickly countered to cover the hot flush of pleasure his declaration elicited. "Then you have lied to other women."

"Yes," he said baldly.

"Did you not like them?"

"I liked some of the women I've been with. But not all. Liking has little to do with lust."

"Did you ever lie to any of those whom you liked?"

"Yes," he said adamantly, unrepentantly.

"But you will not lie to me." The bite of roast beef she had eaten for lunch gored her stomach. "Why not?"

Why wouldn't he tell her that she was beautiful?

She wouldn't believe him then.

She would understand the basis of his purported attraction: money. She would know how to act. What to expect.

She would know what he wanted from her.

Michel rose from the gold brocade couch. Purposefully he stalked her.

The raspy contact of his fingers bolted through her body. It touched places only he would ever touch. *Her breasts. Her clitoris. Her buttocks.*

He cupped her face and lifted it to his, his breath a sultry caress. "Because you don't want me to."

She stared at the black tie knotted at his throat; the heat of his fingers penetrated her flesh. Her teeth. *Her bones.* "How do you know that?"

"I know you, Anne."

He could not possibly know her.

Her desires, yes. But not the woman who had dedicated her life to aging parents rather than risk being ridiculed.

He did not know the woman who out of weakness and cowardliness had heartlessly prolonged pain and suffering.

Anne resolutely met his waiting gaze. "Perhaps I would rather be lusted after than liked."

Michel's face lightened; he smiled, a flash of white, even teeth. "I lust after you, Anne. Lust is not synonymous with liking, but neither does it preclude it."

She determinedly touched the front of his wool trousers to test the validity of his statement.

Heat scorched her hand.

He was hard.

Ready.

A pulse beat in the heart of her palm.

His . . . or hers?

"Did you bring me here because you are ashamed of the way I look?"

The words burst out of her mouth before she could stop them. Anne withdrew her hand in horror.

She didn't want to know—she had had enough truths for one day.

"I brought you here so that you could meet Madame René." Michel did not blink an eyelash at her rash bluntness. "She's a wonderful, courageous woman who has flourished where other women in her circumstances withered. You remind me of her."

Yes, both of them were well past their prime.

"Were you ever her lover?"

Anne cringed. Madame René had to be seventy if she was a day.

"No. But I would have been." Michel's eyes were intent, daring *her,* his procuress, to judge *him,* a man who catered to needy women like herself. "If she had wanted me."

And had paid the price.

Anne focused on the curve of his bottom lip, feeling incredibly naive in this uncomfortable world of exotic beauty and blatant sensuality.

"Madame said that I am too small in the breasts." Her voice was small—almost as small as she felt. "That my waist is thickening. And that my legs are passable. But not to worry, she will do well by me."

He tilted her chin so that she had no choice but to meet his violet gaze. "That is not what she told me," Michel murmured smoothly.

There was no condemnation in either his voice or his face.

"Oh?" Anne drew in a shaky breath. "I would not have credited her with sparing a woman's sensibilities."

Laughter glinted in his eyes, like sunshine rippling on a lake. Brilliant. Blinding. "She said that your breasts are high and firm, like those of a young woman. That your waist is supple. And that you have legs like a racehorse."

Anne remembered . . . the cold draft of air, *and violet fire* . . .

"You saw me," she said breathlessly. "When madame was measuring me."

And she had stood naked save for stockings and her hat with its ridiculous feather that made her feel like a great, clumsy horse.

"I saw you."

By lamplight. By sunlight.

Legs splayed. Feminine lips spread.

"I cannot wear Madame René's creations."

His mouth thinned, *still sensual, still alluring*. "Why not?"

"I'm in mourning." Her throat tightened as she remembered the pain that didn't stop and the exhaustion that always waited. "My parents died ten months ago."

The tension eased out of Michel's face—or perhaps it had never been there. *It was impossible to understand this complex man who claimed he wanted her as badly as she wanted him.* "Is that why you came to me"—his scarred thumbs grated across her cheeks while his fingers burned her ears—"to forget your grief?"

"No." Singeing awareness raced through her. Of his blood

that pulsed in his fingertips; of her blood that thrummed inside her temples. "I came to you out of fear. That I will someday be as lonely and unhappy as they were."

He studied her lips, his gaze a palpable touch. "Yet you nursed them."

"They had no one else."

And neither had she.

"You did not want to go out with me today." Eyelashes lifting, his gaze locked with hers. "Are you ashamed of me?"

Had he heard the couturière?

Did it hurt him when people stared? *Talked?*

How could any woman not find him attractive?

"Women do not pay men ten thousand pounds if they are ashamed of them, Monsieur des Anges," she said firmly.

His violet eyes were unrelenting. "Then why did you cringe in horror when I asked if you would be seen with me?"

He would not allow her dignity. Modesty.

Pride.

What had he said?

Sometimes a lie is all that protects us. But there's no need to lie. We both want. . . . We both need. . . .

Anne stiffened her spine. "I cringed in horror at being seen with you because . . . because everyone shall know that you would not be with me if I did not pay you."

His silky soft lips twisted. "Anne—"

"And because I know that society is not as understanding of a woman's physical needs as you and Madame René are. There will be gossip. Rumors. What few invitations I occasionally receive will stop altogether."

A shrill laugh cut through the muted noise of the city—another customer, cozily ensconced in a private sitting room.

Perhaps she had once been Michel's customer, too.

Immediately she drove the thought out of her head.

She would not allow her insecurities to ruin their short time together. It was time to take responsibility. And initiative.

Anne tentatively cupped her hands over his; his scarred skin was hot and rough against her cheeks where he touched her, and against her palms, where she touched him. "But that is the price I am willing to pay."

"Then you will wear madame's dresses"—Michel's head lowered, close but not close enough—"for the time we have together?"

She instinctively moistened her lips for his kiss. "Yes."

"And afterward, when you are no longer in mourning?"

"Yes," she lied.

The dresses would be wrapped in tissue, packed away in a trunk, and delegated to the attic, there to join the trunks packed with the remnants of her childhood and her coming-out wardrobe.

His mouth grazed hers. "Let's go home."

Michel's home. A house scented with flowers instead of mildew. Passion instead of pain.

Anne's breath quickened. "I cannot take you so soon after. . . . I am raw."

His lips grazed hers again, violet eyes watching her watch him. "There are other ways I can please you."

She grew moist with remembered pleasure, muscles loosening, ache increasing. "You mean"—she swallowed—"like you did earlier."

With lips. Tongue. And teeth.

"I mean"—his lips grazed hers yet again, beautiful eyes starkly staring—"I am going to take that feather out of your hat and tickle your clitoris until you scream for me to stop. But I won't stop, Anne."

For a second Anne couldn't breathe for the vivid image of the white feather adorning her hat held firmly in his long, scarred fingers, and positioned between her yawning thighs.

The muscles in her lower abdomen contracted.

Anne's fingers convulsively dug into his to contain the stab of desire.

But she wanted more than solitary satisfaction.

She wanted the sharing of heartbeats; the mingling of breaths; the joining of their sexes.

"I prefer it when you take your pleasure with me," she said unevenly.

Just when she thought she would explode from the intensity

of his gaze, his touch, *the promise of his kiss,* his thick black lashes lowered. Lightly he licked her lips, a scrape of liquid fire; the scalding heat palpitating against her palms and her cheeks plunged between her legs.

"Then I will show you other ways that a man and a woman can obtain satisfaction," he whispered. "Together."

Unexplored boundaries of passion.

Anticipation. Apprehension.

She had never before realized how alike the two separate emotions were.

Anne licked her lips, tasting his saliva, his breath. *Her uncertainty.* "Can a woman accept a man . . . where you penetrated me with your finger?"

Michel's eyelids slowly lifted.

Scorching heat rocketed through her body.

She did not know if it came from embarrassment at her boldness, or from his gaze and the riveting flare of passion there.

"A woman can take a man in her every orifice," he said hoarsely, fingers squeezing her cheeks, breath searing her lips.

The pressure should hurt, she vaguely realized, but it didn't. All that mattered was the violet of his eyes. The magnetism of his touch. And the image of him taking her where he had previously taken her with his finger.

Remembered sensation rippled through her.

"You said you would tell me what every woman has a right to demand. But what do men have a right to demand?" *How could she possibly return the pleasure he gave her?* "What do you expect from a woman, Michel?"

Michel released her; cold air embraced her cheeks. "I expect everything from you, Anne."

Anne blinked at his unexpected withdrawal.

Turning, he walked away from her. She stood rigidly straight, trying to regain control over her breathing. *Her body.*

She felt rather than heard him come up behind her. "Hold out your right arm."

Anne awkwardly thrust first one arm, then the other into

the sleeves of her cloak. The motion forced her right breast forward . . . her left breast, her linen chemise a rough caress.

The weight of the grenadine cloth settled on her shoulders. It pressed in on her until she could not breathe.

What had she said to turn him away?

Suddenly he stepped in front of her, holding her black silk gloves and beaded reticule.

Not meeting his gaze, she stiffly reached for them.

Michel pulled them back, held them loosely on either side of his groin.

The gray wool trousers bulged between the feminine accessories.

Her gaze shot up to his.

"This is for you, Anne." Face set in unreadable lines, he pressed her gloves and reticule into her hands, his fingers scraping her soft skin, forcing her fingers to close around slippery silk and brittle jet beads. "Money may buy pleasure, but it doesn't make a man hard. When we step out onto the street and people look at us, they will see my erection—not a monetary transaction."

Anne searched his eyes for the truth. "It doesn't bother you that others can see your . . . desire?"

"Why should it?"

Why should it, indeed?

All her life she had camouflaged her needs, afraid to show them for fear of what others would think.

Michel offered her his arm. Underneath the wool jacket lay the muscled reality of masculine flesh.

The streets were crowded with people hurrying to their individual houses or nearby shops to take high tea while vendors frantically tried to tempt them with their goods. They did not notice Anne Aimes, or the man who unashamedly flaunted his arousal for a spinster.

Dark eyes snared hers, slid away. An approaching man, young, obviously wealthy, briefly appraised Michel's groin before his gaze once again leveled on her with open speculation.

There was no ridicule in his eyes. No censure.

Only male appreciation.

The London air, polluted with smoke, raw drainage, and animal leavings, was suddenly clean and pure.

Anne thought of the aigrette bobbing in her hat. And of the use the plume would be put to.

She thought of Michel's flesh, hard and erect. And his remark, bold and direct.

Their steps rang in unison on the cobbled sidewalk. *Every orifice* echoed inside her ears.

A cab instantly pulled up to the curb when Michel raised his hand.

Anne's pupils dilated inside the dim interior of the hack; the springs creaked, tilted, righted, first with her weight, then with his.

Michel smartly closed the cab door behind him.

She pulled her cloak about her to make more room for his shoulder; his hip; his leg. *Her lungs.* "You seem to attract cabdrivers, Monsieur des Anges."

A surge of raw energy bolted through the cramped confines of the hack. Michel's left hand tightened around the door handle as if to wrench it open while his right hand clenched the gold handle of his cane so hard that the reddened welts covering his flesh turned white. At the same time the cab lurched forward.

Too late Anne realized what caused his reaction.

Chapter 8

Michael had not considered the possibility of being taken on a crowded street in the full light of day. *By a cabby.*

Uninterested pedestrians trotted by; vendors shouted out their wares while his cock burned and throbbed as if it were a separate entity, untouched by the looming threat of danger.

His gut clenched with belated understanding: when the time came it wouldn't matter if he was ready.

He gripped the metal door handle; it did not halt the cab.

The asphyxiating odors of old perfume, stale cigar smoke, and damp hay shot to his head in a disorienting rush of energy. Underlying the reek of faceless, nameless customers who would never know the fate of one lone spinster and the man she had hired to take her virginity was the astringent smell of benzine, soap, shampoo, and the sweetness that was Anne herself.

"I beg your pardon." Anne's low, cultured voice was a drum-piercing roar; her shoulder rhythmically pressed and rubbed his right arm, chafing muscles that were stretched taut with tension. "I did not mean to imply that your . . . appearance . . . attracts undue attention."

The cab had two possible destinations. Michael had two choices.

He could grab Anne, open the door, and jump. Or he could wait. And see where the cab carried them.

To death. Or to his town house.

If they jumped, she would be injured, possibly killed, when only minutes earlier her only thoughts had been of the myriad ways a man and a woman could enjoy one another and the orifices through which their mutual satisfaction might be obtained.

It should be *he* who begged *her* forgiveness.

"I told you last night." His breath steamed the window. Familiar buildings appeared through the fogged pane. Disappeared. Appeared. Disappeared. *Death. Desire. Death. Desire.* Inescapable patterns. "There is no need to apologize to me. Not ever."

Sunlight glinted off of a shop window; a shard of light momentarily blinded him.

Unyielding metal bit into his left hand; his right hand fisted around the head of his cane, the gold soft and warm, like Anne's body.

A third choice.

The cane, like the knife and condoms inside his nightstand, was custom-made. With a twist the gold handle pulled out and became the hilt of a short sword.

It would be kinder to kill her himself. Quickly. Before he was forced to watch her beg for death.

As Diane had begged.

"I know what it is like to be an object of curiosity."

Anne's compassion grated his nerves.

Michael's head snapped around.

Her face was luminescent inside the cab's murky interior, pale eyes a glimmer of light.

It had not occurred to her that cabbies were capable of kidnapping—and killing—any more than it had occurred to her that men who were hired to bring women pleasure were capable of kidnapping. *And killing.*

A vein throbbed inside his temple. Blood pulsed and pounded inside his groin.

She had touched him, this spinster who had yet to learn what she wanted. She had cupped her soft, unblemished hands over the backs of his and had not once flinched at the feel of his rough, scarred flesh. She had let him touch her.

And he had brought her to this.

"What do you know about being an object of curiosity?" he asked harshly.

What did she know about lying and cheating and killing?

"A spinster is considered an oddity." Shadow dimmed the glow of Anne's pale eyes; the white plume crowning her black hat danced and shimmied in time with the relentless bump and grind of the carriage wheels. "Especially in the country where people have nothing better to talk about than their neighbors."

Yet she had agreed to stay with him, to be seen with him, knowing that their association would damn her reputation.

Blaring music invaded the cab. A flurry of color and motion flashed outside Anne's window, brass gleaming, drums pounding.

In the blink of an eye it was gone—the ragged street band, the music, the very proof that either had ever existed.

Michael had never spoken the man's name. Not to Gabriel. Not to the madame who had claimed and trained her two angels. If taken, he would simply cease to exist in a world that already thought him dead.

And the cycle of death and desire would be broken.

There would be no more fear. No more carnal hunger that ate at his soul as well as his body.

There would be no one to help Anne.

How could he let the man take her?

The cab veered around a corner, carriage leaning, wood creaking. Anne reached up, grabbed the leather pull.

Too late.

She lunged into him. The layers of grenadine, wool, and whaleboned corset did not protect him from the soft impact of a round, firm breast.

He cursed his cock, which flexed in uncontrollable response. He cursed the man for the fear that only added to the sharpness of desire. He cursed the memories that burst inside his mind like fireworks on Guy Fawkes Day.

He had no illusions about what would happen if he and Anne were taken together. Neither of them would survive.

The instinctive urge to fight, *to escape,* metamorphosed into the primal need for procreation.

Michael and the man were the last of their line. When they died, there would be no one else to carry on the family name.

Anne was the last of her line.

For one galvanizing second he thought about filling her with his seed and pushing her out of the carriage in the hope that she would live, pregnant with his child. She would be a loving mother. Their son, or daughter, would suckle at her breasts, as he had suckled at them, and thrive on her innate goodness, ignorant of the father's sins. Through their offspring he would continue. . . .

As would the man's blood.

Forcibly he reigned in the driving lust to create life out of the endless, senseless destruction. He could not block out the burning imprint of her breast.

"It wasn't your marital status that inspired their gossip," he said stolidly. Women—and men—all too often despised what they wanted. *And wanted what they despised.* "It was your wealth."

"It really doesn't matter what inspires gossip, does it?" she asked quietly. The cracked leather seat bounced and vibrated underneath them, a near painful stimulus in his erect state. "It is still painful."

The left rear carriage wheel hit a hole; the cab dropped heavily before leaping forward.

He could not tell her that words didn't hurt; they did. He could not lie to her and say that someday she would become inured to the pain. If the cabby drove them to the man, there would be no time for her to grow, to love, to laugh.

A row of redbrick town houses sped by, inspiring hope, because the cab had not yet veered off the course to his town house. Breeding rage, because the man, like a cat, toyed with him. And there was nothing he could do about it.

Except watch. And wait.

And ache for release.

"I have touched myself."

Michael's narrow-eyed gaze shifted back to Anne's face. Her right cheek was outlined by the blur of passing buildings.

An invisible vise tightened around his chest.

She was offering him her confidence. Trying to make amends for the pain she thought she had caused him.

"This morning you asked if I had touched my breasts when I imagined a man suckling a woman. I have."

She twisted her reticule. The beads glittered like black diamonds.

"I used to lie in bed at night and imagine you suckling me." Her gaze remained steady, guarded, uncertain of how he would respond to a spinster's secret longings. "And I touched myself."

It was ridiculous to be jealous of a dead man. But Michael was.

A black wave of anger rushed over him.

Anne Aimes had imagined *Michel* suckling her. Not Michael.

No woman had ever cried out his given name at her moment of release.

Always it had been Michel.

Never Michael.

It never would be Michael.

"Wouldn't you rather have the man I used to be?" he asked brutally, wanting to hurt her, wanting to prepare her, wanting to protect her. "Or do you pretend that my scars don't exist?"

The harsh words rang out over the relentless grind of the carriage wheels.

She did not look away from him. "No, I do not."

"No, you do not what?" he asked ruthlessly. "No, you do not pretend that my scars don't exist? Or no, you don't pretend that they matter?"

Her gaze was too perceptive. Too ignorant of her fate. "No, I do not wish you were the man you used to be."

For a gut-wrenching moment Michael wished he were still Michel. *For her sake.*

He wished he were ignorant of the price she would pay. *For his sake.*

He wished he did not know what awaited Anne.

In an hour. A day.

A month.

The man would come.

"Why?" he asked bluntly. Crudely.

After all these years he still did not know *why*.

"Because you make me feel as if I am desirable."

While eighteen years ago Michel had ignored her.

He had hurt his spinster before he had even met her.

The tightly strung wire that his muscles had become quivered—in regret, for the hell he had plunged her into; in hunger, for what could have been under other circumstances.

Responses that, for both their sakes, would best be ignored.

But he couldn't do that, either.

"You *are* desirable, Anne. I saw the way the man on the street looked at you. He wanted you. *I* want you."

The light in her pale blue eyes flickered. Embarrassment that he had witnessed her feminine delight at an unknown man's perusal flowed into vulnerability.

She wanted to believe that she was desirable.

But she still did not.

She wanted to trust him, emotionally as well as physically.

Yet she could not quite bring herself to do that, either.

"You have spoken French only once since you took my virginity." She tilted her chin, denying her embarrassment, her vulnerability, while the cab hurtled forward, its destination set. *And there was nothing he could do to stop it.* "Why is that?"

She was already starting to put the pieces together.

Michael gritted his teeth.

Because he *did* want her more than death itself.

But that wasn't the answer she sought. Or even the question she asked.

Last night she had corrected him when he called her *mon amour. My love.* But not when he called her *chérie.*

Anne wanted the casual French endearments he had given her predecessors—that he had given her before he realized the futility of pretending to be someone he was not.

He forced himself to speak the words she expected. "Would you rather I speak French more often?"

Would death be less painful if it was delivered by Michel?

"I would like you to teach me how to speak French."

Michael's head jerked back, his heart lurching, the cab swaying.

He could not be Michel. Not even knowing that it might be the last wish he could ever grant his spinster. "You already speak it."

Every gently bred woman learned French grammar.

"Not like . . ." Anne resolutely held his gaze. "I want to know other words. Words that do not come from a medical compendium. Scholars define orgasm as a means by which sperm is deposited inside a woman for the purpose of impregnation. They describe a clitoris as a penislike projection which, because of a woman's gender, does not mature into the organ that brings prestige and honor to men. I would like words to express the beauty of sexual union as well as the physiology."

Michael had wanted to know how a well-bred virgin had become conversant with sexual terminology. *Clitoris. Penis.* Terms polite society hid away from their women for fear they would contaminate their souls.

Now he wished like hell he didn't know.

Her knowledge had been gleaned from a medical textbook. Words tainted by death and disease.

"There are English words that are not medical," he said baldly.

"Yes, but English can be crude. I do not feel as if what you did . . . what *we* did . . . is vile. Coition *is* earthy. And primal. I have never felt as close to another person as I felt when you were inside me. French is a beautiful language." She tried to inject lightness into her voice but failed. Anne had not been allowed to take life lightly. "Surely it is more suited for intimacy than English, is it not?"

He had once thought so. Now all he could think about was the grinding progress of the carriage and the pulsating heat of her shoulder, hip, and leg rubbing his.

Two separate rhythms, clocking two separate fates.

Twenty-seven years ago sex had brought Michael back from the edge of insanity. Through the French language he had been able to express his need for comfort. For pleasure. He had basked in the joy of sexuality.

Michel had been born out of that beauty.

Anne was not asking him to be the man he used to be. She was asking him to make her life more bearable.

"What words would you like to know?" he asked hoarsely.

"You kissed me last night," she said determinedly.

"The French have many different words for a kiss." He strained to hear the strike of the horse's hooves to determine either a reduction or an increase in speed. "It depends upon whom one kisses. And where."

"You kissed me between my thighs." Anne's breasts rapidly rose and fell beneath her staid black cloak. "On my clitoris."

The echo of the horse's hooves blended with the pounding of his heart. How far they had traveled since she first climbed into a cab with a man she did not know. *A man she still did not know.*

"A woman's clitoris is called *un bouton d'amour,* a love button." His mouth flooded with the taste of her, the silky hot blend of salty sweet passion. "The type of kiss I gave you there is called *le broute-minou.*"

Anne's gaze skidded away from his. She faced the worn leather interior of the cab; the white egret plume and black hat hid her face from his view.

Michael focused on her window and the reflection of her pale, cameo-perfect profile that was superimposed over passing London landmarks.

They were so close to his town house . . . only a few blocks away. He could not escape the surge of anticipation, even knowing it was too early to tell . . . knowing how carefully orchestrated his hope might be. . . .

Knowing that it would be best if the man took them now, before his spinster became more attached to him . . . and he to her.

"You called your . . . penis . . . *ma bitte.* Are there other words for it?"

A park charged past them—a blur of leafy green trees, twirling parasols, and children chasing a hoop.

He had been young once. Happy. Carefree.

Had Anne?

"There are many words for a man."

A creak of leather alerted him; Anne turned in the seat. Her gaze locked with his, her eyes filled with compelling urgency. "Such as?"

His blood pumped through his veins; the cab rushed through the cobbled streets. There was no turning back.

"Bequille." Crutch. *"Outil."* Tool. *"Bout."* End.

He had by turns used sex as a crutch and a tool. A means to an end that was rapidly approaching . . .

Anne frowned, translating the French slang into English words that made no sense.

He had never heard her laugh.

Diane had not laughed after the man took her. But she had laughed before.

Anne had had no joy, no pleasure. Her entire life had been dedicated to providing comfort for others.

Michael wanted to give her laughter while there was still time.

"A man's penis is also called an *andouille à col roule,"* he said with a calculated ease that denied the pounding inside his chest and groin and the raw, unrelieved pressure that crawled up and down his spine, searching for an outlet.

She stared in blatant disbelief. "The French call a man . . . a sausage with a rolled-down collar?"

He watched her intently, gauging her response. "It is an apt enough comparison."

There was no repulsion in her eyes, only curiosity. "What other words are there?"

She was so serious, this woman who confessed she did not often laugh. So determined to explore the subtle nuances of intimacy.

There were many sex words that, when translated into English, became sublimely ridiculous. He chose a term she could more readily understand.

"Cigare à moustache." Cigar with a mustache.

The imagery was irresistible.

Laughter followed her shock, a clear, husky peal that exploded the gathering darkness inside the cab and twisted about his guts.

Her pale blue eyes sparkled. "What do you prefer?"

His tumescent flesh thickened, hardened, lengthened, nine and a half inches stretching into nineteen and a half inches. He felt as if he would burst through his own skin, like an overripe grape, if he did not soon gain release. *"Bitte,"* he rasped.

All traces of her humor instantly evaporated. Her wide-eyed gaze reflected the evocative memory of her swollen clitoris embracing his rubber-sheathed manhood. *My penis, my cock,* ma bitte.

Suddenly there were only the two of them inside the cab: a spinster with her first lover.

There was no room for death.

"Why do you precede . . . *bitte* . . . with a feminine pronoun . . . as opposed to a masculine one?"

"Bitte is a feminine noun—"

Anne glanced down at his lap.

He did not have to follow her gaze to know that a damp spot, evidence of his arousal, marked his gray wool trousers. Last night he had used it—along with her own feminine essence—to lubricate his manhood to more readily fit it inside a condom.

Her gaze darted up to meet his. She, too, remembered. . . .

A tall, gold brick Georgian town house appeared behind Anne's head, the first in a row that marked his home street.

Michael's muscles coiled for action.

Now.

The cab would stop . . . or it would drive by.

He would take Anne . . . or the man would take him.

The grinding of the carriage wheels filled his head, his body, his sex. His entire being focused on the sound, waiting, waiting . . .

The cab slowed, rattled to a stop.

It was not yet time for either of them to die.

The energy that he had forcibly held in abeyance erupted into naked force. Eyes locking with Anne's, his voice hardened in feral need. "Because it is made for a woman."

He thought about lifting her skirt and taking her there in the cab.

She wouldn't fight him. There was nothing she would not let him do.

Michael wrenched open the door and jumped out, a jarring catalyst of motion. Cool spring air enveloped him.

It did not extinguish the seething turmoil of sexual need.

A creak of springs sounded behind him.

He pivoted and stared, mesmerized.

Poking out her head—downy white plume dancing in the cool breeze—Anne stuck out a narrow half boot and felt for the step.

A picture of her standing in Madame René's dressing room wearing only her hat, stockings, and shoes slammed through him.

She should be dressed in the finest silks and velvets—not grenadine and wool, he thought savagely.

Reaching out, Michael grasped her by the waist and swung her out of the cab. The gold handle of his cane dug into her corseted waist, *just a cane.* A gentleman's accessory; not an assassin's tool.

This time.

Head flying up, eyes wide with surprise, Anne grasped his shoulders.

It was obvious she was not used to being helped out of a carriage. Not used to being complimented. *Wanted.*

But he wanted her. She would never know how much.

Deliberately he pulled her against him until her breasts flattened against his chest and the jointure of her thighs notched his penis.

Her nipples were hard.

He was hard.

"A man's sperm . . ." Anne's breath bathed his lips. Her cultured, husky voice was whisper soft. Sunlight turned the tips of her short, brown eyelashes into gold spikes. "What is it called in French?"

Desire lanced through Michael's testicles.

He knew where this was going.

He knew he should stop her.

But he couldn't.

"Came." He eased her down his body, savoring the weight of her breasts and the press of her stomach, making her feel his hardness . . . his readiness. . . . The heat of her body penetrated her cloak and wool dress; it matched the heat of her breath. *"Sauce. Blanc."*

"Blanc." She tasted the word, feminine need and curiosity fully aroused. "Is your sperm . . . white?"

"It's white," he said roughly. "Hot. Thick."

It swelled inside his testes, straining—

The cabby loudly cleared his throat.

Shamed awareness shone in Anne's eyes. She had allowed a man familiarities in public, her expression said—something that no self-respecting lady allowed.

She recoiled from Michael's arms, attempting to become the self-possessed woman that her appearance proclaimed her to be.

But he knew better.

She had agreed to give him complete access, and that was what he would take. There was no place on her body that he had not touched. That he would not touch again.

Michael released her only long enough to toss a coin to the cabby. Before Anne could further collect her composure and shy away from her natural sensuality, he urged her up the walk. Purposefully he flattened his palm against the small of her back—there, where he had supported her the night before when she straddled his lap and, overcome by his dimensions and her orgasm, had cried out her release.

The memory was as firmly implanted in her mind as it was in his. He could feel the pulse of her recollection all the way through her layers of clothing.

The brass knocker gleamed in the sunlight; no name was etched into it to identify either Michael or Michel as the occupant. The white-enameled door was unlocked; it swung forward on oiled hinges. The sweet perfume of hyacinth welcomed him.

Death, too, possessed a sweet odor. It lurked beneath the stench of rot, luring the unwary.

But there was no beauty in dying.

Or killing.

Anne stepped forward, away from him, when he paused to close the door behind them. Chill air enveloped his fingers where but moments earlier the heat of her body had warmed him.

He forcefully locked the door—a useless precaution; neither locks nor bars would keep out the man—before turning around.

Her spine was rigidly straight. A pale line of skin shone between the stiff black collar of her cloak and her light brown hair, which disappeared underneath the black hat.

What had she been like eighteen years earlier?

How could he have overlooked her in a crowd of simpering debutantes and overperfumed belles?

Bending his head, he lightly nuzzled aside flyaway strands of baby-fine hair, seeking the scent of her underneath the camouflaging odors of benzine, shampoo, and soap.

She stiffened.

Pain spiraled through him. The hunter rejected by his prey.

Michael briefly closed his eyes, his senses fine-tuned to the pulse of her body. "You said you weren't ashamed of me."

"I'm not," she replied in a hushed voice, as if the walls had ears capable of overhearing her lapse of decorum.

And perhaps they did.

"Then you're ashamed of touching me," he said flatly, stepping back, the lover spurned. "Of wanting me."

A quick inhalation of air sliced through the dim stillness inside the foyer. "I'm not."

But she was.

"If you were not, you would look at me. And take me. Openly. Without reserve."

She quickly turned. Shame competed with arousal in her pale eyes. Honesty with self-preservation.

"Is that what you were referring to when you said you expect everything from me?"

He would not think of the man. Not now. Not until the night. "Yes."

Her chin, more round than oval, firmed with determination. "If a woman wanted to kiss a man's *bitte,* what would the French expression be?"

Michael had expected her question in the cab. Now it took him unawares.

He was transfixed by the explicit image her words conjured.

By her desire to taste a scarred whore's pleasure.

It had been five years since a woman had wanted to take him into her mouth.

For a second he thought he would come inside his pants as he had when the madame first caressed him.

"*Bonjour,* monsieur." The sharp, hollow click of hurried footsteps approached them. "Mademoiselle."

Anne's face closed. Once again she became the proper spinster.

And he would not have it. They had so little time. . . .

Michael alertly watched Anne as Raoul deftly took her reticule. He could read her thoughts as clearly as if she spoke them aloud. She had worn the same expression when he introduced her to Madame René.

The butler must know that she had procured Michel's services, she thought.

Her gaze darted lower, to the damp spot up high on Michael's trousers.

A red tide blotched her pale skin. It was not the becoming flush of sexual excitement.

Raoul firmly grasped the gold handle of Michael's cane, white-gloved fingers brushing scarred flesh. "Are we dining in this evening, monsieur?"

Anne's head jerked up.

It had just occurred to her what the literal translation for *sauce,* the French vernacular for a man's sperm, was.

And yes, it was edible, his violet gaze told her.

"Yes," he said evenly. "Mademoiselle and I will be dining in this evening."

Anne's pink tongue darted out, moistened her lips.

Michael's body tightened.

"May I take your *chapeau,* mademoiselle?"

She automatically reached to unpin her hat, then halted midmotion, her gaze trapped by Michael's.

The splotches of red connected so that her entire face was a crimson glow.

Her lips quivered, so very sensitive, responsive to pressure. Nibbles. Licks. Kisses.

They would be equally responsive to the teasing of a feather.

To the kiss of his penis.

Slowly she lowered her arms. "No, thank you. I will keep my hat."

Michael inhaled sharply. Impossibly, he grew harder.

"Très bien." The butler stoically extended a white cotton-gloved hand for Anne's black silk gloves. "Would mademoiselle care to review the menu?"

"No, thank you." Glancing away from Michael, Anne stared at Raoul's black necktie, the cream-painted wall behind him, anything but the butler's eyes. Raoul blankly stared at her hat, not at all interested in her discomfiture. Clumsily she unfastened her cloak. "I am sure whatever the cook prepares will be fine."

"Très bien." Raoul calmly took the black grenadine cloak from her. *"Merci."*

"We will dine at eight, Raoul," Michael said coolly, his gaze never leaving Anne.

"I will inform the cook, monsieur."

Michael held out his hand, inviting Anne to touch him. Openly. Publicly. In the full light of day. Without shame.

Face shadowed by the brim of her hat, she stared at his scars for long seconds. At his flesh, which had caressed her. At his fingers, which had probed the depths of her body.

Squaring her shoulders, she reached out and clasped his hand.

Her touch was electric.

Friends. Lovers.

The bond was complete.

She would not turn away from him again. And he . . . he would protect her.

Somehow. Some way.

Satisfied—sensitive to her sensibilities now that he knew she would not repulse him—he released her hand and unerringly found the arch of her back. Purposely he urged her toward the stairs, his heartbeat counting their steps.

"Monsieur, a delivery came." Behind them, Raoul's voice ricocheted off of the high ceiling and painted walls. "It is in your study."

Michael did not pause. "Thank you. I will attend to it later."

Much later. Death was too close. He needed his spinster to hold it at bay.

Just one more day . . .

Head dipping, aigrette dancing, Anne grasped the intricately wrought-iron banister.

Five years ago the banister had been wooden. Diane had slid down it into his waiting arms, and impaled herself on Michel's waiting cock.

She had wanted nothing to do with Michael's flesh.

Anne furtively glanced at the hard bulge that tented the front of his trousers.

Wondering . . . *what?*

How he would taste?

How she would accommodate him in her other passage?

How soft a feather would feel, caressing the softest part of her body?

The tension inside him coiled tighter, hotter.

Nothing would interfere with their pleasure now.

Anne would give him what he needed: a few hours of respite to strengthen him for the coming night.

He would give her what she needed: memories to sustain her in the aftermath.

"Monsieur!" Raoul's voice came directly behind—*goddamn him.* He was following them. "The man who made the delivery said it is urgent that you read this *lettre.* He said it is from a man whom you recently made the acquaintance of but who is no longer with us."

No longer with us raced up the marble stairs.

The sweet aroma of hyacinth clogged in Michael's throat. Coldness snaked through his veins.

How many more would die before it was over?

The warmth penetrating Anne's wool dress scorched his fingers, living testimony of the man's next victim.

Michael jerked his hand away from the small of her back and pivoted on the mirror-slick floor.

Raoul held out the silver post tray.

There was nothing sinister in the offering. Just the unrelenting reality of the butler's message.

Anne stood motionless beside him. His for the taking. Already marked for another.

Face expressionless, Michael picked up the sealed envelope and ripped it open.

A key fell into the palm of his hand. There was another envelope inside the first. It was simply addressed.

The handwriting was small, neat, feminine.

A note was scrawled underneath the lawyer's name. It was neither small, neat, nor feminine.

The message was blunt: *From one solicitor to another.*

Black dots danced in front of his eyes.

"Please do not feel compelled to keep me entertained." He heard Anne's voice as if through a long, dark tunnel. "I quite understand if you have . . . personal . . . matters to take care of."

Personal matters.

Yes, death was very personal.

The writing on the white vellum paper blurred.

It would be so much easier if he didn't like Anne Aimes.

Had he liked the women in the past who kept the nightmares away?

Had he liked Diane?

"Thank you." Raising his head, he smiled. Anne's pale blue eyes mirrored two smiling faces—Michael, Michel. Michel, Michael. Condensed, there was no difference in their appearance. "I will only be a few minutes. Raoul, show Mademoiselle Aimes to the library."

There were no runners, no rugs, to silence his steps, no carpeting in either his town house or his home in Yorkshire that could ignite in a blazing conflagration.

The man's house was also bare of carpeting.

Twenty-nine years ago he had never known what to expect when he walked into the man's study. Knowing what he was going to walk into now did not alleviate the fear, or the anger.

Impotent emotions.

But unlike the man, Michael was not impotent. His cock continued to pulse and throb.

Inside his study a black trunk squatted beside the marble-topped desk.

He was not surprised at its contents, any more than he was surprised at the contents of the letter inside the second envelope.

Dear Mr. Little:

My meeting with Michel des Anges was quite satisfactory.

I know that you were concerned for my safety. Please do not be. I am well and happier than I have ever been before.

Per the terms of the contract, you may deposit the first quarter of Monsieur des Anges's payment.

I will be available at the below address. As I will remain there for the designated month rather than traveling back and forth between my place of residence and that of Monsieur des Anges, I would greatly appreciate it if you periodically visit my town house to ascertain that everything is as it should be.

Sincerely yours,
Miss Anne Aimes

Michael stared at his address, neatly written at the bottom of the vellum paper. Lowering the letter, he stared down into Little's wide, frightened eyes.

There would be no deposit. The contract had been dissolved.

Its charred remains protruded from Little's blistered, blackened lips.

Death had not brought the solicitor peace.

He had not known why he must die. Neither would Anne.

Michael stared and stared at the little old man whose demise he was responsible for. And he could feel nothing.

No sorrow.

No regret.

Just the pulse of his erection that remained stiff and hard while the blood inside his veins turned to ice.

Tiny images flickered inside Little's fixed pupils: white egret plumes crowning a black felt hat. Pale eyes aglow with sensual awareness. Dark, bruised nipples. Creamy white breasts. Golden brown pubic hair. A tantalizing peep of swollen pink-lips. White garters. Flesh-colored stockings. Black, pointed half boots.

The humanity Michael had clung to throughout the years hovered over him, a ghost that could so easily fade inside the dark hole that was his past.

Little's murder clearly stated the man's intentions.

He would not rest until it was Anne who stared in blank horror. Until it was her flesh that stiffened with rigor mortis.

Until it was her body that waited for disposal.

The man had released Diane. Michael had hoped he would do the same for Anne.

But he would not.

He did not intend to let Anne live—whether she and Michael were taken together or not.

A soft knock splintered the silence.

Not the man.

His minions would not knock.

Michael woodenly closed the trunk lid and relocked it. He pocketed the key. "Come in."

Raoul's graying dark head poked through the door. His nose wrinkled fastidiously. "Did you burn something, monsieur?"

Two solicitors had been burned. The lawyer was dead. The male whore was still alive.

Or was he?

"The merchandise inside the trunk was scorched from a previous fire," Michael said flatly. "What is it that you require, Raoul?"

"Your dinner, monsieur. Shall you have the usual?"

Food.

Dead flesh for the living.

Live worms for the dead.

"I shall have whatever is prepared for Mademoiselle Aimes."

"*Très bien,* monsieur."

The butler's graying, dark head withdrew.

"Raoul."

The butler instantly reappeared. "Monsieur?"

He had bought the Georgian town house eighteen years earlier. Raoul had been in the employ of the previous owner. Michael had allowed the butler to marry the housekeeper; in return Raoul and Marie silently, diligently performed their duties.

They did not question. They did not gossip. When the town house had inexplicably gone up in flames and Diane with it, they had overseen the repairs and stayed on as caretakers.

Michael realized how little he knew about his two principal servants.

"Send a message to Gabriel. Tell him I need him. Tonight. And Raoul—"

The butler stoically met Michael's gaze.

"I do not think I need tell you that I will not welcome any more interruptions."

Bowing, Raoul discreetly withdrew.

Michael stared at the closing door.

He could not let the man take Anne Aimes. When she died, her final thoughts would be of pleasure. Michael would be the last thing she saw. Not the man.

Chapter 9

Anne restlessly perused the rows and rows of leather books lining the library walls. *Beowulf. Canterbury Tales. Le Morte D'Arthur,* an Englishman's account of King Arthur and the man and woman who betrayed him.

The butler's voice continued to ring inside her ears: *no longer with us.*

A euphemism for death, as if the deceased relocated and carelessly forgot to pack their bodies.

She lightly ran a finger over embossed gold lettering. Shakespeare . . . Charles Dickens. *Wuthering Heights,* by Emily Brontë . . . The leather spine was buckled with wear.

Anne could not imagine Michel reading a romance.

She could not imagine a man who was named for his ability to satisfy a woman being vulnerable.

To a spinster's words.

A spinster's body.

A spinster's needs.

To death.

The smell of expensive leather and freshly cut lilacs surged through her.

Death had no place in a house filled with flowers and pleasure.

Anne whirled around, evading the past, the present. Death was an inescapable reality.

Afternoon sunshine checkered the polished oak floor. Gilded chaise lounges upholstered in dark blue silk cast uncompromising shadows; ormolu-applied pedestal tables stood at attention beside each lounge chair, daunting reminders of another era, another culture. Bone-china lamps covered with dark blue and gold fleur-de-lis-patterned silk shades glowed in the fading light.

Eyes widening, she halted; her bustle swayed back and forth underneath her dress.

Michel leaned against the door, eyes hooded, watching her.

She forgot to breathe.

He did not look like the man who had confessed his need for a woman. Or who had propelled her toward the stairs with unmistakable intent.

His violet eyes were flat. Dead. Like the marble eyes in the stuffed owl decorating the foyer in her parents' town house.

He looked, she thought, like a man who had never enjoyed the pleasures of intimacy.

He looked like the butler her solicitor had hired.

Deadly. Dangerous.

"You kept the hat on."

Michel's observation was harsh, discordant.

Anne was abruptly, acutely aware of the white plume that crowned her hat, and of how he must interpret the fact that she wore it still. "Yes."

"Men don't expect women to kiss them."

Her head shot back in surprise. "I beg your pardon?"

"You wanted to know what I expect from a woman."

"You don't expect a woman to kiss you?" she asked carefully.

"No," he said flatly.

She swallowed. "I see."

Electricity rode the air like a gathering storm.

"Don't you want to know what I expect from a woman, Mademoiselle Aimes?"

Anne inwardly cringed at the impersonal form of French address.

"Yes." She stiffened her spine. "I do want to know. Otherwise I would not have asked."

"I expect a woman to lick me. Suck me. Bite me," he said in that curiously harsh yet distant voice. "The same as I did to you last night. And again this morning, when I brought you to orgasm."

It was a direct challenge.

Last night he had teased her with his lips, tongue, and teeth. This morning he had satisfied her with the same tools.

He knew what to do to a woman, how best to please her, whereas she knew nothing about men, or how best to please him.

She struggled to reconcile the man before her with the one who had urged her to accept him as her lover.

She could not.

In the carriage he had been abrupt, angry at circumstances he had no control over, yet which had forever altered his life.

Emotions she could relate to.

She did not know how to respond to the man standing in front of her.

Her short fingernails dug into the palms of her hands. Belatedly she remembered digging them into Michel's back last night. *Had she marked him?* "An acquaintance of yours . . . passed away?" she asked stiffly, hating the euphemism but unable to bring herself to utter the word *died*.

"Yes."

"Please accept my condolences. I quite understand if you would prefer privacy. . . ."

Michel continued staring at her for long seconds, until even her heartbeat fumbled.

"It was not unexpected," he replied finally.

Pushing away from the door, he strode stiff-leggedly toward the white marble fireplace and squatted down.

Anne remembered the pile of white ashes in Mr. Little's iron fireplace. She would not have thought the solicitor the type of man to indulge in the extravagance of burning a fire in April.

She would not have thought to find a Frenchman's library filled with English titles.

Yet Michel's was.

The sharp strike of a safety match pierced the palpitating silence. A faint waft of sulfur mingled with the smell of leather and lilacs.

Rising so quickly that he stumbled, Michel jerkily stepped

away before turning his back toward the flickering yellow fire that licked at the black coals.

For one fleeting second his life was clearly delineated on his face: the pain he had suffered five years earlier, his flesh eaten by flame. The fear he experienced still, forced to daily handle a substance that had caused him unimaginable suffering.

The loss of someone who was far more dear than a mere acquaintance.

Anne had lived with death for many, many years before it had actually taken her parents. When it had finally come, the relief she had felt had been more of a betrayal than the actual demise of the only two people she loved. But he had obviously not been prepared.

Michel had forced her to accept her loneliness. In return he had unselfishly given her comfort—with words, with pleasure. *He had made her laugh.*

He did not deserve to mourn in solitude.

Anne offered him the only solace she suspected he would accept. "How does a woman ask a man if she may lick him . . . suck him . . . bite him?"

"Men are not shy," he said, coldly provocative, the stallion Madame René had called him. "If a woman wants a man, all she has to do is tell him."

Her heartbeat accelerated. "I want you, Michel."

An ember popped in the fireplace.

Michel flinched, as if bracing himself for pain. Lowering his lashes, he suggestively reached for the front of his trousers. "How do you want me, Anne?"

"In front of the window," she replied evenly. Beneath her dress her knees threatened to collapse at the actuality of giving pleasure to a man whose services she had purchased for her own pleasure. "Facing the sunlight. So that I can see you."

His nostrils flared, scarred fingers stilling.

"Taking a man's penis inside your mouth is not like taking his tongue. You may not like the taste of sex." Rawness overrode the crudeness in his voice, remnants of memories devoid of joy. "Not all women do."

"But you enjoy kissing a woman's genitals," she said with a calm certainty that she was far from feeling.

"Yes, I do."

"Why?"

"Because I know that it pleases a woman. Sex is the taste of pleasure."

He did not have to say that it had been five years since a woman had cared to please him. *To taste him.*

It was all there in his stark violet eyes.

"I want to taste you, Michel. To feel your heartbeat against my lips, my tongue. I, too, want to lose myself in another's pleasure."

Long seconds passed, the silence broken only by the crackling of the spreading flame, the pounding of her heart, and the memory of his voice. Telling her he had felt her heartbeat against his lips, his tongue . . .

Just when she thought that he would refuse her, he silently, wordlessly walked toward the large bay window, into the afternoon sunlight. A gilded round table held a large Ming vase filled with lavender lilacs. He halted a few feet in front of it, his right profile facing her, his body wreathed in golden light.

Heart tripping inside her chest, heels clicking on the sun-checkered floor, she closed the distance separating them and stepped between him and the window.

Warmth caressed her exposed nape. Tension weighted the dust motes.

"I don't want you to regret the time we've spent together," Michel said tautly.

The scars on his right cheek and temple were raw in the glare of the sunlight.

Anne ignored them. "I do not regret my decision."

He reached for the buttons fastening his trousers.

She experienced a curious sense of déjà vu.

"No," she impulsively protested.

He paused, eyelashes lifting, his gaze impaling hers.

"No?" he asked softly.

He had dared her to unfasten his trousers last night—a virgin who did not know what to expect.

She now knew what to expect.

"Please. Allow me."

She wanted to bury, now and forever, the memories of death and disease.

Anne did not fumble with his buttons as she had the night before. The hardness behind the scratchy wool was inviting, familiar.

It was for her, he had said.

Not because she paid him. But because he desired her.

Kneeling, dress and petticoats cushioning her knees, she reached into the open vent, finding wiry hair; humid heat; unmistakable male arousal.

A faint whiff of something—something that had been scorched—teased her nostrils. It was immediately gone, replaced by the clean, musky odor of masculine flesh and the pervasive sweetness of lilac. Sunlight danced along the length of his erect penis, revealing every vein, every gradation of color. A curlicue of black hair. Darkening skin that ripened into dewy plum.

Gently she grasped him, encircled the first five inches. A thin thread of silvery arousal glistened on the engorged purple head that protruded from her fingers.

He did not look like a sausage. He did not look like a cigar.

He did not look like the shriveled mass of desiccated flesh that had been her father.

Michel was what she would remember in the forthcoming years.

Anne traced the path of moisture; the plum-shaped crown was slippery smooth. A faint pulse throbbed underneath his skin.

The moisture in her mouth dried up with sudden apprehension at taking him into her mouth. Licking him. Sucking him.

Her fingers tightened; she studied the tiny slit that looked like an eye. It wept a lonely tear. "Is it necessary that I take all of you inside my mouth?"

"No." She could feel his stare; his voice was strained, still harsh but no longer remote. "Just the first couple of inches."

Slowly, carefully, she grazed the throbbing head with her lips.

His flesh jerked.

Anne snapped backward.

Michel's hands were fisted at his side. His head was thrown back. The muscles in his exposed throat were corded, as if he were in supreme agony—or utter ecstasy.

Leaning forward, she tentatively nuzzled him as he had nuzzled her. Inhaled his scent as he had inhaled hers.

It was not offensive.

Closing her eyes, she tasted him, there where his flesh throbbed like a heartbeat.

He tasted . . . clean. Faintly salty.

Anne hesitantly took the thick, plum-shaped tip between her lips, her mouth opening wider, wider still until she encompassed his full circumference.

It was awkward, but not uncomfortable.

He flexed inside the circle of her fingers, as if in approval.

A murmur of surprised pleasure rose inside her throat.

Large, scar-roughened hands banded her neck.

Anne started. Jerking back, she glanced up.

Michel did not loosen his hold.

His eyelids were heavy, a slash of black lashes. Underneath them his pupils were a pinprick of darkness that swallowed the light; his violet irises glittered. "Do you like it?"

"Yes," she said in all honesty.

"Do you know what will happen if you continue?"

She stared at the purple crown that pulsed and throbbed and wept the tears that he did not. "You will ejaculate."

"Inside your mouth," he affirmed.

The thought should repulse her.

It didn't.

Leaning forward, she planted a kiss on the velvety tip of his *bitte*—a beautiful French word for a beautiful Frenchman. Then she swallowed as much of him as she could comfortably take.

One ridged hand slid free of her neck. A heartbeat later a weight depressed her hat. Steel slipped through her hair—the hat pin.

A shiver of alarm coursed down her spine.

Her head snapped back and up.

Michel held the hat pin. Light played along the sharp steel, fluttered along the glistening wetness of his flesh.

Trust me, he had said.

But she didn't.

It was so difficult to trust when all her life she had been warned not to.

Anne took a deep breath. "Tell me what to do. How to do it."

The steel hat pin winked.

Hollows indented his cheeks; the raw-looking scars lining his high cheekbone and temple whitened. "Take me in your mouth."

"Say it in French." She heard her voice over the drum of her heartbeat. "Talk to me like you did the others. . . ."

The women who were beautiful. Gay. Frivolous.

Everything she was not.

For a long second even the rhythmical pounding inside her fist stopped. Sunlight ebbed and swelled around them, defining glistening flesh, gray wool, white linen, and shiny metal.

Across the library the burning coals ceased to snap and pop.

And then . . .

"Prends-moi dans la bouche." Take me into your mouth.

Closing her eyes, she took him into her mouth. The steel pin continued to glint in her mind's eye.

"L'eche-moi." Lick me.

She licked him.

"Mords-moi." Bite me.

She gently nibbled on him.

"Suce-moi." Suck me.

She sucked him.

"Plus profond." Deeper.

She took him deeper, lips working against the circle of her fingers.

"Plus fort." Harder.

She drew deeply on the silky hard flesh inside her mouth, as he had drawn on her breast. A woman taking sustenance from a man.

Did he feel this closeness when he suckled a woman? she wondered.

Had he felt it when he suckled *her?*

His scar-roughened fingers dug into the base of her head.

"Plus vite." Faster.

Anne felt the fragility of her neck, the masculine strength in his hand. The feminine power of her touch.

She took him faster, trembling on the verge of discovery, utterly lost in the taste and texture of Michel des Anges.

His flesh hardened. Thickened.

Something was happening. Something quite incredible.

It felt as if he were about to explode inside her mouth.

A sharp ping resounded beside her. Vaguely she identified it as the hat pin bouncing on the wooden floor. At the same time both of Michel's hands clamped about her neck and he hoarsely shouted, *"N'arrête pas!* Jesus! Don't stop!"

Liquid spurted against the back of her throat.

It was hot. Thick.

Exhilarating. Empowering.

It was the essence of Michel's pleasure.

Anne instinctively swallowed.

And yes, she *did* like it.

Sauce. Blanc. Came.

The French terms rolled on her tongue.

Her hat flew off the top of her head. Suddenly she was standing, blinking in surprise. Strong fingers tangled in her hair, dislodging the pins securing her bun. Hair slithered down her back.

Michel's face was flushed; his eyes were narrow shards of violet. "I won't hurt you," he whispered fiercely.

"You didn't hurt me," she reassured him shakily, equally enthralled by both the wonder of his orgasm and her ability to effect it. "I—"

His dark face swooped down. He stole the words from her mouth, and then he stole her breath, lips grinding against hers, tongue plunging between her teeth.

She was arrested by the unexpected fervor of his embrace. Or perhaps it was fear that held her immobile.

This, she realized with a frisson of alarm, was the difference between a lover and a man employed to ensure a woman's satisfaction.

This was a man out of control.

This was a man's passion.

"I won't hurt you," he repeated raggedly, inside her mouth, against her lips. More hair cascaded down her back; a tiny rain of *pings,* impacting hairpins, reverberated over the harsh sound of his breathing and the thudding cadence of her heartbeat. "I promise. No matter what, I won't hurt you. Kiss me. Kiss me back. Suck my tongue like you did my *bitte.*"

Anne tentatively reached up and kissed him back, suckling his tongue as she had suckled his manhood.

She grabbed his shoulders at the sudden loosening of her dress, her corset. . . .

"The servants—"

His hand flattened against her lower back. "Will not intrude."

The thin cotton chemise did not shield her from the heat of his skin. A matching ball of heat glowed inside her stomach.

It was ridiculous, of course, but she fancied she could feel his sperm inside her. It was every bit as hot as the pressure molding her spine. *The breath gusting against her cheek.* His tongue filling her mouth. *The masculine flesh prodding her abdomen.*

Anne imagined that heat spurting deep inside her vagina, jetting against her womb as it had jetted against the back of her throat.

Gasping for oxygen, she tore her mouth away from the scalding furnace that was his mouth.

"Have you ever ejaculated inside a woman's vagina without benefit of a French letter?"

The words were out of her mouth before she could stop them.

Michel stilled, violet eyes watchful, intensity banked. A man once again in control of his passion. "Yes."

Anne's heartbeat fluttered. *How quickly he recovered from intimacy.*

She firmed her chin. "Is there another means of protection, then, that may be used to prevent conception?"

His irises were translucent in the sunlight, like colored glass. His contracted pupils were as black as jet beads. "Yes."

"What?"

"There are things that you can use. Devices that fit up inside you."

"Do they hurt?"

"No."

"Do they lessen a woman's pleasure?"

"I have been told that they do not."

"Where does a woman obtain these devices?"

"Through a physician."

She frowned. "Not through a chemist?"

"The most effective contraceptive requires an examination so that the proper size can be prescribed."

Anne did not need to ask what part of a woman's anatomy a physician examined in order to prescribe this mysterious device.

It was impossible to think of physicians and the pain they wrought when she was pressed this closely to his body.

She lowered her gaze. Blood rapidly pulsed through the artery underneath his jawbone. An answering rhythm pulsed deep inside her. "Thank you."

"For what?"

"For your honesty."

The blood pumped more quickly through the vein. She saw the muscles in his throat contract as he prepared to speak, but suddenly she did not want to hear what he said.

"And for sharing your pleasure," she blurted out. The back of her throat burned slightly, as if she had swallowed salt water. "It was quite educational."

And redeeming.

She would never again think of a man's sperm as being solely intended to impregnate a woman.

"I have not finished sharing my pleasure with you," he murmured huskily, fingers kneading her spine. Her bustle did not stop the path of erotic sensation. "Or contributing to your education."

Her hair felt heavy and hot. The afternoon sunlight no doubt illuminated every single strand of gray.

"Please do not feel compelled to reciprocate my attentions. I am more than content."

"But I am compelled." He nudged her stomach; he was hard. Erect. "I told you what I would do. And I won't be content until I do it."

He had promised to tickle her clitoris with a feather until she screamed for him to stop. *But he wouldn't stop.*

Heaven knew, she didn't want him to stop. Not now. Not ever.

But that was the price of a liaison.

It did not last forever.

"And afterward?" She continued to watch the thrumming and throbbing of the blood pumping through his artery. "Will you show me how to accept you in my other orifice?"

"Not today."

Startled, she glanced up. "Why not?"

The heat inside Michel's eyes impaled her. "There are other things I want to do. Other avenues I want to explore."

Anne stared into his gaze . . . and felt as if she would incinerate. "I believe one of the chaise lounges will offer an interesting variation to a bed."

"But I don't want you on a chaise lounge."

She dug her fingers into his shoulders, wanting to touch his naked flesh. Wanting him to touch her naked flesh. *Wanting to give him whatever he wanted.* "What do you want, Michel?"

"I want you sitting in a wing chair. Naked. Here. Facing the sunlight. With a leg over each chair arm so that you are completely open when I tease you with the feather. Inside. And out."

One . . . two . . .

Michael waited on the balcony, staring at the dim balls of gaslights that burned throughout London, and counted the distant bongs.

He pictured Anne asleep in his bed, her hand curled against her cheek.

And he felt again the vibrating hums of pleasure she had emitted while sucking his cock.

A sigh of motion sounded behind him. It was followed by the click of a closing door.

"You drugged her."

Gabriel's voice was coldly matter-of-fact.

Michael did not turn around. Nor did he respond to the question that was no question.

There had been no other alternative. He had not wanted to chance Anne's being awake when Gabriel arrived, so he had added a drop of laudanum to her after-dinner glass of wine. Then he had drunk the remainder of the bottle of wine from the container of her body and loved her to sleep.

"You used your key," he said instead, squelching a spurt of possessive anger that Gabriel had trespassed into his bedroom, observing Anne and the unmistakable heaviness of her slumber. While she dreamed, hopefully, of the pleasure he had given her. And the pleasure she had given him.

Michael/Michel. Michel/Michael.

For a brief moment his spinster had brought the two together.

And thanked him for his pleasure.

"You didn't summon me to take her." Gabriel was as stealthy as a cat. Michael mentally gauged his distance by his voice. "Or did you?"

It was too late to send Anne away.

Wispy black clouds trailed across the half-moon that lightened the starless sky.

"I summoned you to dispose of the solicitor's body," Michael said flatly.

"Did you kill him?"

"Do you need to ask?" he evenly countered.

Gabriel stepped up to the balcony rail that Michael gripped with both hands. "Why don't you dispose of him yourself?"

"I can't leave Anne."

"Why not?" Gabriel prodded.

Sunlight reflected off of the moon, lending it radiance.

Anne's steel hat pin had been equally reflective of sunlight. The joy she had taken in pleasing him had made her face shine with an inner radiance no less brilliant than the light illuminating the moon.

Her mouth had tasted of him. Of his sperm.

Of her enjoyment in pleasing a scarred whore.

He had not tasted himself on a woman in five years.

Michael imagined the saltiness of his sperm mingled with the sweetness of her arousal—and fought the need to go back inside his bedchamber and share with her the intoxicating flavor of a man and a woman's mutual satisfaction.

"Because he will kill her," he said finally, bleakly. "And I cannot."

Sharp, furious barking broke up the night.

He listened to stray dogs fight—for food? territory? a female?—and knew he was no different from a mongrel.

Michael had spent the last twenty-seven years looking for a home. A woman.

Food that wouldn't turn his stomach.

He had loved Diane's laughter and passion.

Diane had loved his expertise and stamina.

He had never expected her to thank him. And she hadn't.

A yelping whimper punctuated the end of the battle.

"Go to the police," Gabriel said quietly.

Michael bit back a snarl. He turned his head, his gaze catching Gabriel's. "Little is stuffed inside a trunk that just happens to be in my study. Do you think the police are going to believe he was delivered to me by accident?"

Gabriel's eyes glowed in the moonlight, pale, like Anne's. With none of her softness. Her openness.

"What do you want, Michael?"

What do you want, Michel?

The truth pressed in on him.

Yesterday he would have answered differently. But this wasn't yesterday.

And tomorrow might never come.

"I want Anne." He inhaled cold, dew-laden air and acrid coal smoke. "I want more time with her."

"Is that all?" Gabriel asked ironically.

"No. I want to hire some of your men. I need a driver. A groom. Guards to watch the house."

"They could be killed."

More deaths piled at his feet.

"Everyone has a price. Offer them a thousand pounds each—"

"They would kill *you*, for that amount of money—"

"And tell them that if Anne is killed—or abducted—that they won't receive a farthing," Michael finished implacably. "And *I* will kill them."

"What if it is you who is killed?"

A spark of rebellion briefly flamed, then died.

There was no future for a man like him. It was too late to want to live.

"If Anne is safe, take the funds out of my estate and pay them. Everything I have is deeded to you."

A sharp exhalation tore through the night air, a brief mist of silvery breath. "Sometimes I could kill you myself, Michael."

Michael smiled mockingly. "You can't kill a man who's already dead, Gabriel."

"Have you ever killed a man, *mon vieux?*"

Men, women, and children were dead because of him.

"Yes."

"No, Michael. I mean *kill* a man. Deliberately taking his life. Hearing his breath rattle in his throat. Feeling his blood on you, hot and slippery. Like sex. Knowing that for better or for worse, he's dead. Because of you."

All he could see of Gabriel was the halo of his hair. Pale, perfect skin. A patrician nose. And the glittering darkness in his eyes that owed nothing to the night.

A passage learned in childhood when cramming for Eton flitted through his mind. *And flights of angels sing thee to thy rest.*

Shakespeare. *Hamlet*. Act five, scene two.

He remembered the author. The title of the book. The act it was taken from.

But he couldn't remember the face of his tutor. His parents. His sisters.

The man had taken the memories away.

"If you don't want to risk your men, Gabriel, I'll use a service."

"You can't have both, Michael."

Michael stiffened. Turning, he fully faced Gabriel. "What exactly can't I have, *mon frère?*"

"Dying won't save Anne Aimes."

The damp, cold night air seeped through his bones. "How do you know that?"

"I'm Gabriel." Michael did not have to see Gabriel's face to recognize his taunting smile. "God's messenger."

Chapter 10

Layer by layer, Anne dragged free of the suffocating darkness that banded her breasts and anchored her thighs. Hot, prickly heat crowded her neck; it gusted warm, moist air. The rhythmic soughing overrode the distant ring of a handbell.

Memories flitted through her sleep-drugged thoughts, vivid splashes of color overlying the gray light that pierced her eyelids.

Crimson blood. Peacock blue velvet. Darkly veined, plum-tipped flesh. A white, wet feather. Gold-rimmed china. Burgundy red wine . . .

A vague pounding commenced inside her temples. Hazy, dreamlike images lurked beneath the dull pain.

Michel had teased her with wine. . . .

No. He had teased her with the wine *bottle.* Cool glass sliding, gliding, penetrating. *Filling her with liquid.*

It had been cold instead of hot. Thin rather than thick.

He had drunk from her body as if she were the finest of goblets.

Anne suddenly became aware of the stickiness between her thighs.

And knew it had been no dream.

Burgundy wine coated her tongue; heavy, sweet, with an underlying bitterness.

Her eyelids flew open.

An arm tightened about her breasts; at the same time a leg hitched up higher, pressing on her lower abdomen.

She simultaneously became aware that it was Michel who weighted her down, not sleep. And that she had been awakened by the need to relieve herself, not by the ring of her mother's handbell.

Tenderness ripped through her chest—along with a burst of crystal-clear memories, sights and sounds unmarred by wine or sleep.

Anne had tasted this man. Suckled him. Brought him to orgasm.

She whose only accomplishment was nursing.

Now he lay sleeping beside her. *On top of her.*

And she could not even engage in the luxury of basking in the uniquely intimate experience.

Feeling subtly cheated and slightly disoriented, as if her thoughts and her body were disconnected, she tentatively wriggled out from underneath the heavy weight of his arm and leg, skin and hair sliding on the silk sheet.

How young a woman felt with her hair hanging loose as opposed to having it secured in a tight bun or braided in a single rope, she thought inanely. Freed at last, absurdly bereft at the loss of the bone-melting warmth that had cocooned her, she glanced at Michel.

His shoulder was darkly masculine against the cream-colored silk sheet and leaf green velvet spread. The left side of his face was buried in the pillow; morning stubble shadowed his right cheek. His eyelids remained closed in sleep, lashes a silky black fan.

He looked . . . vulnerable. Seductive. Everything any woman could possibly desire.

And he was all hers for the next twenty-six days.

A spinster's lover.

Holding her breath for fear of waking him, she curiously touched his cheek.

It was bristly. Endearingly masculine.

Moving her finger up, she lightly skimmed the puckered ridge of scars edging his high cheekbone.

Michel winced.

Lassitude scattering, Anne snatched her hand back.

She didn't want to wake him.

There were other things to do. Other avenues to explore. Fears to conquer that without Michel she would never have had the courage to overcome.

She slid out of bed.

Michael clutched the crumpled silk sheet in his hand to stop himself from reaching out and grabbing Anne.

This was her first morning awakening in his arms. Yesterday, after convincing her to stay with him, he had left his bedchamber on a pretext in order to provide her time to take care of personal matters.

She was new to intimacy. She still needed a semblance of privacy.

He knew it. He didn't have to like it.

His cheek burned where she had touched him. The stubble on his cheek. His scars.

Forcing himself to lie as she had left him, he listened to the soft pad of her feet crossing the floor; the bathroom door softly opened, clicked shut. A few minutes later he heard the muted flush of the toilet. The rush of running water. Minute splashes. The sharp click of a toothbrush knocking against the rim of the porcelain sink.

Morning sounds.

He had listened to such sounds thousands of times, lying in bed while a woman took care of her toilet.

Diane had sung while she performed her ablutions.

Anne neatly, efficiently took care of her needs. As she had taken care of his.

Was she shocked in the light of day at the unconventional methods of lovemaking he had introduced her to?

Did she remember every single detail—as he did?

How long would it be before Little's absence was noted?

Would Anne mourn the solicitor?

Would she mourn Michael?

The bathroom door opened with a telltale click.

Michael held perfectly still, every nerve in his body tensed, waiting for what she would do next.

Anne padded across the room to the chaise lounge. Clothing

rustled—wool drawers, a linen chemise, wool petticoats. Everything he had removed from her before showing her how a fine wine was best imbibed.

Anticipation roiled inside him.

Her corset was not the variety that a woman could lace up by herself. Furthermore, the gown she had worn yesterday buttoned down the back. She would need to wake him in order to fully dress.

The door to the wardrobe squeaked.

Michael did not have to look to know that her staid dresses, skirts, and bodices hung side by side with his clothing.

More rustling.

More footsteps.

A soft swish, the depression of a cushion.

He imagined Anne sitting on the yellow silk-upholstered chaise lounge, her prim, dowdy skirt pushed up, pale, slender hands pulling on flesh-colored stockings, smoothing up plain white garters until they snapped around her shapely thighs.

His semierect flesh burgeoned into hard arousal.

He mentally followed her progress to the dressing table.

She had not commented on the absence of mirrors in his house. Had never once complained of any inconvenience.

Perhaps he would buy a mirror for her.

Immediately he discarded the notion.

She didn't need a looking glass. *He* would be her lady's maid. Her mirror. Everything she needed.

Michael could feel sudden hesitation.

She had found her toothbrush that Marie, the housekeeper, had unpacked. But there was only one hairbrush on the dresser.

His.

He wanted her to hold the carved amber handle in her hand, sink the bristles into her hair. To remember that he had held the amber handle in his hand. That he had brushed her hair the day before.

And would do so again when she was ready to crawl back into bed and partake of morning pleasures.

He did not know when she picked up the brush, only when

she put it down, a faint clink of amber on wood. A tiny scraping filled the following silence; she scrambled to scoop up a sliding hairpin.

A smile tugged at his lips.

She was putting up her hair without a mirror.

Anne was nothing if not self-sufficient.

He allowed her to slip out the bedroom door into the hallway.

It was best that she breakfast alone. With her mind free of the clouding effects of sexual satiation and wine, she would be more inquisitive.

Michael relaxed, his erection a not-unpleasant throb. Gabriel's men—and his own servants—would keep her safe until he joined her.

Rolling over, he threw back the covers. Motion reminded him that his erection was not strictly a result of desire.

Anne's corset lay on the chaise lounge.

Amusement lit up his eyes.

His staid spinster was indeed becoming liberated.

Dark shadows filled the bathroom. The French walnut toilet seat was a lifeless brown in the dim light. It sat flatly on the embossed, ivory-tinted porcelain-and-turquoise commode. A sure sign that a woman was in residence.

Leaning down, he lifted the lid for his own convenience. He reminded himself he would have to remember to put it back down. For Anne's convenience.

Shaking himself dry, he jerked the brass pull before stepping over to the sink.

A tin of matches waited beside a box of tissues. Gritting his teeth, he struck a match and lifted the hurricane globe off the brass wall sconce above the sink. Hurriedly he touched the yellow flame to the wick before clumsily replacing the globe and lighting the wall sconce on the left side of the sink.

Anne had seen his fear the day before when he had lit the coals in the library fireplace. She had offered him solace and never once understood the danger she had been in.

He blew out the match and tossed it into the toilet.

Stoppering the porcelain basin with a brass-plated rubber plug, he twisted the ivory taps until water rushed out of the twin brass spouts and hot steam curled upward.

A side drawer in the French oak cabinet underneath the sink yielded a shaving mug, brush, and straight razor. He dipped the brush underneath the hot water spout before plunging it into the mug and working up suds from the cake of soap in the bottom. Setting the mug on the gold-veined marble counter, he twisted off the taps and splashed his face and neck with water. Deftly he lathered his dampened skin.

Michael did not hire a valet. He did not want another man looking at him when he could not.

Or perhaps he no longer trusted baring his throat.

Snapping open the straight razor, he angled it to carefully shave his neck.

He imagined cutting the man's throat. Imagined his blood. Hot and slippery, yes, but not like sex.

Pleasure was a part of life, not death.

Michael shaved his left cheek. His right. Five practiced swipes apiece. Sucking in his lips, he shaved his chin. His upper lip. . . .

Little's burned, scorched mouth formed in the swirling mist.

Son of a bitch!

The straight razor drew blood. He could feel it welling up.

Suddenly anxious to join Anne, he quickly rinsed his neck and face, then returned the shaving articles to the side drawer. The styptic pencil burned, a physical reminder of the fire that had eaten his flesh and killed Little.

Of the fate that awaited Anne if he failed to protect her.

He wrenched open the cabinet drawer directly underneath the sink and froze.

The sight of Anne's plain, wooden-handled toothbrush, still damp, lying beside his own ivory-handled one, brought an unexpected tightness to his chest.

Quickly he brushed his teeth, tossed his toothbrush into the drawer, blew out the two lamps, and rushed out the door. *Damn.* He swung back around to drop the wooden seat onto the commode.

Pale brown hair wound through the bristles in his brush; they lay over a single black strand of hair.

A surge of unadulterated masculine possessiveness was knocked short.

Anne's hat was gone.

He had brought both it, the hat pin, and her hairpins up the night before.

And now they were all gone.

Anne would not take her hat unless she planned on journeying outside his town house.

Raoul did not know that a coach and driver waited at the local livery for Michael's use.

She would take a cab.

And there would be *no one* to protect her.

Michael grabbed the clothes he had tossed onto the floor by the bed after Gabriel had departed. The time it took him to dress was counted by the blood pumping through his heart. Right shoe on. *Bloody hell,* he couldn't unknot the laces on the left shoe.

He pictured Anne stuffed inside a trunk. But he knew it would not be a trunk the man laid her in.

The knot came undone. Shoving his foot inside the shoe—cursing anew at the time it took to tie the lace—he raced out of his bedchamber, footsteps ricocheting up and down the length of the dark hallway.

Reason dictated that his spinster would be in the breakfast room. She wasn't wearing a corset.

Women like Anne didn't go out without a corset.

The last twenty-nine years had taught Michael that reason had little to do with reality.

He took the steps three at a time. Sliding—*goddamn the marble*—he grabbed the wrought-iron banister to regain his balance.

No footmen stood guard near the foyer. Or by any other door.

The small breakfast room at the end of the town house was empty.

Michael threw open the library door.

Marie dropped her feather duster in an unprecedented display of emotion. "*Ma foi!* Monsieur, you startled me! I will only be a moment. If you—"

"Where's Anne?" he interrupted harshly.

Disapproval shone in the housekeeper's brown eyes; it was quickly replaced by Gaelic stoicism. "Mademoiselle Aimes, she is not here, monsieur."

Marie either did not approve of Michael resuming his former profession. Or she did not approve of Anne.

Or perhaps she had never approved of Michael.

The previous owner had been a man of title. Of respectability.

Every man has a price.

So, too, did every woman.

Sweat broke out on his forehead. "Where did she go?"

Marie retrieved the feather duster from the floor, face composed, emotionless. "*Je ne sais pas,* monsieur."

He bit back a curse. "Did you talk to her?"

"*Non.*"

"Did Raoul?"

"*Je ne sais pas.*"

I do not know.

Michael couldn't decide if she was lying or telling the truth.

Gabriel's words in the early morning mocked him: *You can't have both, Michael.*

Pivoting, he strode through the hallway, heartbeat outdistancing his strides.

Where the bloody hell was Raoul?

"Raoul!" he roared down the narrow stairs leading to the kitchen.

The butler appeared at the foot of the steps. He clutched a linen towel and a silver serving platter. At another time Michael would have found Raoul's astonishment humorous. Suave, sophisticated Michel des Anges had never before raised his voice to a servant.

Raoul raced up the stairs, face creased in convincing concern. "Monsieur! *Pardonnez-moi,* the footmen and I, we were just polishing the silver—"

Michael cut off his apology. "Where is Mademoiselle Aimes?"

"She is gone, monsieur."

Had *Raoul* been bribed?

He clung to his self-control. "Where?"

"She did not say. I hailed a cab—"

Michael stalked out of the front door.

No pedestrians loitered nearby. No men disguised as street sweepers or chair menders or vendors lurked about.

There was no one guarding the town house.

His first thought was that Gabriel's men had been killed.

He prayed they had. But he knew they had not.

Too late he understood Gabriel's taunting remark that he was God's messenger.

But it wasn't God who had sent him.

Gabriel had not placed men to guard either the town house or Anne.

Every man has a price, Michael had told Gabriel.

He wondered what Gabriel's price had been.

Chapter 11

Anne stared at the flickering circle of light reflected on the ceiling and tried very hard not to think about thc probing fingers that were not Michel's. A gas lamp hissed and popped in the silence. It heated parts that were never meant to be so exposed.

She had sworn never to visit a physician. Never to let a doctor prod her, to hurt her as her parents had been hurt.

Yet here she lay on a padded leather table, dressed only in a voluminous white gown, with her feet secured in metal stirrups, being both prodded and, if not exactly hurt, certainly being made to feel uncomfortable.

"I am going to introduce a speculum into your vagina, Mrs. Jones. You will feel a bit of a pinch. Please try to relax. It will be only a moment longer now."

Anne winced—yes, it pinched—and wondered if her Dover housekeeper would mind that she had borrowed her name.

Her fingernails dug into the unfeeling leather.

The speculum was harder than glass. Colder. *It did not belong inside a spinster.*

Her heart hammered against her ribs, urging her to run, to scream. Anything to escape the indignity of what she was enduring.

She thought of Michel. What had he thought when he woke and found her gone?

She thought of her parents' former London physician, and his blistering censure when she had asked him to measure her for a device that fit inside a woman to prevent contraception. His nurse, while escorting her out of his office, had whispered the name and address of a gynecologist, that new breed of doctor who specialized in a woman's intimate health.

Dr. Joseph Atwood.

What Michel had called a "device," the gynecologist called a diaphragm.

Her parents' former physician had ranted that prophylactics harbored the ruin of womankind in particular and society in general. Dr. Atwood had acted as if it were the most natural thing in the world for a woman to request a contraceptive device.

And perhaps it was.

If she, plain, dowdy spinster, sought a feminine form of protection, how many other women did?

"You may sit up now, Mrs. Jones."

Anne snapped her feet out of the stirrups and sat up.

The gynecologist leaned over the gray metal counter beside the examination table; his tweed frock coat strained across his shoulders. Metal clinked on metal. Running water splashed. Deftly he grabbed a folded white towel and dried his hands. Tossing it into an open canvas hamper, he turned and smiled.

His hazel eyes were kind. Nonjudgmental.

As if he had not noticed her lack of a wedding band.

"I will send in my nurse to assist you."

There was no need for assistance. She did not wear a corset.

"That is not necessary," she said, gripping the edge of the table.

"Very well. Please join me in my office when you are ready."

His departing footsteps a decisive dismissal, he exited the small examining room.

Anne swiftly pulled on her underclothes. It seemed days instead of hours since she had dressed in Michel's bedchamber while he lay sleeping, impervious to her intention.

Would he be pleased at her initiative? she wondered.

Hurriedly she buttoned her black wool bodice.

Her fingers trembled. *Her whole body trembled.*

With victory—at overcoming her fear.

Or perhaps she trembled with humiliation—at exposing her body to a man other than Michel.

Or perhaps she merely trembled with anticipation at the thought of Michel's flesh inside her with no rubber to separate them.

A mirror hung on the door.

Anne's cheeks were flushed.

She almost looked pretty, she thought. Wisps of hair escaped her makeshift bun. It softened her face.

Deftly she pushed home loosened pins. Setting the black, featherless hat onto her head, she secured it with the hat pin.

Heels echoing tinnily on the wooden floor—hesitant rather than decisive—she grabbed her black gloves and beaded reticule off the shiny metal counter. Taking a deep breath, she swung open the door.

Dr. Atwood sat at a massive, black marble-topped desk, balding head bowed. Overhead, a gas chandelier spit and spewed. A window framed the desk and the physician; outside, the sky was an unrelieved gray.

It was going to rain.

The faint, singsong grind of carriage wheels drifted up from the street; it was interspersed by the muted shouts of vendors and the scratch of a steel nib scribbling across paper.

A small, rose-colored tin sat on the gynecologist's desk near his elbow. Beside the metal container sat a flesh-colored wax model that reminded her of an etching in her medical compendium. It looked rather like—

Scalding heat flooded her cheeks.

It was a model of a woman's interior organs.

He glanced up at her approach. "Please be seated, Mrs. Jones."

Anne perched on the edge of a black, wing-back leather chair, carefully averting her gaze from the sculpture.

The gynecologist held up a rimmed, circular piece of rubber in his left hand. "This is a diaphragm." He reached out, and touched the wax mold with his right hand. "This is a woman's cervix. The diaphragm fits over the cervix—here, and here—rather like a hat. In order to prevent conception it must be positioned prior to sexual congress and left in place a minimum of six hours afterward."

She squeezed her reticule. Never had her parents' physicians spoken so frankly. "Yes. I understand."

"A woman's vagina is shortened when she draws her legs up." He placed the circular piece of rubber on his desk; it blindly stared up at her. "A diaphragm is more easily positioned either while squatting or else while standing with one knee elevated and the foot resting on a stool or a chair."

Anne jerked her head up. His directions were all very well and fine, but . . . "By what means does a woman introduce the diaphragm into her . . . person?"

"By the aid of her fingers, Mrs. Jones."

It could have been a twinkle in his hazel eyes. Or it could have been Anne's own embarrassment that colored her vision.

"I see."

Dr. Atwood handed her the small, rose-colored tin. "Your diaphragm is enclosed. Do you have any further questions?"

Anne accepted the tin box and stuffed it inside her reticule. Metal collided with metal. *The tin of French letters.* She stood up in a rush of wool petticoats and skirt. "No, thank you. You have been most helpful."

He extended the sheet of paper he had earlier been writing on. "You may pay my secretary."

Four women occupied the gynecologist's outer office: three patients and one secretary.

They were all younger than herself. Two of the three were obviously pregnant.

Anne tried to imagine the three patients—their shoulders were squared, spines the required three inches away from the back of the hard leather chairs they sat in, hands folded over their reticules—petitioning the doctor for a diaphragm.

She could not.

She tried to imagine them enjoying a man's sexual embrace.

She could not imagine that either.

The secretary—auburn hair free of silver—smiled. She wore a gold band on her left hand. "Please come back, Mrs. Jones."

Anne forced down a twinge of guilt.

She didn't enjoy lying. No matter what the circumstances.

Nodding her head, she grabbed her cloak off of the coatrack. Six umbrellas stood to attention in the umbrella stand.

At the end of the dimly lit hallway beside the stairs, caged doors jerked open. Two women stepped out. Heads close, they conferred in soft whispers as they passed Anne.

Feeling suddenly very daring and modern, Anne stepped inside the metal cage and nodded at the gold-braided, dark red-liveried man.

The lift down took her breath away.

It had been many years since she had ridden an elevator. With each passing second she felt lighter.

She smiled.

She felt elevated. *Elated.* Not at all like a thirty-six-year-old spinster. As if all the years of disease and death had been magically erased by a circular piece of rubber.

Outside the office building the air was saturated with humidity. Carriages of every size and description sped through the street. Men and women crowded the sidewalk; they looked neither left nor right as they hurried past each other.

Unlike her, they carried umbrellas. Folded. Bullets pointed down. Prepared for inclement weather.

As Anne was prepared for the man who was her lover in deed if not fact.

She realized with a peculiar pang that the words she had written to her solicitor in order to lay his worry to rest were true: she had never before been this happy.

Anne was suddenly assailed by an overwhelming desire to see Michel. To replace the gynecologist's touch with his.

If she hurried, she could find a cab before the rain broke.

Running down the steps, unconfined breasts bobbing in a most unspinsterlike manner, she darted around a group of soberly dressed men—medical students perhaps; the hospital was only another street over—

Searing heat exploded between her shoulder blades. Breath escaping her lungs in an audible whoosh, Anne catapulted forward into the street, arms flailing to regain her balance.

Sound and motion erupted around her. From the Clarence cab

bearing down on her: "Git th' 'ell out o' th' way, ye bleedin' cow!" From the very air surrounding her: Big Ben bonging.

She had a startled image of the cabby standing up in the box, shouting. His black hat flew off of his head, as if tossed by an invisible hand. Immediately a shrill whinny snared her attention.

Anne stared into dark eyes rolling in a white sea of terror.

The horse pulling the four-wheeled cab was fully aware of the imminent collision of woman and equine. Unable to stop it.

As Anne was unable to stop it.

She was going to be trampled underneath its hooves, she thought in a paralyzing flash of clarity.

The horror of pending death was chased by numbing disbelief.

She simply could not die now.

She wasn't wearing a corset.

She hadn't tried out the diaphragm.

Images darted through her head, a summary of her life.

She saw her parents' former physician, his bloated face purple with outrage: *You are an insult to your sex, Miss Aimes, and you insult me by your presence.*

She saw Michel, his face illuminated with morning sunshine: *Stay with me. Or we will both regret it for as long as we live.*

She saw her mother, her arthritis-crippled hand reaching out.

Beckoning.

Beseeching.

Chapter 12

" 'Ere now!"

Between one blink of dark, bloodshot equine eyes and another, Anne was hauled backward. The horse plunged past her, carriage whipping at her cloak. A ghostly face pressed against the cab window, hollow eyes briefly catching her gaze.

Suddenly the sky opened up. The cab was gone. And gray, soot-laden rain misted her vision.

Big Ben continued to strike the time.

Death knolls.

The village bells had rung during her parents' funeral. It had rained then, too.

A black bowler hat sat in the middle of the street: the cabby's hat. A carriage wheel had crushed it.

Anne swirled around—heart pounding, breath choking; *someone had pushed her*—and stared eye-to-eye at an unkempt man of indeterminate years. Greasy brown hair stuck out from underneath his tattered sporting hat. Tiny drops of water beaded on his dirt-encrusted face.

"Thar ain't no way t' git a 'ack, ma'am," he said sternly. "Ye coud git 'urt 'oppin' out in th' middle o' th' strait, ye coud."

Her spine between her shoulder blades burned and throbbed, robbing her of oxygen. It did not stop the tide of heat that flashed through her like a kerosene-doused fire.

She had almost been killed. And this—*this filthy man*—thought she had deliberately jumped into the cab's path?

Anne opened her mouth to shout at him—she who had never

before shouted in anger—only to remember that he had saved her life.

Her jaw snapped shut.

Big Ben's deafening tolls abruptly died. Air rushed into her oxygen-deprived lungs. The singsong grind of carriage wheels filled her ears. And once again Anne was in control of her emotions, alert as she had always been.

For a stranger to harm her.

For society to laugh at her clumsiness.

Pedestrians hurried past the undignified spectacle that a destitute man and a lone, disheveled spinster presented. Their faces were shielded by black umbrellas that before the blow which had sent her catapulting into the street had been folded in expectation of . . . what? Rain, or an innocent bystander? Did they scurry to escape the cold drizzle—or the perpetration of a near-fatal collision?

There was only one person who knew for certain.

Silver arced through the gray rain. Her emaciated savior deftly caught the tossed coin.

"You may leave now." The voice behind her was cold. Hard. Clipped. The voice of a man who was used to issuing orders. "The lady is safe."

The street man grinned, winked. Grabbing a dilapidated broom off the sidewalk, he turned and raced away.

It dawned on Anne that the throbbing between her shoulder blades could as easily have been caused by a broom handle as by the tip of an umbrella.

She started forward. "Wait one second—"

"I told you you're safe."

The unkempt street sweeper disappeared behind a wall of dark cloaks and black umbrellas.

Anne turned around in a rush of grenadine, wool, and bouncing bustle. The stranger did not seem to comprehend the fact that she had been pushed in front of a cab. *And someone was responsible.* Quite possibly the street sweeper—*whom he had rewarded.* "That man—"

The words froze in her throat.

The tall man who stood over her was breathtakingly beautiful. Rain wreathed his fashionable black bowler hat and pearled his face. His double-breasted, gray wool reefer jacket was of the best cut. But it was not the chiseled perfection of his features or his elegant attire that caused Anne's heartbeat to stutter and her throat to lock shut.

Silver-gray eyes regarded her flatly. "You were saying?" he asked politely.

Cool rain misted her burning cheeks.

Smoky, candlelit darkness had haloed his bare blond head and dimmed his gray eyes, but there was no mistaking those too handsome features.

This man had greeted her at the entrance to the House of Gabriel. Then he had escorted her to Michel's table.

Her heart raced to make up for the missed beat.

Had he followed them?

Had he followed *her?*

He lightly held a silver-handled cane between black-gloved fingers.

Had he *pushed her?*

"You are fortunate he did not swipe your reticule."

Anne remembered the diaphragm inside her reticule.

Her reticule was looped about her wrist; otherwise it, like the cabby's black hat, would now be residing in the street.

Overrun by carriages.

She clutched her black-beaded bag to her chest. "I beg your pardon?"

"The street sweeper could have easily stolen it. Instead he pushed you," he offered imperturbably.

For a second Anne could not tell if it was fear or rain that trickled down her spine.

She stepped back. "You saw him?" she asked. Forcefully she swallowed the rest of her sentence: *and did nothing to stop him?*

He stepped forward. "It's a common enough practice among those who live off the streets. One pushes a woman—or an elderly gentleman—rescues them, and is rewarded with coin. No one is hurt. They buy gin and bread. And they survive another day."

But she almost *had not* survived.

She remembered the sheen of fear in the horse's eyes.

She remembered the undiluted terror she had felt at the thought of dying.

Without trying out the diaphragm.

Anne struggled to remain the calm, rational woman she had always believed herself to be. *Before* she had embarked on the liaison with Michel des Anges.

"I see," she said. He spoke as if it were commonplace for an obviously well-to-do man to watch a woman be accosted and do nothing to prevent it. *And perhaps in London it was.* "If you will excuse me, I must be on my way—"

"You have received a shock. There is a pastry shop nearby. I insist upon buying you a cup of tea."

Anne took another step back. "Thank you, that is not necessary."

The beautiful, elegant stranger followed her. "But it is necessary."

She no longer mistook the coldness that sped down her back for rain: it was fear, pure and simple.

"There really is no need to trouble yourself—"

"I am Michel's friend, mademoiselle. He would not be pleased if I were remiss with your welfare."

Mademoiselle.

The man did not sound French. *Until he spoke it.*

Michel did not sound French. Until *he* spoke it.

Two women and one man waited on the street corner for an omnibus. Avoiding Anne's gaze, they turned their backs toward her and huddled underneath their shared umbrella.

Anne took another step backward. She squared her shoulders. *She was not a coward.* "I will tell Monsieur des Anges of your concern."

The blond-haired man stepped closer, his breath a silvery plume of vapor. "Do you not wish to know more about Michel, mademoiselle?"

She could not stop an involuntary retreat. "Friends do not bear tales, monsieur."

The man paused in his pursuit. "I love him, too, mademoiselle."

The misty drizzle turned to a downpour.

There was no thunder to herald the change. No lightning. Just an electric tingle of awareness.

Anne paused in her retreat, eyes wide.

In all her years she had never heard anyone say they loved another. Not husband to wife. Not mother to child.

Cold water slashed her face. "I do not love Monsieur des Anges."

A matching rivulet of water trickled down the blond-haired man's flawless face. "Every woman who has ever been with Michel has loved him, mademoiselle."

But Michel had not loved them, he did not need to add. Michel had loved only one woman.

And she was dead.

Rain dripped off the brim of her round black felt hat, featherless now. *What had Michel done with the feather after he had pleasured her?* she wondered inanely. "Did you follow me?"

Rain dripped off the brim of the stranger's black felt bowler hat. "Yes."

Oh, God.

She had never before realized a woman's nipples hardened with fear.

They did.

Every inhalation, every exhalation, caused her linen shift to abrade her uncorseted breasts.

Anne fought to regulate her breathing. "Why?"

"I do not want Michel to be hurt."

She blinked away a blinding drop of rain.

The dangerous encounter was becoming increasingly farcical.

Surely she had not heard the stranger correctly.

"You think I am going to hurt Monsieur des Anges?" she asked incredulously.

"Michel has not had a procuress since the fire that scarred him." The blond-haired man's gray eyes remained cold, flat, devoid of emotion. His skin gleamed like wet alabaster. "He is more vulnerable than you know."

Anne remembered the warm play of sunshine on Michel's manhood. The silver glint of her hat pin. His unleashed passion: *I won't hurt you.*

The memory was instantly replaced by the impersonal touch of the gynecologist's probing fingers and chill metal instrument.

Physicians had listened to her mother's heart through the protective covering of a nightgown or chemise. Never had she been subjected to such a thoroughly humiliating examination as that which Anne had endured.

A lump rose inside her throat.

She was more vulnerable than she had ever known.

Before Michel she would never, ever have bared her body. Especially to a doctor.

"I would be happy to receive you at"—if he had followed her then he knew where she was currently residing—"Monsieur des Anges's town house. We may then include him in our discussion."

The stranger's gray eyes remained inscrutable, a part of the cold and the rain—silver ice to counter Michel's violet fire. "Are you afraid of me, mademoiselle?"

"No, of course not," she lied.

"Then you are ashamed to be seen with Michel's friends."

The stranger's face was closed, expressionless: waiting for rejection.

As Michel had been prepared for rejection when he accused her of being ashamed of touching him. *Wanting him.*

All at once she felt ridiculous, standing in the rain without an umbrella to protect her from even the most basic elements.

Wet hair straggled down her back.

What was she afraid of?

No man would have designs on a woman her age. Especially one who was as disheveled and untidy as she now was.

There was nothing the stranger could do to her in public.

Nothing more than a street sweeper had done, an inner voice jeered.

Anne stiffened her spine.

She was cold. She was wet.

She wanted to hear whatever the stranger could tell her about Michel.

"Very well, monsieur. I would be delighted to take tea with you."

"Thank you." He did not offer her his arm. "The pastry shop is this way."

He was as tall as Michel. Perhaps taller, Anne thought as he adjusted his stride to match hers. The two men both moved with effortless grace.

They passed fewer and fewer people on the streets. Gaslights illuminated unfamiliar shop windows. Clerks and customers freely ranged within, faces distorted by the water-sluiced glass, unaware of Anne Aimes; of where she had come from or where she was going.

Water poured down her face, her collar.

Panic overcame her resolution.

Some would claim that a woman who wore no corset and who carried upon her person a diaphragm and a tin of French letters deserved no better than she got. It occurred to her that perhaps those people were correct.

No doubt many men knew Michel. Men who were not his friends.

Perhaps the silver-eyed man had followed Anne when she retrieved her clothes. And had then visited her solicitor.

Perhaps he knew who she was.

Perhaps Mr. Little had already received a note demanding money for her ransom.

Without warning, the stranger stopped. Water rolled off of his pale, alabaster skin. "You should be frightened, mademoiselle. A lone woman should never accompany a stranger."

Anne's breath stopped in her lungs.

Stepping around her, he opened a sturdy wooden door.

The aroma of freshly baked pastries and brewed coffee slapped her in the face. Inside, gas-filled balls of white glass brightly lit a crowded restaurant. A baby cried. Women laughed. Men talked in a raucous roar.

She made no move to step inside.

"You are safe here, mademoiselle." Silver eyes speculatively gauged her. "It is tea I desire. I assume that is what you also desire."

Anger warmed her cheeks. She stepped inside.

White-aproned waiters darted back and forth between white-enameled wrought-iron tables. Journeymen, clerks, and laborers sat side by side. Women laughed easily, feeding babies or themselves. Two children raced around a table while their mothers—or their nannies—waited out the rain over a pot of tea.

Anne marginally relaxed.

The pastry shop was comfortable rather than fashionable. She would not be recognized.

The stranger did not wait to be seated. Instead he gestured for Anne to precede him to an empty table at the back of the room.

If she dared, his eyes silently challenged.

When she reached their destination, he pulled out a chair. "Please be seated."

"Thank you." Anne perched on the edge of the hard, metal chair, awkwardly shifted to allow him to push it forward. Her bustle dug into her derriere.

The child's incessant shrieks were enervating.

She bit her lip, acutely aware of the icy water that continued to trickle down her overheated face and neck. Sodden lanks of hair had escaped her bun.

A bowler hat dropped onto the enameled table, wilted black on chipped white. The stranger slid onto the chair opposite her. Silvery highlights shone in the hair on top of his head that had been protected from the rain. Silently he handed her his handkerchief.

Anne automatically accepted it, blotted her nose and cheeks dry. Hurriedly she offered it back.

He did not take it.

She stiffly withdrew her hand. "I will have it laundered and returned to you."

"Handkerchiefs are plentiful, mademoiselle. I assure you I can afford the loss of one."

He did not seem at all disturbed by the unrestrained ruckus

surrounding them. Nor did he appear uncomfortable amidst London's lower middle class.

Slowly he pulled off his black kid gloves, revealing fingers that were long, pale, and slender. Perfect hands to match a perfect face. No doubt he had a perfect body as well.

The wet cotton balled inside her fist. She was not certain which was more thoroughly soaked—his handkerchief or her silk glove. "Are you in the same profession as Monsieur des Anges?" she asked baldly.

Hot blood pricked the tips of her ears at her directness.

"We have both enjoyed women." He dropped his gloves on top of his hat. Silver-gray eyes snared hers. "I have been told that I am every bit as good as Michel is. Would you care to test my expertise?"

The hot blood that burned her ears scorched a trail all the way down to her toes. Anne pushed the wrought-iron chair backward, metal scraping tile. "You are insulting, sir."

"I am asking an honest question, mademoiselle." The blond-haired man held perfectly still, his voice alone latching onto her. "You sought out Michel. Why not me?"

Why not me? whipped through the drone of voices, the shrillness of laughter, and the child's unrelenting cries.

Anne was momentarily arrested by the lash of pain in the stranger's voice.

This beautiful, perfect man hurt.

As Michel hurt. Scarred by fire.

As Anne hurt. A wallflower who had never bloomed.

It was inconceivable that the three of them should be victims of the same needs: the simple desire to be wanted.

The floor tilted underneath her chair at the dizzying thought that he could be hers. For a price.

If she wanted him.

The floor immediately righted at the realization that her nipples were beaded from cold, not temptation.

"I saw Michel when I made my London debut," she offered quietly.

She waited for his response, still poised to flee.

"If you had seen me first, who would you have chosen?"

An underlying intensity rang in the stranger's voice.

An honest question, he had said.

He deserved an honest answer.

Anne held his gaze and did not lie. "Michel."

"Why?"

"His eyes," she responded truthfully. "They burn with passion."

Whereas the gray eyes staring at her now burned with silver fire but no passion.

Michel had said that he was attracted by a woman's sexual needs. She could not even begin to imagine what would attract this man.

"What is your pleasure, mademoiselle?" he asked softly.

Her head snapped back at the suggestive question that held no seduction.

"I have told you my pleasure, monsieur."

"But you have not told the waiter what it is that you wish."

Anne suddenly became aware of the young, fair-haired waiter who hovered several steps back from their table. He appeared afraid to stand any closer.

His trepidation was contagious.

Michel had offered her friendship as well as intimacy. By discussing him with the stranger, she betrayed him. By not discussing him, she would never know . . . so many things.

"I will have tea, please."

"Very well, ma'am."

The stranger's eyes gleamed pure silver. "I will have . . . whatever the lady is having."

The waiter departed as if the hounds of hell were nipping at his heels.

"Are you, too, named for your ability to make women see angels?" she asked recklessly, wanting to see behind the mask of the man who claimed to be Michel's friend but yet who was so unlike him.

"No." His lips twisted in a travesty of a smile. "There is only one man named for his ability to please women."

Anne could not stop the rush of scalding blood that flooded her cheeks. "Yet you claim that your skills are equally proficient. What name are you known by?"

All semblance of his smile died. "I am Gabriel, mademoiselle."

Gabriel.

"Are you the proprietor of the House of Gabriel?"

"Yes."

A wave of mortification rushed over her.

"Then you do not . . . that is, you do not solicit clients."

"No, not anymore," he murmured provocatively. His silvery gray eyes coldly watched her. "But perhaps, like Michel, no one has recently propositioned me. Would you care to know my price, mademoiselle?"

He was deliberately trying to discomfit her.

Or perhaps he was belittling her.

Because she was plain. Yet she had the same needs as did two beautiful men.

"Why do you call me mademoiselle?" she asked sharply. "I have not told you my marital status."

"Married women come to my house every night, dissatisfied with their husband's prowess. You had not the look."

Pride would not let her glance away from the blond-haired man. "What did I have the look of, monsieur?"

"A virgin."

Not for anything would she give him the satisfaction of knowing he had correctly labeled her a virgin spinster. "And now?"

"Your skin glows with satisfaction. You look like a woman who revels in her sexuality. Do you want to know how Michel became a prostitute?"

Heat mushroomed through her body.

Yes, she wanted to know how Michel came to be what he now was.

Contrarily, she did not want to admit her curiosity to the man who called himself Gabriel.

"How long has Monsieur des Anges lived in England?" she asked instead.

"Eighteen years."

Anne was momentarily taken aback. Michel had made his debut into English society at the same time that she had.

She quickly rallied. "How long have you known Monsieur des Anges?"

"Twenty-seven years."

"You knew him in France, then."

"We knew each other in France," he reiterated politely, watching her.

Anne raised her chin, refusing to ask the question he knew she wanted answered. "Michel is French for Michael. You say your name is Gabriel. You are both named after archangels. Are they your true names?"

"Michel is French for Michael," he replied calmly, waiting . . . "And my given name is Gabriel."

Anne weighed the truth of his statement.

It was highly improbable that two Frenchmen, *two friends,* both of whom had sold their services to women, would bear the names of angels.

"What surname do you go by?"

"I do not need a surname, mademoiselle." Contempt laced his voice. "I am Gabriel. Ask any gentleman—and a surprising number of ladies—and they will know me."

Anne bristled. "You don't like the men and women who come to your establishment."

"Sin is like cockroaches. It comes out in the night."

"Perhaps the people who come to you do not consider their needs a sin."

He leaned over the small round table. "Do you, mademoiselle?"

"They should not be, should they?" she countered.

A familiar expression darkened his pale face.

She had seen that expression on Michel's face.

Part pain. Part regret.

Relentlessness.

"Ask the question, mademoiselle."

Anne's heartbeat accelerated.

"You claim Monsieur des Anges is your friend. Why are you intent upon talking about him behind his back?"

"I want you to understand."

Understand what?

She suddenly noticed that the baby's wailing had subsided. A gust of cold wind swept through the room.

A customer had exited. Or entered.

"Very well. How did you and Monsieur des Anges enter into your previous professions?"

"We met on a road to Paris. Two runaways. Neither of us had any money or food. A madame—a bawd, if you will—took us in. She fed us, clothed us, and taught us how best we could pay her back."

Runaways.

"How old were you?"

He had long, thick, dark eyelashes. They did not blink at her question. "Thirteen."

She felt the blood drain from her face. "You were only children."

His lips curled in a mocking smile. She had seen that smile on Michel's lips. "Michel thrived on it, mademoiselle. He loved the women, the sexual excess. Don't ever think otherwise."

Anne could readily believe Michel had.

"But you did not."

Suddenly the waiter was between them. Dishes clattered; silverware rattled. The fair-headed young man nervously slid a plain white cup and saucer in front of Anne, then Gabriel. They were made out of stoneware rather than china; designed for utility rather than beauty. More dishes followed. A lemon wedge rolled off of a small white bowl onto the table.

Anne sat back to allow him room to align a rolled-up white linen napkin beside her saucer. Gabriel did not sit back.

The waiter's hands visibly shook as he set Gabriel's place. Without asking, the effeminate-looking young man grabbed the white porcelain teapot and poured.

Steaming brown liquid cascaded into her saucer.

"I will pour," she shortly ordered. "You may leave us."

The teapot thudded onto the metal tabletop. "Very well, ma'am."

Feeling every bit as nervous as the waiter, she grasped the curved handle of the teapot. Gabriel obligingly held up his saucer and cup.

As if he had not admitted to living off the street. Like the street sweeper lived.

As if he had not admitted to being forced into prostitution at the age of thirteen.

Numbly she wondered why she was so shocked.

The age of consent for an English girl was thirteen. She could sell her favors and those who purchased them would be considered legal, law-abiding citizens.

Why could not men be victimized by society as well as women?

Hot steam misted the air; she filled his cup before filling hers. Carefully she set the heavy stoneware teapot down on the edge of the table.

Anne's gaze skidded away from his. He did not look forty; neither did Michel. Yet if they had met twenty-seven years earlier when they were thirteen, that was the age both men were. "Would you care for cream, monsieur?"

"No, thank you."

"Sugar?"

"Three lumps, please."

Thank you. Please. How polite the two of them were.

She dropped the prescribed sugar lumps into his cup, and added two to her own. He did not wait to be offered lemon, but reached for it himself, fingers long, strong, elegant.

"I neither want nor need your pity, mademoiselle."

Anne carefully unrolled her napkin and draped it across her lap. "Nor do I offer it to you."

"I did not take you as a woman who would hide from the truth."

Anne realized she still clutched his handkerchief. At the same time she realized she still wore her gloves.

It was the height of bad manners to wear gloves while taking tea.

Dropping the wet handkerchief into her reticule, she peeled off her gloves and shoved them underneath her napkin before answering. "I do not pity you, monsieur." Squarely she met his gaze. "I admire you."

"You admire me, mademoiselle?" he asked softly, cup poised between the saucer and his beautiful, chiseled mouth.

A cold shiver raced down her spine.

Dimly she noted that he held his cup in his left hand.

"Admire you," she repeated firmly. "Many people in your circumstances would not have been so successful. You now own your own business. A very prosperous one, I am sure."

His silver eyes turned gunmetal gray. He returned his cup to the saucer. An answering clink of cups colliding with saucers surrounded them. "And you think that I should be proud of my establishment?"

Anne stirred her tea once, a quick turn of her wrist. "I am very grateful that there are establishments like yours." Carefully she set her teaspoon on the edge of her saucer. "Men and women are not supposed to require the services you provide. But obviously we do; otherwise you would not be in the business you are in. And that, monsieur, would be the shame."

Gabriel sat perfectly still. "Do you know why the waiter was so nervous, mademoiselle?"

"No, I do not."

"He frequents the House of Gabriel."

"I would think your prices are too steep for a waiter."

"He does not come to buy a woman's services."

Anne tried to contain her surprise. Forcibly she restrained herself from turning and looking for the fair-haired young man who had waited upon them. He was hardly more than a boy. "Women purchase his services?"

Gabriel leaned across the table, his gaze pinning her. Hot steam framed his face. His silvery eyes were arctic. "*Men* purchase his services."

It took several seconds for the significance of his words to register.

She instinctively resisted what he was implying.

The look in his eyes did not allow her the luxury of resistance.

He wanted to shock her.

He wanted her to be repulsed.

Swallowing both shock and repulsion, she managed, "Does he enjoy it?"

"Perhaps. Some do."

Lifting her cup, her little finger crooked at the prerequisite angle, she took a sip of tea.

Anne was used to translucent bone china. The stoneware was thicker; unfamiliar. The scalding liquid inside brought tears to her eyes.

She resolutely replaced the cup into the saucer. "If he does not, why does he do it?"

"Do you know the price of a loaf of bread?"

Her silence was answer enough.

"A quartern loaf costs seven pence. Do you know what a room rents for?"

Anne's lips tightened.

She knew what cab fare cost: sixpence a mile. She knew the cost of a pair of silk stockings: five shillings.

She did not know what it cost simply to survive.

"What would you choose, mademoiselle, given the choice of starving in the streets or sleeping at night in a bed with a full belly?"

She saw the emaciated street sweeper in her mind's eye. He had pushed her in front of an oncoming carriage for a silver shilling.

He could just as easily have received a copper penny for his efforts.

Never had she wanted for food, clothes, a bed—*security.*

"But the waiter has a job," she protested.

"It pays twelve shillings a week. Rich men pay fortunes for certain young men."

Sudden understanding cut through her. "For beautiful young men."

"Yes."

For *fair-headed,* beautiful young men, she did not need to add.

Men like Gabriel.

If she damned the boy's actions, she damned her own. She damned Michel. And she damned the man sitting across from her.

She would not be a hypocrite.

Her reticule contained a diaphragm and a tin of French letters, both testament to her lack of respectability.

Anne stiffened her spine, her unconfined breasts further proof of her lapsing morals. "Then I hope that the waiter will someday possess enough money so that he will no longer feel compelled to engage in activities he finds unpleasant. And I hope that he will then find someone who will give him pleasure. To make up for everything he endured."

Gabriel's cold alabaster skin paled. He pushed back his chair and stood up. "It is time to leave, mademoiselle. We are late."

Chapter 13

Gabriel was not at the night house. No one there had seen him since midnight.

Michael flung open the rain-shrouded door to his town house.

Raoul jumped around in surprise, a pair of small scissors in his right hand and a withered purple bud in his left. His swarthy face paled. "Monsieur!"

Michael strode past him toward the veined marble stairs. He did not bother closing the front door behind him; he would be leaving soon enough.

Footsteps hurried after him.

"Monsieur! The water! Monsieur! The mud!" The butler's distress rolled over Michael; it did not affect him. Everything was dispensable: the town house, Raoul, *Anne*. "Monsieur—Monsieur Gabriel is in the library!"

Michael halted.

Gabriel. In the library.

The cold rage burning inside him found an outlet.

Noiselessly he pivoted. Raoul raced ahead of him to open the library door.

Gold gleamed in the gray light. The embossed leather books had not been damaged by the flames or smoke. They alone remained familiar.

The library door closed behind him with a gentle swish. A hard click followed, metal notching metal.

Flickering motion danced in the corner of his eye: fire.

Michael turned on a rush of pure energy.

Gabriel stood facing the fireplace, his blond hair a silver halo in the glimmering dance of light and shadow.

A less perceptive man would not have noticed the slight stiffening of his back.

A less perceptive man would inhabit hell in flesh as well as in spirit.

"Where's Anne?"

Michael's voice was soft. It penetrated the four corners of the library.

Slowly Gabriel turned, his face serene. God's messenger boy.

He casually held a silver-handled cane.

It had been made by the same artisan who had fashioned Michael's cane.

Silently they surveyed one another while the pattering rain and the burning coals closed around them.

Front to back. Back to front.

There was no place to hide. No place to run.

Judgment Day had come.

"She's upstairs, changing into dry clothes," Gabriel said finally.

His voice was equally soft. It, too, filled the library.

Michael was not fooled.

"You didn't post any of your men."

Orange and blue flames outlined Gabriel's legs. Dangerous. Unpredictable. "No."

"But *you* stood watch, didn't you?"

"Yes."

"Waiting for Anne."

"Yes."

He had waited. Watched. And followed.

Agony ripped through Michael.

Goddamn him.

Gabriel was his only friend. And he had betrayed him.

Not to the man. But to his woman.

"Why?"

Gabriel did not pretend to misunderstand him.

"I wanted to see what it was that you were willing to die for."

Michael could feel his hackles rise. Memories of moonlight

and dogs flitted through his mind—strays fighting over a bone, territory—*a woman.*

"You were so sure that I would let her leave my side?" he taunted.

"You can't watch her every minute." Gabriel was not drawn by Michael's anger. "You know that, or you wouldn't want my men to protect her."

Yes, Gabriel would wait for that one lone minute, Michael thought savagely. Endlessly. Tirelessly. Until Anne left the town house unescorted.

And she had.

His hands clenched into fists.

He knew he couldn't watch over her all the time. *But he didn't want to know it.*

He wanted to think that he could protect her.

He needed to believe that he could protect her.

There had to exist one small factor in his life that he could control.

"Where did she go?"

Gabriel shrugged. "London proper."

Shopping?

"How did you persuade her to come back with you?"

"A beggar pushed her in front of a hack."

And rescued her for a reward.

But beggars weren't always quick enough to save their victims.

For a second he couldn't breathe.

Anne could have died, and he would not have been able to stop it. He would not even have known about it—until it was too late.

It was already too late.

He gritted his teeth. "What did you tell her?"

"I asked her if she would like to test my expertise in bed."

A coal exploded in the fireplace.

"You son of a bitch."

Michael had felt many things for Gabriel throughout the years they had been together. He had never felt hatred.

Until now.

He hated his games.

He hated his perfect, unmarred skin.

Gabriel lightly fingered the silver handle of his cane that, when twisted, became the hilt of a sword. "Don't you want to know what she said, Michael?"

Was Anne changing clothes . . . or packing to go?

"Do I?" he asked tightly.

"She said she saw you when she made her debut."

Once. Eighteen years ago. At a ball.

A vivid image of Olivia Hendall-Grayson, Countess Raleigh—Michael's first English procuress—flashed before his eyes. She liked beautiful young men. So did her husband.

The same memories were reflected in Gabriel's eyes.

Different women. Different men.

Years of pleasure. Years of pain.

A smile twisted Gabriel's lips. "Don't you want to know what I asked her then, Michael?"

Michael, too, had learned the art of patience.

"What did you ask, Gabriel?"

"I asked her which of us she would prefer if it had been me she had seen first."

The rage and the pain caught in Michael's chest.

In all the twenty-seven years they had been together, Gabriel had never once talked about the choices that had been taken from them or the choices they themselves had made.

"What did she say?" he asked softly.

"You, Michael. She would have chosen you. Because of your eyes."

Bitter irony twisted Michael's lips.

He had flirted with English society for thirteen years and no one had recognized his eyes.

"I told her how you became a whore."

The burning coals snapped and popped behind Gabriel. Behind Michael a sheet of rain pelted the bay window.

"And did you tell her how much I loved it?"

Gabriel's stare did not falter. "Yes."

"Did you tell her what you are, Gabriel?"

"She knows."

The breath whistled out of Michael's lungs. "You brought her back to me. Why?"

"She believes I should take pride in my house." Shadow darkened Gabriel's face. "That men and women require its services."

Michael stilled.

Anne had pulled away from him rather than suffer his touch in public.

He fought down a black wave of jealousy.

This was a side of his spinster he had not seen—perhaps would never see.

"Why did she say that?" he asked dispassionately.

"I took her to a pastry shop. Timothy works there."

Timothy, like Gabriel, had been borne homeless. English rather than French. A nameless bastard in any language. Gabriel had found him a job, that he might learn a trade other than whoring.

Had Anne been shocked? Repulsed?

Her own life had cheated her of choices. Did she understand that life also cheated others of choices?

When it was time, which of the two needs would she remember?

The need for sex?

Or the need for vengeance?

"I wasn't going to bring her back to you, Michael."

Michael had not expected him to. "I know."

"Do you know what else she said?"

Michael no longer knew what to expect.

"She said that she hopes Timothy will someday find someone who will give him pleasure. To make up for everything he has endured."

Emotion coiled inside Michael's gut.

Regret; for the internal scars that did not heal. Relief; that Anne had seen the worst Gabriel could offer. And had accepted the wounded world of two worn-out whores.

"It's over, Gabriel," Michael said quietly. "I know you've killed. I know who you killed. And I know why."

"How do you know who I've killed?"

There was only polite interest in Gabriel's voice. The air between them quickened with tension.

"I know because I saw what he did to you. I would have killed him myself if you had not," Michael returned evenly. "Sell the house. Start a new life."

"Are you suggesting we engage in a *ménage à trois, mon frère?*" Gabriel mocked.

Michael did not have to answer. He dropped the veils of pretense and for one moment allowed the man he was to openly surface.

He wanted. He needed.

He would not share his spinster.

Not even with Gabriel.

"Go to her, Michael." The mockery left Gabriel's eyes. He suddenly looked tired, his perfect skin drawn like fine parchment. "No one will hurt her tonight."

"And you know this because you are . . . God's messenger?" Michael asked, his eyes narrowed, wanting to believe.

Knowing that everything had a price.

Gabriel was as close to a brother as he had ever had. There was nothing the man could give him that he did not already have.

Was there?

"I know it because I'm your friend, Michael."

There was no warmth in Gabriel's silver eyes. No sign of friendship.

The words were enough.

They had to be.

He had not been able to kill Anne. His spinster.

He did not know if he would be able to kill Gabriel. His friend.

Michael turned and opened the library door. Raoul was in the foyer, pruning the potted hyacinth. A maid in a white cap with a white pinafore pinned to her black dress energetically mopped the floor. Anne was upstairs . . . doing what?

Something cold and wet slithered down his cheek.

He stared at the mirror-shiny oak floor. And realized he had tracked in mud and rain.

His hair was plastered to his head. His shirt underneath his open coat stuck to his body.

Anne had accepted Gabriel.

He wanted her to accept *him*. To cry out the name Diane had refused to utter: Michael.

He wanted to touch her. To reassure himself that she was safe.

For one more night.

Anne was not in his bedchamber.

The sweet perfume of the roses on the nightstand weighted the air. Rose petal-stamped boxes were piled on the yellow silk-upholstered chaise lounge.

Rose petals were Madame René's trademark. A symbol of fading youth and fallen virtue.

The first of Anne's new clothes had arrived while he was out. While she was out.

There were so many things he wanted to do for her. To do *to* her.

Where was she?

Steam drifted out from underneath the bathroom door.

Michael thrust it open.

The breath was knocked out of his lungs at the sight of Anne. Even as it registered in his mind that she stood naked, left foot resting on the toilet seat, head bowed, spine curved, right hand disappearing between her splayed thighs, she lurched upright, her neck twisting around in alarm.

Startled awareness shone in her eyes. Crimson embarrassment followed. It painted her face; her neck.

Clearly she had not expected anyone to interrupt her.

Gurgling water from the draining bathtub filled the silence.

Had she been aroused by Gabriel's beauty? he wondered, waiting for the pain to strike even as his body readied to satisfy her.

"I . . ." Anne licked her lips, her pink tongue pale in comparison to the bright red that blotched her cheeks. "I was positioning my diaphragm."

He remembered her questions after she had given him the gift of fellatio: asking if he had ever ejaculated inside a woman's vagina without benefit of a French letter. *Asking if there were other means of protection that could be used to prevent conception.*

The pain struck him with the force of the carriage that could so easily have killed her.

She had not gone shopping; she had visited a physician.

"You want to take my sperm into your body?" he asked hoarsely.

"Yes."

Michael's heart skipped a beat. She could have died. All for the sake of feeling a whore's naked flesh. *A whore's seed.* "Shall I assist you?"

Remembered failure at fitting a condom over his penis flitted over her face.

Her lips tightened with resolution. "No, thank you."

She waited for him to leave, to accord her the privacy in which to prepare herself for the man whom she believed was her lover.

The last of the bathwater slurped down the drain.

He did not leave.

Uncertainty flared in her pale eyes. "I have never done this before."

Michael could not say the same. He had watched one woman so prepare herself: Diane.

He did not think of Diane when he looked at Anne.

Long seconds passed while his spinster wordlessly wrestled with decorum, trying to decide whether to be the uninhibited woman she longed to be or to safely hide behind modesty.

Michael chose for her.

"Finish. Now. Or I will," he said softly.

"Do you enjoy watching a woman introduce a foreign object into her body, monsieur?" she asked defensively.

Another time he would smile at her naïveté. *Not now.*

"Yes, I do," he said deliberately. "Do you not enjoy having me watch you?"

She did not answer.

She did not need to.

They all needed to be wanted: Anne, Michael. *Gabriel.*

Self-consciousness screaming in her every muscle, her every tendon, Anne turned back to her task.

He should warn her that French letters were more than contraceptive devices. That if he were another man she might end up with a condition far worse than pregnancy.

He knew he wasn't going to.

She offered him an intimacy he had long given up hope of ever experiencing again.

Shrugging off his wet wool jacket, Michael stepped forward to more closely watch Anne as she struggled to position the diaphragm over her cervix. She was determined to win the battle between rubber and flesh.

He stared at the minute play of muscles in her back. At the water-darkened clumps of hair that clung to her skin. At her rounded buttocks, moist and flushed from her bath.

His chest tightened. His testicles tightened.

She was heart-stoppingly vulnerable, bowed over with no means of defense—gut-wrenchingly beautiful, preparing to take his sperm.

Unable to resist the temptation she presented, he lightly stroked a finger up the dark crevice between her buttocks, splayed his hand across the sensitive skin at the base of her spine.

Anne instinctively arched into his touch.

He smiled, a sexual grimace of masculine satisfaction. "I lied." *About so many things.* "I've never felt anything as soft as your skin. Silk velvet doesn't breathe. It doesn't pulse with need. But you do. Every time I touch you I can feel your passion. Tell me what you're feeling, Anne. You told me you have imagined that I suckled you. And that you touched your breasts when you did so. Did you ever imagine taking me inside you? Did you ever put your fingers inside you when you wondered what it would be like to lie with me?"

She stiffened in silent protest.

Michael lightly feathered the soft vee of skin above the dark crevice between her buttocks with his thumb. "Lovers, Anne, can share anything," he murmured. *Except the truth.* "Did you?"

"No." Her voice was muffled.

"Did you want to?"

"Yes."

A pulse frantically beat against his thumb. The palm of his hand. *Inside his penis.*

"Why didn't you?"

"I was afraid that I . . . that I would compromise my virginity."

Starting at the base of her spine, slowly working upward, he gently massaged her vertebrae, one at a time. He remembered the taut circle of flesh he had massaged—*ruptured*—less than forty-eight hours earlier. "When our liaison is over, will you put your fingers inside you when you remember me?"

"I don't know."

She didn't know . . . if she would insert her fingers inside her body to ease the ache of loneliness? he wondered. Or she didn't know if she would do so and remember him, a scarred whore who betrayed her trust?

"Will you take another man?" he pressed.

"No," she quickly denied.

Michael could not squelch the burst of primal satisfaction her response elicited.

He did not want another man doing to her the things he had done to her. *The things she had done to him* . . .

A purple shadow marred the pale, smooth skin between Anne's shoulder blades.

He gently touched it. "You have a bruise."

She shuddered. In pain? In memory? "A street sweeper pushed me."

A street sweeper . . .

The throbbing inside his cock crawled up his body and lodged in his temples.

A wisp of steam circled Anne's bowed head. The skin underneath his fingers continued to bunch and stretch.

The bruise had been caused by a blunt object.

Gabriel had said a beggar had pushed her.

There was no reason for a street sweeper to resort to violence for the penny he would receive. No reason at all to strike her with a broom when a hand would attract far less attention.

One more night, Gabriel had promised.

A messenger boy. *But not God's . . .*

Jagged pain twisted inside his intestines.

Had Gabriel, like Michael, been unable to kill Anne Aimes, a spinster whose only crime was wanting to be touched?

Leaning over, he kissed her bruise, lightly laved it with his tongue, silently apologizing for the injury two fallen angels had brought her.

Would continue to bring her.

Contrition was not a deterrent.

Straightening, he unbuttoned his trousers. The backs of his scar-roughened fingers teased the velvety plump softness of her buttocks. "Tell me when you're finished."

"What are you doing?" she asked huskily. Underneath her desire she was restive.

"Readying myself for you," he rasped, easing out his erect penis.

Anne shot up, her back impacting his chest. The icy, sodden linen of his shirt clung to her warm skin.

Michael's hand snaked out and latched onto her left leg before she could lower it. "Don't. Don't turn away from me."

Her leg quivered. "You're cold. And wet."

But she didn't pull away.

A spinster's needs . . . a whore's needs.

He had one more night to fulfill them.

Gritting his teeth, he bent his knees.

She was hot. Wet. The silky soft lips of her labia parted in welcome.

Anne's breath audibly caught in her throat. "The physician said that a woman's vagina is shortened in this position."

"Yes."

Gently he notched his sex to hers.

The liquid heat of her body raced up his spine.

Anne clenched her muscles.

"Relax," he whispered.

"I am," she swiftly returned.

She was afraid.

So was he.

"I don't want to hurt you, Anne. Help me."

Help me hold on for one more night.

"How?"

"Touch yourself." He swirled the head of his penis around the taut ring of her vagina. Flesh on flesh. Essence commingling. Male. Female. *Whore. Spinster.* "Show me how you touch yourself when you think of me."

She stiffened in shock. "I can't."

"You can." He reached for her right hand and brought it up to her breast.

Her fingers fisted in rejection.

"I'm going to penetrate you," he said raggedly, "and when I do, I want you to touch yourself. In the future, I want you to remember. I want you to feel the softness here—" Pressing her hand against her breast, Michel thrust through the ring of her taut flesh. Anne gasped, her fingers involuntarily opening to stop the pain. "And remember the hardness inside you."

As Michael would remember.

This moment. This day.

The man had taken everything . . . *Everything but this night.*

He kneaded Anne's hand, forcing her to knead her breast, and eased inside her another inch.

She clenched around him, tighter than a fist. A spinster who had tasted the pleasures of the flesh but had yet to experience the pain of its betrayal.

Seven dead, *two more to go. . . .*

"Is your nipple hard, Anne? Tell me. *Dites moi.*"

The French slipped out naturally. A remnant of the man he had used to be.

Her vagina squeezed and nipped his invading flesh.

"Yes."

"If I release your thigh, will you stay open for me?"

The muscles in her leg corded beneath his fingers. "Yes."

"And will you take all of me?"

If given a choice, would she take Michael as well as Michel?

Would she take the man who hurt as well as the man who hurt her?

"I will try."

Had Gabriel tried?

Tentatively he released her thigh.

Anne left her leg in position. Tiny ripples contracted her vagina.

He cupped his hand over her lower stomach, feeling her softness, her heat, her internal contractions.

Not enough.

Groin curving to cup her buttocks, he eased another inch inside her.

"Wait!" she gasped, head rearing back, body quivering.

Michael paused, shaking on the outside. *The inside.*

He nuzzled her ear. Trying to ease her fear. His fear. "What is it?"

"The diaphragm—"

He stilled, fighting a stab of hope, of wanting to survive. *Even if through a child.* "Is it in position?"

"No. Yes. I don't remember feeling this full."

Michael remembered. . . .

Silver-eyed laughter, Gabriel watching a clumsy, half-starved English boy swipe a loaf of French bread.

Michael remembered. . . .

Stinging sweat blinding him as he worked over the madame, learning how to please a woman.

Michael remembered. . . .

Long, endless hours, waiting for day to end and darkness to descend, his head pressed close to Gabriel's in a shuttered room as he taught the French boy how to read and write.

To be the gentleman neither of them was meant to be.

He thrust home, burying the memories.

Anne's muscles struggled to adjust to full penetration, milking him like a hungry mouth.

Heaven. Hell.

Revelations. Truth revealed.

Michael pressed his lips against her temple. "Shhh. It's all right."

More lies.

"I . . . You feel different."

Whereas she felt all too familiar. His only link to sanity in a world gone totally insane.

"This is me," he murmured rawly. "My flesh. Not rubber."

Slowly he pulled out, making of her flesh a vacuum.

"Can you feel it?" she panted.

He felt it.

The pleasure of her. Embracing him.

The pain building inside. Waiting for release.

He felt it all.

Michael thrust deep inside Anne, making her feel it all.

The pain. The pleasure.

What had the man given Gabriel that Michael could not?

Anne leaned into his lips, his body, his cock, taking him. *All of him.*

"I want to know—" Her voice caught on a gasp.

He stared down at the pure profile of her nose. Moisture beaded on her lashes. Damp hair tickled his scarred cheek.

"What?" She bore down, drawing a gasp from him. "What do you want to know?"

"I want to know what it feels like for a man when he's inside a woman. Like this."

Blindly he reached down, burned flesh sifting through damp, springy pubic hair. He gently grasped her swollen clitoris between his thumb and forefinger. She was soft and silky on the outside; inside was a core of hardness that matched his own. A pulse beat inside her. Around his cock. Between his fingers. "You want to know what I feel, Anne Aimes?"

"Yes." She took a deep breath; their hands clamped over her breast rose and fell in unison. "Yes, I do."

"I feel this," he whispered. "You squeezing me. Pulsing around me. Expanding with every heartbeat."

Gently, rhythmically, he pumped her engorged flesh, showing her what he felt.

Wondering how long Gabriel had lied. Days? Weeks? *Years?*

Would Anne feel this same sense of betrayal?

"Match my rhythm." He pushed up inside her, hard, wanting to plow into her so deeply that there was no man, no Gabriel—only Anne and Michael. "When I squeeze your clitoris, squeeze my *bitte*. Now. I'm pulling out. Squeeze me."

He squeezed her, feeling her life throb between his fingers. *It could so easily be extinguished.*

"Michel—" Anne flinched.

"Shhh. Relax. Hold me, like I'm holding you. . . . You wanted to know what I feel when I'm inside you. This is what I feel. You gripping me. Harder. *Harder*. Like this . . . *Yes*. Now relax. Squeeze me, release me, like a heartbeat. Yes, *God, yes*. That's it. *C'est bon,*" he crooned, sinking into the rhythm, pumping, thrusting, fingers relaxing, contracting, *up,* down, *in,* out, just the two of them locked together, one body, one sex. "Feel how good you make me feel, Anne. . . ."

Seeking the warmth of her neck, he rubbed his right cheek back and forth, back and forth, inhaling her scent, absorbing her softness, her passion.

The essence that was Anne Aimes.

But for how long?

Ragged breathing harmonized with the cadence of their bodies. Hers. His. He could feel her wetness. Hear his hardness hammering into her.

A crystal droplet of water dripped onto her left breast.

Rain? Sweat?

Tears?

He had cried when the man took him. Once.

The man had laughed.

Michael had never cried since.

Wrapping his arm around her, trapping her hand against her breast, he pulled Anne back against him until her resistance and his shirt melted and all that existed was the thrust of his penis into her vagina and the throb of her clitoris melding with his fingers, no past, no future—

Time exploded.

He felt it in his manhood; he felt it with his fingers. He felt it against his lips and his tongue, her voice crying out. "Michel! Oh, God! Michel! God, Michel, Michel, Michel!"

He sank his teeth into Anne's neck to stop her words, his words: *my name is Michael.*

Diane waited in Michael's dreams, flesh blackening from heat, blond hair a tangle of flames. Just as he had last seen her.

"I love you, Michel."

"Don't do this, Diane. Please. Let me help you. I can help you, goddamn it. Give me a chance!"

"You can't help me, mon amour, *but you can join me. You can join us all."*

Michael recoiled from the clasp of her fingers but he could not withdraw from her touch, could not separate her hands from his. Her flesh destroyed his just as his past had destroyed her.

Thick smoke filled his nostrils—Diane's breath. *"We wait for you, Michel."*

Little appeared behind Diane, lips charred, glazed eyes staring. Accusing.

Arms surrounded Michael, his knees, his waist, his shoulders, his neck. Child, adult, female, male, everyone he loved embraced him. And they were all dead.

Fire licked his cheek—Diane's tongue. *"Do you know what he did to us, Michel?"*

Michael wanted to scream. He wanted to vomit. He wanted to deny the truth.

In the end he could do neither.

"Yes. I know what he did to you."

He knew what the man had done to all of them.

But most especially he knew what the man had done to Diane.

Michael had been only a child when the man took him.

Diane had been a woman, with a woman's body and a woman's needs.

The man had taken it all away from her. Just as he had taken Michael's childhood.

Suddenly it was Gabriel who held him rather than Diane. It was Gabriel's skin that blackened; Gabriel's blond hair that turned into blue and orange flames.

He leaned his smoldering face against Michael's. *"Do you know what* I *have done, Michael?"*

Chapter 14

Hatred had ruled him all of his life, beating inside his chest like the heart of a trapped animal. It was the only thing that had kept him alive these last twenty-nine years.

It was the only reason that he now served in hell.

Expertly he steered the wooden wheelchair out of the metal lift. The man inside it did not make a sound, back straight as his legs were not.

The top of the stairway was only ten feet behind them. It would be so simple to turn the wheelchair around.

Perspiration beaded his forehead.

The mental image of turning the wheelchair around was so vivid in his mind that he could hear the rattle of the chair and the man's surprised exclamation: *What do you think you're doing?*

I'm going to kill you, sir.

His imagination stopped there.

The words would not incite the fear that he so intensely imagined: they would incite laughter.

The man knew he did not have the courage to face up to the consequences of his actions—either past or present.

"It is a bit chilly for this time of year, don't you think, old chap?"

He gritted his teeth at the familiar, mocking voice. *The man knew what he was thinking.*

Staring at the polished mahogany floor instead of the back of the man's head, which was covered in thick gray hair, he politely answered, "Yes, sir."

Face expressionless lest he give away the seething hatred and do what he still imagined doing, he pushed the wheelchair down the shadowed hallway, away from unbearable temptation. Opposing rows of closed mahogany doors witnessed the man's safe passage.

Brass and crystal wall sconces lined the richly paneled corridor. Harsh electric light illuminated priceless paintings in gilded frames, a Chippendale table here, a rose damask-covered rococo chair there.

The man was fond of claiming it had belonged to Napoleon I, another master of men. It guarded the second to the last door.

Smoothly parking the wheelchair, he quickly, efficiently pulled the brake before turning away to swing open the door to the man's bedchamber.

Heavy maroon drapes flanked either side of a hand-crafted mahogany wood fireplace; they were pulled against the encroaching night. Yellow flames blazed inside the grate. The bedcovers were turned down, fine white linen cutting across thick maroon velvet. A book lay on the mahogany nightstand beside a Tiffany lamp, gold-edged pages gleaming in a circle of light. Tall footposts painted columns of shadow onto the wall.

Everything was as it should be.

The man sat as he had left him, gray-haired head turning neither left nor right. Silently, grimly, he released the brake on the wheelchair and pushed it across the threshold.

"I will sit by the fire. You may bathe me there."

"Very good, sir."

He did not know which ordeal was the most repulsive: washing the man in a bathtub or giving him a sponge bath.

"But first I require the urinal."

He stiffened. Revulsion crawled along his skin.

It was an unnecessary task, one that the man was quite capable of doing on his own.

The man was punishing him for his wayward thoughts.

He clenched his hands.

God Almighty. At times like these he didn't care if he did hang.

But it wasn't dying that bothered him. It was what came after death that scared him shitless.

Retrieving the metal urinal from the adjoining bathroom, he knelt in front of the fire at the foot of the wheelchair.

He could feel the man's eyes on him, could feel his limp flesh underneath the tailored wool clothing. Behind him the fire crackled and snapped; heat seared his back. Holding his breath, he lifted the man's penis out of the dual vents of his underwear and trousers, angled the urinal to catch the flow.

The marble clock on the mantel loudly ticked away the seconds. And then . . . a dribble of yellow fluid trickled down the side of the cold metal.

"Clean me; there's a good boy." The man's voice was smug.

A wave of light-headedness assailed him.

The bastard.

He played with him the way a cat played with an injured rabbit. Cruelly. Deliberately. Sure that the animal cannot escape.

Hands shaking, he reached into his pocket for a tissue, cursorily dabbed the head of the man's penis before dropping it inside the metal container.

"I do not need a bath, after all. I wish to retire."

Breathing lightly through his mouth, he readjusted the man's clothing, stood up with the urinal clenched in his hand.

The man tilted his head back, eyes shining in creased, leathery skin. "Do you not wish to thank me for relieving you of a heinous duty?"

For a timeless second he thought about telling the man exactly what he wished.

He wished the man's death.

He wished the man's interment.

He wished the man's rotting flesh filled with worms.

"Thank you, sir," he said woodenly.

Inside the all-white, antiseptic-looking bathroom, he dumped the contents of the urinal inside the commode. Briefly he rested his forehead against the mirror over the sink while he rinsed out the metal container.

At times he wondered if pain and paralysis had driven the man insane. But then he would look into his faded violet eyes and see the truth.

The last twenty-nine years had taught him there was no God. But he still believed in Satan.

The man was evil through and through.

A shudder passed through his body.

He would not let the man destroy him. All he had to endure was a few more minutes. When the man was abed, he would be free to seek consolation.

He prepared the man in silence—undressing him, sliding over his head a flannel nightshirt, lifting him onto the goose down-filled mattress, adjusting the pillows underneath his gray-haired head, tucking the covers about his withered legs. The man was content, his thoughts occupied by his latest quarry. Forcefully he focused on the nightly rituals he had performed for twenty-nine years instead of on the overwhelming desire to snatch up the pillow or the covers and press them over that dry, wrinkled face until it was no more and he was free.

The hair on his neck prickled. Glancing up, he froze underneath the man's icy gaze.

"Have you made arrangements for the servants to leave on holiday tomorrow morning?"

"Yes."

"The coffins, are they set up?"

He slowly straightened, careful to mask his fear and repugnance. "They are ready."

"And are you glad to be back in Dover after your London sojourn?"

"Yes. Sir." He forced himself to be obsequious when all he wanted to do was kill the man and be done with it.

He had killed so many. Why did he hesitate?

But he knew why he hesitated. Fear kept him obedient like the trained dogs that guarded the estate.

"Shall you need anything else, sir?"

The man's bloodless lips curled in a taunting smile. "Has Mrs. Ghetty given you a conscience?"

His vertebrae felt fused. Like the man's.

It had been only a matter of time before his trysts with the widowed cook were discovered. No doubt one of the many servants who, inspired by generous wages, had felt duty-bound to relate the news that the valet of the poor, crippled master raided rather more than the kitchen larders.

Mrs. Ghetty had given him affection, perhaps even love, but she had not given him a conscience.

If she had, he would not carry out the man's plans.

But he would carry them out. And pray that the man died soon of natural causes.

The wheels had been set in motion. Nothing would stop them now.

"Everything has been done according to your instructions," he said tonelessly.

The man's satisfaction permeated the bedchamber. "Excellent. You may go fuck my cook now."

He turned, paused, hand grasping the doorknob. The question was torn out of him. "Why?"

There was no sane reason for the sequence of events, either past or present.

Reaching out, the man grasped the leather book. Dismissing him. His question. His worth as a fellow human being.

He had not expected an answer.

He did not receive one.

All he could do was follow the man's instructions and hope that he did not give in to the rage.

Chapter 15

A shadow imprinted his eyelids. It was accompanied by a breath of sound.

Death awaiting.

Michael awakened spontaneously. He stared up into Raoul's face.

Sleep vanished in a rush of belated alertness.

The earthy scents of sex, sweat, and roses filled his nostrils. Pale pink dawn filtered through the thin, yellow silk drapes.

Like the rain, his night was over.

The butler's face was haggard, his features blurred by the dim glow of the oil lamp. A nightcap perched on his head, white knitted wool a stark contrast against his dark skin. His body was wrapped in a plaid robe.

He did not look like a man on a mission of murder. A cursory appraisal revealed that Raoul did not openly carry a gun or a knife.

"What is it?" Michael asked flatly, pitching his voice low.

Anne's head was pillowed on his left arm; her soft buttocks pressed against his hip. Her breathing was deep; she slept the sleep of exhaustion, her body sated, filled with his seed.

He did not want to wake her if it was not necessary.

If it *was* necessary . . . Michael would never reach the nightstand quickly enough to save her.

Slowly, gently, he eased his arm out from underneath her head. It was numb from lack of circulation. "What is it?" he asked again, barely more than a whisper.

"It is Monsieur Gabriel, monsieur."

Raoul, too, pitched his voice low so as not to disturb the sleeping woman.

Michael tensed. "What about him?"

"A boy delivered a message from a Monsieur Gaston."

Michael's ears pricked with recognition; Gaston was manager at the night house. "And?"

"The boy said that there is a fire at Monsieur Gabriel's. And that Monsieur Gabriel—he is in the fire, monsieur."

The bed reeled underneath Michael.

Gabriel. *In a fire.*

Gabriel. *Burned.*

Gabriel. *The eighth victim.*

Anne dreamed of voices. Then she dreamed Michel tucked the covers around her—as if she were the child she had never been—and chastely kissed her on the cheek, a sigh of silky lips and warm breath. Afterward he blew out the hurricane lamp and left her.

It wasn't a dream.

The sheets were cold. Wet. The flesh between her thighs was hot. *Wet.*

Michel had indeed replaced the gynecologist's touch with his own. Every inch of her skin burned from the scrape of his hair-studded flesh, while her body felt hollowed out. It felt as if he had tunneled his way into the farthest depths of her being.

She laid very still, trying to feel the diaphragm.

She couldn't.

Watery sunshine penetrated the thin, yellow silk drapes.

Thrice now she had awakened in a man's bed.

Thrice Michel had ejaculated inside her, sharing the essence of his pleasure.

A musky odor that was not sweat overlay the sweetness of roses. Tentatively she scooted out of bed, struggling free of silk sheets and tangled hair.

The sheets, too, smelled of the unfamiliar musky odor.

Anne stood up, toes curling on the cold wooden floor. Warm fluid trickled down her thigh.

Michel.

Anne touched the viscous fluid, held up her finger to the muted light.

It was coated with a thick white substance. *Came. Blanc. Sauce.* A man's sperm.

It was the source of the musky odor that permeated the sheets and her body.

She cupped her stomach, remembering the hot spurt of his release, and was suddenly, ravenously hungry.

For fun. For excitement. For love.

All the things that had been denied her. *Until now.*

Acting on pure impulse, she threw back the covers and inspected the sheet. Damp circles marked the evidence of their passion.

Michel had tasted their commingled pleasure. Then he had kissed her, sharing with her the flavor of their mutual ecstasy.

A fastidious spinster would have been repulsed.

But she no longer felt like a spinster. She felt like a woman who had experienced every woman's fantasy.

Delicately she cleaned her finger on the silk, leaving behind her a sign of approval.

Boxes were stacked on top of the yellow silk-upholstered chaise lounge. They were stamped with rose petals, hardly a masculine imprint.

Curious, she lifted the lid off the top box. It contained a bluebell gray silk-and-wool-blend double-breasted jacket with a high, military-style collar and large silver buttons.

Anne investigated the box underneath. She discovered six pairs of silk drawers trimmed with lace and ribbons.

It was Christmas in April.

Madame René included silk chemises, silk petticoats, a black satin corset, silk stockings. A ridiculously frivolous, wireless bustle with five rows of box pleating. Reticule. Hat. Shoes.

Clothes that befitted an attractive woman. Not a drab spinster.

The last box, longer than the rest, contained a bluebell silk-and-wool-blend round skirt. It was bordered with a frill of small pleats and was headed by seven rows of mixed steel and silver braid.

Madame René was a master at blending elegance and simplicity. Well worth the small fortune she had no doubt charged.

She would wear the *couturière*'s creations, Anne decided. Just as soon as she bathed.

Anne stepped up to the mirrorless dresser. A curious pang shot through her chest. Michel had neatly piled her hairpins on top of the dresser.

How many years had it taken the thirteen-year-old boy he had once been to become the sexually adept man he now was?

Slowly she brushed out the tangles from her hair before hurriedly pinning it up. The bathroom wall sconces burned on either side of the marble sink, wicks turned down low.

Another courtesy.

There were so many things she should have asked Michel's silver-eyed, silver-haired friend, she thought, reaching to turn up the light.

The only rooms in the elegant town house that were not occupied by floral arrangements or blooming plants were the bathroom upstairs and the water closet downstairs. Why did a man surround himself with flowers?

Why did a man who was terrified of fire sleep with a burning lamp beside his bed?

Gabriel had been at ease in the pastry shop. Anne could not imagine Michel in similar surroundings, drinking out of a stoneware cup.

How had two such opposite men remained friends for twenty-seven years?

Leaning over the porcelain bathtub, she twisted an ivory tap. She was amazed anew at the steaming hot water that gushed out of the spout.

When she returned to Dover, her first item of business was replacing all of the old plumbing.

The diaphragm was far easier to remove than it had been to position. Rinsing it off, she returned the circle of rubber to the small, rose-colored tin that she had left on the marble counter by the sink.

The bathwater stung pleasantly. Anne stared at the ivory-tinted porcelain-and-turquoise-trimmed commode and wondered if she would ever enter a water closet without remembering the night before.

She had enjoyed him watching her.

Reaching up, she fingered the crook of her neck.

He had bitten her during the height of his climax.

She had even enjoyed that.

Anne quickly washed and dried. Michel was no doubt downstairs. Perhaps after breakfast she would allow him to position the diaphragm. Her lips curved in a smile that was most decidedly unspinsterish. But then again, perhaps not . . .

Briefly she contemplated ringing for a maid to assist her with her dress. She did not.

The only article that required assistance was the black satin corset. Attractive though it was, it was rather pleasant having her breasts and lungs unrestrained by whalebone.

Freedom, she decided, was almost as intoxicating as sexual gratification.

Perhaps, she thought on a wave of giddiness, it was the wearing of corsets that kept women in subjugation.

She opened the bathroom door—only to remember the small tin on the sink.

The diaphragm was featherlight.

What if the maid, when cleaning, decided the tin was empty and discarded it? *What if she opened it and recognized the small circle of rubber for what it was?*

Backtracking, Anne retrieved the rose-colored tin. She opened the nightstand drawer beside the four-poster brass bed to place it beside Michel's tin of French letters.

Sharp metal gleamed beside the stamped image of Graystone's dour face.

Anne remembered the wicked glint of light dancing on the tip of her hat pin. This was far more deadly.

A chill that had nothing to do with the weather raced down her spine.

Her father had kept a gun in his nightstand. For protection, he claimed.

For masculine pride, Anne had surmised.

Why would a man keep a knife by his bed?

Why were her knees suddenly shaking?

She slid her hand inside the drawer. Her fingers encountered something hard. Heavy.

A pistol.

It was more compact than the old-fashioned one her father had possessed.

More blunt.

More lethal.

The metal was smooth and sleek, as if it had been recently polished.

Michel was as adept with weapons as he was with a woman's body.

The thought came out of nowhere. It would not go away.

Every warning Anne's governess had fed her raced through her thoughts.

Children would hurt her because of their envy.

Men would abduct her to ransom her wealth.

Dropping the rose-colored tin into the drawer, she shoved the wood shut so hard that the hurricane lamp rattled and a rain of rose petals fell to the table.

Many men were proficient with weapons. Thieves were more plentiful in London than on the isolated outskirts of Dover.

Michel would not hurt her.

He had said so.

After dropping her hat pin onto the floor.

Anne hurriedly opened the door to the bedchamber that had witnessed her wanton abandon. She came face-to-face with a golden-haired man.

A very handsome golden-haired man. He had cerulean blue eyes.

She bit back a scream.

He was in black livery. A footman. Not an assailant.

The golden-haired footman stepped back and bowed. "Begging your pardon, ma'am. I thought I heard a disturbance. Shall you have breakfast now?"

"Yes. Thank you." She forced a polite smile, nerves screeching the outcry a lady was not allowed to make. "Could you direct me to Monsieur des Anges please?"

"He is not here."

How dim the hallway suddenly seemed. How very silly her earlier fears.

How thin the walls.

If the footman had heard her slam the drawer to the nightstand, there was no question at all that he had heard her scream the night before. As no doubt the other servants had.

She tilted her chin, daring him to think what he would. "Then you may direct me to the breakfast room."

The footman stepped aside, cerulean eyes unreadable. "Of course, ma'am. If you will follow me."

The butler waited for her at the bottom of the steps. Silver gleamed: in his hair, in his white-gloved hand. "Mademoiselle Aimes!"

Tension knotted in her stomach.

He held the silver post tray in front of him. The golden-haired footman waited beside the wrought-iron newel post, a silent witness.

Raoul had similarly offered Michel a post, while she waited, a silent witness.

The missive had not borne good news.

She clutched the black metal balustrade. "Yes?"

"This *lettre* arrived by special delivery, mademoiselle." His dark eyes were politely blank. "It is addressed to you."

Anne breathed a sigh of relief. Mr. Little must have returned from Lincolnshire.

Bowing, Raoul extended the silver tray.

She scooped up the letter. "Thank you."

Stepping down the last step, she turned the white envelope over and read her name.

It was not Mr. Little's busy scrawl. Furthermore, the letter was addressed to her town house.

Anne frowned.

The envelope was stamped, but it had not been mailed in London. There was no return address.

"Ma'am."

She glanced up at the blond footman.

"The breakfast room is this way."

"Thank you."

Anne did not need him for guidance. The delectable odor of ham and bacon drifted down the hallway.

The footman threw open the door to a small, square breakfast room at the end of the corridor. Sunlight sparkled on polished wood and silver. French doors showcased a rectangular garden. Budding rosebushes lined a brick wall.

Another footman—brunet rather than blond, amber-eyed instead of blue—seated her at a round oak table. An oak buffet featured a variety of silver-covered chafing dishes.

"What will be your pleasure, mademoiselle?"

The footman spoke with a decided French accent. The *r* rolled across his tongue.

Heat spread over Anne's cheeks. Did all Frenchmen so cavalierly use the term *pleasure*? "I will have bacon, please. With eggs. And toast."

"Très bien."

English. French. Michel's servants were really no different from her own. More handsome, perhaps, but equally impersonal.

How ridiculous it was to live in fear of a servant's disapproval. No doubt they valued a decent wage far more than they valued their employers' morals.

It was on the tip of her tongue to ask how long he had been in England.

One year? Five?

The butler also spoke with a pronounced accent.

At what point did a Frenchman lose his French accent?

The footman turned away before she could phrase her question.

She carefully opened the sealed letter. It was dated three days hence.

My dear Miss Aimes,

You no doubt do not recall me, but I was a dear friend of your parents. They often visited me before ill health incapacitated them. Please accept my condolences, belated though they are. My own health is precarious. It prevents me from traveling; otherwise I most assuredly would have expressed my sympathies in person.

I would this letter were not necessary. The superintendent of police, apprised of your holiday in London and aware of my former friendship with your family, sought my advice. It is with deep regret that I inform you that your mother's grave has been vandalized in a most monstrous manner. I will not distress you with the details, other than to say it is the work of grisly men. We will await your instructions. Please forward your response and I will make the necessary arrangements that your blessed mother may once again rest in peace.

W. Sturges Bourne

Anne stared at the signature, precisely written with a broad nibbed pen.

William Sturges Bourne was the Earl of Granville. She had never met him, but her parents had spoken of him with the pity that those who enjoy uncertain health reserve for those who in the prime of their life are struck down by misfortune. By the time Anne had reached a presentable age her mother had become bedridden and her parents' visits to the earl had ceased.

A plate slid onto the table in front of her. The smell of bacon and eggs clogged in her throat.

Revulsion sped through her at the thought of her mother's grave being desecrated. What details did the earl not want to distress her with? What necessary arrangements needed to be made so that her mother once again rested in peace?

Anne's first instinct was to contact her solicitor.

She did not need to hear his words to know what he would advise.

"Coffee or tea, mademoiselle?"

Her head jerked up. The handsome brunet footman stood beside her chair, patiently waiting.

Anne realized that her stomach churned with more than revulsion.

She did not want to go back. To once again become immersed in the death and misery that permeated the very grounds of the Dover estate.

Her parents had been dead for ten months.

When would it end?

"I beg your pardon. What did you say?" she asked, mouth dry.

"I asked if mademoiselle would care for coffee or tea."

His amber eyes seemed to say another thing entirely. *Duty . . . or desire?* they seemed to ask. *Selfish pleasure . . . or filial responsibility?*

But in the end there was no choice.

She had let her mother down once. She would not do so again.

"Please send Raoul in."

The liveried footman bowed; at the same time he stepped back out of her vision. "As you will, mademoiselle."

As *she* willed.

Metal clattered behind her. Sunlight warmed her face.

Anne reread the letter.

The wording was old-fashioned. Overly dramatic. A letter written by an old man who no doubt made the antics of some rambunctious schoolchildren into a more heinous crime.

There was no need to be alarmed.

She would arrive and find that her mother's tombstone had been vandalized with paint or some such thing.

Her pain and suffering was over.

As was Anne's.

The tense wire running through her shoulders eased.

She had had the courage to solicit sexual favors. She had then had the courage to endure a gynecologist's examination.

It was time to go back and make her peace with her mother. To forgive both of them.

The contract with Michel was binding. She did not need to choose between duty and desire. There was time enough for both.

"You sent for me, mademoiselle?"

The butler stood in the open doorway, hands behind his back.

Anne folded the letter and straightened her shoulders with resolution. "When will Monsieur des Anges return?"

"I do not know."

Anne knew how long it would take to travel to Dover by coach. *Too long.*

Her heart leaped at her daring.

"I would like a train schedule for Dover, please."

"*Très bien.* I will send a footman to the station."

"I have never ridden on a train." She tilted her chin, defying etiquette, which forbade personal exchanges of any sort between a servant and gentry. *Defying society that forbade the union between a man who was renown for pleasuring women and a spinster who desperately yearned to experience pleasure.* "Is it safe for an unchaperoned woman to travel on one?"

"It is, mademoiselle. Dover is only sixty-three miles away. A short distance. Many of the trains have special compartments for women only. I will see you safely boarded. A coachman or groom may meet you at the Dover station."

Anne swallowed more pride. "My visit is not expected. Would there be a cab available at the station, do you think?"

Raoul stared at a point over her head. "If I may say so, mademoiselle, it would be in your best interests to arrange for transportation before you board the train here in London. It is not safe for a woman to loiter in a station alone."

Dover was a bustling port town. If there was not a cabstand at the station, there were bound to be cabs in the near vicinity. "Then I will just have to take my chances."

"You could always send a telegram, mademoiselle, and arrange for someone to meet you. I could take care of that for you after you board the train."

Such a simple solution.

Her estate bordered the town of Dover. A groom could meet her with a gig.

How sheltered she was.

Not only was she ignorant about the basic economy of the price of bread, but she was dependent upon her servants to arrange her very life.

No more.

"Yes. Thank you. What a splendid suggestion." She smiled warmly. "I would like writing materials, please."

If Michel did not return before she left, she would leave him a letter explaining that it had become necessary that she leave London for a day or so.

Heat flooded her cheeks. *She could not return to Dover without a corset.*

She tilted her chin, knowing that the entire household would soon learn of her lack of proper attire. As society would soon learn of her association with Michel des Anges. "And I will need a maid to help me change."

Raoul bowed, his face hidden from her view. *"Très bien."*

Chapter 16

Smoke and steam spiraled up from the waterlogged ruins of the bedchamber. Michael stared down at the withered, charred body nestled among a bed of ashes and coiled wire springs.

It was unrecognizable.

No silver hair for a halo. No silver eyes to cast mocking barbs.

The skull and face were smashed.

Michael had fought with the fire brigade to extinguish the fire. Then he had fought the firemen to enter the smoking remains of the House of Gabriel.

Too late.

Gabriel had died before the fire ever started.

Dawn had passed. Noon had passed.

The battle was over.

Michael trembled. And did not know why he was so cold when the walls continued to smoke with heat.

"Come away, sir. This place ain't safe. It could tumble down around our ears any minute. Come along, now." Fingers grasped Michael's coat. "There ain't nothin' more to do here."

The emotion he had been unable to feel only seconds earlier fountained through him, a geyser of rage, pain, and grief. He jerked his arm out of the man's grasp. "Get your fucking hand off me."

"Sir, it ain't safe. Please. There ain't nothin' to do for your friend 'ere."

Yes, there was one thing he could do.

He had not been able to save Gabriel from the man. But he could protect him from the collapse of his house.

Leaning over, Michael carefully lifted Gabriel's body into his arms.

Heat seared his hands, his coat, his chest.

Michael did not feel the pain.

Diane had been heavier when he had dragged her out of the blazing inferno that she had turned her bedroom into. But Diane had not been reduced to bones held together by charred skin and sinew.

Slowly, careful not to jar Gabriel, he carried him out of his house, which had brought him no pleasure and now never would.

Michael blinked. Sunlight pierced the overhanging cloud of smoke. The fire brigade had dispersed. Men and women crowded the street, gawking, pointing, talking, laughing. A barrow was parked near the curb. Copper pennies and ginger beer frenziedly exchanged hands.

"Gie' 'im t' us, sir. 'E needs t' rest o'er 'ere, 'e does."

Two men held either end of a stretcher.

Michael protectively tightened his grip; bones ground together. They did not belong to Michael.

Kaleidoscopic images flashed in front of his eyes.

Diane. Her burned body clasped to his chest. Men taking her away from him. Men taking Gabriel away from him.

History repeating itself.

Time to let go.

Michael gently laid Gabriel on the stretcher. The men took him away.

"Monsieur." Gaston stepped up to Michael. His nightshirt was stuffed inside wool trousers; his feet were bare. He twisted his hands. "We could not save him. We tried. We could not save him."

Michael was the only one who could have saved him.

Blood throbbed in his temples. His lungs hurt. His eyes burned. The man must have known about Gabriel. Why had he killed him *now?*

"How many died?" he asked curtly.

"Just Monsieur Gabriel. No one else. The fire . . . it burst out of his *chambre*. We tried, monsieur."

Whereas Michael had taken no precautions to protect his one and only friend.

"Tell the employees that they will be paid through the month."

Month carried over the cacophony of the crowd.

All he had wanted was one month. One woman.

What had Gabriel wanted?

Had he known when the man struck?

Had he experienced an explosion of pain and wondered *why?*

"Our . . . everything, it is gone," Gaston said in a rush. "We have nothing, no money—"

"I told you everyone will be paid," Michael bit out angrily.

He was not prepared to lose Gabriel.

Gaston's face, underneath the soot and smoke, turned crimson. "We have no place to go, monsieur," he said with quiet dignity.

Michael reined in his anger.

Gabriel had taken care of them, his homeless people and French immigrants. Somehow he had always found them work, a place to live—through Michael, through clients. But now Gabriel was dead.

Who would take care of Gabriel's people when Michael died?

"Go to the Hôtel du Piedmonts. I will arrange payment. Tell the concierge what is needed in the way of clothing. He will take care of it."

"*Merci,* monsieur." Gaston's shoulders straightened. "Shall I make arrangements for Monsieur Gabriel?"

Michael had left instructions in his will in the event of his own demise. Had Gabriel?

Did it matter?

Funerals did not bring back the dead.

"No. I will take care of it."

But not now.

Now he had to worry about the living.

Michael no longer knew whom the man would strike. Or when.

Did Gabriel's murderer lurk in the crowd, sipping a ginger beer?

Did he plan another visit tonight?

Would he try to take Anne? Or would he try to kill her?

Michael refused to enter the first two cabs he hailed. The cabbies' loud curses proved their honesty. He climbed into the third cab.

The stench of burned flesh overrode the smells of old leather and damp hay. Roses would not mask the odor.

Silently he let himself into his town house.

He could not smell the hyacinth plant over the reek of Gabriel's burned flesh.

He wanted a bath. He wanted Anne.

He wanted the nightmare to end.

John, a golden-haired footman, stepped out from around the marble staircase and blocked his way.

Michael stopped short.

He had instructed John to guard Anne. Even as he looked into the footman's cerulean blue eyes—eyes that had seen too much poverty and too many perversions—he knew Anne was gone.

The footman calmly reached inside his black jacket. He held out an envelope to Michael. "You have a letter, sir."

Michael tensed. *Goddamn it.* He wouldn't lose her. "Where is she?" he snarled, knowing the answer.

The man had taken everything.

"The letter, sir." John continued to hold out the envelope. "I was told to give it to you."

Michael didn't want to read a fucking letter.

He wanted Anne.

He wanted to know who thought sterling coin was worth so many lives.

"Where's Raoul?"

"I was told to tell you that the letter would explain what you need to know, sir."

Violence would do no good.

John was not afraid of death. Of pain.

He was too much like Gabriel.

With one exception.

He had gotten out of the business before it had taken away his soul.

Michael snatched the envelope out of the footman's hand.

The handwriting was masculine. Familiar.

Michael felt the blood drain out of his head. He ripped open the envelope.

There was no mistaking the handwriting.

A high-pitched hum rang inside his ears.

He remembered Gabriel's body. How weightless it had been.

He remembered Gabriel's face, smashed beyond recognition.

He realized how cleverly he and Anne had both been manipulated. *By lust. By love.*

Michael had walked into the man's trap as easily as Anne now walked into it.

He glanced up. John's face was impassive. "When was this letter delivered?"

"Three hours ago."

While Michael was conveniently away, fighting to save his *friend's* life.

"Who delivered it?"

John did not have to answer.

When would the games end?

"When did Anne leave?"

"Three hours ago."

"Did the *messenger* accompany her?" he snapped.

"No, sir. Raoul did. He escorted her to the train station."

Anne would arrive in Dover in time for tea.

The man would offer her refreshment. And she would drink it.

And there was *nothing* Michael could do to stop it.

"Miss Aimes wrote a letter, sir."

"Where is it?"

"I believe it is in the trash bin, sir. Raoul would know best."

Raoul.

Butler. Caretaker. *Pawn.*

Every man has his price.

He wondered what lie the butler would have fabricated to explain Anne's absence.

How long would Raoul have attempted to delay him?

Bending his head, Michael carefully refolded the letter and

slipped it back into the envelope. Opening his jacket, he slid it inside the pocket slit in the silk lining, thoughts racing, ideas forming.

Slowly he raised his head. "And has Raoul returned from his trip to the train station?" he asked evenly, his gaze pinning the footman.

"He is in the kitchen," John returned imperturbably. He stepped aside.

Michael could not afford to hope. But he did.

For one desperate second he hoped that friendship was stronger than jealousy. Greed. Hate.

"Did he tell you to inform on my butler, John?"

John stared straight ahead. "No, sir. I was concerned for the lady."

Either he lied . . . or he told the truth.

Michael believed him.

No one commanded complete loyalty. The letter in his hand was proof.

Downstairs, the scent of roasting meat filled the air; a beef roast instead of human flesh. Mrs. Banting, his cook; Marie, his housekeeper; and Raoul, his butler, sat at a long, rectangular, maple wood table. The cook, a short, plump woman with apple red cheeks who had always reminded Michael of an elderly fairy he had once seen portrayed in a children's storybook, peeled a potato. Marie, steel-rimmed glasses perched on her nose, wrote in a ledger. A glass and a bottle of gin sat in front of Raoul. Both containers were half-empty.

Or perhaps Raoul saw them as half-full.

The cook was the first to see Michael. She jumped up and awkwardly curtsied, potato in one hand and a paring knife in the other. "Sir."

Marie glanced up, her expression freezing. The tip of her steel nib audibly snapped. Raoul alone remained undisturbed by Michael's presence. He reached out and poured more gin into his glass.

A malicious smile curled Michael's lips.

Raoul's hand visibly shook, belying his unconcern.

He *should* be afraid.

"Mrs. Banting, please get me a box of matches," he politely ordered.

"Yes, sir. Of course, sir. Are you all right, sir? I heard about the fire. Is Mr. Gabriel all right, sir?"

Gin splattered onto the maple wood table. Marie jerked the bottle out of Raoul's hand and slammed it down.

Her hand shook, too.

Which of the two, his butler or his housekeeper, had been most eager to betray him? he wondered.

"The matches, Mrs. Banting. I am waiting."

The cook dropped the knife and potato into a large aluminum bowl filled with peels and potatoes. Wiping her hands on her apron, she hurried across the kitchen and nervously fumbled on a shelf near the black iron cooking stove. She returned with a box of matches, flinching away from his fingers when he took it from her hand.

"Thank you," Michael said gently. "You may leave now."

Bushy gray eyebrows shot up her wrinkled forehead. "But, sir, dinner—"

"Is cooking. I know, Mrs. Banting." Michael refocused on Raoul and Marie. "I won't take long. I have several bottles of an excellent sherry dated 1872. Be so kind as to fetch one from the cellar. I'm sure you will find it much more palatable than gin."

"Now see 'ere," Mrs. Banting protested, revealing her gutter origins, another one of Gabriel's homeless people. "I only 'ave a bit of a nip 'ere and now t' take th' chill out o' me bones—"

Michael did not care if she bathed in gin every night, so long as she performed her duties.

He spared her a glance. Her normally flushed cheeks were pale, revealing a broken network of veins that were the source of her perpetual rosy glow. "Go, Mrs. Banting."

The cook fled. Marie snapped shut her journal and folded her glasses.

Raoul still did not look up.

Michael slid open the box, retrieved a match, struck it, and walked over to the table. He dropped the flaming stick into the glass of gin.

Blue flame swooshed upward.

Marie gasped and jumped up from the table.

The smile twisting Michael's lips widened. "Imagine if I had fed you that match, Raoul."

"He didn't harm her!" Marie shrilled.

For the butler's sake, he hoped not.

"What *did* you do, Raoul?"

Raoul looked up. His eyes were glassy from drink. "I escorted Mademoiselle Aimes to the train station. To protect her."

Michael lit another match. For the first time in five years he relished the yellow teeth that ate wood, paper, *skin.*

"Did you look inside the trunk that you so anxiously apprised me of to see the results of a man being fed fire, I wonder? It's not a pretty sight."

"I do not know what you are talking about. I opened no trunk."

Perhaps not. It had been locked.

How long had the man planned for this moment? How many men had it taken to see it through?

One, two, three, four?

The fire steadily burned.

"Five years ago. How did he know that Lady Wenterton traveled to Brighton?"

"I telegraphed him."

Michael saw Diane's laughing face. She had blown kisses from the train.

It had been the last time he had seen her laugh.

Heat licked Michael's fingers. "Did you know what he was going to do to her?"

Raoul's gaze did not waver from Michael's. "*Non.*"

"But you sent Mademoiselle Aimes to him. Knowing that Lady Wenterton killed herself because of what he had done to her."

"*Oui.*"

"*C'est un mensonge!*" Marie hissed. "She killed herself because she was a whore. No woman can live with herself if she gives up her children!"

Michael ignored her. The man would not.

"Why did you do it, Raoul?"

Raoul's gaze slid away from Michael's. He reached over the blazing glass of gin for the bottle. "*L'argent,* monsieur. We cannot all make our fortunes by selling our bodies."

The glass exploded. Blue fire spit into the air; it simultaneously spread across the maple tabletop in a liquid sheet of blazing heat.

Raoul jumped up, wooden chair careening across the floor, alarmed now that his own life was at stake. He frantically slapped at his flaming shirtsleeve.

Michael dropped the match onto the burning table. "Everything has a price, Raoul. Remember that when next you close your eyes to sleep."

He turned around and walked away.

Neither of them would live long enough to enjoy the money.

The man would see to that.

Chapter 17

Anne had heard that the earl's estate was guarded more securely than Buckingham Palace, yet the gatekeeper had unquestioningly granted her entrance, as had the rail-thin butler.

She followed the butler up the sweeping mahogany staircase. No runner softened their discordant steps. Her silk drawers, chemise, petticoats, and stockings whispered against her skin, her treat to herself, a reminder of the pleasure she had experienced the night before. Black wool rustled about her feet, her concession to her mother, a reminder of the mourning that she was still in.

The earl's home was palatial, a mausoleum of rich wood paneling, priceless paintings, and elegant, antique furniture. Surely a house this large employed a veritable army of servants, she thought uneasily: grooms, gardeners, footmen, parlor maids, housemaids.

Where were they?

An elevator waited at the top of the stairs, metal door barred. Brass and crystal wall sconces dotted the hallway; they emitted glaring electric light. It did not alleviate the darkness of the mahogany wall paneling and floor.

Her footsteps ricocheted down the long, endless corridor. *She should have gone straight to the cemetery,* they cautioned her, and seen for herself what the vandalism was before visiting the earl.

Too late, the butler's footsteps answered: the earl had agreed to see her.

A rose damask-covered rococo chair rigidly stood at attention near the end of the hallway. The butler threw open the door beside it. "Miss Aimes, my lord," he announced before stepping aside to allow her entrance.

Anne clutched her black-beaded reticule.

The back of a gray-haired man faced the doorway. He sat in a wheelchair in front of a massive mahogany fireplace, wooden frame silhouetted by orange and yellow flames. Above his head on the mantelpiece, blue Sèvres vases flanked a sculpted white marble clock. Windows on either side admitted waning sunlight. A tea cart was parked between the earl and a latticed Chippendale armchair.

Every instinct warned her not to enter the bedchamber. Her common sense ridiculed her apprehension.

She was no stranger to the sickroom.

The Earl of Granville was old and crippled. He could not harm her.

He was a former friend of her parents. There was no reason he would *want* to harm her.

Ignoring the warning tingles that trailed up and down her spine, Anne stepped inside. The bedroom door softly closed behind her.

"Welcome to my home, Miss Aimes. I hope you do not mind visiting an old man in his private chambers." The earl did not turn his head. His voice, genial and cultured, clearly carried across the room. "Please come sit beside me."

Anne did not want to take a seat. She wanted to escape back into air that was not tainted with the smell of carbolic disinfectant. Immediately she was ashamed of her thoughts.

The earl had not asked to be an invalid. He, too, had suffered from circumstances outside his control.

"Thank you, Lord Granville. It was very kind of you to see me."

Her shoes clicked a hollow trail across the vast expanse of wooden floor. The tinny echo drove home to her just how isolated the earl's estate was and just how far removed she was from the life she had lived before venturing to London.

In the last few days she had thrice accompanied strange men:

Michel, Gabriel, and the man who had met her at the station, a new groom hired by her bailiff in her absence.

A whimsical smile touched her lips.

And now here she was, visiting a strange man in his bedchamber.

She rounded the latticed armchair; heat blasted the smile off of her face. Gingerly she perched on the edge of the maroon velvet-upholstered seat.

The earl's face was pale with pain and wrinkled with age. She judged him to be in his early seventies. He looked like a man who had had few pleasures in his life—or wanted them. His eyes—faded, rheumy eyes whose color was indistinguishable in the uncertain light—stared at her shrewdly, as if assessing her reaction to his infirmity. "Forgive me for not rising."

Anne's gaze slid away from his. "There is no need to apologize, my lord."

Two gilt-edged cups and saucers rested on the tea cart. A silver-covered serving dish sat between matching cream and sugar containers. It was weighted down by a small stack of folded white linen napkins. Lemon wedges were piled in a small silver bowl. Steam rose from the silver teapot, as if the tea were freshly brewed.

As if the earl had expected her.

Anne fought down a new wave of uneasiness.

A faint, rhythmic click resonated over the monotonous *tick, tick, tick* of the mantel clock.

Her gaze unerringly settled on the earl's right hand; it rested on the thin wooden arm of his wheelchair.

He rolled something between his fingers. Something that gleamed like silver . . . She glimpsed two metal balls. They were somewhat larger than the marbles she had seen village children play with.

A log collapsed in the fireplace; sparks and yellow flame flew up the chimney.

Jerking her gaze back to his, she licked lips that suddenly felt parched. "I want to thank you for your letter, my lord. It was very kind of you to take it upon yourself to notify me of the vandalism to my mother's grave."

"Not at all, Miss Aimes." *Click. Click. Click.* "Your parents were particular friends of mine. We spent many an evening playing piquet."

He smiled. There was something vaguely familiar about that smile. "Would you care for tea, my dear?"

"I do not wish to intrude on your hospitality, my lord. Obviously you are expecting a guest. I will take only a few moments of your time."

"Nonsense. You are not intruding on my hospitality. My guest will not be here for some time," he replied cordially. "Please do me the honor of pouring. You have no idea how much I hoped you would visit when I wrote that unfortunate letter. I do not go out now. It is a lonely life, being old and sick. But then you know that, do you not, my dear?"

Yes, she did know that. Most of the people who had attended her parents' funeral had not visited them in years.

"Thank you." She tugged her black silk gloves off of her fingers and reached for a napkin. "I would enjoy some refreshment."

Anne poured, reminded of another teapot, stoneware instead of silver. Of another man, silver-haired rather than gray. Of eyes staring, probing. *Watching.*

Hair prickling on the nape of her neck, she carefully placed the heavy silver teapot on the tea tray. Lifting her head, she caught his gaze. "Would you care for sugar, Lord Granville? Cream? Lemon?"

A cloud of steam hovered between them.

He smiled blandly. "I will have whatever you have, my dear."

Her lips involuntarily tightened. Gabriel had said much the same thing when the waiter at the pastry shop had taken her order.

He had followed her, Michel's silver-eyed, silver-haired friend. Why did she suddenly feel as if the earl, too, had been spying on her?

Anne added two cubes of sugar to first his cup of tea and then hers. The earl did not touch his. She wished she had followed his example.

It tasted as if she had added bitters rather than sugar.

Hastily she set the delicate bone china cup into its saucer. "You said that my mother's grave had been vandalized in a 'monstrous manner.' Exactly what was the nature of the vandalism, Lord Granville?"

His busy fingers paused. The *tick, tick, tick* of the marble clock was inordinately loud over the roar of the fire. "Is not the tea to your liking, Miss Aimes? Pardon me, servants do take advantage of a crippled old man. I will ring for fresh—"

"No, no, it's fine, really." Anne lifted her cup and forced down another swallow. "Has the superintendent of police—"

"You must miss your mother very much, my dear." His voice cut through hers; he resumed the rhythmical rolling of the two silver balls. "She died two days after your father, I believe. It was very tragic. Most unfortunate."

Anne set her cup down. And lied. "Yes, it was."

Both her father and her mother had been riddled with uncontrollable pain. Their deaths had been a blessing.

"Do you enjoy London, Miss Aimes?"

Click. Click. Click.

Sweat formed on her forehead. The earl seemed unaffected by the blazing heat only a few feet away from them. "Yes, I find that I quite enjoy it, thank you."

"It must have been difficult to tear yourself away from your friends. London is a gay town, not like our staid country life here."

An image of the House of Gabriel flashed through her mind. Of disreputable women and wealthy gentlemen.

Light flickered in the earl's faded eyes. As if he guessed her thoughts. *As if he knew exactly how she had spent her time in London.*

Had gossip spread that quickly?

"The vandalism, Lord Granville," she said firmly.

"Forgive me, an old man's mind sometimes wanders. Do drink your tea, there's a good girl. We don't want it to get cold. Are you quite certain you don't want me to ring for another pot?"

Anne remembered how lonely her parents had been. How eager

for company that rarely came. How pitifully anxious they had been when it did.

She resignedly reached for her cup. The flavor of the tea did not improve with the third sip.

"Have you ever been in love, Miss Aimes?"

"Have you, sir?" she riposted politely.

"Yes, Miss Aimes, I have."

Lord Granville was the second person who confessed to having loved. Man. Woman. Friends. Lovers.

Or perhaps the earl had loved a man. *As a lover.*

She determinedly swallowed another sip of tea.

"Then you are fortunate." She set down her cup with finality. "I do not believe love is a highly prized commodity in our society."

"That is because people are afraid. Money is more material. But you aren't afraid, are you, my dear?"

Yes.

Anne was afraid of many things. Loneliness. Growing old. Dying . . . *alone*. But she did not visit the earl to discuss her fears.

The relentless *click, click, click* was beginning to wear on her nerves.

"You have spoken to the superintendent of police, my lord. Does he have any idea as to who is the culprit?"

"You are uncomfortable talking about love." Speculation flickered in his eyes, and something else, something dark that was gone even as she tried to name it. "Why is that, I wonder?"

Perspiration trickled down her temple. Moisture pooled underneath her breasts.

"I do not think that I am qualified to discuss the subject, Lord Granville," she said stiffly. "Perhaps another day—"

"There is a poem that I often reflect upon," he interrupted trenchantly. "It is by Andrew Marvell. In it a man attempts to convince his lady love to sample the pleasures of the marriage bed. 'The grave's a fine and private place, / but none, I think, do there embrace,' he tells her. It is quite prophetic. Have you ever read the poem?"

The heat that flashed through Anne owed nothing to the roaring fire in front of her. Discussing sexual love with a man who professed to be Michel's friend was one thing; this was another matter entirely.

She crumpled her napkin and dropped it onto the tea cart beside her cup and saucer. "No, I have not. I told my groom I would be only a few minutes. The horse will be restive. If you will excuse me—"

"Spring is such an unpredictable season, is it not?" he cut in smoothly, rheumy eyes guileless. "I confess, I never seem to get warm enough. My manservant took advantage of your visit to have a few moments to himself. Would you mind terribly fetching a quilt from my chest?"

Courtesy demanded that she see to his comfort before she took her leave. "No, of course not."

Stuffing her gloves and reticule between her hip and the chair arm, she stood up and glanced about the long, rectangular bedchamber. It was paneled in the same dark mahogany that lined the hallway. What fire and sunlight the paneling did not consume, the dark four-poster bed did.

"The chest is on the other side of the bed, my dear," he affably instructed her, as if unaware of the social gaffe he had committed or her eagerness to escape. "Against the far wall. The quilt is in the top drawer."

Anne walked into the blessedly cool shadows.

A life-size portrait hung on the wall beside the chest of drawers. A young man leaned against a horse, quirt in hand, chiseled lips curved in a faintly mocking smile.

She had seen that smile before.

The young man had black hair that was curled in a manner considered fashionable in the early 1830s. It looked blue in the dim light.

Anne retrieved the quilt, eyes trained on the portrait. She could almost make out the color of the young man's eyes.

She could almost remember seeing him.

Dancing. Laughing. Weaving through a forest of jewel-colored gowns and black formal wear while the music soared—

"I was rather a handsome chap in my salad days, was I not, Miss Aimes?"

Starting guiltily, Anne turned away from the portrait.

Lord Granville had soundlessly maneuvered his wheelchair to the four-poster bed. He reached for the stained-glass Tiffany lamp on the nightstand. "Some say that my nephew is the spitting image of me. What do you think?"

She thought that his mind wandered.

His nephew had died two years after the accident that had claimed the earl's mobility, his only brother, sister-in-law and three nieces.

Electric light circled him, a very proper old gentleman dressed in a starched white shirt, black tie, tweed wool trousers, and a dark burgundy velvet smoking jacket with black satin lapels. Dropping his hand, he fully faced her. Smiling. Waiting for Anne to tuck the quilt around his wasted legs.

Anne reluctantly complied.

He suddenly did not seem so helpless. *So harmless.*

His legs through the dark green quilt and tweed wool trousers were more bone than flesh. The fingers on his right hand continued to rhythmically move, silver flashing, metal clicking.

Glancing up, she caught his gaze.

The earl's irises were translucent in the lamplight, like violet colored glass. His contracted pupils were as black as jet beads.

It dawned on her who the earl reminded her of when he smiled. *It dawned on her who the man in the portrait reminded her of.*

Anne jerked upright, her heart pounding. "It was unforgivable of me to intrude on you without notice, Lord Granville. Pray do not trouble yourself anymore. I will see myself out."

A satisfied smile blossomed across his aged face. "I am flattered, Miss Aimes. You do see the resemblance."

She backed away on rubbery legs. "I do not know what you are talking about."

"Of course you do, my dear." He continued smiling and rolling the two silver balls between long, shapely fingers. *Click. Click. Click.* His fingers were the same length and breadth as the scarred ones that had fondled her breasts. Massaged her clitoris. *Penetrated her vagina.* "You see the resemblance between me and my nephew. The man whom you paid ten thousand pounds to fuck you."

She bumped into wood. *Hard.* Porcelain rattled; silver clattered.

He stared at her, mildly curious, as if he had not just claimed the most notorious stallion in England for a relative. As if he did not know that she had paid ten thousand pounds. *So his* nephew *would fuck her.*

But he didn't have a legitimate nephew. The boy had died twenty-seven years earlier.

Gossip about her sexual liaison was bound to reach Dover, but not the monetary arrangements.

Mr. Little would not betray a client's confidence. The earl could have obtained his information from only one other source.

Michel des Anges had known all along who she was.

Lies. Everything he had said had all been *lies.*

His desire for friendship. Intimacy. *The pleasure he derived from a spinster's gratification.*

There was only one reason she had been lured back to Dover.

"My mother's grave was not vandalized." Anne held the earl's gaze. Forcefully she tamped down the pain that chuckled and bubbled inside her chest. "Was it, Lord Granville?"

"Wasn't it?" he asked politely.

"While you are to be commended for claiming a by-blow for a nephew, I am afraid you have made a grievous error." She inched around the tea cart, trying to preserve her dignity while keeping her face turned toward the earl. *Another man who had fallen on hard times.* "You may circulate whatever defamation you wish. I will not pay either you or Michel des Anges more than the ten thousand pounds that we agreed upon."

An odd smile played about his lips; it sent a cold shiver shimmying down her back. "I never expected that you would, Miss Aimes."

More lies.

"Then we will forget this day," she said. And knew that she too lied.

She would never forget this day. This moment.

No wonder she had not been able to envision the man who had claimed he wanted to be her lover inside a cheap pastry shop. His blood was more blue, if not as respectable, than was hers.

Had that been what Gabriel had wanted her to understand?

That her *lover* was the bastard nephew of an earl?

Her gloves . . . Ah, there they were, they had slid between the cushion and the chair. She scooped up her reticule—and promptly stumbled forward.

Mortification at her clumsiness scorched her cheeks. She hurriedly straightened, determined to show that she was unscathed by the earl and his nephew's attempt to inveigle money from a love-starved spinster. "Good day, sir."

"I do not think so, Miss Aimes."

Anne ignored the earl. The mahogany floor between her and the door yawned before her. Memories turned her legs to lead, images of her taking Michel into her mouth; of him caressing her back and buttocks while she propped her leg on the toilet seat and fished about inside her vagina.

She had been happy. For three days and nights she had been given more joy than she had known in her entire life.

Anne had always known that no man—especially a man such as Michel des Anges—would want a thirty-six-year-old spinster for more than her money.

Why did the truth hurt so much?

Please, God, she prayed, *just let me get to the door. Don't let me cry in front of this man.*

God answered her prayer.

She gratefully wrenched open the door.

A man dressed in black blocked her progress. He had receding sandy hair.

Recognition slammed through Anne.

He was the butler her solicitor had hired to oversee her London town house. *A picture of English moral rectitude.*

"Shut the door, Frank, there's a good boy. Miss Aimes is not ready for you yet."

Face expressionless, the sandy-haired man obediently pulled

the door closed. Pale features shone in the polished mahogany. They were capped by a black, featherless hat.

Her parents' worst fear was coming to pass: she was being held hostage for ransom.

Heart hammering against her ribs, Anne whirled around. The room whirled with her. "You cannot keep me here against my will. My groom—"

Her jaws snapped together.

Gabriel's voice mocked her. *A lone woman should never accompany a stranger.*

How neatly she had played into their hands.

Isolating herself by staying with Michel. Taking the train with no escort. *Accompanying a man who claimed to be recently hired by her bailiff.*

The earl's faded violet eyes gleamed with malice. "You are very astute, Miss Aimes. Yes, the man who drove you here was hired by me. Or perhaps I should say, he was hired by Frank. Frank is very thorough in these matters."

"My servants are expecting me, Lord Granville. If I do not soon arrive they will summon a constable."

"Come, come, Miss Aimes," he mockingly chided. "You must by now realize that no one is expecting you. Raoul telegraphed me, not your servants. How else do you think I would have been prepared for you?"

How many people did it take to abduct one woman? she wondered on a wave of horror.

A lover. An earl. A blond-haired butler who was not a butler. Jane—had she been an abigail, or an accomplice? Raoul—was *he* a butler?

Was Gabriel a friend of her *lover?* Or simply a beautiful man hired to follow her, to ensure she did not stray or come to harm before her money was harvested?

She remembered the man with the blue-black hair who had stood outside her solicitor's office.

And knew that it had been Michel.

She squared her shoulders. "My solicitor will go to Scotland Yard."

"Your solicitor is dead. His corpse was delivered to my nephew."

Mr. Little. *Dead.*

Anne's heart stopped beating. The clock continued ticking.

"I created a special greeting to accompany the delivery," the earl preened. " 'From one solicitor to another.' Although there are, of course, far more derogatory terms for my nephew. Whore comes to mind. Still, I thought it was a rather clever play on professional titles, don't you?"

Anne saw again the black trunk inside the solicitor's office. Smelled again the stench of charred flesh.

And knew exactly when he had been delivered.

She had comforted Michel—*no, no, Gabriel had confirmed that Michel was Michael in French, not that it was his name. Dear God, she didn't even know the name of the man whose flesh she had taken into her body and her mouth*—for the death of a business acquaintance.

For the death of Mr. Little.

Her heart lurched inside her chest; raced to catch up with the ticking clock.

Incongruously she realized it had not been fear that had hardened her nipples when Gabriel had confronted her in the rain; it had been the cold that had done so.

This was fear, the ice that coursed through her veins. She had no nipples, no limbs, no fingers. Her entire body had been converted into living, breathing terror.

"I will scream." She bit the insides of her cheeks to keep from doing the very thing she threatened to do. "A servant is bound to come to my aid. You cannot hold a woman against her will."

"I beg to differ, Miss Aimes. I have. And I will again. My servants will not hear you. Those who might be sympathetic to your plight, that is. I sent them on a holiday for the next few days. By the time they return, no one will be the wiser."

"I will give you money," she offered desperately. "All the money you wish."

"I have no need of your money."

No need of her money! Then what—

She took a deep breath. She *would not* panic.

"Then what do you want from me?"

"I want you to understand."

Anne cringed at the familiar words. "Understand what?"

"I want you to understand that you cannot escape the consequences of killing your mother."

She gritted her teeth. "I did not . . . kill . . . my mother."

She had not had the courage to.

Her mother had begged her to release her from the pain, *and she had done nothing.*

"Come now, Miss Aimes. You cared for your mother. You nursed her. You slept in a room adjoining hers so that you could minister to her. She was found on the floor, cold and stiff. Did you not hear her fall? Did you not hear her cries for help?"

Pain crowded the fear that thudded throughout her body. She had heard it all before, village whispers deliberately pitched so that she could hear them.

Had Michel secretly laughed at her, when she told him she knew what it was like to be an object of curiosity?

It wasn't her marital status that inspired their gossip, he had told her. It was her *wealth.*

Why hadn't she listened to what he said instead of what she wanted to hear?

"I . . . did not . . . kill . . . my mother," she repeated more stridently.

"Of course you did, my dear. And you will be punished for it. But there are other things you must first understand."

Darkness edged Anne's vision. She swayed, caught the doorknob behind her to prevent herself from falling face-first onto the floor. Her gloves and reticule dropped from suddenly numb fingers, a whisper of sound and a jarring plop. She leaned against the door to keep from collapsing.

Horror clogged her throat. "You put something in the tea."

"Don't worry, Miss Aimes." The earl expertly maneuvered his chair to the tea cart and brushed the napkins off of the lid on the silver serving dish. He carefully lifted it, as if afraid of spilling whatever was inside. "The paralysis will be temporary."

Securing the silver dish on his lap, he rolled the chair toward her. The track of wheels on the wooden floor grated along her spine. "You will not be able to move or speak, but you will be able to hear. And think. And remember."

The wheelchair stopped five feet away from her. He stared up at her, rheumy eyes intent. "Oh, yes, Miss Aimes, you will most definitely be able to think and remember."

"You are insane," she whispered.

This entire situation was insane.

Why would the earl and his illegitimate nephew do this to her if they did not want her money?

The earl watched her speculatively. "Do you know, my dear, that is what those who lack power always say about those who are in power. One becomes quite the philosopher when confined to a wheelchair. A point of example: we all possess one distinguishing quality that will either bring us great joy or immeasurable suffering. Twenty-nine years ago my nephew was a very loving boy. Contrary to what the Greeks taught us, guilt is the other side of love, not hate. Imagine the pain an eleven-year-old boy felt, knowing that he was responsible for the death of his family."

She knew what the earl was doing. *She would not be made to feel guilty.*

The accident that had taken the boy's life had been just that—*an accident.*

Her mother's death had been an accident.

Anne had gone to sleep.

While her mother tried to get out of bed and do the job Anne had refused to do.

She had fallen.

While Anne slept.

She had died.

While Anne slept.

"Yes, I see you do imagine how my nephew felt. Guilt is a wonderfully corrosive sentiment. It did not take him long at all to realize how selfish it was of him to enjoy life when I confronted him with the reality of death." The earl briefly touched the silver-covered dish; his face creased with reminiscent pleasure. "Now imagine Lady Wenterton, a spoiled, beautiful woman who possessed a voracious sexual appetite. There are devices, Miss Aimes, that can create excruciating desire in a woman. No doubt my nephew would have introduced you to such dreadful delights had I allowed him more time. But he was ever a naughty boy."

The last was said with indulgent reproof.

Anne felt herself sliding, sliding, sliding. . . .

Laughter welled up into her throat.

Lady Wenterton . . . *who was she?* Lustful cravings. . . . *Naughty boys who engaged in murder.*

Anne's skirt, bustle, and petticoats bunched up in the small of her back.

The urge to laugh abruptly died.

She sat on the floor, silk stockinged legs stuck out in front of her.

Paralyzed.

Desperately she rallied, trying to fight the drug. To purchase more time. *To understand what was totally incomprehensible.*

The earl and her parents were friends.

Why was he doing this to her?

Her lips were stiff; she forced the words out from between them. "Why was your nephew naughty, Lord Granville?"

"He would not kill you."

Death stared down at her.

Memory danced on the perimeter of Anne's consciousness like light on a hat pin.

Michel leaning against the library door, violet eyes flat. *Dead.*

Michel standing over her, his manhood glistening with her saliva and his arousal, steel hat pin winking.

Michel's fingers firmly gripping the back of her head while she licked and nibbled and suckled him.

Michel's passion: *I won't hurt you. I promise. No matter what, I won't hurt you.*

The earl leaned over and inspected her curiously, as if she were an insect. *Sin and cockroaches . . .*

"My nephew is aware that you are here, Miss Aimes, make no mistake of that. He cannot help you, though he will soon join you. But I digress. Imagine, if you please, this Lady Wenterton whom I mentioned. She quite fancied my nephew. Remember that I said she had a voracious sexual appetite. Imagine being consumed by lustful cravings yet being physically restrained with no means of gaining satisfaction. Imagine what that would do to a woman of her appetites."

Anne could indeed hear. And think. *And remember.*

Lady Wenterton . . . a woman of appetites.

You have never experienced intimate sex . . . or friendship . . . with another woman?

I have known such a relationship. Once. A long, long time ago.

What happened?

She died. Click. *She died.* Click. *She died.* Click.

Anne stared in dawning horror at the earl's right hand and the silver metal balls that rolled round and round between his fingers.

"And now, Miss Aimes, I want you to imagine the plight of a woman in your predicament. You are an amalgam of my nephew and Lady Wenterton. A loving daughter who also possesses a voracious sexual appetite. I can imagine the great guilt you must harbor, having killed your mother so that you would be free to gratify your passions. You have presented me with a unique opportunity."

Anne tried to scream, to argue the logic of accusing a "loving" daughter of murder.

She could not open her jaws.

"You're very tired, Miss Aimes." Silver flashed, metal clicked. The earl's eyes were bright with a malignancy that did not come from disease. "Should you like to hear more Marvell before you retire, I wonder? As I said, his poem is rather prophetic. I am sure you are curious about what I have planned for your chastisement."

Anne reached out to grab the wheelchair, to turn him over, to stop the madness.

She couldn't move; she couldn't speak.

He was going to kill her.

And she didn't know why.

"There's a good girl, don't strain yourself, you'll understand in due time." The earl knew what she was thinking. He did not mask his amusement. "Now listen up. It's really quite clear. 'But at my back I always hear / Time's winged chariot hurrying near: / And yonder all before us lie / Deserts of vast eternity. / Thy beauty shall no more be found; / Nor, in thy marble vault, shall sound / My echoing song; then worms shall try / That long preserved virginity.' "

Worms. *Vaults.*

There should not exist an emotion greater than terror: there did.

The earl laughed congenially. Sympathetically. "You are no longer a virgin, of course, but I'm sure the worms won't mind. Would you care to join your mother now? She's waiting for you."

This could not be happening.

Her mother was buried. She had tossed the first handful of dirt onto the coffin.

He wouldn't bury her alive.

Tears of helplessness welled up in her eyes.

The earl leaned closer. "Yes, I think you are ready. But you must understand: your lust brought you to this. If you had controlled your sexual appetites and stayed in Dover, you would be safe. If my nephew had controlled his lust and remained in Yorkshire, you would be safe. And lastly, Miss Aimes—look at me when I speak to you!—I want you to understand that my nephew is not a bastard."

Malevolence shone in his faded eyes. "How did it feel to be fucked by a dead man?"

Anne at last understood.

Chapter 18

A gift.

Michael clung to the thought.

The letter was a gift.

Gabriel had told him to go to the police. But he had had no evidence other than that which would have incriminated himself. Now he had concrete proof that William Sturges Bourne, the Earl of Granville, was not the benign, harmless cripple that the world believed him to be.

Why wouldn't the superintendent of police act on it?

Light and shadow shimmered around him; it reflected off of the glass topped desk, each flicker a second lost.

The superintendent of police thrust the letter back to Michael, gray wool night cap askew; at the same time he ripped off wire-rimmed glasses with his left hand. "I fail to see the urgency of your visit, sir. Come around the station in the morning. There was no need to wake me up in the middle of the night."

Michael took the letter and counted to three. "Has Mrs. Aimes's grave been vandalized?"

"Not that I know of, no."

"Did you go to the Earl of Granville, telling him that it had?"

"No, I did not, but I fail to see—"

"He has Anne Aimes."

"Now see here, my good man, Lord Granville is a morally responsible gentleman who is confined to a wheelchair. He don't go about abducting women. Miss Aimes is no doubt safely asleep in her bed, where all decent folk should be—"

"No, she's not," Michael brutally interrupted him. And lied

to further convince him of the urgent need to visit the earl. "She telegraphed her servants and told them what train she would be on. A groom met her and drove her to see the earl. She told him to come back and pick her up in an hour. When the groom returned he was not allowed back onto the estate. No one has heard from either her or the earl."

"Her estate is a goodly distance from Lord Granville's." The superintendent's bushy gray side whiskers twitched in his irritation. "No doubt she stayed the night. Visit the old lord in the morning and you'll see for yourself."

"Tomorrow morning is too late," Michael said flatly.

He suspiciously surveyed Michael. "How is it you have this letter, if it was indeed intended for Miss Aimes?"

The superintendent would dismiss him if he told the truth, that a lonely spinster had sought to buy herself a little happiness and instead had been entangled in a twenty-nine-year-old nightmare.

"Miss Aimes was staying in London with mutual friends," Michael lied again. "She did not take the letter with her when she left. Our friends, upon reading it, thought the wording peculiar and contacted me. All I am asking, Superintendent Drake, is that you and a few of your men accompany me to Lord Granville's estate. If Miss Aimes is safe, then you will have the satisfaction of knowing that you have done your best to ensure a woman's safety."

"This is not London, sir. Our lords do not molest our gentlewomen. Get out of here, or I will see that the streets are safe from the likes of you," Drake growled.

The letter made no difference.

The truth rarely did.

Michael refolded the paper and put it back inside his coat. Reaching down, he pulled out an indisputable weapon from his outer pocket. "Perhaps this will persuade you, Superintendent Drake."

Drake's jaw dropped at sight of the Adam's revolving pistol. "Now see here—"

Michael saw too damn much.

The earl was succeeding. *Again.*

He cocked the hammer, effectively silencing Drake. "You are coming with me. Now."

Drake's face turned a shade lighter than his gray hair. His side whiskers trembled. "Who do you think you are, bursting into my house like this?"

"A dead man," Michael said in all sincerity.

"My wife is upstairs."

"All the more reason to cooperate."

"I am expecting my first great-grandchild."

"Then let's not deprive it of a great-grandfather."

Michael alertly watched the older man as he eyed the top drawer in his desk. "I don't want to hurt you or your wife, Superintendent Drake. All I want is to ensure that Miss Aimes is well."

Stepping around the desk, Michael opened the drawer and retrieved the police-issue pistol there, another revolver. Drake averted his gaze away from Michael's scarred skin.

He shoved the superintendent's gun into his left pocket; metal butted metal, an instrument of death knocking against a tin filled with a whore and a spinster's salvation.

"The servant who let me in." Michael withdrew his hand from his pocket. "I want you to tell him to fetch you some clothes. Tell him you have urgent business to attend to."

"Why don't you go out to the earl's estate and see for yourself if Miss Aimes is safe?" Drake blustered.

Because Anne would not survive if the man took Michael.

And that was precisely what the earl planned.

A spinster's life to bag a whore.

"I am not a patient man," Michael said evenly. The revolver did not waver in his hand. "I suggest you hurry."

Drake had sat behind a desk for too long. He would not win in a hand-to-hand struggle with a man twenty years his junior.

He knew it. Michael knew it.

Jerkily the older man stood up. Michael stepped back to allow him to pass.

"No unexpected motions, please, Superintendent Drake. You have far more to lose than I."

The superintendent's steps were hobbled by the muzzle of the gun Michael thrust into his left kidney. When they reached the study door, Michael stepped to the side. "Remember what I said. No one need be hurt. Do not open the door all the way."

Stiffly Drake cracked open the door. "Maynard. Maynard!"

The young footman who had let Michael into the superintendent's house responded quickly. Had he listened at the keyhole? "Yes, sir?"

"There's trouble at the police station, Maynard. Be so good as to grab some clothes for me."

"Sir." The footman was clearly astonished at the constable's request. "Shall I wake your valet?"

"No, no, hurry, man, no time," Drake said, agitation translating as testiness. "I have plans to make."

"Very well, sir."

"Maynard—"

Michael tensed.

"Yes, sir?"

He could feel the superintendent's indecision.

Would the scarred man kill? Or would he run?

Would Drake live to see his great-grandchild? *Or would he die?*

The superintendent of police was not a gambler.

"Careful you don't wake Mrs. Drake," he said gruffly.

"No, sir."

Drake closed the door. He was pale but otherwise composed. "What are you going to do?"

"We are going to gather up some of your men and visit the earl," Michael replied matter-of-factly.

"There's no need to involve anyone else in this distasteful matter."

"There is every need, Superintendent Drake."

"Why?"

"I doubt if the earl would hold a superintendent of police in higher esteem than he does a solicitor."

Drake bristled. "The Earl of Granville is a law-abiding citizen. Which is more, sir, than I can say about you!"

"If he is a law-abiding citizen, he will forgive us our trespass," Michael said dryly.

"You're not from around here." Drake's eyes narrowed intently underneath his bushy gray eyebrows. "I would remember those scars."

Michael did not bother correcting him.

"When your servant knocks, open the door just wide enough to take the clothes. Dismiss him. And hand the clothes to me."

The dim echoes of a Westminster clock chimed a quarter hour.

It was the only sound in the house.

Drake jumped when the footman knocked; the first outward sign of nervousness he had thus far displayed. He jerked open the door.

"Thank you, Maynard. You may go to bed now. I don't know when I shall return home."

"Thank you, sir."

Michael shook the proffered clothing to make sure that they did not contain any concealed weapons before handing them back to the superintendent one at a time: gray woolen drawers; gray woolen vest; starched white cotton shirt; brown wool trousers; orange and brown plaid waistcoat; brown woolen socks; monogrammed handkerchief; and black shoes.

The older man turned his back and stepped into his underwear and trousers before discarding the shield of his robe and nightshirt.

Michael allowed the superintendent the dignity of whatever privacy he could afford him and watched his shadow on the door rather than his bared upper torso. When he turned around, fully clothed, Michael silently held out his braces and brown wool coat.

Drake's footsteps were heavier than Michael's; together they passed through the foyer. Silver framed photographs crowded the dark, rose papered walls and cluttered the cramped occasional tables whose legs were concealed by lace cloths. Michael kept the muzzle of the gun pressed against Drake's left kidney, his own body blocking the pistol from view in case Maynard was more curious than obedient.

The Clarence cab was parked in front of the superintendent's modest brick home. Michael had earlier instructed the cabby as to what he should do. Silently, watchful lest Drake bolt out the opposite door, he climbed in beside the superintendent and braced himself for the journey that had started with a lone spinster's desire.

Flickering gas streetlamps alternately filled the cab with light and darkness. The rhythmical clip-clop of the horse's hooves rang out in the night. Dover was quieter than London, the air more pure.

Home.

It had been twenty-seven years since Michael had been on the earl's estate. Twenty-seven years since he had made his vow.

"I've seen you before." Drake's voice was disembodied in a lull of darkness.

Michael didn't answer.

"You have the look of a Sturges Bourne."

"That isn't possible, is it, Superintendent Drake?" Michael replied remotely. "The earl is the last of the line."

"Men don't always sire children in marriage." Light splintered the darkness, turning black into gray, shadow into flesh. The superintendent peered more closely at Michael. "Are you a bastard come to stir up trouble?"

The cab passed the streetlamp. Gray turned back to black, flesh to shadow.

Yes, he was a bastard. But not through his bloodlines.

Drake's bushy gray side whiskers glowed in the darkness. "Who are you?" he persisted.

Light once again flooded the cab, revealing Michael's scars, his eyes, his features. He smiled. "I told you, Superintendent. I'm a dead man."

Drake jerked back. "That's not possible."

Michael let his silence speak for him. Darkness swallowed the truth.

"Michael Sturges Bourne is dead."

The carriage hit a bump.

"He's buried with his family," Drake insisted.

A carriage traveling from the opposite direction passed the cab; the pounding of hooves filled the alternating light and darkness before fading into the night.

"Why would he bury you if you're not dead?"

Michael pictured the marble tombstone in the family plot.

His name was engraved in it. The date of his birth. The date of his death. The epitaph that was forever burned into his mind just as his scars were burned into his flesh.

Beloved son, brother and nephew.

He wondered if there was a body in his casket, or if it was empty, waiting for him.

"Why have you come back now, after all these years?"

Drake would not shut up until he had some answers.

Michael could at least resolve one of his questions.

"I've come back to kill my uncle."

He was alerted by the rustle of clothing and the squeak of the springs. Drake was preparing to wrench open the cab door and jump out.

Michael jammed the muzzle of his pistol into the superintendent's side. "But that's between me and my uncle. Right now all I care about is Anne Aimes."

"Why are you so certain that he would hurt her?"

"Because he's hurt other women."

Gaslights lit up the arched entrance to the police station. The cab rolled to a stop.

"Who were these other women? What happened to them? If they were harmed, why have their assaults not been reported?"

Why, indeed?

"They are dead, Superintendent Drake."

"If you failed to report their deaths you are guilty of complicity, sir," the superintendent barked.

Michael smiled humorlessly.

No one had believed him as a child.

As an adult. . . .

Diane's family had been too eager to hush up any scandal. They were not interested in learning about the truth.

Drake drummed his fingers on his knee, remembering, perhaps, that no one had seen Michael Sturges Bourne's corpse. Or perhaps he remembered that people were rarely what they seemed.

Even respectable, upstanding citizens.

"If the earl has done what you claim he has done, what makes you so certain he has not already disposed of Miss Aimes's body?" Drake abruptly demanded.

"I know."

He knew exactly what the man had done to her.

"Miss Aimes nursed both her parents. Only a sadistic monster would lure her by writing that her mother's grave had been vandalized."

Michael did not reprove Drake. Nor did he halt him when he opened the cab door and stepped down onto the cobbled street.

Coercion, he realized, could only go so far.

He had forced Drake to the station. He would not be able to force the superintendent to help him.

To help Anne.

He glanced up at the sky, at the glow of the gibbous moon.

It had changed. Two nights earlier he had stood on his balcony in London and stared up at a half-moon.

What would it take to change Drake's mind?

A whore's pride?

Would he beg for Anne?

Had she begged the man?

He threw the cab door open and tossed a florin at the cabby.

Michael blinked at the blaring light inside the station. All sound ceased at his entrance.

Three young, disheveled constables stood around the superintendent, helmet badges shiny, eyes groggy. Drake glanced up at Michael.

"Well?" he asked with acerbic English humor. "Will these be enough? Or should I wake up the entire barracks?"

Michael stilled. The letter inside his pocket burned his chest.

Hope.

"It will do," he said quietly.

Two constables rode as outriders; one drove the police carriage. Michael and Drake rode inside the carriage. The cracked leather seat was hard. Fresh hay lined the floor.

Silently he offered the superintendent his revolver. Equally silent, the superintendent accepted it.

The alternating bursts of light and darkness gave way to an unlighted road. He did not have to look out the window to see the approaching cliffs. Every second, every grinding bump brought him closer to his destination.

He reined in the need to kill the man and concentrated on Anne.

She would need him.

He would not let her down.

"I was the constable on duty when your family was in the accident." The superintendent's voice ruptured the darkness. "It was a shame, them dying that way."

"Yes."

Michael would think about his family later.

"It was an accident," Drake urged gruffly. "I often permitted my grandsons to drive my carriage when we went on outings. It wasn't your fault the carriage went over the cliffs."

"No, it wasn't," Michael agreed tonelessly. He gripped the leather pull by his shoulder. The ascent had started.

The white cliffs of Dover rose three hundred feet high. There had been little left of his parents' carriage when it fell; even less left of their bodies.

The superintendent remained silent for the rest of the journey. The baying of dogs alerted Michael that they approached the estate.

He gritted his teeth.

No dogs had guarded the park twenty-seven years ago. No wrought-iron spikes had topped the twelve foot tall brick wall that enclosed it.

He wondered when the earl had felt it necessary to protect himself. On what year had he started fearing reprisal?

On Michael's fifteenth birthday? Seventeenth? Nineteenth?

The wagon slid to a stop on the gravel.

"Ho, there! You!" an outriding constable shouted. "Open up the gates!"

"Ain't gonna let no one in this time o' th' night."

The gatekeeper's voice was not familiar to Michael. How long had he been employed by the earl? A day? Two days? What hellhole had the man found him in?

"Ye'll let us in, by God!" The dogs viciously barked and snarled at the threat in the constable's voice. "Leash those dogs and open the friggin' gate!"

"Git on wi' ye or I'll gie ye some buckshot to gnaw on!" shouted the gatekeeper.

"We're constables, ye bleedin' lummox!" The second outriding constable spoke up. "Open the gate or we'll give you time to think about it in goal!"

"Bobbies!" The surprise in the gatekeeper's voice was unfeigned. So was the fear.

No one had anticipated the police's intervention.

Not even the man.

"We got business with the Earl of Granville," the second outriding constable said. "Open up!"

Michael waited, muscles coiled, breath suspended. A horse snorted, pawed the gravel. The wagon lurched, stilled, restively awaited the outcome.

A dog growled, whimpered in submission. Creaking metal announced the gatekeeper's compliance.

He had breached the man's security. All it had required was the sacrifice of one spinster.

Blood pumping, heart pounding, he waited out the lifetime that it took for the carriage to traverse the short distance through the park.

Every second would be an hour to Anne, every passing minute another reason to end it once and for all.

The wheels crunched, slid to a halt. Michael threw the carriage door open and jumped out before the two outriding constables could dismount. Bolting up the tiered concrete steps, he beat on the door that had held him prisoner for two years. He could sense motion behind him, could feel the solid presence of three bodies.

"What the—Hold your pounding, you'll wake the dead!" Light switched on beside the door, something new—the man had invested in electricity. The door swung inward. "What do you—"

Michael did not recognize the tall, gaunt man who stood before him, but he recognized his type.

Creatures like he periodically crawled out of opium dens when their habit superseded their funds. They did not care what job they performed or what crime they committed as long as they were paid in sterling coin.

It was obvious the servant recognized Michael. The burn scars would make him an easily identifiable target.

What little color the tall, gaunt man possessed drained away.

The plan had gone awry.

Michael pushed past him into the great hall. He took the mahogany stairs three at a time. Drake's voice ricocheted after Michael. "You, Jemmy! After him, you fool!"

The corridor at the top of the steps was a black, bottomless abyss.

He did not need light to guide his steps. He knew exactly where Anne was, exactly how many steps it took to get there. A man's steps now rather than those of a boy.

He made the physical adjustments.

The corridor was just as endless.

Behind him booted footsteps rang out on the naked wood floor, faltered. "Sir?"

Anne drew Michael on.

Her laughter, that he had only heard once.

Her passion, that he had sampled too briefly.

She was alive.

He could feel it.

A light snapped on underneath a door. The ring of a handbell penetrated the wood. It was followed by a barking voice: "Frank! Frank, get in here now!"

Michael did not pause.

The last door was locked, as he had known it would be.

He threw his body against it. Once. Twice. . . .

Light sliced through the darkness like a miniature beacon. The constable's bull's eye lantern illuminated mahogany wood, careened off Michael and instantly returned, fully spotlighting him. *Damnit, he was running out of time.*

The door crashed open.

He struck a match.

An electric switch was on the inside of the door. Glaring light momentarily blinded him.

A faint, unmistakable odor overpowered the smell of burning sulfur. It wafted down the flight of narrow attic stairs.

Michael fought the churning of his stomach. He fought the fear the familiar smell triggered. He fought the temptation to burn the house to the ground.

Blowing out the match, he let it drop and raced up the steep steps.

The door at the top was locked.

Suddenly another pair of shoulders added to the force of his. Wood splintered; the attic door shot open.

The stench of death took his breath away.

A beam of light cut across a wooden box, danced back and forth through the blackness, briefly caught another rectangular wooden box in its glare before it disappeared altogether. Light exploded overhead, clearly delineating two coffins.

Michael knew which one Anne inhabited.

He could feel her heartbeat, taste her fear.

The lid was nailed down.

He grabbed the hammer that rested on top of the second coffin.

Endless minutes passed while he pried and pulled and gouged and hammered at the nails. No sound came from inside the coffin.

She wasn't dead—there were ample cracks in the wood to admit oxygen. But there were far worse things than death.

White gloved hands joined his scarred hands; they eased into the spaces between the loosening nails. Together he and the constable ripped the lid off the coffin.

Anne lay inside, eyes closed, cheeks wet with tears. She was silently crying. Glistening dark bodies slithered in the folds of her clothes, her hair.

"Jesus God."

For a second Michael thought he had spoken out loud. He felt the warmth of a body crowding his left side.

It was the constable who had spoken.

"She's got worms crawling in there on 'er," the constable gulped, sounding like the young man that he was instead of the model of authority he represented.

Michael did not spare time on the constable's horror. He had experienced his own, twenty-nine years earlier. Now he must get Anne through hers.

"Anne." Leaning down, he grasped her underneath her shoulders and legs and lifted her clear of the coffin. The back of her dress was damp. It did not matter to him, but he knew it would matter to her. "Anne, talk to me. Open your eyes. It's all right. Open your eyes, Anne."

Anne opened her eyes. Her pupils were dilated with terror. Tears continued pouring down her cheeks. "Put me down."

Her voice was hoarse from screaming; begging; sobbing.

There was no room for pride inside a coffin.

Michael carefully set her down. A worm slithered onto her neck.

She screamed. His spinster who had always prided herself on her self-control did not now have any.

Michael wanted to weep.

"It's all right, Anne." Quickly, efficiently, he plucked the earthworms off her. "They can't hurt you. It's all right. Don't. Don't cry. Don't let him do this to you."

But she couldn't stop crying. And Michael knew why.

"Leave us," he roughly commanded.

The young constable was only too eager to escape the stench and the horror.

"Anne. Don't. It's all right. I'm going to make it better." He wrapped his left arm around her and pressed her face against his shoulder, knowing she was going to struggle, knowing he might hurt her, knowing there was no other solution. Hiking up her wool skirt, he slid his hand up the inside of her thigh.

Silk.

She wore a pair of the silk drawers Madame René had delivered.

They were wet; not all of the dampness came from desire.

Anne fought him, as he had expected she would. "Let me go. *What are you doing?*"

"He put something inside you, Anne."

"It's worms! Oh, God, they're everywhere!" She pushed with a strength he would not have thought she possessed. "Let me go! Don't touch me! I can feel them—oh, God, oh, God, oh, God, they're inside me—"

"No." He held her firmly. Tears burned his eyes. "Listen to me, Anne. It's not worms inside you. I promise. It's two silver balls. They create sexual excitation inside a woman. Don't fight me. Please. Let me take them out. . . ."

She wrenched out of his arms.

Michael watched a miracle. On the verge of hysteria, she found the strength to take control. "Please. I can . . . turn around."

He would give her this. For now.

But he would not allow his uncle to destroy her passion or her awakening sensuality. Too much had already been taken away from both of them.

Michael turned around.

Chapter 19

Anne concentrated on two things: not screaming and the bath she would take when she reached her Dover house. Underneath her the carriage churned and writhed. Beside her, Michel—*she still did not know his given name,* did not even remember if she had known it twenty-seven years ago when he supposedly died—burned and throbbed.

No, it was *her* body that burned and throbbed and churned and writhed. While she sat in clothes that were soiled by her own fear. *By her own helplessness.*

She clamped her mouth shut to control the rising hysteria. Nausea roiled in her stomach. "There is no need to escort me to my estate, monsieur. . . ." Her throat was raw; her voice gravelly. The pain did not stop the words rising up inside her. "What do I call you? Monsieur des Anges? The honorable Mr. Sturges Bourne? You are the nephew of an earl. It is important in our society to adhere to protocol. I want to address you by your proper title."

"You are in shock," was the flat rejoinder.

She was babbling, but she was not in shock. Every nerve in her body hummed and sang. Thoughts flitted through her mind like crystal butterflies.

Frank had removed her hat. It remained in the Earl of Granville's bedchamber, as did her gloves and reticule.

The earl still possessed a part of her.

Pressing her hand over her mouth, she stared out the window. Darkness closed around her. *Like a coffin.*

It dawned on her why the man who sat beside her did not sleep in darkness.

She swallowed the bile. "What was in the other coffin? He said—" Her lips trembled uncontrollably as the memories rolled over her. "He said it was my mother."

"It was a dead cat. Or dog. Or rat."

"You would know."

"Yes, I would know."

She wrapped her arms around her torso; the grenadine cloak abraded her fingers. Invisible worms continued to crawl over her skin.

As they crawled over her mother. Her father. *Buried deep in the darkness.*

Anne gagged.

"Put your head down between your knees."

"I am fine," she insisted through clenched teeth. "Please do not trouble yourself over me."

"You will feel better after a bath."

She prayed so. She feared she would never feel better. That her skin would always crawl.

A bitter taste lingered in her mouth.

The tea. Her terror, lying in darkness. The scent of death and the musty odor of worms—

No, if she went that route she would start screaming again.

Anne Aimes. A woman who screamed in passion. *A woman who screamed in fear.*

It did not seem possible that a scant twelve hours earlier she had taken pleasure in the anonymity and swaying comfort of riding on a train. And only hours before that, she had cried out her release and felt this man's answering passion flood her body.

"The second night I was with you," she said abruptly, hoarsely. "You put something in my wine."

"Yes."

"Why?"

"I needed time to make arrangements for your safety."

"Don't lie to me," she said fiercely. "You knew. . . ." She could not make herself go on. "Lady Wenterton. She's the woman you said you cared about. The one you experienced intimate sex . . . and friendship with."

The carriage lurched forward in the darkness. "Yes."

"He did this to her."

"Yes."

"You loved her."

"Yes."

"And you let him do that to her!" Revulsion rocketed through Anne. "How could you?"

"I didn't know he had her." His voice was distant. "I thought she visited her sister. I received telegrams. I didn't know."

"But you knew . . ." Anne took a calming breath. "You knew what he would do to me."

"Yes."

"What did you hope to gain through your deception?"

"Revenge."

Why wouldn't the carriage hurry?

Why wouldn't the pain stop?

Her teeth chattered. With cold. With betrayal. With the repugnance and terror that would not end. "How long did he have Lady Wenterton?"

"Two months."

Anne closed her eyes. She tried to imagine what it would be like to be imprisoned inside a coffin for two months, *consumed by lustful cravings.*

She could not.

Anne opened her eyes and stared at the blur that was his face. "How did she die?"

"Diane sealed her bedchamber door with cloth and turned on the gas in her lamp. An explosion occurred—probably as a result of burning embers in the fireplace. She wanted to die. She did."

There was nothing more to be said.

Lady Wenterton had chosen death over living.

Anne could not blame her.

She huddled back into the corner of the carriage and concentrated on the hard, cracked leather seat, the fresh hay underneath her feet, the bumping grate of the wheels—anything but the darkness and the slippery heat that continued to coil and writhe inside her.

He did not speak.

As if he waited. . . .

For what?

The moment the lurching, swaying motion stopped, Anne wrenched open the coach door and jumped out.

She fell. *Clumsy, clumsy, clumsy old spinster.*

Immediately, strong, scarred hands reached out for her.

Anne shrugged them off and scrambled to her feet.

She had had three nights of passion. She would regret them for as long as she lived.

Her Dover house was dark.

Still.

A giant coffin, waiting.

Anne pounded on the door, forgetting dignity, welcoming the pain, the noise. Trying to run from the memories and the presence of the man behind her.

Why wouldn't he go away?

Her butler threw open the door, a lit candle in his gnarled hand, aged face crunched up in unaccustomed irritation. His jaw dropped. "Miss Anne!"

He was too old for this job, Anne thought irrationally. Tomorrow she would retire him. She would put the estate up for sale and retire all of her servants.

But that was tomorrow.

Anne had to get through the remainder of the night.

She raced up the steps, silk petticoats and wool dress tangling her feet.

"Miss Anne!" chased after her, a spiraling echo. A masculine murmur responded; it drifted up the stairs and through her body.

She did not stop running.

The scent of damp wood, musty air, and carbolic disinfectant permeated the dark paneling lining the hallway and the green wool runner underfoot. It did not alleviate the stench of death that clung to her clothes, her hair, her skin.

So many things were clear now.

The abundance of flowers in his town house. His proclamation of passion.

He had not wanted a woman: he had wanted vengeance.

Anne threw open the door to her bedchamber and scrambled for the matches inside her nightstand drawer. She turned on the gas in her lamp—and for one timeless second thought about Lady Wenterton.

Hurriedly she struck a match, picked up the etched crystal globe, and lit the burner tip. Replacing the globe, she turned the light up as high as it would go.

The walls writhed with shadows.

Anne tore at her bodice. A button cannonaded across the room, soundlessly disappearing into faded green carpeting.

It did not matter. Nothing mattered, except getting out of her clothes.

The ridiculously frivolous, wireless bustle dropped with a muffled swish; her petticoats with a whispering hiss. She was afraid to look, afraid she would find more worms.

The corset.

She could not unlace *the corset.*

Her abigail was asleep in her bed. Anne did not want her maid to see her like this.

Underneath the corset her skin crawled.

Hysteria pushed and clawed inside her, a living entity trying to gain expression.

She would not let the earl do this to her.

Scissors. . . .

Anne frantically rummaged inside her closet for the sewing basket that had not seen the light of day for ten months.

Her mother had thought a lady must occupy herself with needle and thread. Anne had humored her when she sat at her bedside, neatly stitching handkerchiefs that would never be used.

The small twin blades were fashioned to snip threads; they sawed through the black satin, fiber by fiber. She threw both the corset and the scissors at the shadows that would not stop writhing.

It did not stop the coiling inside her.

Flinging the damp, clinging silk chemise over her head—*Oh, God, he had felt and seen her lack of control*—she untied her drawers and kicked them off. Vaguely shocked at her violence, she ripped off her garters and silk stockings.

Her hair—she frenziedly plucked out the pins, leaned over, and shook out the slithering tresses, fingers combing through them over and over.

There was no time to heat the water in the geyser.

Hands trembling, Anne lit the twin wall sconces on either side of the mirror above the bathroom sink.

A disheveled spinster looked out of the glass, silver shining in her pale brown hair. She was all too recognizable.

The earl had shown her *exactly* what distinguishing quality she possessed.

She twisted a plain brass tap. Rust cascaded from the spout. Unable to wait for the narrow copper tub to fill, Anne stepped into it and scrambled to fit under the spout. An icy deluge pounded the back of her head. The water was so cold it took her breath away. Straightening, she reached for a bar of soap and washcloth. She scrubbed her skin and scalp until they were as raw as her throat. When the tub was full, she twisted off the tap and scrubbed some more.

The worms continued to crawl on her body. Inside. *Outside.*

Anne held her head underwater. Her hair floated about her. Alive.

She sat up, gasping for oxygen.

He stood beside the tub, coatless, hatless, gloveless. Michel des Anges, the Honorable Mr. Sturges Bourne. Black hair curled through the opened placket of his white shirt. Stubbly beard darkened his face. The scars edging his cheek were stark white.

Water streaming down her face, Anne slapped her arms over her chest. Vaguely she realized how ridiculous she must appear.

He had seen far more than her breasts.

"Get out. My solicitor—" *Was dead.* What had he done with Mr. Little's body? "I'll make arrangements for the bank to deposit the remainder of your money."

"I don't want your money, Anne." Regret glimmered in his violet eyes, was instantly gone. "I never wanted your money."

He had never wanted her money. *Her passion.*

"Nevertheless—" Her strained voice cracked. She swallowed. "Nevertheless, that is what the contract stipulated. I will honor the terms. Please leave. The servants will talk."

Anne cringed at her hypocrisy.

It was too late to be concerned over what servants would say.

What did it matter what anyone said ever *again?*

Gossip did not paralyze or imprison.

It did not make one scream until one's throat burned and swelled shut.

It did not—

"Get up."

Anne snapped clear of the yawning blackness. "I beg your pardon?"

"I said get up." He reached for the towel on the rack beside the copper tub. "You're turning blue."

"Monsieur des Anges—"

"My name is Michael."

Michel is French for Michael. And my name is Gabriel.

Black hair. Silver hair. *Gray hair.*

"I don't care what you call yourself; get out of my house! For God's sake, haven't you done enough?"

One second she was looking up at him; the next they were eye-to-eye. In one smooth motion he lifted her out of the tub and wrapped the towel around her.

"You're going to listen to me," he grated. "Whether you want to or not."

"So that I can *understand?"* she screamed rawly—and promptly clamped her mouth shut, appalled at her loss of control. She stood wrapped in the towel, her throat on fire, shivering, trembling, hating her weakness, her vulnerability.

Hating that she still wanted him.

While her mother lay dead, food for worms.

"You think you will never recover." Hot breath scorched her face. "You can. You will. I'm going to help you."

She gulped down her revulsion and gripped the towel between her breasts, wrenching control out of his hands. "I don't want your help."

He loomed over her, tall, dark, handsome, everything she had ever wanted in a man. "That is regrettable, Mademoiselle Aimes, because you're going to get it."

"Don't address me in French!" she lashed out, impervious to the pain that slashed her throat. Water crawled down her neck, her shoulders, her arms, her legs, reality unavoidable. "You're not French! You lied to me! You told me you wanted my passion! You didn't want me! You used me!"

"But I do want your passion, Anne." His expression was hard; the violet glitter in his eyes unmistakable. "And you're going to give it to me."

Fear crowded out reason.

He blocked the entrance to the bathroom door; the tub blocked her from behind.

There was no place that was safe.

Nowhere to hide from the truth.

"If you do not step aside, I will—"

"What, Anne?" he asked provocatively. "What will you do?"

What could a woman do to stop a man?

She had not been able to stop the earl.

She had not been able to stop the street sweeper who had knocked her into an oncoming cab.

She had not even been able to control her own body.

The trembling rose up inside her.

"You were going to kill me."

The memory of her hat pin and his saliva-moistened penis glimmered in his violet eyes. "I told you I wouldn't hurt you."

But he *had* hurt her.

"He said you killed your family."

"What did he accuse you of, Anne?"

She did not want to tell him. The words tore out of her throat. "He said I killed my mother."

"Did you?"

Anne slapped him, she who had never raised her hand against

anyone or anything in her life. The slap resounded in the small bathroom, flesh impacting flesh, for no other reason than to hurt. *Because she could.*

She cupped her mouth in horror.

Her fingers tingled; they felt as if they had been impaled with hundreds of tiny needles.

Four fingers imprinted his left cheek underneath the dark stubble. Violet fire flashed down at her. "We were going on a picnic down by the sea, my mother, my father, my three younger sisters, and I. I was eleven years old, preparing to take my exams to enter Eton. My father joked that I was a man, that I should drive him. He gave me the reins to the gig. The reins snapped. The horses wouldn't stop. They ran off the road, across a field, straight toward the edge of the cliff. Out of the blue my uncle rode up. He didn't try to grab the lead horse, to stop them. He reached out. My mother grabbed me and threw me into his arms. His horse reared; it threw us both. My uncle was trampled. I lay on the ground and watched my family go over the cliff. He has taken away everything I have ever cared about, Anne. I'm not going to let him destroy you, too."

Anne slowly brought her hands down. Reins did not snap.

"He killed them."

"Did he?" he parried cynically. "Or did an inexperienced boy lose control and send his family over a cliff?"

Guilt. The other side of love.

"The reins were cut through," she said decisively.

"So where are the reins? There's no proof. He was an earl. My father was the younger son. Why would he kill his brother?"

Anne did not have any doubt whatsoever as to why the earl would kill his brother. "He's insane."

He smiled. There was no humor in it. No warmth. "My uncle is many things, but he is not insane. I never lied to you, save for the fact that I knew who you were before we met. I told you I waited at the night house hoping that the woman who solicited my services would see my scars and still want me. You were the woman I waited for. *You* were the one I hoped would want me. I wanted revenge, Anne, but I wanted your passion far more. I wanted to hold you, to please you. You solicited me. My body. Did you care about me? My wants? My needs? Tell me, Anne Aimes. Who used whom?"

Anne sucked in air at the base unfairness of his accusation. "I did not endanger your life."

"You endangered your life the moment you walked out of the night house with a stranger. There are men who take pleasure in hurting women. Some men take pleasure in killing."

Men like the earl.

For a few moments she had forgotten the horror she had endured. The writhing need inside her body.

His level rejoinder brought it all back.

The horror. The hunger.

Voracious sexual appetites, the earl had said. *Dreadful delights. . . . Your lust brought you to this. If you had controlled your sexual appetites and stayed in Dover, you would be safe. If my nephew had controlled his lust and remained in Yorkshire, you would be safe.*

But she had not stayed in Dover. And Michael Sturges Bourne had not stayed in Yorkshire.

And now here they were.

He stepped aside.

She rushed past him.

She would not be victimized by her needs.

Anne paused on the threshold. The clothes she had strewn about her bedchamber were gone. A white sheet covered the mattress; the two down pillows in their embroidered white cases were plumped. The remainder of the bedcoverings were folded over the foot of the four-poster bed. Yellow flames snapped and crackled inside the Adam's fireplace. A silver tray rested on the nightstand beside the gas lamp.

She blinked in confusion.

The aromatic sweetness of chocolate flavored the air.

Rough cotton brushed her cheeks; her streaming wet hair was pulled back and gently rubbed inside a towel.

Anne jerked away from the gentle ministrations and swirled around.

He held a damp hand towel, violet gaze alert. Watchful. Predatory.

Blue shadow darkened his hair and face.

She had touched the stubble of his beard while he slept. Had kissed that perfect, chiseled mouth.

And did not know who she had touched or kissed.

Michel? Or Michael?

Her heart violently beat inside her breast, *her vagina.* "I don't want you."

Purposefully he reached for the towel she clutched between her breasts. "Now who's lying?"

His fingers were hard; they were roughened with scars.

Anne could run. Or she could confront him.

The power of a woman.

"If I do want you, it is only because of the silver balls."

"I know."

The towel slithered down her body and bunched around her feet. She clenched her hands into fists and endured his examination, fighting humiliation, fighting excitement. His eyes caressed her calves, her thighs, the damp thatch of hair at the jointure of her thighs, her stomach, her breasts.

Every place on her body that he had touched.

Her nipples were hard. She could not lie to herself and say that it was because of the cold.

He had always known how much she wanted him.

"I paid you," she said harshly.

His eyes met hers. Violet flame glinted inside their depths. "I know."

"It's not you I want," she said deliberately, cruelly—hating herself, hating him, hating the earl for destroying the only beauty she had ever experienced. "Any man would do."

The light in his eyes dimmed. Rough, scarred hands cupped her face. "I know."

She opened her mouth to take back the words.

His mouth closed over hers, lips softer than rose petals while the stubble on his chin abraded her skin.

This was what she had wanted, surrounded by death. His kiss. His embrace. *He* was the one she had prayed to God to save her.

She wrenched her head back.

Denying him. Denying herself.

He held her face up to his, his breath feathering her lips. "If you fight me, Anne, I will tie you to the bed. Don't make me use force. Let me help you. Let me show you. . . ."

Anne stiffened. She could not stop the flow of antagonism. "As you showed Lady Wenterton? Did you help her by tying her to the bed?"

His fingers tightened around her head and dug into her wet scalp. "No, but I wish to God that I had. Perhaps then she would still be alive. But she didn't want me to touch her. I respected her wishes. I thought time would heal her. And now she's dead."

Taken from him as his family had been taken from him.

Water dripped down her back, dribbled between her buttocks. The heat of his body scorched her lips, her face, her breasts, her pelvis.

"I am not in danger of taking my life."

"There are many types of death, Anne."

"I didn't ask for this!"

"Neither did I."

"I screamed." The heat of his body did not take away the coldness inside her. "I couldn't stop screaming."

He brushed her lips with his. Slowly. Softly. Seductively. "You're not screaming now."

But she wanted to.

She wanted to open her mouth and scream until there was nothing left to come out of her.

No more fear. No more desire.

Anne didn't close her eyes. She stared at herself in his pupils, a plain, pale-faced woman trapped by her own passion.

Sighing, he closed his eyes, long black lashes a tangle of silk on his cheeks. His tongue thrust into her mouth. The shock of it bolted through her womb.

Anne closed her eyes, her mouth involuntarily opening wider.

The darkness behind her lids writhed.

Suddenly the writhing darkness shifted, tilted, raced up to meet her back and buttocks.

Anne's eyes popped open. She lay on the bed.

White linen fluttered to the floor, revealing a mat of black hair, two small, hard nipples, and contoured muscles.

Michel's chest. *Michael's chest.*

She struggled to sit up, to counteract the roll of her body, hair entangling her, impeding her, robbing her of what little dignity she still possessed. "I will not be forced!"

The mattress sank; he sat beside her, all fluid muscle and masculine temptation. "I have no intention of forcing you."

"You do not think that tying a woman to a bed is force?" Her voice broke, trying to reach a pitch of hysteria it could not make.

Reaching out—corded muscles flexing, metal a piercing clang—he lifted the domed cover off of the silver tray.

She remembered the silver-covered serving dish on the earl's lap. Remembered the worms it had been filled with.

Anne broke free of her hair and bolted upright. Only to stare in surprise at a large silver sauce dish and a banana.

He set the lid onto the floor, mattress shifting, squeaking with his motion, then straightened and dipped a finger into the silver sauce dish. It came out coated with chocolate.

"My uncle was my legal guardian." He studied the chocolate on the tip of his finger with an odd blend of curiosity and contempt on his face. "No one believed me when I told them that the reins snapped. The earl had been trampled trying to save us, I was told. Why would he hurt us, his only living relatives?"

Without warning he reached out and wiped his finger onto her left nipple. The chocolate was smooth as silk; his skin underneath it was rough.

Hot.

It burned.

She jolted back in startled pain.

His violet eyes snared hers. "Stay still, Anne," he warned.

Immediately the chocolate cooled and hardened.

Her nipple throbbed.

"Why are you doing this?" she whispered.

He didn't want her.

Aside from her money, no one wanted a thirty-six-year-old spinster.

But he didn't even want her money.

The gas lamp hissed. Shadow skittered across his features.

"I loved chocolate when I was a child," he said dispassionately.

An ember exploded in the fireplace.

Anne was arrested. It was not her that his violet eyes gazed at.

"I had hot chocolate for breakfast," he said, staring at the boy he had once been. "At lunch. Before I went to sleep. My tutor quickly learned that the promise of a piece of chocolate motivated me to read Shakespeare, conjugate Latin and Greek verbs, even memorize multiplication tables. I hid my prizes and ate them in bed at night so that I wouldn't have to share with my younger sisters. I used to dream about the day I would grow up so that I could have all the chocolate I wanted."

Anne almost smiled at the image of this beautiful, scarred, beard-stubbled man being bribed with chocolate to do his studies. The urge to smile faded at the thought of his younger sisters, dead because of the earl.

As she would have been dead.

He dipped his finger into the sauce dish. "My uncle was ill for several months," he said—and smeared chocolate around her aureole, heat that solidified into a cool crust. A stab of pleasure contracted her womb; the muscles inside her vagina greedily clenched, relaxed, *clenched*. "The horse had crushed his legs and damaged his lower spine. He did not want me near him."

He glanced up, his gaze unexpectedly bright, focused on her instead of the past. "Lie down, Anne."

She suddenly didn't want to hear what he was going to tell her.

She didn't want to know the horrors that he must have endured, living with his uncle.

She didn't want to lie down ever again and remember what it felt like staring up into darkness, helpless to stop the fear and the desire.

She didn't want to forgive this man for the unforgivable.

He had betrayed her trust. *Her passion.*

"He was going to let me die," she hoarsely accused him.

And there had been nothing she could do to stop it.

"Yes."

"Because of you!"

The violet in his eyes flickered. "Did you lie to me, Anne?"

Her breasts jiggled from the force of her breathing. Tiny cracks spread through the hardened chocolate encasing her nipple. "I never lied to you!"

"You said you wanted to know what I felt."

"I did." She fought the memories of his manhood buried inside her, his fingers rhythmically squeezing her clitoris while his penis moved in and out of her body. "You showed me what you felt."

"I am more than a cock, Anne."

Whereas she was exactly what she was: *a plain spinster.*

"I suppose next you are going to say that what we did was more than *fucking!*"

Anne choked on the vulgarity. Or perhaps she choked on the earl's sacrilege at calling what had transpired between a scarred whore and a spinster "fucking."

But she had never considered what they did as "fucking." Any more than she had considered Michel des Anges a whore.

His gaze did not waver from hers. "Lie down."

Her fingernails bit into the palms of her hands. "What do you want from me?"

"I want you to listen. I want you to know the man behind the cock."

Anne couldn't breathe, staring into his violet eyes that all at once belonged to neither Michel, a man named for his ability to please women, nor Michael, a man who was heir to an earldom. All she could do was—

Lie down.

With his long, scarred fingers he brushed her wet hair off of her breasts and her shoulders until it spread over the pillow; he seemed impervious to the threads of gray that twined through it. Reaching out, he dipped his finger in the silver container.

Anne tensed, waiting.

"I sought solace in chocolate when my family died." Hot chocolate glided over her right nipple—a quick burning heat. "With my uncle ill, the servants gave me whatever I wanted."

Anne concentrated on his eyes that impassively stared at her breast and his ministrations rather than the lust that streaked through her body.

"That's how he found me when he unexpectedly visited me one night." He painted her right aureole. "In bed. With chocolate smeared on my face."

Anne glanced down and saw what he saw: chocolate smeared on her breasts.

As it had been smeared on his face when he had been an eleven-year-old child.

But there was nothing childish—or innocent—about the dark, glistening smears on her white breasts.

She glanced up.

The earl had said his nephew had been a very loving boy.

There was no love on his face now.

"He looked at me and asked one question," he continued in that flat monotone. Her aureole cooled, abandoned. He scooped all four fingers inside the silver sauce dish. " 'How much do you love chocolate?' "

Slowly, methodically, he worked the chocolate into the globe of her right breast.

Anne's breath quickened: with distress—with desire.

Liquid arousal trickled out of her vagina.

She clenched her muscles to stop the flow.

It wasn't supposed to be like this.

"The next night Frank wheeled my uncle into my bedchamber." He surveyed his handiwork. "He brought me a chocolate bar. It was filled with worms."

Anne squirmed: at the unwitting sensation arcing between her breasts and her womb—at the image his words conjured.

He worked chocolate into her left breast, smooth heat and grating fingers.

"He asked me if I knew what my mother was eating, buried

underneath the earth in a dark coffin. Worms, he said. He told me if I didn't eat the chocolate bar that Frank would bury me with my mother. I ate it."

"Michel—"

His name burst unbidden from her lips.

"I told you. My name isn't Michel." He raised his eyelashes. His violet irises had been swallowed by the black of his pupils. "It's Michael. The Honorable Michael Sturges Bourne."

But there had been nothing honorable in allowing a woman to solicit his services. *Knowing the price she would have to pay.*

"What he did to you does not excuse what you did to me."

"I loved you, Anne"—he reached for the silver dish rather than the chocolate inside it—"to the best of my ability."

Loved rang out over the snap of the burning logs and the drum of her heartbeat.

"Your friend Gabriel. He knew about the earl."

"Gabriel knew," he agreed evenly.

And dribbled chocolate between her breasts, down her stomach, over her navel.

Everyone had known but her, she thought, anger rising anew. Even the butler had known.

Perhaps even the maid who had helped her into Madame René's black satin corset.

"Don't move, Anne." His voice was dangerously soft, as if he were poised on a precipice.

"What are you going to do?" she asked defiantly, refusing to show her fear—or her desire.

"Make memories," he murmured.

"I already have memories!"

Of death. Of desire.

His gaze held hers, reflecting her pain. Her need.

Her memories.

Of death. *Of desire.*

Melted chocolate and scarred fingers smoothed her stomach, a shock of heat that quickly cooled.

"He started taking his meals with me. Breakfast. Lunch. Dinner." His lashes lowered. Jagged shadows hollowed his cheeks.

Anne raised her head and watched the progress of his fingers, her skin crawling with sensation. "If he noticed that I liked a particular food, he would bring a dish of it to me when I was in bed. I liked kedgeree for breakfast." His middle finger dipped into her navel, a stabbing invasion. "He brought me a bowl of rice that was alive with maggots.

"I liked pasta." He smeared chocolate onto her lower stomach, dipping lower, lower yet into her pubic hair. . . . "He brought me a bowl filled with noodles that wriggled in the sauce. And always reminded me that worms ate my mother. Because of my carelessness she was dead, he claimed. If I did not eat them, I would join her, he said, and be eaten alive. Slowly. They would crawl into my hair. Up my nose. Into my ears. I ate whatever he brought because I was more afraid of being eaten by worms than I was of eating them."

Anne mentally writhed.

"Spread your legs, Anne."

She stared up into his flat, lifeless eyes. "It won't change anything."

"No, but come morning it won't be worms you remember."

She spread her legs—and closed her eyes when he dribbled chocolate onto her clitoris.

Burning heat. Rasping skin.

He worked chocolate into her clitoris, her labia, her clitoris again.

She arched up into his fingers—control perilously strained—only to drop down onto the bed when he left her.

Hot. Wet. Aching for more than chocolate.

For more than fingers.

She anchored herself to the sheet with both hands.

Her head plunked down onto the mattress.

Anne's eyelids flew open.

He stood over her, her pillow in his hands.

She held her breath.

He could kill her just as easily as the earl could have.

Leaning over, body blocking the light, he grabbed the pillow from the opposite side of the bed.

He straightened; light spilled across her. "Lift your hips."

"Why?" she asked shakily.

Afraid to die. Afraid to live.

Yes, Lord Granville, I am afraid, she thought.

"So I can elevate your pelvis."

And she would be open, exposed, with no means to hide the plainness of her body or the carnal needs of a spinster.

"And when I am elevated . . . what are you going to do then?" she asked, trying to control her breathing. *Her desire.*

"You bought me because of my ability to please a woman." His chest rose and fell in cadence with her breathing. "Lift your hips and I guarantee you that I will please you. Come tomorrow, if you wish to terminate the contract, I will not object. But you need me tonight, Anne. What you have never realized is that I need you, too."

Anne lifted her hips.

A network of tiny cracks spread across her breasts and stomach. Cool air enveloped her buttocks. It was replaced by even cooler cotton.

Her pelvis was elevated, jutting forward as if she walked in heels. *Naked.* Her thighs fell apart in lewd invitation.

She had never been more vulnerable. Not the first night he had undressed her. Not when the earl had drugged her.

He grabbed the silver sauce dish and dribbled chocolate on her legs, her toes.

Anne felt like a mummy, covered breasts to feet with the hardening foodstuff. She watched wide-eyed as he put the sauce dish back onto the tray and picked up the banana. Light and shadow caressed his naked arms, skin smooth as dusk; his hands were ridged and scarred. He partially peeled the banana before smearing the outer skin with chocolate.

There was not enough oxygen to fill her lungs.

"You surely do not intend to. . . ."

Her voice trailed off. A vivid image flashed before her eyes.

Of her, *naked.* Of him, *lying between her outspread legs,* dressed in a white linen shirt and trousers, fingers digging into her thighs.

She had wanted him to taste her. Lick her. Tongue her.

And he had.

The pulsating flesh inside her vagina assured her that he would surely do this too.

And she wanted him to.

"Were you fond of bananas?" she asked, unable to suppress the catch in her voice.

"Yes."

And the earl had destroyed even that.

Sitting down on the edge of the bed, he delicately parted the folds of her labia.

Her heart leaped up into her throat.

Cold hardness that was neither flesh nor rubber circled her, prepared her, penetrated her.

She instinctively tightened her muscles, rejecting what the earl had done to him. To her. Rejecting her own perverse nature that had brought her to this while Michel—*Michael*—had done nothing but become an orphaned child.

His dark eyelashes swept upward. "Take it, Anne. I know you ache inside. I can feel the heat of you. You're wet with desire. It's natural, your need to be filled; that's the nature of a woman's body. Let me fill you. Let me give you memories. Of fullness. Of pleasure. . . ."

Gently, firmly, he pushed the banana inside her, holding her stare, overcoming her internal resistance until it lodged deep inside her and her muscles hungrily clenched, holding it in place, and she could not contain a gasp.

Of fullness. *Of pleasure.*

She stared up at him mutely, pierced to the core of her being.

At last she understood the difference between penetration and possession.

Lashes lowering, shielding his eyes, he lightly outlined the slick outer parameters of her vagina. She was stretched taut to accommodate the fruit, quivering, poised as he was poised, waiting for the outcome. . . .

"By the end of that first year, there were few foods that I could stomach. Bread. Raw vegetables. Apples. Pears. Fruits that weren't pulpy or mushy. I was half-starved. He wanted me alive, so he did not tamper with those foods that I could still tolerate. I thought he had done his worst. I was wrong. One night he and Frank came to my bedroom. He said he had a surprise for me in the attic."

He did not have to tell her what the surprise was.

"I thought it was my mother in the coffin. Just as you thought it was your mother. I know what you felt when you were in that coffin, Anne, because I've felt it. Always Frank would come lift me out the next morning before the servants got up. And I would have to spend my day as if nothing were wrong, reading the books my uncle considered necessary for my education. As if my uncle were a saintly man who suffered because he had saved me and who now fed and clothed and educated me. As if I had nothing to fear when every moment I trembled in fear."

He gently, rhythmically prodded the banana, increasing the fullness inside her, fueling the hunger.

"In the beginning I tried telling the servants. They didn't believe me. When my uncle found out . . . I never talked to anyone again. I think I went insane. I think that's how I got the strength one night while I lay in bed, waiting for the man, to climb out of my window and scale the walls and then the stone fence. There were no spikes topping it then. I stowed away on a freight boat to Calais."

Anne sucked in her breath . . . remembering the stone fence surrounding the earl's estate: it was far too high for a boy to scale, spikes or no spikes. Feeling the rhythmical push and pull of the banana: it prodded every fiber in her body. Absorbing the tug of his emotions: they seethed beneath the mask of his face.

"In Calais all I could think about were the nights I'd spent in the coffin. I couldn't sleep. I had nothing to eat. I was caught stealing a loaf of bread. Gabriel upturned a table of pies to distract the baker. Then he and I traveled to Paris. The madame found us. Trained us.

"Sexual pleasure was the only thing in my life that had not been tainted by my uncle. Sex made it possible for me to live, to forget. Gabriel lost his soul, but I found remnants of mine. I learned everything the madame had to teach me, eager for more. Every woman I have ever been with I have learned from. I've learned from you, Anne."

Anne realized that *this* was what Gabriel had tried to tell her.

Michael loved women and sex—not because of the money, or even because of sexual pleasure—but because they were the only things left in his life for him to love.

"What have you learned from me?" she whispered, afraid to move—afraid to break the spell of his confidence; afraid to orgasm—afraid her control would splinter and there would be nothing left of the spinster that she was.

He looked up at her, violet eyes naked.

"I've learned that it's time to get on with my life. Starting now. I'm going to lick every inch of your body. Outside. Inside. You won't remember the worms, and neither will I. Whenever I see chocolate I will think of you. The flavor of your skin. And the pleasure you've shared with me."

Something hot and wet slithered down her temples.

A man should not endure the kind of pain he had survived.

"How did you—" She bit her lip to stop the question, knowing that it had to be asked. "How did you intend upon gaining revenge by accepting my offer?"

"I knew he would take you. Or me. Either way I would gain admission to his estate."

To kill. Or be killed.

But he had not killed his uncle. She had heard the earl's voice through the door as she walked back down the hallway.

Michael had helped her instead.

She expelled an unsteady breath. "How did you get my cook to warm up chocolate for you?"

His violet eyes were suddenly brilliant in the light of the lamp. "I told her you and I were going to enjoy a snack *alfresco.*"

Chocolate. Bananas.

Unexplored boundaries of passion.

Three days ago Anne would have been shocked down to her toes.

"Michael."

He stilled, waiting. The very air seemed to wait.

"How are you going to eat the banana?"

A smile stretched his lips. It slowly widened until his even white teeth flashed, giving her a glimpse of what he must have looked like twenty-nine years earlier, a boy who had yet to learn the guilt that love could cause.

"A nibble at a time, Anne."

Michael started at her toes. He sucked her big toe into his mouth and cleansed it with his tongue.

It was more erotic than a feather. More intimate than a kiss. Electric sensation raced through every nerve inside her body.

He tongued the ultrasensitive skin between her toes.

She gripped the sheet to hold herself down on the bed and not shoot straight up to the ceiling.

Right foot. Left foot.

Just when she thought she was going to do the impossible and orgasm from having her toes suckled, he slid up and nuzzled between her splayed legs, softer-than-silk lips surrounded by sharp bristles. The banana jiggled inside her.

Anne held her breath, her entire world reduced to the fruit that filled her and Michael who tongued her.

He persistently licked and rooted, trying to get to the flesh inside the peel.

Anne's hips surged upward. She could not control the orgasm that ripped through her.

She grabbed for his head, his hair, anything to hold him in place, to pull him closer. . . .

Michael slipped away. He leisurely sampled her right leg.

Anne did not think of coffins.

He licked behind her knee.

She jumped at the bolt of lightning that shot through her.

Immediately he surged forward and kissed her clitoris, his tongue a burning lash.

He licked and licked until she could not restrain her hips; they rose with a will of their own. Michael licked a blazing trail down her labia and nibbled—on her flesh, on the flesh of the banana.

She cried out as another orgasm jolted through her.

He licked her stomach, her breasts, teeth grazing her nipple—"Oh, my God"—ducking down to lave her navel. Abruptly he lifted up to kiss her, tongue filling her mouth as the fruit filled her femininity.

She tasted chocolate. She tasted banana. She tasted herself.

"Say my name," he whispered into her mouth.

Anne swallowed. "Michael."

Michael pushed her thighs more widely apart and settled between them. "Now scream my name."

He alternately licked her clitoris and nibbled on the diminishing banana until she screamed his name, again and again and again, until the banana was gone and he licked the chocolate from her throbbing vagina, not deep enough, not thick enough, *she needed more. . . .*

Suddenly he was kneeling between her legs. Somewhere between the licks and the nibbles he had removed his trousers. Dark chocolate streaked his face, chest and stomach. His manhood jutted out from a black nest of hair, blue veins bulging, purple crown shiny with arousal.

"What are you thinking about now, Anne?" His voice was ragged.

"You." Her voice was equally ragged.

"What do you want me to do?"

"I want you to come inside me. Please."

"Say it in French."

"I don't. . . ." She was not proficient with French at the best of times; she could not think of one single French word at the moment. "I don't know the words."

"I'll give you the words. Tell me . . . *j'ai envie de toi.*"

I want you.

Anne stared up into his beautiful violet eyes. He must know that her French was not that poor.

Her throat tightened. *"J'ai envie de toi."*

Sweat and chocolate glistened on his dark skin. *"J'ai besoin de toi."*

I need you.

Tears burned her eyes.

"J'ai besoin de toi," she repeated.

"Je voudrais faire l'amour avec toi."

"What does that mean?"

"I want to make love to you."

Make love.

The ugliness the earl had created when describing their actions disappeared.

A spinster's common sense held her back. "My diaphragm . . ."

"Trust me."

She *had* trusted him. And he had—

"Je voudrais faire l'amour avec toi."

Michael plunged his fingers inside her vagina. *Deep.* She held still at the abrupt invasion.

He was . . . fitting a diaphragm over her cervix. And then he was coming inside her, *oh,* far larger than the fruit. Larger than his fingers. Coming into her far more deeply than either the fruit or his fingers. Naked flesh pulsing. Throbbing.

She welcomed the weight of his body; the slippery glide of skin, sweat and chocolate. The flood of his pleasure. The fulfillment of hers.

Michael buried his head into the crook of her neck, his beard a prickly rasp. His flesh inside her ebbed. "I never knew why."

Anne remembered so many things, now that her thoughts were free of drugs and desire and revulsion.

Have you ever been in love, Miss Aimes?

Have you, sir?

Yes, Miss Aimes, I have.

The coffin. The worms.

They all related to the poem he had quoted.

"He loved your mother."

Michael stiffened. "He killed my mother."

Nothing is ever simple, Michael had once told her. *Not lust. Not life.*

Neither was love.

Anne squeezed her eyes shut and buried her fingers into his hair; it curled around her skin, warm and vital. "Sometimes I wanted my mother to die . . . so I could sleep. Just one night. Uninterrupted."

"But you didn't kill her."

"No."

Not even when she had begged Anne to do the very thing she could not do.

She waited for the familiar guilt to come; it did not.

Michael lay in her arms for long minutes, his heartbeat slowing against her right breast until it was only a faint tattoo. Finally he stirred; his skin slowly peeled away from hers. "I'll draw us a bath."

Dread twisted inside her stomach.

"What are you going to do after that?"

"I'm going to go kill my uncle."

Chapter 20

The gate stood open. There was no sign of the gatekeeper.

Thugs rarely stuck around when police became involved.

The dogs had been kenneled; they howled in the distance, as if they knew what the dawn would yield. The gelding underneath him fought for air, lungs bellowing, sides heaving, breath gusting pale streams of vapor. It tossed its head in protest at entering through the gate.

Like the horse, Michael wanted to turn around and go back home to Anne.

He dug his heels into its flanks.

Pale pink dawn outlined the Earl of Granville's palatial manor. Lights blazed through the windows like malevolent eyes.

He grimly smiled.

The man was waiting for him. He would not be taken unawares again.

There were no signs indicating that the police had come. Or gone.

Michael did not doubt at all that the superintendent would distastefully wipe the truth off his fingers and thank God for his children, grandchildren and expected great-grandchild. What else could he do? The man had detained a woman. Buried a boy.

Hardly the crimes that constituted a threat to society.

What magistrate would convict a seventy-year-old earl whose wealth and properties were Devon's mainstay?

He swung down from the horse he had taken from Anne's stable and tied the reins to budding shrubbery. Vaguely he registered the uneven crunch of gravel underfoot, the ache in his thighs and the dull ring of his soles as he ascended the concrete steps.

The front door was not locked. No tall, gaunt man who posed as a butler waited behind it.

Warning tingles raced up and down his back.

There was no gatekeeper, no dogs, no guards, and no servants, but someone waited for him.

He could sense their presence, could feel the empty coffins in the attic.

One had been for Anne, but the second one was for him.

Gilt-framed paintings, their subjects stern and forbidding, stared down from the cavernous walls. Potted ferns bordered the grand mahogany staircase.

They did not conceal an assassin. But one waited.

He thought of Anne in her old-fashioned bed, sleeping.

Or did she sleep?

She had made no sound when he had eased her head off of his shoulder and untangled himself from her damp hair.

His spinster had cried silent tears when he had told her about his childhood. He had mourned in his own way, crying sweat and sperm.

She had called his name: *Michael.*

The taste of chocolate was sweet on his tongue. The taste of Anne was so much sweeter.

He didn't want to die, he realized belatedly.

He wanted his spinster.

He wanted to show her everything he had ever learned.

He wanted her to show him everything she'd ever yearned for.

Cold premonition coursed through his body.

Rarely did men get what they wanted.

The pistol weighted his jacket. His heels echoed in the cavernous hallway, taunting him.

Death. Desire. Death. Desire.

Muscles taut, he walked past the stairs, past the elevator whose caged door was open, down the long, endless corridor to the study. A trail of electric lights guided his footsteps.

There were no shadows to hide in. Yet someone watched him.

Michael could feel eyes trained on him as he journeyed back into the past.

Three people walked down the hallway.

The boy who should have died. The man who had pleasured a spinster. And the person who watched Michael Sturges Bourne.

The boy inside him remembered the fear as if it existed now and not twenty-seven years ago. The man who had pleasured his spinster wondered when electricity had been installed. Before or after the earl had abducted Diane?

Had the thought of burning in a gas-ignited fire frightened the earl?

Did he fear roasting in hell?

Had his uncle loved his mother?

Bright light shone beneath the study door.

Michael paused.

No steps followed his. But the third person was there.

The paneled hallway breathed when the watcher did. The wood throbbed in time with the watcher's heartbeat.

Michael prayed that love was stronger than hate. That shared pleasure surpassed shared pain.

Grasping the doorknob, he gently swung open the mahogany door.

A crystal chandelier blazed overhead. The man waited behind his desk. His hellhound stood behind him, servilely attired in black and white livery, face impassive.

A white marble fireplace framed the two men; blue and yellow flames silhouetted their bodies. Michael's gaze fastened onto the taller of the two men.

The hellhound's sandy hair was receding, but otherwise he looked exactly as Michael remembered him.

Michael had never seen him show any emotion.

He had seen cruelty on the man's face, sadistic satisfaction when Michael tossed up his guts or fought a futile battle. But he had never seen anything on the hellhound's face.

"Hello, Frank," he said softly.

Frank did not respond.

"Michael." The earl showed no signs of displeasure that his

fun and games had been interrupted by the superintendent of police. The satin lapels on his burgundy velvet smoking jacket gleamed like black blood. "You took longer than I expected."

How much longer than he had expected?

Twenty-seven years? Five years? Five hours?

Michael dispassionately studied the man's face.

The electric light was not kind.

He had aged beyond recognition. His hair was totally gray. The earl was a seventy-year-old man whose impotence clearly shone in his faded eyes.

"Did you love my mother?" Michael asked, curiously numb now that the moment had arrived.

A delighted smile creased the old man's face.

It had not changed.

Michael had slept with that smile every night the last twenty-nine years. Had awoken to it every morning.

He felt a twinge of regret, that the hatred that had kept him alive had died in the last five hours.

"Miss Aimes." The earl chuckled, a dry wheeze, black satin lapels undulating. "She's a very astute girl. I am surprised she solicited you, Michael. Truly I am. Yes, I loved your mother."

"But you killed her."

The old man's smile widened. He had lost some teeth. "You never listened, Michael. I told you twenty-nine years ago that I did not kill your mother."

The truth.

Michael clearly saw now what he had not been able to see twenty-nine years earlier. He braced himself against the familiar guilt.

It did not matter.

The man would die for Little. Diane. Anne. The child Michael had once been.

But first . . .

"What boy did you bury?"

"No one you knew, Michael. Just a scruffy black-haired boy who sold his life for the promise of food."

The rage unexpectedly struck him. Another life. . . . What was the count?

Eight? Nine?

"You have a penchant for young boys and women. One could almost believe you're a coward, *uncle.*"

The smile on the earl's face disappeared. "I did what I had to do to make sure you wouldn't inherit the title."

"But you enjoyed it, didn't you?" he asked viciously.

"Yes, Michael, I enjoyed it. But never did I enjoy it more than with you. What woman did you most enjoy? Lady Wenterton? Or Miss Aimes? Who do you regret leaving behind the most?"

His spinster.

"What are you afraid of, Uncle William?" Michael asked dispassionately.

"Nothing, Michael. Nothing is worse than what you reduced me to. This is hell, here in this wheelchair." The man cocked his head curiously. "Have you come to kill me, dear boy?"

"Yes, Uncle William, I have come to kill you."

"I rather thought you might have," the man said sympathetically. "Yet I am alive. I never expected you to bring in the constabulary. You had the perfect opportunity to kill me earlier. You didn't, Michael. Why not?"

Michael did not speak. He did not have to.

They both knew his desire for his spinster was stronger than his hatred for the man. Just as they both knew that she would never be safe as long as the man lived.

A smile of understanding bloomed on the earl's face. "You are not a killer, Michael, yet you felt compelled to kill me. It must have been quite frustrating for you all those years, searching for witnesses. Did you hope to see me hang, Michael?"

Michael tried to forgive Michel's ignorance and the wasted years he had spent trying to find evidence that would convict the earl. For the past five years that he had licked his wounds and mourned Diane there was no excuse.

The man was his to kill, not the law, not age.

"Why didn't you kill me twenty-nine years ago, Uncle William?" he asked disinterestedly. "Did you hope that I would someday find a way to end your miserable life?"

"Watching you throughout the years has greatly relieved my misery. I never wanted you to die, dear boy. I wanted you to suffer. I have gone to great lengths to ensure that you do."

Michael pulled out his revolver and aimed it at the man's head.

The man smiled triumphantly.

Cold metal dug into Michael's left temple, the barrel of a pistol.

Michael's aim did not waver. "How much money does it take to satisfy you, Gabriel?"

"I don't kill for money," Gabriel murmured flatly.

Michael felt something shift inside his chest: hope giving way to reality.

The man watched him with malicious curiosity. Frank's face remained impassive.

He knew that Gabriel's face, too, would be impassive. "What is worth twenty-seven years of friendship?"

Hot breath brushed his ear. "Restitution."

"For what?"

"Pleasure. Pain."

Michael's pleasure. Gabriel's pain.

He could feel his blood thrumming against metal—inside his temple, inside his fingers. "You were jealous."

"Yes, Michael, I was jealous. From the first moment I saw you staring inside the baker's shop with hunger in your eyes, I was jealous. If you had asked the baker, he would have given you the bread. But you never asked. You never asked me for help. You never asked the madame. You never asked the women who chose you over me. You never had to ask. Whatever you wanted, we struggled to give it to you."

A fallen angel's pain.

It was time for it to end.

"You promised to look after Anne."

"I promised."

Gabriel had never broken a promise.

"Then have your restitution."

Somewhere deep inside him where he was still capable of feeling, Michael felt satisfaction.

The man's face no longer smiled. He knew he was going to die.

Time ceased to exist. There was regret in death, but there was also freedom.

Slowly he pulled back the hammer. A loud click echoed in his ear, an answering cock.

Death was all around.

The man's lips unexpectedly curled in amusement. "You will not kill me, Michael. Or will you? Will you kill the man who gave you life? Will you kill your father, Michael?"

His mother . . . and his uncle?

Michael paused.

Life had taught him that anything was possible.

His mother had been blond. Beautiful. Vivacious. Full of laughter.

Much like Diane.

Perhaps she had loved this man.

More than her husband.

More than her children.

Perhaps in hell he would find out.

Michael mentally started the count down. *One* . . .

"Don't do it, Michael!"

Another voice—Frank had spoken.

The hellhound had brought his hand out from behind the wheelchair. He trained a pistol on Michael.

Michael did not glance at the pistol; it would be much like his own. Much like the one that pressed against his left temple. Both Colt and Adam revolvers were equipped with double-locks—self-cocking, for rapid fire, or manual-cocking, for accurate single fire. At close quarters either action would efficiently kill. He stared instead at Frank's face.

It wasn't expressionless. It was filled with fear.

Sweat glistened on his forehead.

Jesus. Did a hellhound feel affection for his master?

Grim humor worked its way up inside Michael. "I can only

die once, Frank. Let's see whose bullet hits first. Yours. Gabriel's. Or mine."

He refocused on the earl.

Two . . .

"He didn't kill your family." The man's face did not show surprise at Frank's interruption. "I did!"

Michael had hunted down every single servant who had worked on the estate of the man whom he believed had been his father. No one had mentioned Frank.

Michael dispassionately studied the earl. "Why would you kill them, Frank?"

"Yes, tell him, Frank." The man couldn't contain his glee at destroying another person's life.

"I cut the reins," Frank confessed.

The truth at last.

Michael remembered the thundering of the horses' hooves. The terror that had hammered inside his chest while his father pried the leather reins from between his hands. Shrill girlish screams. His mother crying out. The abrupt cessation of sound when the gig went over the cliff.

"Why?" Michael asked hoarsely.

"I was a drifter," Frank related jerkily. "Your father hired me. A day later he found me drunk on the job, so he dismissed me. I knew he was taking the gig. I cut the reins."

It was not the gun that weighted Michael's arm.

He stared at the man, the emotion he had strove to distance himself from swelling over him.

All through the years he had believed either he killed his family, or the man did.

The earl openly flaunted his satisfaction.

"You knew," Michael gritted. "All those years you knew Frank was responsible for their deaths and you blamed me."

"You did kill her," the earl gloated. "She wasn't supposed to attend the picnic. She was supposed to beg off due to some minor indisposition. Instead she accompanied my spineless brother and you and your sniveling sisters. When I arrived at my brother's home, Frank was sobering up. He felt guilty. He sobbed out the whole sorry story and begged me to go after him. If your mother had not been on the carriage I would not have wasted my time. But she was. And I had her in my reach. I would have saved her, but she threw you into my arms. Yes, I loved your mother, and she chose you over me. You did kill her, Michael. Every day I live with her death."

Michael had not believed anything would ever again surprise him.

He had been wrong.

So many people had died . . . *because of a mother's love.*

The earl leaned forward in his chair, a sharp protest of squeaking wood. "You've never killed, Michael; I killed before you were born. Some call it expansionism, some call it God's supremacy, but really war is just a gentleman's sport. I could have eliminated you so easily, but I wanted you to know what it felt like, having the woman you loved reject you. So I waited, and watched.

"You were quite the stud, weren't you, nephew? How did it feel to have Lady Wenterton turn away from you? You were burned in her eagerness to escape a life with you, and I rejoiced in your pain. In your suffering. At last you knew what it was like to have a woman turn away from you, to die while you could do nothing to stop her death.

"But I knew, Michael, that someday you would recover from your burns. I knew you would want another woman, whore that you are. Imagine my delight when Miss Aimes solicited you, disfigured though you were. How did it feel knowing that you had to choose between Miss Aimes and me?

"Yes, I know exactly how much you want to kill me. You'll enjoy it, Michael. Pull the trigger, and die knowing that you're no different than I am."

The count down ended. *Three . . .*

Michael felt a sigh of air, a whisper of a kiss.

Gabriel, who had not touched anyone in so long Michael ached for him, kissed him on his scarred cheek.

A messenger's kiss of death.

"For you, Michael," he murmured.

A deafening blast resounded in his ears. The earl's head exploded. Blood and gray matter sprayed the air.

The bullet had not come from Michael's pistol.

Frank froze. Michael watched the life drain out of him.

Just another pawn.

Crimson speckled his paper-white face. A glob of gray matter slid down his stiff black coat.

Twenty-nine years of hell was over.

Frank's arm dropped. Michael lowered his pistol.

Gabriel stepped back—God's messenger, not the man's.

"He was dying." Frank dumbly stared down at the old man who had ruled them all. "In a few more months he would have been dead and it all would have been over."

Michael almost felt pity for the hellhound.

Frank lifted his head and stared at Michael.

There was no regret on his face. No remorse for the lives he had taken.

"He's not your father," Frank said dully.

Michael believed him.

"Your mother didn't love him. That's why he couldn't forgive you."

Perhaps Anne had been right. Perhaps the old man had been insane.

The police would investigate.

What would Frank tell them?

What would Michael tell them?

Michael turned.

"The cook." Frank's voice halted him as he stepped toward the door where Gabriel waited, his hair a silver halo. "Her name is Mrs. Ghetty. There is a letter underneath my mattress. The earl sent the servants on holiday so that—"

So that Michael and the woman he had taken pleasure in could be killed with no witnesses.

"When she returns, tell her where the letter is. Tell her it is for her. Tell her she will be taken care of."

Michael didn't turn around. "You can tell her yourself."

"The earl's solicitor has in his possession a sealed envelope.

In that envelope is a signed confession in which I admit to cutting the reins that caused the death of your family. The solicitor's instructions are to open it in the event he dies an untimely death. No doubt there are other letters that detail the crimes I have committed while in the earl's service. I am not going to prison."

And so he, too, would die.

Michael's gaze locked with Gabriel's. The two men walked out of the earl's study.

A shot rang through the dawn. The echo followed them down the hallway.

The sound of justice.

The hollow click of their footsteps did not falter.

A man stood at the front door, his back as straight as an eighty-five-year-old man bowed by arthritis could stand. "My lord. Shall I go for the constable?"

The old butler was too dignified not to receive a like amount of dignity.

Denby had known Michael's father. Had watched him grow up into a man while his older brother grew up into a monster.

Had he known what the earl had done to Michael?

"Is there no other servant here, Denby?"

"They are on holiday, sir. Save for the pot boy. I feared he was coming down with measles, so I would not let him go. But he is well now."

Was Denby aware of what the earl had done to Anne?

"Did you not think it strange, Denby, when Miss Aimes visited the earl but did not leave?"

"I was not aware of a visitor, my lord," he replied, dignity intact. "That is, until I heard the commotion with you and the constable. The earl hired a temporary butler so that I could nurse the pot boy and get some rest. My bones have been troubling me of late."

No one would have questioned the death of an eighty-five-year-old servant and a small pot boy.

The earl's secret would have been safe.

"Have the pot boy fetch a constable, Denby."

"When he arrives, what shall I tell him, my lord?"

"Tell him the truth. That the earl has been killed and that Frank put a bullet through his own head after the deed was done."

Denby blinked. "Shall you be back, my lord?"

"No, I won't be back."

"You're the last of the line."

Michael pictured Anne, covered in chocolate.

"No, Denby, I'm the first of my line."

"What will happen to the estate, my lord?"

"I'm sure the earl left provisions for you. If not, contact me through Miss Aimes. She will know where to find me."

If she still wanted to find him.

Denby stood his ground. "You're an earl, sir. This is your home now. You have responsibilities."

"You are confused, Denby," Michael said gently. "I am not an earl. Michael Sturges Bourne is dead. Don't ever forget that. If the superintendent of police asks you, tell him the blood line has ended."

Denby blinked. "The Sturges Bourne name is an old one, sir. An honored one. You are making a mistake."

It wouldn't be the first mistake Michael had made.

"When Mrs. Ghetty returns, tell her that Frank left her a letter underneath his mattress. Tell her he loved her. Will you do that for me, Denby?"

"Yes, sir." It could have been tears in his eyes. Or perhaps it was age that filmed them. "Good-bye, sir."

Denby closed the door behind Michael and Gabriel, a sharp click of closure.

The sky was pale pink. Michael's breath steamed in the chill morning air.

Sharp sensation filled him, witnessing another day. "What did the man offer you?" he asked, throat suddenly tight.

"The second man."

Gabriel did not have to elaborate.

Two men had raped him, not one as Michael had believed.

Cold air rasped his lungs. "You never asked for my help either, Gabriel."

Gabriel threw his head back and stared at the sky, as if searching for something. "Perhaps I didn't believe I deserved help, Michael."

"Who was the man in the fire?"

"Did you think I was dead?" he asked, breath a silver cloud.

"Yes."

Gabriel lowered his head and met Michael's gaze. "Did you mourn me?"

"Yes."

"Yet you thought that I would kill you."

In the end . . . "Yes."

"Frank came to the house a week ago," he said neutrally. "I was to deliver a letter to Miss Aimes. If she did not voluntarily visit the earl, I was to get her there by whatever means were necessary, while at the same time creating a diversion to forestall you."

And then he was supposed to kill Michael.

"You copied the letter that he had written for Anne."

"If you had not been able to convince the police to assist you, neither of us would be alive, Michael. He had planned for every contingency."

Except one.

The man had not taken into consideration the friendship between two male whores.

"He was mine to kill, Gabriel."

"Do you know, Michael, in twenty-seven years you haven't changed. You're still hungry. Killing takes that away. I find that I like the fact that one of us can still feel. You may hate me for what I did, but hatred is better than feeling nothing."

"You don't feel anything, *mon vieux?*" Michael asked.

Gabriel's answer was simple, blunt; unequivocal. "No."

Michael did not correct him. Sometimes lies *were* the only thing that protected one.

"What will you do, now that your house is gone?"

"Build another one."

"You think the second man will come to you?"

"I know he will."

Michael walked down the stone steps. The horse, a plain brown sorrel in the pink light, had eaten the buds off of the shrub. He grabbed the reins and forcibly pulled its head away from its breakfast.

"Michael."

He looked up. Gabriel stood at the top of the steps, hair a silver halo in the new dawn.

"I didn't push Anne Aimes. Nor did I kill a man to take my place in the fire. He was a beggar I'd found dead in the gutter. I didn't think you would spend all day rummaging around the ashes. If you had not been so damned sentimental, you would have gotten to her sooner."

Michael put his foot in the stirrup and vaulted onto the horse.

He suddenly felt light-headed. His right cheek burned.

The kiss of an angel.

"I lied to you, Gabriel."

"I am shocked, *mon frère.*"

Gabriel had withdrawn back into his shell.

"I told you that the man had killed everyone I loved. I was wrong. You were there."

He kicked the horse into a gallop.

Gabriel would make his own way back to London. But what would Anne do? He had told her that come the morrow she could cancel their contract and he wouldn't object.

Michael Sturges Bourne wouldn't. But Michael had long ago given up any claims to being a gentleman.

The gate stood open, as he'd left it. A plain, square brougham waited on the other side. The coachman sat in the box, staring straight ahead. A groom stood by the lead horse.

The gelding shook its head, hooves prancing, mane flying.

It recognized the groom and the horses.

Michael's heartbeat raced faster than his thoughts.

His spinster believed he had used her. *And he had.*

She believed he had killed his uncle. *And he would have.*

The groom looked up at him. "Miss Aimes said that I should take your horse, sir."

Tossing the reins to the groom, Michael dismounted and swung open the carriage door.

Anne sat with her feet firmly together. She wore a black wool cloak and a plain black bonnet. A picnic basket sat on her lap.

There was no condemnation in her eyes. "Is he dead?"

He stiffened his knees to keep them from buckling. "Yes."

"I thought you would like transportation back to London." Her voice was more husky than usual, polite as it had been in the night house. She clutched the woven handle of the basket. "This is not my best coach, but it is comfortable."

"Are you accompanying me?"

"Yes." She tilted her chin, as if afraid that he would object. "We do have a contract."

He didn't want her because of a goddamn contract.

He would take what he could get.

Before she could change her mind, he jumped into the carriage and slammed shut the door. The coach lurched, moved backward, forward, slowly turned in a creaking circle.

Michael stared at the dark leather interior opposite him. Anne's hip pressed against his.

He would not lie again.

"I didn't kill him."

"You said he was dead."

"Gabriel killed him."

He could feel her thoughts cataloging the sequence of events.

"Did he push me?"

"No."

"He loves you."

Scalding tears pricked his eyelids. "I know." And for want of anything else to say, he asked, "What's in the basket?"

"Chocolate bars and bananas," she said stiltedly. "It's a long journey by coach. I thought you might get hungry."

Emotion welled deep inside his chest.

Laughter. Tears.

He wanted to snicker like the eleven-year-old boy he had once been. He wanted to weep the tears he had been unable to cry these past twenty-nine years.

It was truly over.

The man was dead and Michael was alive. A sudden throb inside his groin reminded him of just how alive he was.

Reaching out, he scooped Anne up and deposited her onto his lap. The basket went flying. He wrapped his arms around her and buried his face in the crook of her neck. Underneath the harsh benzene cleaning agent that permeated her clothes, her skin faintly smelled of chocolate, of her passion, of his passion. "You were right. It's time for breakfast."